THE CENTER
OF EVERYTHING

Laura Moriarty

THE CENTER
OF EVERYTHING

HYPERION NEW YORK

Copyright © 2003 Laura Moriarty

Library of Congress Cataloging-in-Publication Data

Moriarty, Laura.
    The center of everything / Laura Moriarty.— 1st ed.
      p. cm.
    ISBN 1-4013-0031-6
    1. Girls—Fiction.   2. Kansas—Fiction.   3. First loves—Fiction.   4. Grandmothers—Fiction.
5. Single mothers—Fiction.   6. Gifted children—Fiction.   7. Mothers and daughters—Fiction.
I. Title.

PS3613.O75 C46   2003
813'.6—dc21

                                  2002032898

Hyperion books are available for special promotions and premiums. For details contact Hyperion Special Markets, 77 West 66th Street, 11th floor, New York, New York 10023, or call 212-456-0133.

FIRST EDITION

10 9 8 7 6 5 4 3 2 1

Acknowledgments

First and foremost, I want to thank Elias Kulukundis and Phillips Exeter Academy for creating the George Bennett Fellowship for Creative Writing. The Fellowship allowed me the time and space I needed to complete this novel, and I will always be grateful for Exeter's wonderfully supportive community.

I'm grateful for the people I've met at Hyperion: Leigh Haber, Ben Loehnen, Ellen Archer, and Bob Miller have been tirelessly enthusiastic and supportive. I also want to thank my agent, Jennifer Rudolph Walsh, for taking a chance on a new writer.

Julie Daggett, Carolyn Doty, Tom Lorenz, Alice Lieberman, Amy Stuber, and Tina Schwarz read earlier drafts of this book and gave me thoughtful feedback. All of these people had their own work to do, and I appreciate the time they spent helping me.

I should also thank my mom, who paid more than a few months' worth of student loan bills when things got dicey. And I've got to thank Mary Lamboley, who gave me her old car when she probably could have sold it. (I'm sad to say the car just gave out last summer, but it got me from Kansas to New Hampshire, no problem.)

It's a wonderful thing to find pure generosity in people; I've been fortunate enough to find it many, many times.

THE CENTER
OF EVERYTHING

*R*ONALD REAGAN IS ON TELEVISION, giving a speech because he wants to be president. He has the voice of a nice person, and something in his hair that makes it shiny under the lights. I change the channel, but it's still him, just from a different angle.

The people in the audience wear cowboy hats with REAGAN printed on the front, and they clap and blow horns every time he stops talking, so much that sometimes he has to put his hands up so they'll be quiet and hear what he's going to say next. Nancy Reagan sits behind him, smiling and wearing a peach-colored dress with a bow on one of the shoulders, no cowboy hat. She claps too, but only after everyone else has started, so it looks like while he is talking, she is maybe thinking about something else.

"She's a mannequin," my mother says, pointing a spatula at the television. "She freaks me out."

My mother is maybe the opposite of Nancy Reagan. I could never imagine her wearing the peach dress with the bow on it because she wears blue jeans and usually her gray sweatshirt. And she always listens to what everyone says, even people sitting in the next booth in restaurants who probably don't want her to listen. Right now, she's supposed to be in the kitchen, making us grilled cheese sandwiches for dinner, but she came out to the front room when she heard Ronald Reagan's voice, and now she's just standing there with the spatula, looking at the television and shaking her head until I can smell smoke coming from the kitchen, the bread starting to burn.

She smells it too, runs back. *"Zing!"* she says. When she kisses me sometimes she says *"Smack!"*

The people listening to Ronald Reagan in the audience yell *"Hip hip, hooray! Hip hip, hooray!"* and wave their cowboy hats at the camera as it moves around the room. Finally Ronald Reagan laughs and says, "I think you're playing our song." And this just makes people yell more.

My grandmother Eileen was here last week, and she said she remembered back when Ronald Reagan was an actor in movies, so handsome you'd faint if you ever got the chance to see him up close. She's worried about him being president, though, because his middle name is Wilson, which means he has six letters in each of his three names, and if you've read Revelations, that alone is enough to give you the shivers. But she's going to vote for him anyway, because she says he's the one person who can maybe make everything right again and he's not afraid of the Communists. Really, she says, the grand finale is coming one way or another, through him or through somebody else. The important thing is to be ready.

My mother says not to listen to Eileen about things like this. Six is just a number, she says, bigger than five, smaller than seven, and there are enough real reasons to worry about Ronald Reagan without bringing in imaginary ones.

"What's he saying now?" she yells. She's standing on top of a chair, waving a dishtowel in front of the smoke detector.

But I can't talk and listen at the same time, so I just listen, and Ronald Reagan says God put America between two oceans on purpose, to help the freedom fighters in Afghanistan and the Christians and Jews behind the Iron Curtain. I don't understand this, how a curtain can be iron. There was a metal fold-out wall between our classrooms last year at school; usually it was shut, but when Mrs. West or Mrs. Blackmore was sick, the one who wasn't sick could unhook the latch and push it back so it folded up and we would all just be in one big room together.

No, my mother says, "Iron Curtain" is a figure of speech. There's not really a curtain anywhere.

She brings the grilled cheese sandwiches out on a plate, burned on the edges but still okay to eat, one of her long red hairs in the melted cheese of mine. "Sorry, sorry," she says, picking it out. "It won't kill you."

Ronald Reagan says he wants everyone to begin this crusade joined together in a moment of silence, and really you know he means praying to God. The people in cowboy hats take them off and bow their heads, but my mother keeps eating her sandwich. She doesn't like Ronald Reagan because she thinks he'll get us all blown up with nuclear bombs. She says all somebody has to do is get mad and push a button and we'll all be dead within half an hour, all the houses melted, the whales cooked in the sea, and Eileen can think she'll hear angels singing all she wants, but really she won't be able to hear a damn thing because she'll be just as dead as everybody else. She says she used to not worry so much about things like this, but now she has me, and the idea of somebody pushing this button makes her crazy, makes her scared when she hears even an airplane in the sky.

I tell her if we had half an hour, we could go downstairs the way we do when the tornado sirens go off. We don't have our own basement, but there's a storage space underneath our apartment building, and my mother has a key. There would even be enough time to go outside and wave people down on the highway, tell them they better get inside. I would stay outside until I could see the missiles, and then I would run back and have my mother shut the door behind me.

My mother says no, Evelyn, it wouldn't work like that. A nuclear bomb would blow up the basement too. Just one bomb in Wichita or even Kansas City would be enough to get us, even all the way out here. If the bombs start going off, they'll get everyone, she says. It'll be curtains for us all.

But the next time Eileen is here she says yes, Evelyn, sometimes it does work like that. Whenever a lot of people get killed, there are always a few people who don't.

We are sitting at the kitchen table, Eileen and I, eating the barbecued ribs she brought with her from Wichita. She says when she was a little girl in Alabama, a tornado came, and her family lived while other families died. She'd been standing outside looking up at the sky as it got darker, feeling the raindrops turn into tiny balls of hail that stung when they landed on the backs of her arms, and then she looked up and saw a cloud turning over on itself and filling up the sky, like smoke coming out the windows of a burning building. And then a man not wearing any shoes blew right past her, his feet not touching the ground, his legs moving like he was riding a bicycle.

"He looked at me," Eileen says. "He looked right into my eyes."

She turned and saw the funnel then, dark and thin like a snake. Her father grabbed her around the waist and carried her down to the cellar, and he kept his arms tight around her and her mother while the house rattled and shook over their heads.

"It sounded like a train," Eileen says. "Just like a train going right over us."

My mother rolls her eyes and says that's what everyone always says about tornados. She's standing behind Eileen, doing dishes. She won't eat the ribs with us. She doesn't eat meat since she started working at Peterson's.

Eileen says maybe because that's exactly what tornados sound like, and when it was over, she and her father and mother came out to nothing but quiet, and already the sun was shining through the clouds. The air was pale green, she says, the color of the ocean, and she could see the flying man's shoeless feet sticking straight up out of the ground, as if he had dived into the earth.

Eileen's neighbors died too. They had two daughters. Before the tornado, Eileen played with one of the daughters, but not the other one because she was special and couldn't walk. When the tornado came, they went down to their basement too, carried the special daughter with them, but even so the whole family, even the chickens they kept in the yard if you want to count them, ended up dead, sucked up into the funnel or crushed under the ceiling of their cellar with their hands on top of their heads.

Eileen cries when she gets to this part of the story.

"The Gates were on the right," she says, her small hands pressed together, pointing to her right. "And the Braggs were on the left." She points to her left. "But when we came out, it was just us. Our house wasn't . . . even . . . *touched*."

I try to imagine it, a tornado hopping over her house at just the right moment, like a skip in a record. "You were lucky, Eileen."

She shakes her head, wiping her eyes. "Not lucky, Evelyn. We were spared."

My mother turns around so only I can see her face and puts her soapy hands around her own throat, sticking her tongue out to one side like she is choking. Eileen is somehow able to see her doing this, though she does not turn her head.

"Think what you like, Tina," she says, picking her rib back up, her eyes already dry again. "Think what you like."

My mother doesn't like cigarettes, so Eileen has to go outside and sit on the front step when she wants to smoke. She smokes Virginia Slims out of the right side of her mouth because the left side doesn't move. Something's wrong with it. When she's happy, only the right side of her mouth goes up and it looks as if she's making a funny face. She is only forty-five, and she says as much as she loves me, she doesn't feel like a grandmother yet. This is why I call her Eileen.

I go outside with her sometimes, and she tells me that the real problem with my mother is that she believes everything she sees, but really, Eileen says, they can put anything on television these days. There are pictures of astronauts standing on the moon, but they have been faked by the government, and if you look closely, you can tell. There aren't even any stars in the background, but people are just too stupid to notice. The scientists want us to think that they know more than they really do, but really, the stars are where the angels live and also a way for God to see you, even at night. If you do something wrong, or even think it, he'll know.

She wants us to come visit her in Wichita sometime, to come with her to her church. But we have never gone, and when Eileen isn't there to listen, my mother says it's because one crazy person in my life is enough. I don't need to meet the people from Eileen's church.

But when my mother isn't there to listen, Eileen says yes, actually, I do. When we're outside on the step, she lowers her voice so my mother can't hear what she's saying and tells me I have to believe that Jesus Christ died on the cross for my sins even before I was around to make them. She says it's very important that I believe this all the time, every single second of the day, because if I'm a believer when I die, I will go to heaven, but if I die a doubter, I will go to hell and I will be on fire for the rest of everything. If I am walking down the street and I start to doubt just a little, if I just start to wonder if Jesus and heaven is a story that somebody made up and a bus comes around the corner and hits me before I'm a believer again, too bad. She says she loves me so much that she can't stand to think of this happening to me, so it's very important that I always believe and never doubt.

"What about my mother?" I ask. "What will happen to her?"

Eileen frowns, taking a drag off her cigarette. "She'll go to hell, honey, if she keeps making fun. I know it's sad, but those are the rules."

Men like my mother. They run after her with socks if she drops them from the laundry basket, and they dig into their pockets and wallets for change when we run short in the checkout line at the store. The bag boys are only in high school, but they found out her name. When we go through the line they smile and say, "Hi Tina."

She is almost beautiful, her eyes large and blue like Eileen's, and so many straight, white teeth in her smile. But she's got a bad nose. It's thin like Eileen's but longer, with a bump, like someone tried to pick her up by it before she was done drying. She sometimes looks cross-eyed, both eyes maybe trying to see over the bump. But she also makes herself cross-eyed on purpose when she's telling a joke, and she does it slowly, so it's difficult to tell where being cross-eyed for real stops and where the joke starts. And this makes her funny, I think. People laugh more at her jokes than they would if somebody else said the same thing.

I have a normal nose, without the bump, but I have to wear glasses, and underneath them my eyes are brown and turned downward, drooping, so I look like I'm sad or tired even when I'm not. Brad Browning at school has asked me, "Why are you always so sleepy, Evelyn? Why don't you just take a nap?" But my mother says she thinks sad sleepy eyes are pretty. She crosses her eyes and says, "Let's just say if your father didn't have sad brown eyes you probably wouldn't be here today."

But I don't think most people think sad-looking eyes are pretty. Brad Browning says I look like the plastic basset hounds at grocery stores that you can put quarters in to give money to the Humane Society. There is a chance I could grow up to be ugly, and this is one of many things I worry about.

My mother works at Peterson's Pet Food, right across from the slaughterhouse on Highway 59. Her boss at Peterson's is Mr. Mitchell, and he's also her friend, even though he's old. My mother says his hair is salt and pepper, not gray, and she thinks he's still handsome. Don't call him old, she says.

Two of Mr. Mitchell's fingernails are purple, with some of the nail missing and yellow where the white should be. My mother says this happened when Denise Fishbone the knucklehead got her hair caught in the grinder, and Mr. Mitchell reached in and yanked it out, just in time.

"He saved her," she says. "Saved her life. Two more seconds and she would have been a goner." She drags a red fingernail across her neck, making a slicing sound, her eyes bulging.

Mr. Mitchell saved us too. When the bus service got canceled, he gave us a car. Just like that. He said it was just sitting there anyway, making his yard look trashy and his wife mad. But when he first drove it over to give to us, my mother didn't believe it. She stood in the doorway, watching his face.

"You're going to give me a car? For free?"

He smiled, first at her, and then down at me. "I've got the new truck now, so I don't really need it." He held out the key in one of his big hands. "It's the trickle-down theory, Tina. Embrace it."

For a moment my mother did not move. She only looked at him, as if she were waiting for something else, some more information. And then she leaned forward quickly and kissed him on his forehead, her hands in his salt-and-pepper hair. "This is unbelievable!" she yelled, running to the Volkswagen. "Too good to be true!"

"Exactly, Tina," he said, laughing now, walking behind her. "I might just be giving you a headache. It's an old car. It's got some problems."

"No, no." She rolled down the window as soon as she got inside, waving us over. "Come on, both of you. Let's go for a ride."

So we did. We drove up and down the highway, the three of us, a Frank Sinatra tape in the stereo. Mr. Mitchell sat in the passenger seat, telling my mother when to shift. When she went too fast, the car would shimmy back and forth, and Mr. Mitchell would turn around and look at me like he was scared, but really I knew he wasn't.

The Volkswagen is okay from the outside, but on the inside, it's no good. There's an alarm that's supposed to tell us that our seat belts aren't on, and since there aren't any seat belts anymore, the alarm stays on all the time. This sound makes me crazy. Also the stereo is broken. The Frank Sinatra tape is stuck inside it, and the off switch doesn't work, so when the car starts, the stereo comes on automatically, and it can play only that tape. You can't even turn it down.

"Well," my mother says. "You get what you get."

I liked the Frank Sinatra songs at first, but now I'm sick of them. I'm sick of "Love and Marriage," sick of "Witchcraft," sick of "Three Coins in the Fountain." I tell my mother I'm so tired of Frank Sinatra that if I saw him walking down the street, I would turn around and run the other way.

She rolls down her window and asks if I would like some cheese to go with my whine. "Beggars can't be choosers," she says. "We need this car."

It's true. We live just off the side of the highway in an apartment complex called Treeline Colonies, four flat-roofed, black and brown units of eight apartments each, sixty-three miles from Wichita, three miles from Kerrville. There aren't any sidewalks, and even if there were, there wouldn't be anywhere to walk on them.

My mother says the rent is cheap cheap cheap at Treeline Colonies because they were going to put more buildings around it and then somebody lost all their money and that was the end of that. There are four units in Treeline Colonies, A, B, C, and D. We live in Unit C. The people on the upper floors get a balcony, but we don't. My mother says balconies are just something to fall off of. She says she can see where they get the "Colony" part of Treeline Colonies, because that's exactly what it feels like, a colony out in the middle of nowhere, waiting for reinforcements. She doesn't see where they got the "Treeline," though, because there aren't any trees except for the two redbuds in front of Unit A that still need to be propped up with string and sticks. But I am starting to see that things get named wrong all the time. Rhode Island, for instance. Indians. There's a strip mall in Kerrville called Pine Ridge Shopping Plaza, but there aren't any pines, and there isn't a ridge.

"See, Evelyn?" my mother asks. She has to yell so I can hear her over Frank Sinatra. "See? You never can tell what your luck is. The bus gets canceled, so then somebody gives us a car. A bad thing turns into a good thing, just like that."

She snaps her fingers. Just like that.

But the Volkswagen always breaks down, so much that when the tow truck men get out of their trucks now they smile and say, "Hi Tina." Mr. Mitchell has to give my mother rides home from work in his big red truck, and when I get home from school, he's still there, standing in back of the Volkswagen, looking down at the engine with his arms crossed. He says that cars are like people, and you have to get to know them before you can fix them. He talks about the Volkswagen as if it is a person, a woman, with feelings that can be hurt. "Let's see what's troubling her, squirrel," he says to me, but really, this is all he does. I think maybe he is afraid to touch the engine, with two of his fingernails already gone. And then my mother makes sandwiches or spaghetti and we all three sit out on the step and eat it, looking at the car.

Mr. Mitchell likes to do tricks for me, like pretending he can pull his thumb off with one hand, then put it back on. I am too old for this. I know his thumb is really tucked behind his hand, that things can look one way and be another, depending on where you're standing.

On our way to the grocery store one afternoon, the numbers on the dash turn to 250,000 miles. Frank Sinatra is singing "You Make Me Feel So Young," and my mother says isn't that a coincidence.

But maybe now, finally, the Volkswagen has had enough. My mother has to use both hands to pull the stick shift, and when we stop at red lights, it takes too long to get it back into first. On a cold and rainy day in late April, the gear sticks for too long, and when people start honking she gets out of the car, her arms straight above her head, and yells, "Shut up! Just shut the fuck up! I'm doing the best I can!" She says "fuck" right in front of me. When she gets back in the car, she looks like a crazy woman, her curly hair flying all around her.

The man at the garage says a new clutch is going to cost three hundred and fifty dollars, and that is just the beginning. There's also the transmission. At home, she sits at the kitchen table, making long lists of numbers on yellow notebook paper, subtracting and adding, rubbing her eyes.

"Why don't you ask Eileen for money?" I ask. "She'll give it to you."

She looks at me, and now there is nothing funny about her face. She tells me no one ever just gives anyone anything. She tells me to go to bed.

The next time Eileen comes over, she brings a strawberry jelly roll, so buttery and sugary I tell her I am going to pass out from happiness when I take a bite. I pretend to faint, and lie down on the floor, shaking for a moment and then lying still. Eileen thinks this is funny, but my mother is too worried about the three hundred and fifty dollars, and has not laughed at anything all day.

Eileen is almost out the door when my mother finally asks. Instead of answering yes or no she comes back in and sits down at the table across from my mother, her arms folded in her lap.

"He sees my checkbook, Tina."

"Can't you just make something up?"

Eileen stares at my mother for a moment, like she is waiting for my mother to laugh or at least smile. When she doesn't, Eileen looks down at her hands and shakes her head. "If you want his money, you're going to have to come see him. That's reasonable. That's fair."

They're talking about my grandfather. He doesn't visit us. I've never met him. My mother takes her plate to the sink and turns on the water. Eileen stares and stares, but still my mother won't say anything else. It's mean to do this, to pretend someone isn't there when they are.

"You know, Tina, most people don't go giving money to daughters who don't talk to them."

My mother comes back over to the table to get my plate, not looking at Eileen.

"You going to ask *her* father for the money, Tina?" Eileen tilts her head at me. "Do you even know where he is?"

My mother says nothing to this either, and she gets a very serious look on her face. She bends down and looks under the table, then up at the ceiling. She peers into the hallway. "No. Now that you mention it . . . ," she says, scratching her head. She looks at me. "Oh my God, where is he?"

Finally, for the first time all night, she is smiling. It's just a joke. The sad-eyed man who was my father left two months before I was even born. There's no way he's under the table. I laugh, but this time Eileen doesn't. She stands up to leave again, picking up her keys.

"He'll give you the money, Tina," she says. "You just have to ask."

The only good thing about Treeline Colonies is the flat roof. There's a stairway in the back of the building and a door that opens to the roof, but my mother says this door is for maintenance men who know what they're doing and not ten-year-old girls who don't know what it's like to fall three stories off a roof and have their heads go *splat* on the pavement. But I like to go up there in the evening, watching the sky turn from blue to pink to violet, seeing the first twinkling stars of night.

I just did a report on Venus at school, so I know where it is in the sky.

It's the closest planet, made up mostly of vaporous gases. Ms. Fairchild says that no one could live on Venus. It's covered with clouds, but the clouds are poisonous, and the poison would kill you as soon as you breathed it, and anyway it's too hot. The stars are balls of hydrogen and helium and fire, just like our sun, and no one could live there either.

Ms. Fairchild says people used to think the Earth was flat, with an edge you could fall off of. They thought the sky was just a big dome, and that the sun moved across it every day, pulled by a man with a chariot. It's easy to look back now and say, "Oh, you dummies," but when I'm up on the roof, watching the sun disappear behind the fields on the other side of the highway, I can see how they would think that. If everybody I ever met told me the Earth was flat and that somebody pulled the sun across the sky with a chariot and nobody told me anything else, I would have believed them. Or, if no one would have told me anything, and I had to come up with an idea myself, I would have thought that the sun went into a giant slot in the Earth at night, like bread into a toaster.

I watch the cars on the highway, their red taillights getting brighter as the sky grows dark. Two deer move quickly through the corn, just their ears showing over the green stalks. There are more deer out, now that it's spring. Sometimes they try to cross the highway. I saw one get hit by a car last year. The police came and took the body away, and Eileen said they were going to sell it to people who would eat it. A dark line of blood stayed on the road until it rained.

I hear my mother's voice from below. "I know you're up there, Evelyn. You've got two minutes to get back in here. Two minutes."

When I get down, I find her back in her bedroom, lying on her stomach, reading a book. She used to just watch television after dinner, falling asleep on the green couch and then waking up again to ask me what time it was, but now she says she is tired of watching television and letting her brain turn to mush. Last week, she went to the library and checked out a stack of books, and now she falls asleep while she is reading. She is still on the first one, *The Grapes of Wrath*, and she says it isn't nearly as bad as it was when she had to read it in high school, but of course, then she was busy getting pregnant. She had all the wrath she needed, ha ha.

"I don't want you on the roof," she says. "How many times do I have to tell you?"

"Okay."

"You could really hurt yourself. You go up there again and I'll ground you. No TV. No radio."

"Okay." I say this in a mean way. She's bugging me.

"Okay then. Do you want to get your homework and bring it in here?"

"I did it at school."

She rolls her eyes. "Of course you did."

I crawl up on the bed next to her. I am not supposed to read over her shoulder because I read more quickly than she does, and it makes her mad when I get to the end of the page and look up and hum, waiting for her to turn it.

"Mom?"

"Yes."

"Are we going to be able to fix the car?"

She squints, but does not look up from the book. "I don't know."

"Are we going to Wichita to get the money from your dad?" I am kicking my feet up and down on the bed. She crosses her leg over mine, makes me stop.

"I don't know," she says.

"What happened to Eileen's mouth?"

"She married my father," she says, quickly, half smiling, like it's a joke she just made up. But even as she says it her voice trails off, catches at the end. She looks up from her book, her eyes on mine.

"He hit her?"

She nods. "A long time ago. Yes."

"Why?"

"I'm not sure. I wasn't there."

She shuts the book with her finger inside it to mark the place, waiting, and I know this means I can ask whatever else I want. I know I want to know something, but I can't think of how to ask it. I know you'd have to hit someone pretty hard to do that to somebody's mouth. You'd have to be really mad.

I've been that mad. I wanted to hit Brad Browning last week. He was standing right in front of me, smiling, and he wouldn't stop saying mean things, and I could feel my hand ball up in a fist. It was like electricity, lifting my arm up for me. And then Ms. Fairchild was behind us, calling us in from recess.

Maybe it was like this. Maybe Eileen was saying something bad to my grandfather over and over again, and no one was standing behind him, telling him it was time to go back in.

two

WHEN I GET HOME FROM school the next day, my mother tells me we're going to Wichita.

"We're just going for dinner." She is brushing her teeth, hard and fast, looking at me in the mirror. She looks right at my eyes, knows where they are even though it's just a reflection. "We'll be back by eight." She spits and rinses, turns around. "Do I look okay?"

I tell her yes, though I'm not sure this is true. She's wearing a yellow dress with a high collar, a slip underneath it. She isn't wearing makeup, and her curly hair is pulled back with two of my barrettes. I like her better the other way, in the gray sweatshirt, or, when she's dressed up, with lipstick that matches her clothes.

She makes me change into a pink dress that I hate, a present from Eileen from last Christmas. It itches, and I know I look stupid. When it's time to go, I run to the Volkswagen with my head down, my arms in front of my face. Mr. Rowley is outside, sitting in a lawn chair in front of Unit B. Kevin and Travis Rowley stand in front of him. They are playing some kind of game, taking turns throwing a white-handled knife in between each other's feet, their legs spread wide. Kevin and Travis are usually fighting, and although the knife throwing is just a game, the fighting is real. Yesterday I saw

Travis running out the Rowleys' door, a magazine tucked under his arm, Kevin running right after him yelling, *"You shit! You little shit!,"* and grabbing Travis's ankle just as he started to jump down the stairs. Travis went flying forward, his ankle still in Kevin's hand, his head and arms falling on the concrete with a *smack* that I could hear even through my window. They rolled over each other for a while, their hands on each other's necks, until Mr. Rowley came out and told them to knock it off. When they got up, there was blood on the sidewalk, and Kevin had the magazine.

Today, when they see me, they stop throwing the knife. Both of them look at Mr. Rowley.

"Well hello there, little Evelyn," Mr. Rowley calls out. "What a nice dress. Where's your pretty mother?"

Mr. Rowley always wants to know where my mother is. Don't tell him, she says. Don't say anything. So I go to the car without saying anything and wait for her to come out.

Mr. Rowley stands up, watching our door. He's in love with my mother, but not in a good way. He used to be drunk most of the time and sometimes he would fall asleep on our front step instead of in his own house. I would have to step over him in the morning, and even then he would wake up and move his mouth like there was a lemon inside it and say, "Oh. Evelyn. Where's your pretty mother?"

The Rowleys moved here last year from Wisconsin, and Mr. Rowley said he made steel there, until one day he went to work and there was a padlock on the door. He used to have a T-shirt that said MEN OF STEEL! WISCONSIN STEEL! But he doesn't have it anymore because he set it on fire. I saw him do it. He was barbecuing out on their balcony and all of a sudden he took the shirt off and squirted lighter fluid on it and then got out a match. The shirt went *poof!* into a bright little ball, and he threw it off the balcony down onto the parking lot. No one's car was there, but he didn't look to see either way before he threw it.

He stopped drinking last year because of AA, and he doesn't sleep on our step or set things on fire anymore, but he still always wants to know where my mother is. Sometimes when she walks out to the Volkswagen in the parking lot, he whistles at her or growls like a tiger, limping along beside her, even though she won't look at him and she is a fast walker, so it's hard for him to keep up. My mother says we can never, ever, make fun of Mr.

Rowley's limp, even though he's a pain in the butt, because that happened to him in Vietnam when he was only eighteen years old.

But, she says, we don't have to talk to him either.

He has a tattoo on his shoulder, a picture of a dancing naked lady with breasts like staring eyeballs, CARMEN written underneath in blurring blue letters. Mrs. Rowley's name is Becky. She's very thin, and she wears eyeglasses with a gold chain that loops down on each side of her face. She is not a very nice person. I don't have to see her so much, except when she is walking their poodle, Jackie O, and then she does not say hello but just stands there, watching me like she is a frog and I am a fly and if I get too close to her, that's it. She will not let me pet Jackie O because she says Jackie has a nervous condition that I will only aggravate. But I think Mrs. Rowley is the one with the nervous condition. She leans her head over their balcony sometimes and says, "Please don't jump rope on the pavement because I can hear the *skip skip skip,* and it's very annoying." I tell my mother when Mrs. Rowley was little, someone must have told her if you don't have anything nice to say, don't say anything at all, only she got confused, got it backwards. Only talk if you are going to say something mean.

My mother says oh well, Mrs. Rowley has problems of her own.

My mother also says it's unfortunate the way Mr. Rowley acts toward women, not just because he's married but because he's the father of two growing boys, and you can already see where that's going. Kevin Rowley is in eighth grade and already he tries to whistle at her the way his father does. One time when he did it my mother said, "What a good little parrot. Want a cracker?"

But the younger one, Travis, doesn't ever whistle. Every time I see him, he's biting his bottom lip like he's either mad or trying not to say what he's thinking. He's in fifth grade, one grade above me. We ride the same bus, but he has only talked to me one time. Last year there was a contest at school to see who could do multiplication and division tables the fastest. Each teacher picked the best math person out of their class by playing Around the World, which means whoever is sitting in one of the corners in the front row stands up next to the person behind them, and the teacher asks something like "Twelve times eight?" Whoever answers first wins and gets to go on to the next person, and if you beat everybody in the room, one by one, then you've gone Around the World and you're the winner. I won out of my class, but I also got in trouble and Ms. Ferro said I would be disqualified if I kept getting excited and yelling out the answers so loud it hurt her ears. Calm down, Evelyn, she said. It's math. The right answer is the right answer, whether you yell it or not.

After lunch, I got to go down to the library to do Around the World against all the people who won out of their homerooms, and Travis Rowley was there. I was thinking it wasn't very fair that I had to go against fourth and fifth graders, but they weren't as fast as you would think. I got in trouble for yelling again, but I went almost all the way Around the World again until I got to Travis, who you wouldn't think would be very smart, only reading comic books and throwing knives around with his brother. But he was. We kept tying. He did not yell out the answers the way I did, but he said them very quickly, somehow pushing the right answers out of his mouth while still biting his bottom lip. He kept his thumbs hooked in the front pockets of his jeans and looked down at his shoes the whole time, and I could hear him like a softer echo of my own voice, his voice muffled, hard to hear.

"Sixty-three."

"One hundred and forty-four."

"Six."

"Thirty-two."

"Seven."

"Forty-nine."

After a while, Mr. Leland, the principal, stopped looking down at his cards and just asked us whatever came into his head, his eyes shifting between Travis's mouth and mine. "Six times twelve. Fifty-four divided by six. Eighty-four divided by twelve. Six times seven. Three times eleven."

And we just kept going and going and going. Mr. Leland told me that I could hold on to the table in front of me if that would help me not jump or clap every time I answered. He told Travis he would have to speak up, and he told me to be a little more quiet. Calm down, honey, he said. It's just a game. But by then I couldn't calm down because, more than anything, I like to win things, and it didn't seem fair that I could beat everybody else and then still not win just because of one person. If you don't win things, you lose them, and I think the way I feel when I lose must be the way it feels to be dead.

So I was thinking about winning, how much I wanted to win, clenching my hands so tightly my fingers hurt and that's when Mr. Leland said, "Thirty-nine divided by three!" and Travis won.

I didn't know the thirteens at all. We hadn't even done them yet.

All he got was a piece of paper that said he won and Mr. Leland shaking his hand. He sort of smiled when he got the paper, but then he just went right back to biting his bottom lip. I was mad, looking at the piece of paper I almost got but didn't.

And then Travis turned around and said, "Nice job, kiddo," and even though this is all he has ever said to me and all he probably will ever say to me my entire life, I felt better. I've never seen him say that much to anyone.

He shoplifts. A month ago, there was a police cruiser parked outside of Unit B, and I saw him getting out of the back, wearing a sweatshirt hood over his head, but you could still see it was him because he has curly brown hair that my mother calls corkscrews, and no one else I know has it. So now, twice a week, the school bus drops Travis Rowley off at the group home for boys in town instead of at our stop.

He's still doing it though, shoplifting. Last week I saw him in the Kwikshop when I was with my mother, his hands moving quickly, pushing two comic books into the sleeves of the blue sweatshirt. He reads these comic books on the bus, a ski hat pulled down over his hair. They are mostly comic books with covers of superheroes in masks and colorful body suits, swinging from ropes, shooting lightning out of their fingers, with names like *Dark Avenger* and *Captain Victory*.

My mother calls Travis the little one, even though he isn't really that little. She looks out the window sometimes and says, "That little one, when he gets older, look out. He'll be the one getting whistles. He will break hearts."

When she finally comes out to the car, she has her sunglasses on and so in the yellow dress, she looks like she is in disguise, a movie star trying not to be recognized. She walks quickly, looking straight ahead, but Mr. Rowley has already gotten up from his lawn chair.

"You're looking good, Tina."

She keeps walking, so he stays where he is and starts to clap. Kevin and Travis have stopped throwing the knife. They turn around, watching.

"Jesus, Tina," Mr. Rowley says, scratching his beard. "Your ass looks like a bell ringing, I swear to God."

She gets in the car and shuts the door.

"Ding dong!" Mr. Rowley yells, still clapping. "Ding dinga dong!"

The engine starts up, no problem, Frank Sinatra on the stereo singing "My Way." She gives the stick shift a good tug, using both hands. There is a loud, straining sound, like someone turning on a vacuum cleaner, but the stick won't move. The Rowleys watch.

"Please," she says, her hand on the dashboard. She's talking to the car. "Please?"

Mr. Rowley walks closer, leaning on his good leg. Travis and Kevin follow and stand behind him, looking at the Volkswagen with serious faces, Kevin still holding the white-handled knife. They are shirtless, both of them, their chests smooth and already tan. My mother is still trying to move the gearshift. It doesn't give, and it doesn't give. Mr. Rowley is still just standing there, waiting for her to let him help.

"I just need to get it into first," she says finally. She pushes herself up out of her seat. The yellow dress is already wrinkled in the back. "It does this when I start it sometimes."

Mr. Rowley nods and lowers himself into the car, holding his bad knee with his hand. He steps on the clutch pedal, and the stick moves into first right away even though he is using only one hand, the ball of muscle in his arm sliding down like the bulge of a mouse inside a boa constrictor.

My mother says thank you, not looking at him, but up at the sky. Travis sees me looking at him, and he meets my eyes without smiling before I can look away. "Yup," Mr. Rowley says, patting the dashboard. "But you need a new clutch. I hope you're not trying to go far."

He tells her she will have to put her foot down on the clutch pedal while his foot is still on it so the car won't stall again, and I can see by her face she is worried this is a trick. She holds on to the door and puts her right foot on the pedal, and Mr. Rowley slides out behind her, using the door as leverage, his hands right next to hers as he pulls himself up. I am waiting for him to say something or even worse, but he doesn't. He stretches his good leg out of the car, and then the other. My mother slides back into the seat, the engine humming now, ready to go.

We watch Mr. Rowley walk back across the parking lot, Travis and Kevin behind him. He swings his arms, his hands rounded into loose fists. The limp looks like a bounce.

· · ·

The sky is a bright, bright blue, almost turquoise, with no clouds, the sun still high, and I am excited just to be on the highway, going this fast. I hang my head out the window the way a dog would, the spring breeze blowing hard on my face as we sail along on I-35 past grain elevators and rest stops, clusters of cows behind barbed-wire fences and fields of blue stem grass that look so green I can't stand it. Frank Sinatra is singing "I've Got the World on a String," for the second time since we left, but it's so pretty out I don't care.

"I knew a girl who fell right out of the car hanging her head out the window like that," my mother says. "She went *splat*." She pulls me back in the car by my arm. "Listen, you know we're going to see my father. Your grandfather."

"Okay," I say, but I'm still looking out the window, at a red tractor moving slowly along a tan-and-brown-striped field. There are butterflies already, monarchs. Ms. Fairchild said the monarchs come through Kansas every spring, millions of them, moving north with the birds. Or maybe the birds move with them.

"My father and I haven't talked for a while. Evelyn? Are you listening?"

I look at her and nod.

She talks quickly. She says her father is a lot older than Eileen, and that he grew up on a farm in Nebraska. He was in the Korean War before he met Eileen, when Eileen was still just a teenager, and he has a Bronze Star because when he was in the war another man got shot, and my grandfather carried him seven miles to a hospital. On the way there, he got shot too, but he didn't put the other man down.

"He's a hard worker," she says, only one hand on the steering wheel now. The other one is up by her mouth, her thumbnail between her teeth.

She keeps talking. She has six younger brothers and sisters, but only four of them will be there today because one of them, Stephen, is in the army in Virginia and another one, Theresa, is married in Texas with babies of her own. But I'll meet four of them today. She counts them off on her fingers— Daniel, Joe, Stephanie, and Beth—my aunts and uncles, she says. I won't need to call them that, and probably shouldn't. Beth is younger than I am, so that would be a little weird. They live in a nice house. Her father works at Boeing now. He helps make airplanes.

"Where did the bullet go?"

"In the arm," she says, looking in the rearview mirror. She has it tilted at an angle where she can see her eyes, not the cars behind her. "And he's missing a finger. He lost it working in the winter. Frostbite."

"Which finger?" I look down at my hands.

"His pinkie." She wiggles her own pinkie at me. "Don't stare at it when you see him."

I try to imagine it, what he will look like, a four-fingered hand over his arm where the bullet went in, nice enough to carry another man when he himself was bleeding, mean enough to do what he did to Eileen's mouth. But I know I can't really imagine him, the way he will look. It's like trying to imagine my own father, always someone to make up, knowing that whatever way I try to imagine him I am probably wrong, at least about something.

"Why doesn't he come over to visit like Eileen does?"

She smiles, tilting her head back and forth. "He doesn't like me very much."

I watch her face. "Why not?"

"Next question, please." She glances up at the mirror.

"Is he nice?"

She rubs her lips together. "He has a temper."

"You have a temper."

She looks at me. "No. No I don't."

"Is he going to talk about Jesus all the time like Eileen?"

She smiles. "Yes. But he likes to talk about God more. Eileen loves Jesus, and he loves God. That's why they get along."

I hang my arm out the window, waving it in the wind. "Who do you love?"

She laughs, putting her sunglasses back on. "I love you, Evaloo. I do I do."

Eileen and my nine-fingered grandfather have a real house and a real yard. The house is green with white trim, on the turnaround of a dead-end street. An American flag hangs in the front, and a tiny gold eagle is perched on the front of their mailbox. One side of the house is two stories with a brown front door, and the other side is a two-car garage. The other houses on their street have this same shape, but they are painted different colors, some brown, some white, some light yellow with brick. Shade trees rise over the backs of the houses, one with a tire swing hanging down. There are kids riding on bikes and skateboards, none of them wearing pink dresses. Two women sit on chairs on the lawn next to Eileen's. They look up from their magazines when our Volkswagen pulls into Eileen's driveway, Frank Sinatra floating out the windows.

"It'll be fine," my mother says, even though I haven't said anything. She holds my hand when we walk up the driveway, her hand tight around mine.

The doormat is a picture of Jesus holding out his arms and smiling, WELCOME stamped in cursive over his smiling face. It looks like I am standing on Jesus, my white shoes on his neck, and this seems like it could bring bad luck. I step off.

A boy opens the door. He is tall and thin, all throat and elbows, wearing a mesh football shirt and shorts. The visor of his baseball hat knocks into my mother's forehead when he hugs her.

"Daniel! Oh my God! Oh my God!" She holds him away from her, squeezing his shoulders. "You've gotten so big! You're taller than I am."

"Well shit, Tina, I'm about seventeen." He bends down and looks at me. He has Eileen's nose, and a retainer. "Hey, is this my niece?" He looks up at my mother. "She looks like you. Weird."

We follow him inside. There is baby blue carpeting everywhere, two girls stretched out on it, playing Chinese checkers. They look up at us, saying nothing. They also have Eileen's bony nose, my mother's dark red curls pulled back from their faces with plastic bands.

"This is Stephanie," he says, pointing at the older one. "And this is Beth."

Aunt Beth. She could be eight. Daniel makes hand signals for them to stand up, like a policeman waving traffic through a stoplight. They do not stand up, but they smile, and when they do, they look like small, flat-chested versions of my mother. They look more like her than I do.

"Hi," the older one says. The younger one, Beth, says nothing. She's just a watcher.

"Hi," my mother says. "It's okay if you don't remember us. I came by once when you were still just a baby, Beth. Evelyn was just a toddler, maybe three." She nods at Stephanie. "You two played together, out in the yard. But there's no way you could remember."

They say nothing. Daniel comes back, handing each of us a glass of ice water. My mother is smiling in a way that looks like it would hurt if you did it for a long time. "I used to baby-sit him," she says, pointing at Daniel. "How do you like that?"

Another boy walks in the front door, this one younger than Daniel, and he has a dog on a leash. He has the same red hair, and the same nose. The dog is a German shepherd with a pink collar, and when it sees me and my mother it starts barking, its teeth sharp and yellowy white. My mother puts both hands on my shoulders, and pulls me behind her.

The boy has to hold the pink leash with both hands. "No, Rita! No! Stop barking!"

Daniel takes the leash, dragging the dog away. He uses his foot to push the dog behind a door, shutting it quickly. "Guess Rita doesn't know you're family," he says, leaning against the door. He smiles, and again there is the metal retainer. But Rita is still barking, throwing her weight against the door, so it sounds like someone kicking. "Dad's new dog," he says.

My mother looks at the door. "Where's Marilyn?"

"He had to put her down. Hip problems."

"Oh." She looks at the other boy. "Well, God, I guess you're Joe."

The other boy nods, says hi, and my mother laughs. And then they all four just stand there, staring at us like we have just come down from Mars, like we have green heads and noses where our eyes should be. Rita is still barking, growling, trying to sniff us through the small opening under the door. The water that Daniel gave me smells and tastes like soap.

My mother clears her throat, her hand on the back of her neck. "This is a little strange, isn't it? I know it feels strange for me."

Only Daniel smiles back. She turns to him, lowering her voice. "Is he here?"

"No, he's still at work," Daniel says. "Man, this is going to be *in*-tense, isn't it?"

I hear Eileen's voice from a different room. "Is that them? Are they here?" She walks into the entryway, carrying a wooden spoon with mashed potatoes on the end of it. When she sees me, she looks down at the dress and makes a squealing sound, leaning down to give me a tight hug. "Did you all meet Evelyn? Isn't she just beautiful?"

All four of them look at me carefully, but say nothing.

"Well, she is, stupids," she says, kissing the top of my head. She hands the spoon to Daniel and tells him to go in the kitchen and make sure the potatoes stay warm but don't burn. She tells Beth and Stephanie to set the table.

"You two come with me," she says, and leads us into another room. It's not a kitchen, and there isn't a TV in it, so I'm not sure what it's for. A piano sits in one corner, a gold sofa and two matching chairs in another. Someone has spilled something on the baby blue carpet that stained, something brown or dark green in the shape of a boot. I sit next to my mother on the gold sofa, little pillows on each side of us. Eileen sits in one of the chairs.

"I'm just so glad you two are here," she says. "So glad." She claps her hands and bounces a little, like she is riding in a car on a bumpy road.

My mother smiles with her lips together. She looks around the room, at the oil painting of the ocean crashing onto rocks above the piano, the gauzy gold curtains in the windows. She picks up one of the pillows, fingering its baby blue fringe.

"This room is exactly the same," she says. "Time warp."

"Some things are different."

"Let's hope so."

Eileen reaches over to my mother's face, smoothing down her hair. "Just be nice, Tina. Just be nice and everything will be okay."

"I'll be nice if he'll be nice."

Eileen frowns and looks away.

My grandfather is a very big man, broad shouldered and so tall that he has to duck when he first comes through the door. My eyes go right to where his pinkie should be, and it's true: there's just a little white stub there, the end smoothed over with pink, dimpled flesh. He sees me looking and wiggles it at me before he even says hello.

"Hi," I say, still looking at the stub.

"Hi yourself."

He looks much older than Eileen; a flap of skin hangs between his chin and his neck, and one of his eyes has a red vein zigzagging across the white part. His hair is dark red, cut short like a soldier's, and he's wearing a white shirt with a blue striped tie. Rita stands behind him, watching us, no longer barking.

"This is Evelyn," my mother says.

He nods at me, smiling, and then looks back at my mother. "It's good to see you again, dear, so grown up." His voice is very low. I can hear the ticking of my mother's watch, her wrist just below my ear, her hands still on my shoulders.

He starts to pull on his tie, loosening it, unbuttoning his sleeves and rolling them up. Eileen bulges her eyes at him.

"I'm glad you've come here today, Tina," he says, very slowly. "Your mother has missed you."

My mother nods, rolling her lips between her teeth. If the whole night goes like this, people speaking so slowly and with such long spaces in between, it will seem like forever. I wish my mother and I were already back at home right now, sitting in front of the television, eating grilled cheese.

He clears his throat. "You've been missed."

"Thanks, Dad." She's still standing behind me, her hands heavy on my shoulders. Eileen catches my eye and winks.

Beth and Stephanie appear in the doorway. "Table's set," Stephanie says. Neither of them looks at me. They are both watching my grandfather's face.

"You girls get a chance to talk to your sister?" he asks. "And little Evelyn here?"

They nod, and then it's quiet again. We are all just standing around. If I could think of anything to say, anything at all, I would say it. I can tell by looking at Beth and Stephanie that they are trying to think of something to say too.

Beth looks at my mother. "Where's the horse?"

"What?" my mother asks.

My grandfather laughs, then stops quickly. "What are you talking about?"

Beth squints up at him. "You said the horse was coming tonight. The little horse."

Eileen begins to move toward the kitchen, waving for us to follow. But my mother stays still, her fingers drumming on my shoulders. "The little horse?" she asks. "A little horse was coming?"

He shakes his head. "I don't know what you're talking about, Beth. But that's enough of that."

My mother turns her head out the window so she is no longer looking at her father or Eileen, and now I can't see her face.

"Okay, okay," Eileen says, clapping her hands, a teacher at the end of recess. "No more talking about horses. Let's go eat."

We go into the other room and sit down around the table. It's a table for six people, but someone has pulled the piano bench up to the table to make room for two more people, and my mother and I sit there.

Nobody talks. Eileen uses silver tongs to give everyone some salad, and there is sound only when they tap against a plate.

But then my grandfather starts laughing about something. When I look up, he winks at me and wrinkles his nose. "Well aren't you just a little pumpkin?" he asks.

I am not certain how to answer this. Am I a little pumpkin? I turn to my mother, but her head is bent down as if she were praying with her eyes open, staring at her reflection on her shiny white plate.

After a while, he answers for me, still grinning. "You are. You're just a little pumpkin."

Eileen leaves and comes back with the ham. My grandfather smiles at my mother, but she's still looking down at her plate, so she doesn't see. Eileen puts two thick pieces of ham on everyone's plate, so there is ham on one side, salad on the other. I pick up my fork, but my mother pokes my knee under the table, shaking her head no.

"I'd like to say the grace tonight," my grandfather says. He waits until we have all closed our eyes and bowed our heads, just like Ronald Reagan. But instead of a moment of silence, he talks. He thanks God for getting me and my mother to Wichita safely, and for putting food on the table, and for the roof over our heads, and he says thank you for blessed reunions, and blessed returns. When he says amen, Eileen looks up at us, her crooked mouth in a wide smile, and she says amen too.

Everyone else starts to eat, but my mother is still just looking at her plate, her hands pressed against the piano bench. She taps her foot against one of the legs of the table, hard enough so the ice cubes in my glass clink together.

My grandfather's temples move as he chews, his eyes wide. He looks at my mother, then glances at Eileen. "Well I saw that German car out there," he says. "We can look into fixing it, but it might be better to try to just get you-all a new one altogether. Get something a little more reliable."

My mother looks up. "Who's the horse?"

He stops chewing for just a moment, staring at her. But he says nothing, and after a while he starts chewing again, looking down at his plate as if she didn't say anything at all. "Maybe a good Ford. Chrysler."

My mother doesn't look at him. She pretends he isn't there. He looks at me and smiles. "What grade are you in now, sweetheart?"

I am not sure if I should answer, but he is looking at me, waiting. "Fourth," I say.

"Fourth! Just one grade above Beth. How nice."

"Who's the horse?" my mother asks.

He swallows and points his fork at my mother, but doesn't look at her. "Tina, I heard you-all needed money, and I'm willing to help you out. Just drop the horse business. Just drop it."

She lowers her head. Daniel and Stephanie catch each other's eye, and something about the way they do this makes me think of the deer in the corn field across the highway.

"I got Italian dressing," Eileen says. "Tina, for the life of me, I couldn't remember if you liked Italian or Ranch."

My mother doesn't say anything to this, and so it is quiet for a while except for the sound of people chewing. Still she isn't eating, just sitting there. I put a cucumber slice in my mouth, and I am chewing it as carefully as I can when I hear a high-pitched humming sound, almost like the seat belt alarm in the Volkswagen. When I look at my mother, the humming gets louder, and I know it's her.

People are still chewing, acting like they don't hear. But she gets louder and louder, even with her mouth closed. Finally, the chewing stops.

"Tina?" Eileen says. "You okay, honey?"

My mother closes her eyes, and tilts her chin all the way back. She opens her mouth wide, and the humming sound turns into a long, slow whinny.

I am amazed by how good she is at this, how much she sounds like a horse.

My grandfather puts down his fork, his face like a rock. She neighs again, and Rita comes out from underneath the table, her ears pointed, tilting her head at the sound.

"Daniel, will you pass the salad dressing?" Eileen asks. "That's right. Fourth. Just one year ahead of Beth, and one year behind Stephanie. Isn't that something? Isn't that something, Stephanie?"

Stephanie nods quickly. But my mother neighs again, this time even louder, more high-pitched. Rita starts to whimper, watching her closely.

"Drop it, Tina," my grandfather says. "I'm warning you."

"Not a horse, of course," she says, no smile now. "You called me a whore."

He puts his fork down. "Don't talk like that in my house." He is speaking softly and quickly, and it's difficult to hear him.

"You said it! You're the one who said it!" She leans back and laughs, holding out her arms. "Thanks for the introduction!"

He looks at Eileen. "Get her to stop."

"Tina—" Eileen reaches over me, almost touching my mother's hand. "Tina, please."

"I'm a *mother*," she says. "I've raised a *child* by myself. And that's what you have to say about me? Still?" She waits, but no one says anything. "I feel *sorry* for you, then. I really do."

There are veins on my grandfather's forehead that I did not see before. I can see them rising, filling up with blood. He grips the table with both hands, holding on so tightly that his nine fingers turn white, like the table will fly away from him if he lets go. "Tina," he says, slowly, carefully, still looking at Eileen. "I'm willing to forgive you. I suggest you start to show some appreciation for that, given the present situation you have gotten yourself into."

"Forgive me," she says. "Oh that's so big of you. What a nice man you are."

"Tina, honey." Eileen's voice is just above a whisper, pleading. "Let's just try . . ."

"No." She pulls her hand away, standing up. "I gave it a try, but I see that things are the same. Come on, Evelyn. Come on. Let's go. We're leaving." She claps the way Eileen did. No more talking about horses. She pushes the bench back from the table, and now we are up, moving quickly down the baby-blue-carpeted hallway, back toward the front door. I hear his heavy footsteps behind us, his low voice yelling. "This is my house. I'll say what I want when I'm right!"

But we are already out the door, moving down the stairs to the car. I worry he will chase us, but when we get outside, he stays at the top of the steps, holding on to the little black railing. My mother unlocks my door for me, and once I am inside, she turns and looks up at him. For a moment, they both stand where they are, staring at each other. He is breathing heavily, his eyes steady on hers.

"Then don't come back." He crosses his arms in front of him and brings them down quickly, like an umpire in baseball. "That's it!"

My mother rolls her eyes. "You know, fuck you," she says, pointing up at him. "Fuck you for calling me that. I don't *want* to come back, okay?"

The women in the lawn chairs in the other yard have pushed up their sunglasses and put down their magazines.

My grandfather holds his hand up like he is going to wave good-bye, but then brings it down, swatting the air like he is sick of us anyway, like he has had enough. I don't know if he thinks I'm a little pumpkin anymore or not, but it doesn't matter. I'm on her side now. He made her cry.

He goes back inside, Eileen passing him in the doorway. She touches him on the shoulder and jogs across the yard toward us, her hand over her mouth.

"Tina, don't leave like this," she says, holding the edge of my mother's window. "You don't want to leave it like this."

"Yes I do, Mom. Okay? Let go."

"But honey, this might be your last chance." She is speaking softly, reaching into the car to smooth my mother's hair. "Come back inside, and the three of us can sit down and talk. Tina, in his mind, you did something wrong, okay? But we've been talking a lot, and he wants to forgive. He wants to forgive you, baby."

My mother puts her hands in front of her face. There are tears on her neck now, seeping into the collar of the yellow dress. She hiccups, wiping her face on her shoulder. "He thinks I'm a bad person, and I'm not." She thumps her hand against her chest, and then the steering wheel. "And it feels like I'm sick, Mom. It really does. We're leaving, okay? Just let us go."

She turns the key in the ignition, and the seat belt alarm and Frank Sinatra come on. Eileen lets go of the window, giving me a little wave, her other hand cupped over her mouth. My mother pulls on the gearshift once with both hands, and we roll away. The house grows smaller and smaller in the rearview mirror, until we turn, and then it's just gone.

She can't drive straight. There's a stoplight up ahead on a yellow light, and she steps on the gas, trying to make it, but it turns red long before we get there.

"We're never going back there, Evelyn, I promise you that," she says, looking up at the light. She wipes her nose with the skirt of her dress. "Never again."

"Okay." I reach over to pat her on the knee. "It's okay, Mom. Don't cry."

She smiles then. She isn't really crying now, but her nose is still running. She leans over and kisses me on top of my head. Someone honks. The light has turned green. She tries to shift into first, but the gear won't move. More horns.

She tugs harder, and again she tries to talk to the Volkswagen like it can hear her. *Come on, baby,* she says. Cars start to go around us, people yelling out their windows. Finally the gear pops into first, the engine racing. "Okay," she says, making a sharp turn at the next corner. "We're going to take a shortcut. No more red lights."

We turn onto a gravel road, and soon there are no more buildings, just fields of wheat. We drive and drive, going right over potholes, a dead possum. We are going too fast. Rocks kick up and hit the underside of the Volkswagen, like popcorn popping.

Suddenly, she slows. She leans forward, looking up. "Evelyn, do you see that? Up ahead?"

I squint, trying to see. To the left, maybe a quarter of a mile away, there's a whirling blur of something dark, rolling down from the cloudless twilight, like a column of smoke moving down instead of up.

"What is that?"

If there were clouds, it could be a tornado. It's that big, moving that quickly. But there aren't any clouds. The day is cooling into night, and already I can see Venus, low on the horizon. The whirling blur is coming from nowhere, like a puff of smoke for something to step out of, a genie or a witch.

We get closer, and I can see it's not really a cloud, but a swarm of many small things, moving together. Mrs. Stanley said that one time grasshoppers came down from the sky and ate up all the Mormons' crops in Utah, and they almost all starved to death. Eileen told me this had also happened to the Egyptians, only they were called locusts back then, and the Egyptians had deserved it.

My mother stops the car. "Oh my God. Honey, I think they're birds."

I lean my head out my window, pushing up my glasses. She's right; it's some kind of small, dark bird, thousands of them, maybe millions. They fall on the field below like rocks, shrieking, covering the still green stalks for as far as I can see, until the field itself looks like it is moving, or like this is the spot where all black birds come from, out of a crack in the earth.

"Oh my God," my mother says. She says it again as a shadow passes over us, darkening the car. It's more birds, an entire cloud of them, blocking out the sun. They form a stripe across the sky that starts out thin and thickens as they spiral downward, on top of the birds already there. My mother rolls her window the rest of the way down, and we sit and watch, silent. It's like watching lightning. It's beautiful, the sky full of an energy I can feel in my fingers. But I have an uneasy feeling in my stomach, listening to their shrieks. Anything could happen now. The Earth could spin out of its orbit and crash into the moon.

We watch. There are too many of them, and I can see now they are fighting, pecking one another out of the way. Some of them, the ones on the bottom maybe, the ones who were there first, are maybe getting killed, smashed flat by the weight of all the birds still falling from the sky.

Suddenly, they begin to slowly funnel back up, forming thick lines again, moving in the opposite direction from where they came. They fly up in waves, in pulses, and I wonder what makes them do this, how they decide who will go when.

"Wow," my mother says, and then she says it again.

She starts the engine, giving the gearshift a tug. It doesn't move. "No," she says. She tugs again. I try to help. "We can't get stuck here," she says, slapping the dashboard. "No!"

But the Volkswagen doesn't hear her. It doesn't feel the slap, and it doesn't care. I look out the window, and there is nothing, not one light on the horizon, and I get the uneasy feeling again. I press my hands together and pray to God to make the Volkswagen move, but this does not work.

She gives up after a while, turning off the engine so at least Frank Sinatra will quit singing.

"What should we do?" I ask.

"I don't know." She looks up at her eyes in the rearview mirror. One of my barrettes has come loose from her hair, dangling down by her ear. "Let me think for a minute."

The field to our left is mostly dirt now, picked clean, only a few strips of stalk left over. But the field to our right is untouched, the corn still growing in neat, green rows. On the far side of the sky, I see the birds again. Their shadows pass the setting sun before they vanish for good, leaving us behind.

$\mathcal{W}$E ABANDON THE VOLKSWAGEN, LEAVE it right there on the side of the road, dead and unburied. We walk over a small hill, and then we can see three houses, far away from the road and from each other. My mother spends a long time looking at each one and then points to a white house with a white fence and says, "That one." It's farther than it looks, and by the time we step on the creaking front porch there are lightning bugs, the sky dark with night.

The lady who answers the door opens it only an inch, just enough to see us with one of her light blue eyes. She says she will call someone for us, but does not invite us in. "Who is it you'd like me to call, dear?" she asks.

My mother opens her mouth to speak, but no words come out.

"Eileen," I say.

My mother shakes her head and writes something on a gum wrapper from her purse. "Could you please call Merle Mitchell? It'll be long distance to Kerrville, I think. I can give you some money."

"No no," the lady says, taking the wrapper. "It's fine." She shuts the door behind her, locks it.

I look up at my mother. "She's acting like we're *killers*."

"Well, we could be for all she knows. How is she supposed to know?"

I look at our reflection in the window, and I realize that it is true: neither of us looks like a normal person. I am still wearing the stupid pink-and-white dress, and my mother looks a little crazy, the barrette still hanging down by her ear, trails of mascara under her eyes from when she was crying.

"That's exactly right," she says. "If ever some people come knocking on our door and I'm not home, I don't want you to let them in either. I don't even want you to answer the door."

"But what if their car broke down?"

"Too bad for them."

The lady opens the door just an inch again and tells us Mr. Mitchell said he would leave right away. We can wait on the porch, she says. She'll leave the light on.

"Thank you so much," my mother says. "Thank you."

The lady shuts the door, opens it again, and asks if she can bring us a bowl of ice cream.

I ask what kind, and my mother pinches the back of my elbow. I can see the lady's mouth through the door, her lips bluish and thin. "Um, I'm not sure, dear," she says. "I'll have to check and see what we have." My mother says she'll just have a glass of water, if that isn't too much trouble.

When the door shuts again, she tells me it's rude to ask what kind, and that beggars can't be choosers. I'm sick of her saying this to me.

"We're not beggars," I say. "Our car just broke down."

The lady comes back with a bowl of mint chocolate chip ice cream and a glass of water, and since we are sitting on the steps now, she has to stretch to pass it to us so she can stay inside, keeping one foot behind the door, like a baseball player getting ready to steal home. I tell her thank you, and she smiles. She is younger than I thought she was, wearing an apron over a flowered dress, tennis shoes on her feet.

"Say thank you," my mother whispers.

"I already said it."

"Say it again."

I say thank you again.

"Certainly," the lady says, and shuts the door again. We both look down at the green ice cream.

"I don't like mint chocolate chip," I say.

My mother nods. "Yes. I know."

"It's the only kind I don't like."

She closes her eyes. "Yes, Evelyn, I know."

She says she will eat the ice cream if I won't, and that when Mr. Mitchell comes, we can ask him to take us someplace to eat, as long as his wife isn't with him. If his wife is with him, she says, we won't say anything at all.

"Why not?"

"Because I said so." She points up at the sky. "Look, see that up there? That's the Big Dipper."

She's telling me this like she's teaching me something new, but of course I know the Big Dipper. It's the easiest one. I also know the Little Dipper, Cassiopeia, and Orion's Belt. Ms. Fairchild said the stars in the constellations are not really close together; it only looks that way because they are so far away from us. They only make shapes if you are looking at them from Earth. If you were looking at the Big Dipper from another solar system, she said, it would look like something else, or maybe like nothing at all.

I can hear cicadas from the field across the road, the sound a plastic straw makes when you bend it, back and forth, back and forth. Moths circle the porch light over our heads, and I watch them, my head resting in my mother's lap. They are like the birds, fluttering and flapping on top of one another, trying to get inside. The bottom of the bulb is dark with the silhouettes of moths already dead, their wings still against the glass.

I wake to headlights shining on my face, the sound of Mr. Mitchell's truck. He kills the engine and steps out, squinting to see us on the porch.

"Oh Merle," my mother says. "Thank you so much. I'm sorry we had to call you out here. Come on, Evelyn. It's time to go."

"Don't be sorry!" he yells. Even when Mr. Mitchell yells, it's in a nice way, the way Santa Claus yells "Ho Ho Ho" outside of Wal-Mart at Christmas. "What the hell are you-all doing sitting outside is what I'd like to know. Didn't they let you wait inside?"

My mother puts a finger to her lips. "Shh. It's just an older woman. She was scared, I think."

He picks me up and carries me down the steps of the porch, my mother walking behind us. "Come on, squirrel," he says. "We'll get you home."

I squint into the headlights and see the outline of someone sitting in the passenger seat. It's a woman, Mr. Mitchell's wife. She gets out of the truck to let us in, and I see she is short, halfway between my mother and me, with broad shoulders. Her hair is cut close around her head, like a little hat, and she looks at us with small, staring eyes.

"Hello," my mother says. "Thank you so much for coming all the way out here. This is my daughter, Evelyn."

Mrs. Mitchell smiles quickly at me, but her small eyes stay on my mother, even as she leans down to pop the front seat of the truck forward for us. I get in behind the driver's seat next to a bag of dog food. My mother sits behind Mrs. Mitchell, her legs folded, her chin resting on her knees.

Mr. Mitchell jogs around the front of the truck and slides in, whistling. "So, Tina, what do you think happened?" He looks over his shoulder while he backs out of the driveway, and when he catches my eye, he winks.

"The clutch gave out. I can't get it into first. I knew it was going to happen, but I thought I could make it to Wichita and back."

"Why didn't you tell me you needed a car? I would have loaned you the truck."

Mrs. Mitchell makes a quick, hissing sound with her tongue, like water sprinkled on a hot pan. We drive on in silence, until the back of the Volks-wagen appears in the headlights.

"Do you want me to take a look at it?" Mr. Mitchell asks, pulling up behind it. "I could try to fiddle with the clutch a bit."

Mrs. Mitchell turns on the overhead light and holds her watch up underneath it.

"Oh, that's okay, Merle," my mother says. "I feel bad enough, dragging you both out here."

Mr. Mitchell says, "Don't be ridiculous," but Mrs. Mitchell says nothing. From where I sit, I can see only one side of her face, gray and unmoving. She is looking straight ahead, squinting at the white Volkswagen bug.

"That's our car," she says, like no one else knows this. She looks at Mr. Mitchell with her small eyes. "You gave them our car?" Mr. Mitchell gets out of the truck, letting the door slam behind him. We watch him pop open the back of the Volkswagen and stand there, looking at it and shaking his head. I'm scared to talk. Mrs. Mitchell is not saying anything, but something about her, something invisible coming out of the back of her head like ultraviolet rays, makes me scared to move, even my head, even my mouth. My mother isn't moving either.

Mrs. Mitchell reaches up to the rearview mirror, tilting it so she can see my mother's face. "So, uh . . . Tina," she says. The way she says this makes it sound like just my mother's name is something bad, something you don't want to be called. "You don't have any family or anyone who could have come and picked you up?"

My mother waits so long to answer that at first I think she won't, but then she clears her throat and says, "Well, if I had, I suppose I would have called them."

"I suppose. How long have you been working for Merle?"

"About four years."

Out of the corner of my eye, I can see my mother is actually biting her tongue, the pink tip of it sticking out from between her teeth. She reaches over the front seat and opens Mr. Mitchell's door.

"Let me out, Evelyn."

I get out quickly, shutting the door behind us.

"No," she says. "You get back in. I need to talk to Mr. Mitchell."

"With her? No way."

"Get in now."

I get back in the truck. Mrs. Mitchell and I watch my mother walk over to Mr. Mitchell, her body making a shadow like the number eight in the headlights. I'm hungry, and I'm sick of this day. If I were at home, I would be in bed by now, asleep or reading Nancy Drew, my teeth brushed, my hair wet from the shower. They shouldn't have left me in the truck alone with Mrs. Mitchell. The keys are still in the ignition. She could drive away, take me with her.

"So, Evelyn . . . It's Evelyn, isn't it?" she asks, turning around, smiling with only her mouth. "Why did you-all go to Wichita?"

"To see Eileen."

"Who's Eileen?"

"My grandmother."

My mother and Mr. Mitchell are both peering into the engine of the car, winged insects swirling around their heads. My mother says something, and he laughs.

"So, where's your daddy?"

"Huh?"

"Your father. Where is he?"

I shrug my shoulders. I don't want to talk to her anymore.

She clicks her tongue, frowns. "Do you know who your daddy is, honey?"

I stare at her. She stares back, the muscles in her face tight and still. She reaches over the seat and tries to pat me on the hand. She has a diamond ring, a white flicker in the darkness. "You poor thing," she says. "It's not your fault."

Mr. Mitchell and my mother walk slowly back to the truck, Mr. Mitchell with his hands in his pockets, looking down at his feet. When Mrs. Mitchell gets out of the truck to let my mother in, she doesn't look at my mother, and my mother doesn't look at her.

"If that car was a horse, I'd have shot it long ago," Mr. Mitchell says, starting up the truck's loud engine. "Even if you get the clutch figured out, the transmission's bound to go next."

"Well," my mother says. "At least it got me to work."

"Yeah. I'll give you a ride until we can find something else for you."

My mother says thank you, but it is difficult to hear her because Mrs. Mitchell makes another hissing sound. Mr. Mitchell turns toward her, braking the truck so quickly that we all slide forward and then jerk back. He and Mrs. Mitchell look at each other, unblinking, for maybe three seconds.

But it seems longer, sitting in the backseat.

And now I know my mother shouldn't have called Mr. Mitchell for a ride, even if it meant we had to hitchhike, or call the police. Now Mr. and Mrs. Mitchell are in a fight, staring at each other right in front of us like they hate each other even though they're married. I've seen my mother and Eileen look at each other like this, eyes flat, mouths unmoving, a long stare that looks like hate but could be something else, and nothing you want to get in between.

$\mathcal{M}$R. MITCHELL IS GOING TO pick my mother up for work early, fifteen minutes before my bus comes. She has to give me a key to wear around my neck so I can lock the door behind me, and she tells me not to answer the door, not for anyone. She thinks I will die the moment she leaves, that I'll let people in from off the highway, turn on the iron to start a fire. I remind her that it will be summer soon, and then I'll be home by myself all the time.

"Don't even talk about that," she says, her hand over her eyes. "I can't think about that now."

I'm excited because today is the day of the science fair, and I finally get to bring my lima bean plants to school. I used empty milk cartons for containers, and I made a label for each one with red Magic Marker on masking tape: DARK, IN SUNLIGHT, DARK WITH MIRACLE-GRO, or IN SUNLIGHT WITH MIRACLE-GRO. I planted the seeds less than a month ago, pushing the seeds into the soil with my finger, and already the two that were in sunlight are actual plants, the leaves like small, waving hands. The one with Miracle-Gro in the soil is a darker green, the stem two inches taller than the other ones. Before she leaves, my mother helps me tape them inside a box so they won't get smashed on the bus.

Ms. Fairchild had been very particular that we should have a poster to go with our project, and it had to be a triptych, she said, a poster folded into thirds so it could stand up on its side. I got a piece of yellow poster board at the Kwikshop the same day I bought the lima bean seeds, and I tried just bending it into thirds, but it wouldn't stay up. So I cut it into thirds and taped it with masking tape on the back. Now it stands up on its side when it's unfolded, but it's crooked.

On the board, Ms. Fairchild had written HYPOTHESIS, OBJECTIVE, METHOD, OBSERVATIONS, and CONCLUSION. I copied these same words onto the yellow poster board, and I like how they look, very official. Under OBSERVATION, I have made a graph charting the growth of each plant in inches per week. So even though my poster is crooked, I'm pleased with the way it looks, and also with the lima bean plants themselves. I am amazed that anything came out of the soil at all, green and healthy, something coming out of nothing. On the bus, I show my poster to a second grader. I explain the graph to her, opening the box so she can see the plants for herself. She says it's nice, reaching into the box to touch the leaves.

The student with the best project gets to go to Topeka this summer to be in the state Science Fair, and if you win that, you get to go to Washington, D.C., and meet Ronald Reagan. I would love, more than anything, to meet Ronald Reagan, to see him in person, making his jokes. There is a chance that this could happen. I usually have the highest score on science tests. The only person who ever beats me is Traci Carmichael. She is smart, and she is also popular, and usually you don't get to be both. But she has always been popular, and this year you can actually see it because of friendship pins. They are just safety pins with beads pushed onto them in different colors, and you are supposed to have your own design and then bring them to school in a plastic bag to give to all your friends. I don't know who started it, but last year no one had them, and this year everyone does. Or the girls do. Boys don't.

When someone gives you a pin, you stick it on your shoelace, so people will know you have friends. I don't know who started it, but now you have to have at least one friendship pin if you're a girl or it looks like no one likes you. I have two: one from Patty Pollo, one from Star Sweeny. Traci Carmichael has nineteen. I count them when she stands by my desk, sharpening her pencils.

She also has four different OP sweatshirts, with matching ribbons for her braids. Other people have one or two of these sweatshirts—Brad Browning has three—but only Traci has four. They are just normal sweatshirts, with hoods and sometimes pockets and palm trees painted on the back, but they say OP on them, and this is what matters. I asked my mother for one for Christmas, but she said no. You could get just as good a sweatshirt without a palm tree on it for half the price, she said, and who needs a goddamn palm tree in the middle of Kansas anyway? She said "OP" stands for Over Priced, in her opinion anyway. But it doesn't. It stands for Ocean Pacific, and I wish I had one.

Traci Carmichael's house is the last stop the bus makes in the morning. She lives in a redbrick house, a porch swing in front, twelve different windows on just the front side. I can't imagine what it would be like to live there, in all that space. She doesn't have any brothers or sisters. I picture Traci at one end of the house, having to call to her mother at the other end, her hands cupped around her mouth.

I know Traci's mother, and I don't like her because of registration day. There was a long line to sign up for lunches, and the Carmichaels got there after we did. When Mrs. Carmichael saw the line, she said in a loud voice that she didn't appreciate the poor management that had led to such a long line on such a hot day, when some people were busy and had things to do. My mother and I were standing behind Robby Hernandez and his mother, and when they got up to the front of the line, Mrs. Carmichael was standing right next to them because of the way the line wound around itself. The Hernandezes had just gotten up to the counter when Mrs. Carmichael leaned forward, jingling her car keys to get the registration lady's attention, and said, "Excuse me, but don't you think the people who are actually paying for the lunches should get to go first?"

The registration lady said she didn't know, and Mrs. Carmichael said it only seemed fair, and then Brad Browning's mother raised her hand like she was in school and said she had just been thinking the same thing, the same thing exactly. They were both wearing sleeveless shirts and sweaters with the sleeves tied around their shoulders. My mother watched them talking, sweat trickling down her forehead, no sweater. I get free lunches too, and we were next in line.

The registration lady said she might as well finish up with Mrs. Hernandez, since she was already up at the front of the line, but by then Robby had turned what they were saying into Spanish and Mrs. Hernandez went straight to the back of the line, pulling him behind her, without anyone saying another word about it. So we had to go to the back of the line too. Mrs. Hernandez put on a pair of sunglasses even though we were inside, and I could tell she was crying, or at least trying not to, her mouth closed tight like she would never open it again.

When Traci and her mother got to the front of the line, my mother was too mad to talk. She stood very still, her arms crossed, her eyes trained on the back of Mrs. Carmichael's head as if just by looking at it, she could make it explode.

So when the bus pulls up to Traci's brick house with the porch swing and she isn't there, I'm glad, because maybe Traci is sick and won't be able to be in the science fair. Libby Masterson is Traci's next-door neighbor, and she isn't at her stop either, which makes sense, because she does everything Traci tells her to, and if Traci called her and said, "Don't go to school tomorrow," Libby probably wouldn't.

I know you're not supposed to be glad when other people get sick, but I have been sick of Traci for a long time. And it's not like you can make someone sick just by wishing for it. Eileen says you can make sick people better by praying for them. But I don't know if it works the other way.

I'm surprised by how much I like Ms. Fairchild, because she is old, and not pretty and her breath always smells like coffee. She has been teaching at Free State Elementary for twenty-nine years, which is longer than even my mother has been alive, and she has one dress for every day of the week, a Monday dress, a Tuesday dress, a Wednesday dress, and so on. She never mixes up the order. Star Sweeny makes fun of her for this, but I like it.

The first time I saw her, though, I thought, *Oh no.* I wished I would have gotten into Mrs. Blake's class, the other fourth-grade teacher, young and pretty, with straight blond hair that curves under her chin. She got married just last year, and some of the fourth graders from last year got to sing "Going to the Chapel" in her wedding. She wears high heels and bright sweaters and gold earrings shaped like little suns or little snowflakes, depending on the weather.

Ms. Fairchild, my teacher, has big eyebrows and short black hair cut like a pilgrim's. Her hair never moves, even in the breeze, and she does not wear earrings. When I first saw Mrs. Blake and Ms. Fairchild standing next to each other on the playground the first day of school, it was easy to think that Ms. Fairchild was unlucky.

But it turns out that Mrs. Blake is a screamer. We can hear her from our room, her shrill voice saying *Stop that! Stop that this instant!* When this happens, Ms. Fairchild walks across the room in her flat, soundless shoes to shut the door. She does not yell, and if we are good, she tells stories at the end of class about people who can turn into trees whenever they want, and pets that talk when their owners aren't home. Sometimes she reads out of a book, and sometimes she doesn't have to.

Today she is wearing a green dress with white buttons, the Friday dress. She looks at me carrying in my triptych poster and my box of plants, and she smiles. She tells me to put them on the shelf by the window. Star is already standing by the window next to a cookie sheet covered with aluminum foil and a mound of something that looks like dried mud.

"What is it?" I ask.

"It's a volcano. I'm going to make it explode." She doesn't have a triptych, not even a regular poster. Star is always getting in trouble, getting sent to the office for saying "fuck" like it's just a regular word you can say. She came to Kerrville from Florida last year because a hurricane blew down her family's house, and they had to move to Kansas to live with her aunt and uncle. She has long blond hair, and she wears Dr. Scholl's sandals and earrings that make it look like she has pierced ears even though she doesn't. They are just tiny magnets, one on each side of her earlobes, strong enough to stick to each other through the skin. She let me wear them once, for an hour.

Star mostly spends her time with boys, because the girls in our class don't like her. She makes things up, and you have to be listening carefully, or you won't know. She said her cousin had been killed by a poisonous butterfly, right here in Kansas; she said she once saw a man lick an envelope and get such a bad paper cut on his tongue that it actually rolled right out of his mouth and landed on the floor, and that on the floor, it looked like a large strawberry, one you could pick up and eat; she said when they lived in Florida her dad had killed the most dangerous kind of snake in the world, the dreaded Monty Python, which could kill you just by looking at you long enough to make you look back. Patty Pollo and I are the only two girls in the class who will still talk to Star, and Patty doesn't really count because she will talk to anyone because she says God loves everyone, even liars.

Brad Browning walks in, carrying a small flat board with a battery, wires, and a tiny lightbulb taped to it. He's wearing a new OP sweatshirt, a purple one.

"What's this?" Ms. Fairchild asks.

"It's a circuit." He looks up at her, blinking quickly. "My dad helped me."

"Where's your triptych?"

He blinks again. "My what?"

She frowns. More people come in, and the ledge by the window slowly fills up with projects. No one else has made a triptych, but they are good projects, some of them, better than mine. Stephen Maefield made an aluminum-can crusher. He says it can be used to crush aluminum cans, but also many other things. Vera Miles has a prism. She takes it out of her pocket and holds it up to the light, and a lovely rainbow appears on the floor, red blurring into orange blurring into yellow blurring into short bands of green, blue, and purple. I think it's beautiful, but I can see Ms. Fairchild is getting mad because no one has a triptych.

Ray Watley has a piece of cardboard with dead bugs pinned to it with colored thumbtacks. They are labeled underneath, but they are not even the real names of the bugs. They say things like BUG FOUND IN DRAIN OF BATHTUB and MOTH KILLED WITH SPRAY. There are at least thirty bugs pinned to the cardboard, and when he shows it to Ms. Fairchild, she makes a face and says, "Just put it by the window."

Libby Masterson shows up after all, carrying a small velvet bag with a yellow string around the top. It is full of rocks, she says, special rocks, and Ms. Fairchild asks her to take them out of the bag and spread them out on the shelf. Libby doesn't have a triptych either, but the rocks are beautiful. Some are blue and glossy, smooth to hold. Some look like normal ugly rocks on the outside, but they've been sliced open like oranges, and inside they are lovely, full of lavender crystals that sparkle in the light.

Ms. Fairchild shakes her head. "Libby, did you just go out and buy these rocks? Did you get these at the mall?"

Libby looks down at her shoes, so many friendship pins on them you can hardly see the laces. "Yes, ma'am."

"What's your hypothesis?"

Libby frowns, looking at the rocks. "Traci's on her way in," she says. "Her mom gave us a ride. She's helping her carry her thing in." She doesn't notice that I'm still holding one of the smooth blue rocks. I slip it into my pocket. There's a knock on the door and a "Helllooooo?" It's Traci and Mrs. Carmichael, holding a rectangular-shaped wooden object between them. Mrs. Carmichael is wearing a sweater tied around her shoulders again, a red one that matches the belt on her pants, and she smiles at Ms. Fairchild, making a face like Traci's project is too heavy for them to even carry. Ms. Fairchild knows Mrs. Carmichael because she's in the PTA and because when there's a holiday, she brings cupcakes for our class.

Ms. Fairchild moves across the room quickly and helps them stand the wooden thing on one end, and then you can see it really is a triptych, made out of wood, five or six times the size of mine, not crooked. There are actual hinges in between the panels, the kind you would see on a door. It still smells like sawdust. I try to imagine Traci working in the garage of her redbrick house, with a chain saw or some other large tool, cutting away at the wood, plastic goggles pulled down over her face.

"Very impressive," Ms. Fairchild says.

Mrs. Carmichael smiles at Traci. "That's just part one. We've got to go back for part two."

While they are gone, the rest of us stand around, looking at Traci's triptych. She has used large amounts of red glitter and glue to write SEISMOGRAPHS AND EARTHQUAKES across the top. Below, she has written what seismographs do and what a Richter scale is. There are color pictures of the aftermaths of famous earthquakes—San Francisco, Italy. Underneath each picture is the number that particular earthquake got on the Richter scale.

It's impressive enough on its own. We are all still looking at it when Traci and Mrs. Carmichael come back in, carrying something metal between them with a spring sticking out of the top. Ms. Fairchild goes to help them, but Mrs. Carmichael holds up her hand.

"It's not heavy," she says. "I just didn't want Traci to drop it after so much work. She's been a slave to this thing for the last month." When they have moved the metal thing to the ledge by the window, she turns to Traci, says, "Bye, sugar," and leaves.

"What is it?" Ray Watley asks.

"It's a seismograph," Traci says, pushing her braids behind her shoulders.

She waits until Ms. Fairchild is looking and then flips a switch. A roll of paper from an adding machine revolves slowly, letting out paper at one end, which Traci holds with one hand. Now you can see that the spring has a pen attached to the end of it, positioned so it makes one long, straight line on the paper. Traci's blue-gray eyes watch ours.

"Now jump," she says, pointing at Libby. Libby jumps, her braids that are supposed to be just like Traci's but aren't really flying up behind her. There is a small wave in the line, a tiny bump.

It's impossible not to say "ahhh," though I try not to. Traci smiles. "Now three people jump, and it'll get bigger." Three people jump. She shows us the paper.

"Yours is the best," Brad Browning tells her. No one says anything, but already, I know it's true. Traci will get to meet Ronald Reagan. Ronald Reagan will get to meet Traci.

Star says she wants to make her volcano go off now, and Ms. Fairchild says fine, as long as it doesn't really explode the way a volcano would. They are usually enemies. Star goes to her backpack and takes out a bottle of vinegar, red food coloring, and a box of Arm & Hammer baking soda. She pours a little of each in, one at a time, through a funnel into the mouth of the clay mud thing that is supposed to look like a volcano but doesn't at all. We stand in a circle around it, waiting. Nothing comes out, and she has to keep adding more. Finally, there is a small, oozing trickle of red.

"That's gross," Ray Watley says. "It looks like blood."

"More will come out," she says. "Just wait."

While we are waiting, Traci turns to look at my plants and the yellow triptych on the windowsill. Her eyes move slowly over the words, and I try not to watch. I'm embarrassed by it now, how crooked it is, how small.

"Is that yours?" she asks.

I nod, watching her carefully.

"It's nice," she says, and turns back around.

Star finally pours the rest of the bottle of vinegar into the volcano. When she does this, there is a crackling sound beneath, like aluminum foil being shaken, and then finally the mixture comes back out again in red blobs, rolling down the clay mound onto the cookie sheet, dripping onto the floor.

"It's like throw up!" Ray yells. He's very happy about this. "It's like blood and puke!"

Ms. Fairchild clears her throat and claps her hands twice. "That's enough. That's enough," she says, reaching for the paper towels. She makes us go back to our seats, warning us not to step in the lava from Star's volcano, which really does look like blood and maybe throw up. When she finishes with the paper towels, she stands at the front of the room, unsmiling, her hands on her hips.

"I have to say I'm a little disappointed. When I gave you this assignment in March, I clearly explained the rules. Only two people actually brought in a triptych the way you were supposed to."

Traci looks down at her lap, trying not to smile.

"And while Traci's is very impressive, I'm afraid only Evelyn's follows the procedure outlined in the rules for the Kansas State Science Fair. You have to have an experiment. You have to have a hypothesis, an objective, a method, observations, and a conclusion. You have to follow directions." She crosses her arms, her black eyebrows pushed down low. "Sometimes I don't think you children listen to me at all."

No one says anything. Her dark eyes rest on mine for just an instant. I am the only one who followed directions, and this is turning out to be the most important thing of all. There's a chance I could win, and it's like something sweet almost touching my tongue. Eileen says if you want something very much you can pray for it, and that gets God on your side, which helps a lot.

So I do. *Please, God, let me be the one to go to Topeka. Please.* I imagine God sitting in front of a computer with blinking lights, putting on headphones when my voice comes in like a radio frequency from far away. He turns dials, adjusts the headphones, watching words flash on a screen: *Bucknow, Evelyn. Kerrville, Kansas, U.S. Fourth Grade. Science Fair.*

"Many of you showed wonderful creativity and imagination with your projects. But I'm afraid many of you let your parents do most of the work." She looks at Brad Browning. "I'm going to send Evelyn Bucknow to represent our school in Topeka, because her work is clearly her own, and because she followed the rules."

I am silent, knowing this is probably the best thing to be right now. But in my head I say thank you to God. I imagine him taking off his headphones, chuckling to himself. *No problem, Evelyn. No problem.*

Traci raises her hand.

"Traci?"

"It's not fair," she says, lowering her hand.

"Traci's is the best," Libby agrees. I stay facing forward. But I can see other people are nodding, looking at Traci's triptych by the window, standing almost four feet high on its own. Ray Watley stomps his foot, and the seismograph records it.

Traci crosses her arms and leans back in her chair. She is steady, calm, but I can see tears in her blue-gray eyes. "My parents didn't do all the work, if that's what you're saying. My dad helped me with the wood, but it was my idea. I worked hard on that. I worked really hard."

Ms. Fairchild shakes her head. "I'm sorry, Traci. The rules for the contest are very specific."

"It's not fair," she says again. Ray glares at me and gives me the finger from under his desk.

I say nothing. It is fair, of course.

Ms. Fairchild says she wants us to leave our projects by the window for all of next week, and then we can take them home. She takes a Polaroid camera out of her desk drawer and takes pictures of each of our projects, but she takes several pictures of mine, getting a close-up of each plant.

Before lunch, she goes to her desk and pulls out an envelope, handing it to me with a smile. Inside is a crisp, new twenty-dollar bill. This is good enough, plenty, but then she reaches into her desk again and pulls out a trophy, brassy gold with a small gold statue of a woman holding a bowling ball at the top, SCIENCE FAIR WINNER taped across the bottom. When she gives it to me, she acts like people should clap, but no one does.

But when Randy, the bus driver, sees the trophy, he's impressed. "Hey, hey, hey, what have we got here?" he asks, swinging open the doors. "Looks like somebody won an Oscar."

"Science fair," I tell him.

Randy is the nicest bus driver our route has ever had—he is much better than Stella from the year before. Stella had bright yellow hair with a black strip across the top, and she kept a broom behind her seat. If we got too noisy, or if someone stood up before the bus came to a complete stop, she would stop the bus quickly and bang the top of the broomstick against the metal ceiling and yell that if we didn't shut up, she would wreck the bus on purpose, and break all of our little necks, and then she would be the only one laughing, ha ha ha. But then Traci Carmichael told her mother about Stella, and the next day, Stella was gone.

Randy is a big improvement. He brought little paper cups of candy corn for us on Halloween, handing them out one by one as we stepped on the bus. He gave out candy canes at Christmas. He plays country music on the radio, and he sings along to the words, his voice low and deep. Sometimes when we have to stop for a train, he turns off the radio and sings "This Train Is Bound for Glory," and everyone stops talking and just listens.

He points at my trophy. "For the plants you had with you this morning?"

I nod.

He smiles. He's missing teeth, but it's okay, because he's nice. "Congratulations, honey."

Traci and Libby are sitting in the front, and when I walk by, they stop talking and watch me, their mouths flat and small. Travis Rowley is already sitting in the very back seat, reading a comic book, his shoes sticking out into the aisle. One of his shoes says DARK along the toe, and the other one says AVENGER. He does not look up when I sit down.

Victor Veltkamp asks if he can hold the trophy. He is only a first grader, with a nose that always runs, but he is a little scary because already he knows the names of different kinds of machine guns, and he talks about them and pretends he is holding them, even when he is just sitting in his seat by himself, when no one is listening. "Man!" he says, picking up the trophy by its base, swinging it slowly, like he is a batter, warming up. "This things is heavy. You could really clock somebody with this thing. I mean, you could just..." He swings it again, *"Bam!"*

I am about to take the trophy back from him when I feel someone staring at me, the way you can feel someone staring even before you look. You don't see them, you don't hear them, but you know they're there. I look up and see that Traci has moved to the seat in front of me. She has been sitting there for a while, watching me with her blue-gray eyes, her small, pointed chin resting on the back of the seat.

Already I can feel my heart starting to pound, my fingers twitching. "What?"

She is very calm, her eyes even on mine. "It's not fair that you won," she says. She looks at the trophy that Victor Veltkamp is still swinging in his arms and then back at me. "Yours was nothing compared to mine. She made you the winner because she felt sorry for you. Anyone can see that." She is almost smiling now. If I do anything, look away only for a moment, she will think I believe her.

Victor aims the trophy at her like it's a gun for him to shoot her with. "She won and you lost," he says. "Too bad."

But Traci ignores him, looking only at me. "All the teachers know you don't have a dad," she says. "They feel sorry for you. They know your mom works in a factory making dog food and that your poster was the most you could afford. They know you don't have anyone to help you." She shrugs her shoulders. She is wearing her OP sweatshirt today, the blue one, palm trees on the front. "That's sad, fine. But that doesn't make you the winner."

Everyone is watching. I don't know how she knows I don't have a dad, but now she is saying that everyone knows this. I wonder if this is something I should have been more careful about keeping a secret. I think about her seismograph, so amazing, detecting every tremor in the room.

"I won because I followed directions," I say, but I can hear the shakiness in my own voice. I don't even know if this is true. I am very aware of Travis now, of everyone, all of them listening to this, to Traci telling me I am someone to feel sorry for. The bus stops at a railroad crossing even though there isn't a train, Randy singing "Kansas City, Kansas City, here I come."

She shakes her head. "I think it's okay for teachers to feel bad for you, but it's not fair when poor people get more than they should just because somebody feels sorry for them."

Victor Veltkamp wipes his nose with his hand and looks at me. "Hit her," he says. "You need to hit her for saying that."

And now, the moment he says this, I know I will hit her. I feel the electricity moving up and down my arms, my fingers twitching, my hand rising up to her face. My hand hits her cheek, and I'm surprised at how much it hurts my hand, how her cheek doesn't give way.

"Ouch!" I am the one to say it.

We stare at each other, both of us stunned. She puts her hand to her cheek, her eyes wide. And then, quickly, she is on me, grabbing my ear with one hand. She hits me on the mouth with the other, her fist solid and sharp.

I see a burst of color, red and blue, little sparks going off in darkness. My glasses are gone. I reach forward, swinging. Libby is yelling something from the front of the bus.

The bus stops, and we roll into the aisle like just one body, her fingernails pushed into the skin of my arms. I have her by the hair, one of her braids wrapped around my fingers twice. Victor is yelling words of encouragement, and I can smell the mud on the floor of the aisle, my face pressed up against it. My free hand moves up and down like a hammer until I feel her teeth biting into the skin at the bottom of my fist.

And then I feel myself rising, being picked up, one of Randy's large hands under each of my arms. "That's enough!" he yells. "That's enough!" He pushes me into a seat on the other side of the aisle. Traci stands up and tries to come at me again, but Randy pushes her back. She is crying, yelling something. The braid I was pulling on has come unraveled, and half of her hair hangs in front of her face, kinked up and wild.

"You girls STOP IT! Stop it RIGHT NOW!" He points at Traci, and then at me. His John Deere hat has fallen off, and I see, for the first time, that he is bald. We are all realizing this at the same time, looking up at him. He reaches down for his hat, and puts it back on with a shaking hand.

"YOU, Bucknow, to the back of the bus, NOW. YOU, Carmichael, to the very front, NOW! I won't have this bullshit on my bus. You're both kicked off for a week."

Randy gives me a look then, a look to let me know we aren't friends anymore, and this is the worst part of the whole thing, even though my lips sting so much that it is everything I can do not to cry right there in front of everyone. I get up and creep to the back of the bus, tasting the blood on my lips. Traci is still crying in the front, stupid Libby Masterson consoling her.

Victor Veltkamp hands me my glasses, the frames bent, the lenses unbroken. "Good job," he whispers. "Nice work."

But the other kids only stare at me, at the blood trickling down my chin now, soaking through my white shirt that was new from Eileen for Easter. Randy turns off the country music. We ride along with no sound, except for Traci's crying. The bus stops in front of Juvenile Corrections, and when Travis Rowley stands up to get off, I don't look up.

Randy does not say good-bye to Traci when she gets off at her stop, and he doesn't say good-bye to me when I get off at mine. I forget the trophy, leave it on the bus.

My mother is alarmed and very nice to me at first. She says, "Oh, baby, what happened?" in a worried voice, and before I can answer, she is pressing a wet washcloth against my mouth. But when I tell her, she narrows her eyes, and takes her hand away from the washcloth so I have to hold it myself.

"You started it?"

"She was saying things." I touch my cheek lightly, marveling at the swelling that is already there, the tenderness. I will have a swollen lip, perhaps a black eye.

"But you hit her first?"

I say nothing, keeping the washcloth up against my mouth. My mother groans and covers her face with her hands, looking at me from between her fingers.

"And I'm kicked off the bus for a week."

This part of the story seems the most difficult for her to take in. I watch red, comma-shaped splotches form on her throat and cheeks. "Go stand on the other side of the room, Evelyn. Hurry."

"Why?"

She exhales, slowly. "Because if you don't, I may kill you."

I go to the other side of the room. She walks around the kitchen, her arms moving up and down like she is trying to fly. She counts to ten three times in a row, all ten numbers coming out in just one breath.

"I'm sorry," I say.

"Great. How are you going to get to school?"

"I don't know."

"Great."

"Mr. Mitchell?"

She laughs, but there's no smile in it. "I don't think so." She puts another washcloth under the faucet and presses it against my mouth. "He can't even give me rides anymore, okay? We're screwed."

Something is wrong. Usually when I get home, she still smells like Peterson's. But now she is already wearing jeans and the gray sweatshirt, her hair wet from the shower.

"Why can't he give you rides?"

"Don't worry about it."

I take the washcloth off my lip, looking down at the small circles of blood seeping into the cloth. If there was a fight between my mother and Mrs. Mitchell, my mother, younger and taller, would probably win. But maybe not. Mrs. Mitchell's diamond ring would cut across my mother's face, leaving blood, a long, deep scratch. My mother has no rings, and would have to fight bare-handed.

"Evelyn, keep the washcloth up." She pushes my hand against my face hard enough to make my head jerk back, and she moves her hand away quickly and goes back to the other side of the room. We look at each other, saying nothing.

five

I WAIT UNTIL THE NEXT day, when she isn't so mad, to tell her I won the science fair. We are in the bathroom, and she is still wearing her nightgown, dabbing stinging peroxide on the cut on my lip, but when she hears this, she stops and almost smiles.

"Out of the whole class?"

I nod.

"Then stick with lima beans, Rocky," she says, touching the cotton ball to my lip. "Stay out of the ring."

She says she will figure out a way for us to get to Topeka when the time comes, and I shouldn't worry about that at all. But there is no way to get anywhere right now, to work or to school, so when Monday comes, we both just stay home. It should be fun, but it isn't. All day there is a steady, gray rain that makes me want to sleep. We eat peanut butter and Wonder Bread. We watch game shows that run into each other until the whole day is gone. The school calls in the afternoon, telling her I'm not there, wanting to know why.

"She's sick," my mother tells them, switching the phone to her other ear.

They want to know what kind of sick. My mother frowns and looks down at me. "Carsick. She'll be back next week."

We walk to the Kwikshop across the highway, and the manager tells my mother no, they aren't hiring, but maybe something will open up in the fall. She buys milk and a box of oatmeal. At home, she calls restaurants, hotels, and banks. She tells secretaries and answering machines that she can't type, but she can talk talk talk, to just about anybody, and that she will also need a ride to and from work. She will learn to type, she says. She is a fast learner. No one calls back. After a while, she stops calling and just looks out the window, watching the rain.

On Tuesday, Mr. Mitchell knocks on the door, holding a bag from Taco Bell. "Hi," he says, his eyes on my mother's face.

We eat together at the table. He tells me he made the tacos himself, and that the people at Taco Bell let him come in and use their kitchen anytime. My mother laughs, her hand over her mouth. I understand he is not supposed to be here, that his being here is somehow illegal. But he's here anyway, like Mrs. Mitchell stopped existing, not just here, but anywhere. She didn't win the fight after all. She made him choose, and he chose us.

The next day, he comes back, this time carrying paper sacks of groceries from his truck, holding a red umbrella between his head and his shoulder. He is wet with rain and breathing hard by the time he gets to our door. "Ho ho ho," he says, his hand on top of my head.

I take one of the bags from him and look inside. Canned green beans. Frozen broccoli. But also ice cream, chocolate syrup. He lifts a head of lettuce out of another bag, two bars of soap.

"You don't have to do this, Merle," my mother says. She takes a dishtowel and dabs at the rain on his cheeks. They are standing close to each other, my mother looking up.

"I want to do this," he says. He takes the rest of the groceries out of the bag, lifting them out and setting them down carefully, the broccoli, the beans, the soap, the ice cream, the paper towels, and everything else until it is all spread out on the counter before us like a display in a window, so we can see just how much he means this, how much he wants to help.

With the groceries, it's better, but I still don't like missing school. I miss the library, and the large, lit globe in Mr. Pohl's room. I miss science. Ms. Fairchild showed us a movie the week before about a plant growing, the film sped up so much that you could watch the plant grow from a seed to a tall, leafy plant in less than a minute. It looked like it was exploding. I think about my lima bean plants, dying on the ledge by the window, no one giving them water.

I'm worried Ms. Fairchild knows about the fight. Traci is probably not missing school, because her mother has a red station wagon with a bumper sticker that says PROUD PARENT OF AN HONOR ROLL STUDENT, and I have seen her drop Traci off in front of the school on the mornings when she misses the bus. I tell my mother this, and she frowns and says life isn't always fair. Or maybe it is, she adds, because I hit Traci first. Just walk away next time, she says. Turn the other cheek.

Wednesday afternoon the phone rings, and it's Mrs. Carmichael.

"Do you want to speak to my mother?" I ask.

"No, Evelyn," she says. "I want to speak to you." She wants to know if I know that Traci had her clothes stolen from her gym locker while she was playing volleyball today, including her heart-shaped gold necklace that her grandmother gave her for Christmas. Someone, Mrs. Carmichael says, *some-one*, walked into the girls' changing room and broke the lock on Traci's locker, and walked right out with everything. Did I know that?

"No," I say. I am thinking about the smooth blue rock I took from Libby's rock collection. This is all I have. "I didn't."

"Can I speak with your mother?"

My mother gets on the phone and listens for a while, frowning, looking at me and then out the window. She tells Mrs. Carmichael that yes, I have been home all week. No, she says, there is no way I could have gotten to school. Yes, she is sure. Absolutely. Yes. Good-bye now. Good-bye. She hangs up while Mrs. Carmichael is still talking.

"What a bitch," she says. "What? Does she think I'm lying? Maybe some-one else hates her brat."

But I know that I am the only one who hates Traci Carmichael. And it's hard to imagine that anyone would really be able to walk right into the girls' locker room and break the lock to steal her clothes, that someone could be that fearless. There is a chance she herself hid them, just to get me in trouble.

The next morning, it's still raining, a cool breeze lifting the sheets pinned to my window. I stay in bed late because I can, because there's nothing else to do. I am tired of not being able to go to school, staying home all day and watching game shows.

There is something red on my floor, some unfamiliar cloth. I sit up in bed, squinting. There's a palm tree on it.

In an instant I am awake, kneeling at the foot of my bed. A red OP sweatshirt lies by the foot of my bed, folded neatly on top of a pair of white A. Smile jeans. There is also a pair of red Keds, friendship pins covering the laces.

I stare down at the shoes, scared to touch them. They shouldn't be here in the first place, and it seems like they could easily disappear, or maybe explode. There are smiley faces drawn on the white rims of the shoes. I unfold the sweatshirt carefully, tracing the line of the palm tree with my finger. It feels like I did steal the clothes now. My fingers twitch with fear and excitement. There are people who sleepwalk, people who get up in the middle of the night and do crazy things without even knowing it themselves.

The gold heart necklace is in the pocket of the jeans.

I pull back the sheet from the window and look out across the parking lot to Unit B. Mr. Rowley is sitting on his balcony even though it's raining, drinking coffee and looking down at the pavement.

I was out on a bathroom pass once and saw Travis Rowley walking through the empty hallways, his fingers running up and down the locks of lockers, like someone who plays piano and doesn't need to look at the keys.

I start to watch for him more carefully. He does not have to go to Juvenile Corrections on Fridays, and the bus drops him off at three-thirty, Randy waving at him from the window. He stops in at the Kwikshop and reappears a moment later, crossing the highway, his arms crisscrossed over his jacket like he is trying to keep something from falling out. Later, he comes back outside and sits on the stairs of Unit B, his curly head bent over a *MAD* magazine, a large Coke from the Kwikshop by his side.

Travis Rowley, thief, breaker of locks, my own dark avenger and first true love.

I hide Traci's clothes in my bottom drawer, covering them with my old dolls, headless Barbies, the pink-and-white dress that I had to wear to Wichita. But late at night, when I'm sure my mother is asleep, I take them out again. I slip the Keds on my feet and walk around my room in slow circles, the friendship pins glinting in the glow of my nightlight. My own shoes are getting small on me, my toes curled against the canvas, but Traci's shoes fit perfectly. I wish I could wear them to school, but even wearing them in my room seems dangerous. There is a chance that Travis Rowley did not steal the clothes for me after all. Perhaps Traci planted them here, and she will show up with her mother and the police, and they will fling open the door and say, "A-ha!"

And in the daytime, I have to be careful of my mother, now that she is home all the time, putting away laundry in my room instead of leaving it on the table, opening my door in the mornings to raise my window shade and kiss me on the forehead, saying, "What's the story, morning glory?"

I realize this is what my mother is really like when she is not tired. When she worked at Peterson's with Mr. Mitchell, she had to wake up at six every morning. By seven o'clock at night, she was yawning, doing the dishes, standing over the sink with her eyes closed. Now she sleeps in until eight, and she cooks the eggs and bacon that Mr. Mitchell bought, humming along with the radio. She plays hangman at the kitchen table with me after dinner, and we go on walks when it isn't raining. I was so sad two days ago, but now my mother is in a good mood and there are groceries in the cabinets and Traci Carmichael's clothes are hidden in my drawer because Travis Rowley stole them for me, and now I am so happy I can't even remember why I would ever be sad.

When the weekend comes, it's still raining. My mother gets out her old records—Fleetwood Mac and Elton John. I like the song "Rocket Man," about the man who travels in a rocket, but he's sad because he misses the Earth so much and he misses his wife. I wonder what that would be like, to be up in a rocket, so far away from the Earth that you would miss it. Being up by the stars would be pretty in its own way, but there wouldn't be any trees, or deer, or thunderstorms. Eileen says when she leaves the Earth she won't miss it at all because she's going to a better place. But I think I would miss it a lot, even on rainy days like this.

When I go back to school on Monday, there is only a small cut on my lip, already healing over with a maroon scab, and the black eye is gone. When Ms. Fairchild sees me, she puts her hands on her hips and shakes her head. "My goodness, child, where have you been? I'd given you up for dead."

"Sick," I tell her.

She looks hard at me. "Five whole days you were gone. That's too much. Tell your mother if you miss this much again, she needs to call me."

Traci Carmichael is watching all of this from her seat in the third row, wearing a white OP sweatshirt, not nearly as nice as the red one folded in my bottom drawer. She looks at Libby Masterson, but neither of them say anything. She still has a scratch on her neck, and I am glad about this. *I did that.*

We do worksheets, story problems about what time trains will arrive if they are going so many miles per hour. It's not a contest. Ms. Fairchild doesn't say anything about the winner being whoever finishes their worksheet first. But today I know I must be the first one done, especially because it's math, and the answers are always the same. It has nothing to do with people feeling sorry for you. I finish my worksheet, and when I stand up to turn it in, I look at Traci's paper and see she is only halfway done.

Ms. Fairchild looks over my answers. "Good. Good," she whispers. "The others are still working, so here's another worksheet."

I go back to my desk, and I can see Traci is hurrying now, looking up at me quickly. There.

When the bell rings, Ms. Fairchild touches me on the arm. "Would you stay after, dear? I'd like us to have a little chat."

"I can't miss my bus," I tell her. It seems to me we have already chatted.

She nods once. "This will only take a moment, Evelyn. Keep your seat."

When everyone else has gone, she sits down in the chair next to mine, crossing her legs. The chair is too small for an adult, and she wears black stockings even though it is late May. Sitting there, smiling, her black legs crossed over each other, with her black helmet hair, she looks a little like a spider.

"You know the science fair is in July," she says. "In Topeka."

"I know."

She nods at me, squinting. "I just want to make sure you'll be able to make it, Evelyn. Your mother will be able to take you?"

"She will."

She looks at her fingernails. She bites them, and they are pale and ragged, sickly looking. "It's a big honor to represent the whole school. You wouldn't want to miss it. I'd be glad to take you myself."

I watch her carefully, wondering if she feels sorry for me, if she knows I don't have a father. "I don't need a ride. My mom said she would take me. Thanks though."

I stand up to go, but Ms. Fairchild shakes her head and points back at my chair. "Evelyn, I know your mother cares about you in her own way. But I want to be very clear with you about something." She pauses, recrossing her legs so I can hear it, nylon sliding against nylon. "You have to understand that you're not the same as she is. You've been given a little gift." She points to the place where her hair touches the edge of her glasses. "Right here." She taps twice, and I think of the fairy godmother in *Cinderella,* tapping pumpkins with her wand exactly two times, causing stars to shoot out, wishes to be granted. She leans forward, her breath smelling of coffee, her teeth straight but yellowed. "People who don't have this gift often don't understand how important it is to nurture it, to help it grow. Do you see what I mean?"

Out the window, I can see the long block of orange school buses pulling up to the curb, engines idling, doors sliding open. I have been given a little gift.

"So I hope your mother can take you. But if she can't, you still need to go. You need to call me up, and I'll come get you."

I nod. She takes off her glasses, still looking at me. I take off my glasses too, because for a moment I think she is going to place them on my eyes, the way you place a crown on someone's head when they become queen. *Welcome to being smart. This is how it goes.* But she only rubs her eyes and puts them back on, yawning. "You can't miss any more school, Evelyn, not with your potential. Your mother is very nice, but you're not the same kind of people. You have a different future in front of you." She taps the side of her head again. "You've been blessed."

I forget about the buses. It's important, what's happening, the beginning of something. It's the way stories start. Someone is blessed, picked out as special by someone who can tell, their luckiness planted deep inside them, sure as a seed.

I watch Travis, but I have to pretend not to. I glance at him in the hallways, and walk by his locker when I can, just close enough so that if he wanted to say something to me, he could. I hope to get a wave, or even a secret wink to let me know for certain that he is the one who stole Traci's clothes and crept into my room through the window, placing them on my floor as I slept. But I get nothing, or sometimes just a quick nod. He smokes cigarettes by the shrubs at lunch with other boys, and does not look at me at all. He gets detention often, and is not always on the bus.

But now that I am blessed I am getting bolder. Sometimes I watch him just long enough for him to turn around and see me watching. Maybe I will be the one to wink.

Mr. Mitchell is still coming over in the daytime. He's not there when I get home from school, but the refrigerator and cabinets are full of new and interesting groceries. My mother, smiling and rested, waits for me at the bus stop, and on the walk home she asks about school, about the bus, about staying away from Traci Carmichael and turning the other cheek, her hand on the back of my shoulder.

I look in her room one day and see one of the posts of her white wooden bed frame has splintered off, like a branch of a tree struck by lightning. Half the mattress has fallen through the bed frame, lying on the floor. When I ask her what happened, she scratches her head and looks like she doesn't remember. She does not cross her eyes.

"It just broke," she says. "I'll fix it later."

I look back at the bed, and then up at her. "How did it break?"

"It just broke."

"It just broke?"

She shrugs. "I was jumping on it."

"Why?"

"You know, just for fun." She pulls the door shut, nudging me out of the way. I watch her walk back down the hallway. When Star got to stay over, and we wanted to jump on my bed so we would get dizzy and fall over, my mother said no. Absolutely not. Furniture is expensive, she said, and beds aren't made for jumping.

Calm down and play a quieter game, she said. No more horseplay.

I try to imagine my mother jumping on her bed, ignoring her own rules. She would put her red hair back in a ponytail and take her shoes off, her bare feet flying high in the air. I am certain that Mr. Mitchell was there with her when the bed broke; that's why she shut the door to her room. I picture them jumping together, holding hands, Mr. Mitchell so much older, but still able to whisper something in her bouncing ear that could make her throw back her head and laugh.

· · ·

Mrs. Rowley is so thin and bony looking that sometimes I think just a very loud sound could make her shatter, all her bones splintering up like a cracked vase, then falling to the ground. So it's a good thing she's usually the one being loud. She's a screamer, and although the people above us are loud, she's the loudest. When she's mad, we can hear what she's saying, even though she lives in a different unit and there is a whole parking lot in between. She is mad most of the time, and we know exactly why. Kevin and Travis and Mr. Rowley don't help her clean up. They live like roaches. They treat her with no respect, she says, and she is getting just a little tired of it.

But just like we know things about her, she knows things about us. She's a watcher, the kind of watcher who wants you to know she's watching. On the morning of the last day of school, she opens the door as I'm walking to the bus stop, Jackie O growling in her bony arms. "That man sure does spend a lot of time over at your house during the day, doesn't he?"

I try to look over her shoulder, to see if Travis is behind her, inside. He's been getting rides to school with Kevin's friends in the morning, in an orange car with mud flaps painted with white silhouettes of naked women.

"I asked you a question," she says. "I see that big truck of his parked out here for about an hour each side of noon almost every single day." She smooths back Jackie O's ears. "Is that what she does now? Sit around all day, waiting for him to come over?"

I swing my backpack over my shoulder. "Sounds like that's what you do."

"Don't you sass me. Don't you sass. Who is he?"

"That's her boss. They're having lunch."

"Ha," she says. "I bet they are."

I start to walk away, but she calls after me, Jackie O barking in her arms. "You tell your mother that this is a decent neighborhood. You tell her this is a place for families. We don't need any sort of indecency around here."

My mother says that when Mrs. Rowley is mean, which is generally the case, it is really because she is just unhappy, and who could blame her with a husband like that, and Travis always in so much trouble. She says this is really the only reason people are ever mean—they have something hurting inside of them, a claw of unhappiness scratching at their hearts, and it hurts them so much that sometimes they have to push it right out of their mouths to scratch someone else, just to give themselves a rest, a moment of relief.

I look into Mrs. Rowley's deep-set eyes, burning at me from behind her glasses with the gold chain looping down beneath them, and I think that what my mother says could very well be true. We can hear Mrs. Rowley's unhappiness through our walls almost every night, yelling at Kevin and Travis, at Mr. Rowley, what sometimes sounds like strangled cries, but mostly just sounds like screaming.

At school, Ms. Fairchild tells us to have a good summer, but also to continue to feed our minds. She says she has a crystal ball, and that she will be able to look into it over the summer months to see which of us are being good, which of us are being bad, which of us are reading good books, and which ones of us are throwing our lives away watching television or some other kind of nonsense. She says if she doesn't like what she sees in her crystal ball, she will cast a spell and cause our hair to turn green.

She shows us a picture of her grandnephew in California, tanned and happy, his blond hair tinted light green. "See?" she says.

"It's from the chlorine," Star whispers, rolling her eyes.

Before recess, Ms. Fairchild hands me a slip of paper.

Kansas State Fourth Grade Science Fair 1982
Washington School Gymnasium
July 21   2:00 P.M.

On the bottom, she's written GOOD LUCK and her home phone number.

I am on the monkey bars when I see Star waving at me from behind the school. "Listen, I'm going to the fucking park," she whispers. "You want to come?"

I think of Ms. Fairchild, my hair turning green. "We'll get in trouble."

"What are they going to do to us? It's the last day." She moves her eyebrows up and down, her magnetic earrings glimmering in the sunlight. "I do it all the time, and I've never gotten caught."

Ms. Fairchild is standing by the basketball court. Her head turns slowly back and forth across the playground, like the light in a lighthouse. Even if she doesn't catch me leaving, she will see my empty chair when the class goes back in from recess. She will push her skinny lips together and breathe out through her nose, shaking her head at the empty chair, disappointed, worried that I've already forgotten about being blessed.

But I also know that this afternoon, Traci Carmichael's mother is coming in as room mother, giving out cupcakes for everyone because it's the last day.

On Valentine's Day, she brought in white cupcakes with pink icing, a candy heart with red words placed on top of each one. Mine said LOVE YOU and Star's said TOO CUTE. But that was before the fight, before Traci's clothes were stolen. I don't know if Mrs. Carmichael will give me a cupcake now. It would be terrible if she didn't, if I were the only one who didn't get a cupcake.

Star says there's a park we can go to, that we can play in the sprinklers. "I do it all the time," she says again, pushing back her hair. "Evelyn, you should try to have some fucking fun now and then."

"Okay," I say. "I'll go."

We run to the chain-link fence, crouching low. Once over it, we cross a ravine and creep through backyards, staying away from barking dogs and people watering their lawns. I take off my shoes and walk barefoot in the grass, thinking about how good it feels in between my toes, and Star does the same thing, carrying one Dr. Scholl's sandal in each hand. It's a good day to be outside. Nickel-sized balls of cotton drift down from the cottonwood trees by the river, floating slowly in the warm breeze and covering the ground, so that it looks like a gentle snow falling, even though the grass beneath our feet is warm as early June.

"Fuck, it's hot," Star says.

She's right about the sprinklers in Rocket Park. Seven sprinklers sputter out arches of cool water, little rainbows in the mist of each one. Only two older girls are in the park, wearing bikinis and smoking cigarettes, stretched out on beach towels. One lies on her stomach, propped up on her elbows. The other one is pregnant, lying on her back and smoking a cigarette, so much baby oil rubbed on her round belly that it glistens in the sunlight.

Star runs out in front of me, dodging the spray of the sprinkler long enough to get behind it and take aim. I scream when I feel the first slap of cold water on my shoulder, and then on the side of my face. The sunbathing girls look up and glare at us, even though their radio is playing music that is louder than we are. They talk for a moment, glare at us again, and the unpregnant one helps the pregnant one to her feet. They fold up their towels, turn off their music, get in their car, and drive away.

"Pregnant women aren't supposed to be around sprinklers," Star says. "It can be bad for the baby. That's why they left."

I am the one to discover we can pull the sprinklers right out of the ground. We do this, chasing each other as far as the hose will stretch. We slide into stretches of mud, rinse ourselves off, then slide in the mud again. It's wonderful. The sun moves across the sky. I begin to get tired, feeling the first pinpricks of a sunburn on my nose and shoulders. We are both dripping wet, our hair sticking to the sides of our faces. And then the sprinklers turn off, all at once, slowing to a trickle and then nothing. Star stops running and looks at me, the dry sprinkler still in her hand.

"I'm hungry," she says. We have missed lunch.

"What do you usually do?"

"I don't know. I've never done this before."

We go to Arby's, and I spend six dollars of the science fair money because Star hasn't brought any. We sit shivering in a booth with a sunny window, our wet clothes too cold for the air-conditioning, dipping salty fries into ketchup.

"This is great," Star says. She doesn't chew with her mouth closed. "When I grow up, I'm going out to eat like this every single day."

"That'd be expensive," I say. Six dollars, gone, just like that.

"I'll be rich. I'll be a stewardess."

"They aren't rich."

She rolls her eyes. "They are. We had one come and talk to us on career day in Florida. She said the only bad part of her job was that she had to sleep in hotel rooms and eat out in restaurants all the time. That's what she was *complaining* about."

There are five french fries left. Star puts them all in her mouth at the same time and swallows, looking at me the whole time. "So I was like, if that's the worst thing, let me at it. You'll never hear me complain about it. No cooking, no dishes. Plus you get to fly all over the fucking world. And all the pilots fall in love with you."

"Did she say that?"

She pushes her hair back over her shoulder. "No, but you know that's what happens." She reaches for her Coke, poking a straw into the lid. "The only thing is, you have to be careful not to get fat. If you get even a little bit fat, they'll fire you."

"Why?"

Star swallows, her eyes scanning the restaurant. "It's bad for the plane . . . if the stewardesses are fat." She sees me squinting and looks away. "Anyway, it's a rule."

I look out the window. Right there, on the street in front of the Arby's, is Mr. Mitchell, wearing a Royals baseball hat, easing out of his truck. He stops to put money in the meter, fishing in the pockets of his jeans for change.

"What?" Star asks. "What are you looking at?"

"It's a friend of my mom's."

"Like a boyfriend?" She moves to my side of the booth so she can see him.

"Kind of," I say. He takes his baseball hat off and wipes sweat from off his forehead, looking right at our window. If he sees us, he doesn't show it.

"He's too fucking old for your mom," Star says.

We watch him walk into the flower shop across the street. He smiles and holds the door open for two women coming out.

"Do you think he's buying flowers for your mom?" Star asks. She is almost sitting on me now, waiting, trying to get a good look. We wait, watching the door, not looking away. No one has ever gotten my mother flowers.

The glass door of the flower shop opens again, and Mr. Mitchell steps out carrying red roses, their stems wrapped in green paper. Star and I look at each other, mouths open, eyes wide. For a while, there are no words, nothing we can say. We watch him get back in his truck, Star clutching my sunburned arm.

"Roses mean love. He must love her," she says, nodding the way she does when she talks, whether she's lying or not.

My mother meets me at the bus stop, wearing a blue dress that is too hot for the day. She is also sunburned, especially on her nose and cheeks.

"You're going to get a big surprise," I tell her. I am so excited about the roses I could blow up. The whole way back to school and then home on the bus, I have been imagining her taking them into her arms, saying, "Oh Merle," like a woman in a soap opera, smiling at what she knows they mean.

But my mother frowns and says she doesn't need any more surprises. When we get inside, she looks at me, squinting. She wants to know why my shoes are wet, how I got sunburned.

"They took us to the park," I say. "They do that on the last day."

Her eyebrow moves up. "I didn't hear anything about a park."

There is a knock at the door. Mr. Mitchell, wearing no baseball hat and a different shirt from before, is on the other side of the screen, holding not roses, but a box of pizza. He cups his hands against the screen to see inside. "Shakey's Pizza," he says.

I run to open the door for him and reach up to see inside the box, to see if it's pepperoni. He holds it high above my head, laughing. "Uh, Miss, that'll be eleven ninety-five with tax," he says. "Uh, Miss, you can't have the pizza until you pay."

"Evelyn," my mother says, holding the door open for him, "did you ever think to stop and say hello to him before you started grabbing? Were you raised in a barn?"

I stop jumping. "Hi."

"Hi, squirrel." He tousles my hair with his free hand. "If you hold on a moment, I'll set this down on the table and let you dig in." He looks up and smiles at my mother as she walks around the counter to get a knife, running her hands through her hair.

"I wasn't expecting you this evening," she says. "I'm just a mess."

"Sorry to stop by without calling. I ended up having to come back into town, and I thought I'd see if you-all wanted to have dinner. I didn't mean to interrupt. If you want me to come back later . . ."

"No no," she says. "Don't be silly. I just need to take a quick shower. I walked down to Pine Ridge because I heard they were hiring."

He makes a face. "You walked that far in this heat?"

"It wasn't bad going there, just coming back."

"Were they hiring?"

"They took my application. They wanted to know if I had a car."

"Oh," Mr. Mitchell says. "Well, maybe they'll call."

"Maybe." She shakes her head, looks down at her sunburned hands. Only the tops of her hands are red; the palms are still white.

"If they don't," he says, "we'll work something out."

My mother gives him a long look, smiling slowly.

He tells her if she wants to jump in the shower, he will help me make a salad so it will be ready when she comes out. She likes this idea and disappears down the hallway, humming to herself. He takes lettuce, carrots, cucumbers, and tomatoes out of the refrigerator. He gets a bowl down from the cabinet above the sink. He knows where everything is.

"Okay, squirrel," he says, lifting me up on the counter. "Your job is to tear up the lettuce. You think you can handle that?"

"Aren't you going to wash it first?"

"Huh? Oh yeah." He holds the head of lettuce under the faucet and hands it back to me. He scrapes and chops the carrots, whistling "On Top of Old Smokey." I don't know how long he is going to wait to bring in the roses, if he is going to do it in front of me or not.

He starts to sing, making up words that are wrong.

On top of Old Smokey, all covered with cheese
I ate a bad hot dog, threw up on my knees.

He laughs, and I laugh too. It would be nice if Mr. Mitchell came to live with us. I wouldn't mind if he moved right in with us and married my mother. It wouldn't even be so bad if we just kept going on this way, with him living somewhere else but coming by sometimes to give us pizzas and flowers, cutting up carrots while my mother takes a shower.

He asks me why I am so sunburned. I tell him they took us to the park. When lying, it is important to keep all your lies the same.

Mr. Mitchell looks up at me and smiles again. "You're a good kid," he says. "I like having you around."

I hear the shower water turn on. "When are you going to give her the roses?"

He looks up. "Huh?"

I roll my eyes. "The roses you bought today. From the flower shop."

He yells "ouch" and "dammit," and I look down to see he has slipped with the knife and cut his thumb, the one on the same hand as the two purple fingernails. He looks away and puts his thumb in his mouth. "What do you mean?" he mumbles.

"I saw you today. I saw you buying roses." I am surprising him by how much I know. "Where are they?"

He turns and looks at me, and when his blue eyes meet mine, they flinch. "How did you see me buying roses?"

He sounds angry, like I am in trouble, and I wonder if he knows I am lying about the teachers taking us to the park. "I was at Arby's, after we went to the park. I saw you come out of the flower shop. You bought roses."

He takes his thumb out of his mouth, holds it under the faucet, and asks me what I was doing at Arby's on a school day, the cut from his thumb turning the water from the faucet pink before it rushes down the drain. He has a ring too, just a gold band though, no diamond.

"Oh. They were for your wife?"

He shuts the faucet off and rubs his eyes. He looks up at me and then down, shaking his head. I can feel my mind stretching, putting pictures together very quickly. I see Mr. Mitchell carrying the roses out of the shop, then going home and giving them to his short, small-eyed wife. *Oh Merle, thank you*. She would put them in a vase on a table in their house. She could be looking at the roses in the vase right now, this very moment, her nose against their red petals.

He must not hate Mrs. Mitchell after all. He might love her again, maybe as much as he loves my mother, but in a different way. Or maybe the same way, at different times. Or perhaps he doesn't really love either of them at all. I feel bad for him, standing there, looking down into the sink. "Don't worry," I say. "I won't tell her."

"Aw Jesus," he whispers, his hand over his eyes. He grabs a paper towel and wraps it tightly around his thumb, so it looks like a little finger puppet, a tiny mummy. "Evelyn, I . . ." His eyes move around the kitchen, like it is someplace new to him, a place he doesn't know. "Okay," he says. "I better go. Shit. I need to leave. I need to just leave right now. I'm sorry, honey. I'm so sorry."

He kisses me on the forehead, picks up his keys, and walks out, gently closing the door behind him.

"Where'd he go?" my mother asks. She is wearing a tight flowered dress with no sleeves, her hair wet, slicked back, water dripping down on her sunburned shoulders. She is wearing red lipstick and perfume that smells like strawberries.

"He's gone." I pick at a piece of melted cheese on the side of the pizza box. "He left the pizza."

She looks at the pizza and then at me. "What do you mean gone? Where did he go?"

"I guess he had to go home."

She sits down on the couch, looking around the room like she thinks maybe I am lying and actually he is still here, only hiding. "Did he use the telephone?"

"No."

"Did he say he'd forgotten something?"

"No."

She crosses her arms, looking at me. "That doesn't make any sense, Evelyn."

"Do you want some pizza?"

She stands up, her hands on her hips. Her hair has already started to dry in the warm breeze coming in through the screen door, red curlicues springing up around her forehead. "Evelyn, did you say something to him?"

"No." I pick up a piece of pizza. I won't tell her about the roses. It will just make her sad. He shouldn't have been coming over here anyway.

"That just makes no sense to me. No sense at all." She rubs her lips together. "What did you say to him?"

"Nothing."

We hear a car. My mother runs to the window, but it's only Mr. Platt from Unit D, his El Dorado slinking onto the highway. "Well that's great," she says. "Just great."

"Have some pizza, Mom."

She watches me, saying nothing. "I'm not hungry, Evelyn." She goes back to her room and closes the door.

I am sitting on the front step when she comes out from her room an hour later, her cheeks tear-stained, her sunburn worse. She sits down next to me, holding a slice of pizza, the pepperoni picked off. "Hey there, you," she says.

I nod, squinting into the Rowleys' front window. They are sitting at a table, all four of them, the glow of a television flickering in the corner of the room. Mrs. Rowley turns and sees me looking in, my mother sitting next to me. She gets up and closes the curtains.

My mother is no longer crying, but she looks bad, the skin on her nose starting to peel. Her hair has dried funny, one side flat against her face, the other side still curly. She looks at my burned arms and face, frowning. She goes inside and comes back out with a jar of cold cream.

"You're really burned, Evelyn," she says, rubbing the cream onto my shoulders. This is what smelled like strawberries, the cream. It feels good on my skin, taking away the sting. "If you would have told me they were taking you to the park, I would have made you wear sunscreen."

"You're burned too," I remind her. "I'm sorry Mr. Mitchell left."

She stops rubbing, her fingers still on my back. "Well, if you don't know why he left, you've got nothing to be sorry for."

I don't say anything. She rubs some cream on her own throat and the backs of her hands. "So what's my surprise?"

"What?"

"My surprise. You said I was going to get a big surprise tonight. And now I could use one."

I look back at the Rowleys' window, the closed curtain. "Later," I say, trying to think.

She gives my leg a poke. She's trying hard to smile. "Tell me now. I want my surprise now."

I think of the roses in Mrs. Mitchell's vase. He is at home with his wife now, maybe sitting with her at a table. He maybe sings for her. Maybe he tells her the same jokes.

"Later," I say. "You'll get it later."

My mother goes inside to watch television, but I stay out on the step, trying to figure out what to do. I consider giving her Traci Carmichael's heart-shaped locket, but then I think about what would happen if Mrs. Carmichael ever saw her with it, maybe in the grocery store, how terrible that would be.

Mr. Rowley and Kevin come out of their apartment, both of them patting their stomachs like they have eaten too much. "Why so glum, chum?" Mr. Rowley asks, but he does not wait for an answer. They get into Mr. Rowley's car and drive away.

The door opens again, and Travis steps outside, leaning over their balcony. Someone has cut off all his curls. Now his ears look like handles for his face.

"What's the matter?" he asks. He is talking to me. It takes me too long to believe this, and already he is turning around, starting to go back inside.

"I screwed something up," I yell. I wave for him to come over, the way a crossing guard tells you it's okay to walk across the street. To my surprise, this works. He closes the door behind him and walks quickly down the wooden staircase of Unit B, his hands in the front pockets of his jeans.

At first I do not think I will even be able to stand up, but then I am standing, walking across the parking lot toward him. He looks at me, waiting, his green eyes large, far away from each other, like the eyes of a fish. "I need a surprise for my mother," I say. "By tonight. And I don't have one."

He tilts his head. "Is it her birthday?"

"Kind of. Something like that." It's strange to actually be talking to him face-to-face, like he is just another person. He has become almost like just a story in my head now, someone I made up to make me feel better, to have something to do. There are little gold flecks in the green of his eyes, and they are looking right at me. *That little one, when he gets older, look out.*

He squints across the highway. "There's the Kwikshop. You could get her something there."

"It needs to be something nice. I have eight dollars."

"You can get her something nice, then. There's stuff there girls would like." He turns and starts walking. "Come on. I'll go with you."

Again, it's difficult to move. The afternoon has gone so badly that it seems unlikely that something this good could happen at the end of it. But here it is, standing in front of me, good on the heels of bad.

He turns around, zipping up the front of his sweatshirt. "But if you want to go, we have to go now. I've got to be back before my dad and Kevin get home. I'm supposed to be grounded."

"What about your mom?"

He makes a face. "*The Wizard of Oz* is on. She'll be camped out all night."

I smile. My mother is also watching it, lying on the couch underneath the quilt Eileen gave her for Christmas. She tried to get me to watch it with her, but I'm sick of it. It's on every year, and I've seen it so many times that I can say the lines right along with the movie, from "Auntie Em, Auntie Em" to "I'll get you, my little pretty," down the yellow brick road and back again to the scary flying monkeys who turn out to be people and then back off to see the Wizard who is really just an old man who is very nice but not exactly dependable to "You had the answer inside you all the time, Dorothy, just click your heels three times." My mother said, "Okay, Evelyn, you've seen it before. I get the picture."

She said she knew all the lines by heart too, but she still wanted to watch it. She pulled the quilt up to her eyes, but when Dorothy started to sing "Somewhere Over the Rainbow," she knew I could see she was crying, and she said it was just because she liked the song.

Mrs. Rowley doesn't like my mother, and my mother doesn't like her; they won't speak to each other face-to-face. But I like the idea of them watching the same movie in different houses, both of them so wrapped up in the same old story they won't even notice we're gone.

· · ·

When we walk into the Kwikshop, the bells tied to the door handle jingle, and Carlotta, the woman who works there evenings, looks up from her magazine and frowns.

"Where are your mothers?" she asks, holding up her hand flat out to us, like STOP. Her fingernails are long, painted red, filed sharp like arrows. "We don't want you kids coming in here without mothers."

"We don't have mothers," Travis says, already moving down one of the aisles. "We're orphans."

Carlotta can't see him, so she glares at me. "Yeah, you're hilarious, buddy," she says. "You steal one thing, and I call the police."

"We're not here to steal," I tell her. "I have money." I reach into my pocket and bring out the wad of bills, all that is left from the twenty dollars. She leans over the counter and eyes the money, and I can't help but stare. Carlotta is an interesting person to look at on any day because of all the colors on her skin: pink blush streaked across her cheeks and not rubbed in, red glossed lips, and yellow teeth. But on this day, there's even more: two large hickeys sit on her neck just over the line between her orange smock and her throat. They're blue and bruised at the center, green around the edges. She sees me staring, and her hand goes to her throat.

"Hmm. Well, I'll be watching you both." She points up to the circular mirrors in each corner of the ceiling. "I can see you at every point in the store."

"Can you see me now?" Travis asks. His voice is coming from the aisle with the corn chips.

"Yes," Carlotta says.

"What am I doing?" he asks.

"Bothering me."

Travis stands up, leaning on the handle of one of the glass refrigerator doors. "You could get her a pop," he says. "Everybody likes pop."

"It has to be nicer than that." I look around the front aisles. Sewing kits. Sunglasses. Tiny jars of instant coffee. Work gloves. My mother has use for none of these things. Superglue. Rows of doughnuts, crackers, and animal cookies. Aspirin. Cough drops.

"Get her sunglasses," Travis says. "Everybody likes sunglasses."

"She already has some."

Two workmen come in to pay for gas and cigarettes, wearing khaki overalls and yellow gloves. One of them moves very slowly, his eyes on Carlotta's neck. She looks flustered, trying to work the register and watch us at the same time.

"I see how you two are spreading out," she yells. "I can watch you both at the same time." She smiles at the man buying cigarettes. "Kids."

A Kwikshop Supergulp mug sits next to the cash register, filled with miniature long-stemmed roses, each one wrapped in plastic with a red bow around the top. A white card in front of the cup reads THE GIFT OF A RED ROSE IS A TRADITIONAL WAY TO SAY "I LOVE YOU" in Magic Marker. One rose costs a dollar fifty.

"Yeah, that's nice," Travis says, slapping two quarters on the counter. He is already drinking a Dr Pepper. "Get her flowers. Girls like flowers."

I peel back the plastic wrap and sniff the top of the rose. No smell. "Are these even real?" I ask. Travis has moved to the back of the store again.

"Yeah they're real," she says. "They're just tiny. Who're you trying to buy something for?"

"My mom."

Carlotta stops chewing her gum. "Hmm. That's kind of sweet. Is it her birthday or something?"

"No. She's just sad."

She frowns. Carlotta knows who my mother is, and I know she likes her. My mother comes in to buy milk when she can't get to the store in town, and she leaves pennies in the bowl that says TAKE A PENNY, ADD A PENNY. Carlotta likes my mother's hair, and has told her this, several times. "Those curls," she tells her. "You can't get that from a permanent wave. It's just not the same."

"Why's your mama sad, hon?"

"She just is."

"Well, a flower is enough, then. If any of my kids ever bought me even a flower, even a fake tiny flower like this, I'd fall over dead. I'd be like—" She gasps and makes a croaking sound, her eyes wide.

I shake my head. "It's not enough."

She blows a bubble, large and light purple. "You could make her a care package. Put a lot of little stuff in there, you know?" She gets a brown cardboard box out from under the register and sets it on the counter. She is able to hold it with just her nails, not touching it with her fingers at all. "Now you just fill it up with lots of little stuff she might like. We'll put the flower in last, so it doesn't get smushed."

I like this idea, and collect small items from each aisle: a tester bottle of White Rain shampoo. A can of Pepsi. A pink cord to hold her sunglasses around her neck when she isn't wearing them, and a black wristwatch, water resistant up to two hundred feet. An air freshener, shaped like a flower with a smiling face in the center. Travis suggests beef jerky. I have never seen my mother eat beef jerky, but he says it's good, and it's only thirty-five cents.

"What's her horoscope sign?" Carlotta asks.

"I don't know."

She blows another purple bubble and looks at me as if I am a bad person. "When's her birthday?"

"December twenty-eighth."

"Hmm. Capricorn. No wonder she's down." She reaches across the counter and picks up a small green tube that says CAPRICORN. "See, this unrolls into a piece of paper with all her astrological information. It can guide her through her whole year—career, family, romance, money. . . . It's a dollar."

I nod quickly, put it in the box.

"I'm a Capricorn too," she whispers, leaning closer, the hickeys on her throat moving up and down like small, uneven eyes. "Good things are coming our way, this summer. You tell your mama that. This summer belongs to the goat, hands down."

I pick up the green roll again, holding it more carefully now. *This summer belongs to the goat.* I like knowing that my mother will have a good summer, that the next three months are already certain, printed and rolled up into a wand.

"You could get her a magazine," Travis says.

"I'm out of money."

"Here," Carlotta says. "Take my *People*. I'm already done reading it, and it looks new."

"Thanks," I say. On the cover, a man is carrying a woman wearing a ruffled pink dress with white tights, and the words say WHODUNIT ON *DYNASTY*?

"I'm done with it. No biggie." She goes to work on the cash register, her fingernails clicking against the buttons. "Okay, that's seven dollars and ninety-five cents, with tax."

I give her all of my bills. She gives me back a nickel.

"Well, there you go," she says. "That's nice of you to want to give something to your mom. I used to have kids, and I guess they were sweet to me too once." She leans her elbows on the counter. "Now they've gotten big and they don't give me shit."

Carlotta does not look old enough to have grown children. I tell her this, and she smiles and says I'm a little sweetie, and that I made her day. But I didn't say it to be nice. I said it because she really doesn't look that old.

I follow Travis out the door, the string of bells jangling behind us.

Once we're out of the store, Travis begins unloading various items from the pockets of his jeans and the sleeves of his sweatshirt: five packs of gum, Tic Tacs, and a lightbulb.

"Here," he says. "Give this gum to your mom."

"You stole all of that? Just then? I was standing right by you."

He wiggles his fingers. "Magic," he says. He opens my mother's care package and puts the gum inside. And now I know for certain, without asking, that he is the one who took Traci's clothes. I also know it is better not to say this. It's just something we both know.

"Why do you steal things?"

He thinks for a moment before answering, turning the lightbulb from hand to hand. "Because I want to get things I don't have money for."

"But you just gave me some of the things you stole."

"So?"

"So you must not have wanted them."

"I wanted them so I could give them to you." He shrugs. "I don't know."

When we get to the highway, Travis pinches the skin at my elbow, as if I will run in front of a car if left on my own. Once we are on the other side, he stops walking, cupping his finger and thumb around his mouth. "I think it makes me feel better somehow, stealing. Like I get something for nothing, and it makes up for other times. You get something for nothing for all the times you just get nothing."

"Oh." I don't know what else to say. I know stealing is wrong, but lying is wrong too. I've already lied three times today, and the day isn't over.

"Like I was in a bad mood because my dad and Kevin went to this fucking baseball game without me because I'm grounded. But now I feel better."

"But that's why you got grounded in the first place."

His handle ears rise up when he smiles. "Yeah."

We round the corner and stop walking at the same time. My mother and Mrs. Rowley are both standing outside, their hands on their hips. They are not talking, but they are standing closer to each other than would usually be allowed. My mother sees me first.

"Where have you been, Evelyn? Jesus, I thought you'd been stolen."

"We went to the Kwikshop to get you presents," Travis says. He is not supposed to tell her this part. It's supposed to be a surprise.

Her eyes squeeze shut, and when she opens them, she is looking only at me. "You went across the highway? Don't do that. Don't ever do that."

Mrs. Rowley moves quickly across the parking lot and grabs Travis by the elbow and the back of his neck. "And I told you to stay away from them," she whispers, pushing him up the steps.

"What?" my mother asks. The Rowleys' door slams shut, and she turns to me. "What does she mean by that?"

"I don't know," I say, although I know it's because of Mr. Mitchell's truck, because this is a neighborhood for decent families, which does not include people jumping on beds. This is the fourth lie. I walk back inside, and she follows. *The Wizard of Oz* is still on. Dorothy has just met the scarecrow. I hand her the box. "Here," I say. "It's your surprise."

She tilts her head, eyes narrowed, suspicious. "It's not my birthday."

"I know."

She frowns and shakes the box lightly. "It's not a kitten or anything, is it? It's not going to be something that jumps up at me? I won't think that's funny, Evelyn. I'm telling you now."

"No, Mom, it's nice. I just got you a present. That's all."

She puts a hand on her hip. "Why?"

"Because I love you."

She nods, rolling her tongue across her top lip. "Good," she says. "Good to know somebody does." She opens the box carefully, pulling out the gum, then the rose wrapped in plastic.

"There's more," I say, watching her eyes. "Much more."

She sets the rose on the table and pulls out the *People*. "Huh," she says, her voice high. Next comes the beef jerky and the air freshener. She sets each present on the table: the horoscope roll, the Pepsi, the shampoo, the watch. She pulls the sunglasses strap out last, holding it in front of her.

"What is this?"

"It'll keep your sunglasses around your neck, so you won't lose them."

"Ahhhh." She sets it down on the table and looks at all the things together, smiling steadily now. "Well, this was very nice of you, Evelyn, to get me all this."

"Do you like it?"

"Yes. Yes I do." She laughs. "These are all very useful things. Why just today I was thinking I needed to get more shampoo."

"And now you've got it."

"And now I've got it." She picks up the beef jerky and tries to sniff it through the wrapper. "This must have cost you a lot of money."

"I wanted to get you a surprise."

"Right, the surprise. I've had a lot of surprises today. But this was a nice one." She kisses me on the forehead and tells me that after my shower, if I want, we can watch the rest of *The Wizard of Oz* together. We can each have some beef jerky.

It's a nice feeling, giving her this. And later, sitting on the floor in front of the television, my mother combing through my wet hair, everything is okay again, at least for a little while. So maybe Travis is right, and sometimes you really can cancel out the bad with the good. Even if you have to lie, or maybe steal, it's worth it to have a few moments when you're happy, making up for bad times, taking what you can.

~

six

*W*E KNOW SOMETHING IS WRONG when the Rowleys' is so quiet. Two nights ago, it was very loud, even for them, but now there's nothing. No screaming, no slamming doors. We notice the difference right away.

Mr. Rowley normally leaves for work about eight every morning, a ring of keys jangling from the side of his belt, sipping hot coffee from a mug that says I'D RATHER BE TROUTING. But now there is no sign of him, and we have not seen his car for days.

We still see Mrs. Rowley in the window sometimes, Jackie O in her arms. She holds her tightly, up by her neck, and stands there while Jackie O licks her chin. When she sees us looking, she moves away from the window and pulls the curtains down.

"Either he left or she ate him," my mother says.

On the third day of quiet, still no sign of Mr. Rowley or his car, Travis comes outside with Jackie O, holding her leash with just one finger, his sweatshirt hood pulled over his hair and eyes.

I lean my head out the door and say hello. He waves back, and I start to walk across the parking lot toward him, but Jackie O barks and growls, showing me her tiny teeth.

"Calm down," he says. "Evelyn's nice." He has to pick her up so I can come closer, and as he stands there with the dog in the crook of his arm, for the first time, I can see how he looks like his mother, his skin pulled tight around his face. His hair is growing back, turning into curls again.

"My dad left," he says, looking down, his fingers working to pull a bur out of Jackie O's ear. "He went to West Virginia and he's not coming back. He took Kevin."

I bend forward to see inside his hood. His eyes are dry, his heart-shaped mouth closed tight. My mother guessed that Mr. Rowley might have left, but this is worse than we thought. We did not think he would take just Kevin, leaving Travis behind. Jackie O is still barking at me, shrill and loud.

Travis picks her up so her head is pointed away from me, his hand over her eyes, and sits down on the step, leaving enough room for me.

"I'm sorry," I say, sitting down. It's all I can think of. "You're sure he won't come back?"

Travis nods. He says Mr. Rowley woke him up two days ago, came in and sat down on Travis's bed and said, "Wake up, son," just like that. He told him he and Kevin were leaving, that they had already packed. He had been planning to leave for a long time. He had been unhappy with Mrs. Rowley for a long time. He said he had only been waiting for the last day of school because he didn't want to pull Kevin out in the middle of the school year. It was the last day of school for Travis too, but he did not mention this.

He told Travis he had to leave or he would start drinking again. He and Kevin were going to go live with Travis's Uncle Bobby and Aunt Terry in West Virginia until he could get settled enough to live on his own. He couldn't take Travis too because of the fighting and because of the stealing. They would be living off the charity of others. They couldn't afford any trouble. He would miss Travis very much, but this was what he had to do, or he just wasn't going to make it.

Travis puts Jackie O on the ground, and she walks closer to me, sniffing my feet. I can't think of anything good to say. My dad left, I know, but that was before I was born. It would be worse if they knew you, and left all the same.

He picks up a piece of bark, grinding it into the concrete step. "We fight a lot, me and Kevin."

"I know," I say. "I've seen you."

"My mom said that wasn't the real reason, though. She said she made him leave me with her. She said he was going to take both of us, but that she made him at least leave me." He looks up at me quickly. "He's going to send us money, still. He said he'd send five hundred dollars a month, no matter what. And I can come live with them as soon as he gets his own house."

I am still trying to think of the right thing to say, the thing that will make him feel better. *Maybe he'll come back. You don't want him to start drinking again, and maybe this way he won't. Five hundred dollars is a lot of money.* But none of these seem right. Really, I know nothing will make him feel better. There is nothing to do or say but just sit beside him on the step, and wait until he has told me everything, so we will both know the entire story, and never need it explained again.

"That makes me so goddamn mad," my mother says. She is looking out the window across the parking lot, as if Mr. Rowley is still standing in it, waiting for her to come out. "You don't just take one child and leave the other. You don't leave, period."

Ever since Mr. Rowley and Kevin left, the light in Travis's room stays on late, and it is on even in the morning when I first wake up. My mother says this breaks her heart.

"Maybe he's just reading," I say. "He likes to read."

"He's waiting," she says. "And that fucker isn't coming back."

My mother has gotten a new job at the Blue Market grocery store in the Pine Ridge Shopping Plaza. She is not worried about the walk, but she doesn't like the idea of leaving me alone for eight hours, plus the two hours it will take to walk there and back. Last summer she worked at Peterson's, but the library was on the way, and in the morning she would drop me off in the Volkswagen with a sandwich, a thermos, and a bag of Fritos. I want to do that again now, but the library is on the other side of town from the store, too far away to walk.

"I'll be fine," I tell her. "I'm not a baby."

She chews her thumbnail, looking out the window at the cars on the highway. "No," she says. "You're going to have to come to work with me. Travis can come too if he likes. Have him ask his mom, and tell him he'll need to pack a lunch." She looks at me and shrugs. "Sorry. That's the best I can come up with right now."

Surprisingly, Mrs. Rowley says yes. Or at least this is what Travis tells us.

She does not pack him a lunch, but Travis shows up at our door at eight o'clock. My mother makes a lunch for him.

The walk to the store is long and hot, cars honking as they pass us on the highway. But once we get to the store, it's nice. Travis and I go in before my mother so they won't think we are with her, and we sit on our knees in the air-conditioned aisles, reading magazines, but never for very long at one time. We have been instructed to keep moving, to not stay in one place long enough for anyone to notice us. We are allowed to go anywhere in the strip mall, as long as we don't go onto the main road, and we check in with my mother every half hour. Checking in must be done in secret, so my mother will not get in trouble. At quarter till and at quarter past, Travis and I are to stand in the front of the store by the cash registers, until we are sure that she sees us. We know she sees us when she tugs on her ear twice; that's the signal. After that, we are free to go for thirty more minutes. We are not to talk to strangers. We are not, under any circumstances, to go up to her while she is working, unless one of us is bleeding. And for God's sake, she says, almost every morning, looking at both of us. Please don't steal anything. Please. If we screw this up, that's it.

She's worried we'll be bored, but there are plenty of things to do. There is a pet store to the right of the parking lot, with tiny bunnies jumping around a big pen on the floor, and there are also puppies that cost four hundred dollars, and kittens, and fish, and even a large, hairy tarantula with a sign on its aquarium that says DO NOT TAP ON GLASS!!!! We spend most of our time there until Travis taps on the glass, and we are told to leave.

But there is also an arcade, dark and cool as a cave. We play Pac-Man and Space Invaders, and already Travis and I both have the high score on two of the machines. We ask people we don't know in the parking lot for quarters. It is my idea, and I am better at it than Travis, stopping people coming out of the store. I can make myself cry, saying I need to call my parents but don't have any change. I look for old people to ask, thinking they will have softer hearts. No one ever says no.

After three days of this, Travis says he doesn't want to do it anymore. It's wrong, he says, taking old people's quarters.

I am hurt by this. I feel stupid, or maybe like a bad person. "It's the same as stealing," I tell him. "You steal."

He considers this, then shakes his head. "It's different."

We go back to the store, read more magazines. Travis finds *Carrie* by Stephen King, and we take turns reading it to each other in scary voices. A man with a bow tie asks us if he can help us with something. No, we say. We're fine.

"Well," he says. "Run along now."

At quarter till and quarter past, we stop whatever we are doing and go to the front of the store, where my mother stands in her green smock and yellow name tag that says HI! I'M TINA! I'M HERE TO HELP YOU SAVE BIG!, punching numbers into a machine, asking questions of customers who some- times answer her, sometimes not. *How are you doing today? Paper or plastic? I like your shirt. Did you get that around here? Is this stuff any good? I haven't tried it.*

She says it makes the day go faster, to try to talk to people, to make them remember she's a person, to make herself remember too. But sometimes they don't want to talk to her, or they look surprised when she starts talking, like she is part of the cash register, not supposed to talk.

One morning she wakes up sick, running to the bathroom. She tries to go in to work anyway, but we walk for only ten minutes along the shoulder of the highway when she stops and looks at us, her hand on her stomach, and says we have to go back home.

"Do you want some juice?" Travis asks. He holds out the thermos my mother bought for him.

"No," she says. "No."

She is sick again the next day, and the day after that, and then her boss at Blue Market calls and tells her not to come back.

So she doesn't. She stays home and walks around in her bathrobe, looking at the television but not watching it. She lies on the couch with one hand over her stomach, the other one over her eyes.

"What are you going to do?" I ask. She needs to have a job.

"I don't know," she says.

It is hot summer now, too sticky and miserable in the daytime to be outside for more than a minute. Travis comes over, and we sit by the fan in my window, sucking grape Popsicles. I show him my lima bean plants, my triptych, and my graph. The two plants that have been in sunlight are even taller now, and I had to replant them in bigger containers.

"This one had fertilizer," I tell him, touching the leaves of the larger plant. "See?"

"Huh," he says. But I can look at his face and see he is only being nice, trying to act interested.

Even when my mother's stomach stops bothering her, she stays in her nightgown all day, unshowered. She walks around the house making a weird, high-pitched groaning sound, almost like she's trying to be a horse again. When she does this, and we are in the same room, it's difficult for me to read or hear the television.

"What's the matter?" I ask.

"What isn't the matter?" she answers.

She tries to call Mr. Mitchell at her old job. She leaves messages for him, telling the person on the phone to tell him it's urgent. Finally, someone calls back and says he doesn't work there anymore, that he has moved away some-where with his wife. She holds the phone away from her ear and looks at it, like she can see the person on the other end through the holes in the earpiece.

I stay back in my room to get away from her, reading the books Ms. Fairchild gave me last year in a brown paper grocery sack. They are mostly Judy Blume books, *Tales of a Fourth Grade Nothing, Are You There God? It's Me, Margaret*, but there is also *Anne Frank: The Diary of a Young Girl*. I save this one for last because Ms. Fairchild told me the story already, and I know it's a true story, a real diary of a girl who gets killed in a war. It ends without having an ending because the Nazis come get her before she has time to finish it. All of a sudden, it just stops.

It's sad reading her diary, because the whole time she's locked up in the attic she keeps saying maybe the war will end so they will get to come out and live like normal people again, but you know, when you're reading it, that it won't. You know the whole time she's going to die. If it weren't a real diary, but just a story that someone made up, she would have lived, and maybe married Peter. But since it's a true story, anything can happen, even the very worst.

Travis starts walking back down to Pine Ridge, spending the long after-noons there by himself, and then with other kids he meets there, older kids with skateboards and BMX bikes. He stops by and asks me to come too.

"No," my mother says, not even looking at me. "You'll get hit by a car."

In July, the gas company cuts us off, but this isn't so bad because it's too hot for hot water anyway. I wear my swimsuit all day, jumping in and out of the shower, shrieking when the cold water hits my back. My mother tells me to be quiet. She says she has a lot on her mind, and that I shouldn't try so hard to get on her very last nerve.

I wake up one morning and see her sitting on the kitchen floor, the window fan blowing on her face, a ketchup stain on the front of her night-gown. You're supposed to sleep in your bed.

"How are we going to get to Topeka?" I ask.

"What?" She says this like she doesn't really want to know what I asked. I turn off the fan, and she opens her eyes.

"You said you'd figure out some way to get me to Topeka for the science fair. You promised. Ms. Fairchild said she would take me if you wouldn't, but you told me you would and it's in four days."

"I'll figure something out," she says, closing her eyes again. "But later. Not right now." She has turned ugly, her nightgown stained, her skin oily, her hair dark.

"You keep saying that. What's wrong with you? Are you sick?"

She opens her eyes. They are dull, glazed over. "I said I'd figure something out and I will, okay? Please go away, just for a minute." She reaches behind me and turns the fan back on.

I stand over her. I cannot go away, even just for a minute. I have to go to Topeka. I have been blessed. "My shoes are too small," I tell her. "I need new shoes."

She says nothing.

"Did you hear me? I need new shoes. They're hurting my feet." I stomp my foot, hard, right next to where her hand is on the floor. She doesn't move.

"I HATE YOU!"

"Good," she says. "Good."

Eileen is the one to drive us to Topeka. Two days before the science fair, my mother and I walk across the highway to use the pay phone at the Kwikshop to call her, and it sounds like my mother is calling to get her hair cut by someone she doesn't know: "Can you do it? Yes, nine o'clock. We'll be waiting for you," her voice flat, her eyes watching the cars on the highway.

I won't let her hold my hand when we go back across the highway, so she grabs me by the arm.

The morning of the science fair, she is sick again; I can hear her throwing up in the bathroom. I knock on the door. "Are you sick again?"

"I'm fine. Is Eileen here yet?"

"No." I wait. "If you're sick, you don't have to go. Eileen can take me."

She opens the door and looks down at me, trying to smile. She is wearing a dress, and for the first time in over a month, she looks normal, clean. "Get serious, Evelyn. I'm fine. I wouldn't miss this for the world." But then she cups her hand over her mouth and shuts the door again.

Eileen arrives, wearing a long white dress with little roses all over it, her hair pulled back in a single braid. "How's my baby?" she asks. She leans down to hug me, and I breathe her in, her cigarette smell. "Oh, I missed you, sweetie. I really did."

"Mom's sick," I tell her. "She's been throwing up."

But my mother is already behind me, saying she is fine, just a bit queasy. Eileen's hand goes to my mother's forehead. "You sure, Tina?"

"I'm fine. God, Mom, you look so pretty. That's a great dress."

"Oh, this is old," Eileen says. She leans forward and kisses her on the cheek. It's as if they were never in a fight. As if Wichita never happened.

My mother looks down at my feet, squinting.

"Evelyn, what shoes are those? Since when do you have red shoes? What are those pins all over them?"

I look her in the eye. "Star gave them to me."

My mother looks confused, and I am worried, because sometimes she can be very smart about things. "My shoes are too small, remember? I've been telling you that. I need a new pair."

She frowns. "Well now you have those, Evelyn. Now you have those."

Eileen's Oldsmobile has air-conditioning, and when we pull onto the highway, she cranks it up so high I get goose bumps, even though it's over a hundred degrees outside, the sky a cloudless blue. A small statue of Jesus in a white robe is glued to her dashboard, one hand raised up like he is waving.

"Are you my lucky lady today?" Eileen asks, catching my eye in the rearview mirror.

"I am," I tell her, wriggling my toes in Traci's shoes. I am lucky, but also I have been working hard. I purchased three pieces of poster board for a new triptych, and this one is so large I have to fold it into thirds just to get it into the backseat of Eileen's car. I have made a new graph as well, this time using different-colored Magic Markers to chart the growth of each plant. And again I have followed Ms. Fairchild's directions carefully, with neat labels on the required sections.

I am hoping that in Topeka, there will again be the problem of people not following directions, not having their triptychs divided into HYPOTHESIS, OBJECTIVE, METHOD, OBSERVATIONS, and CONCLUSION. When I meet Ronald Reagan, he will laugh his wonderful laugh and say, "I'm so glad that at least some kids today know how to follow directions." He will give me jelly beans, and people will take pictures of me shaking his hand in the Oval Office.

Eileen asks my mother if she is feeling better, and she says she is.

Eileen asks my mother if she knows what made her so sick: Did she eat some bad food? My mother shrugs and doesn't answer. Eileen turns on the radio, Jerry Falwell's *Old Time Gospel Hour*. The leaves of the lima bean plants tremble in the breeze of the air-conditioning.

I look out my window, down at the yellow lines whizzing under us in the middle of the highway. There is nothing but fields of wheat on each side of the road, their feathery tops swirling in the heat. Last year, Ms. Fairchild read some of *My Antonia* to us. She said she wanted us to see Kansas and Nebraska the way it is in the book, beautiful, a breadbasket that feeds so many people. She said Kansas is beautiful if you look at it the right way, and that we shouldn't believe anything other people try to say about it. *The abundance of it,* she said, spreading her arms in her Wednesday dress, as if she were holding something large.

I like living in Kansas, not just because of the wheat, but because it's right in the center. If you look at a map of the world, the United States is usually right in the middle, and Kansas is in the middle of that. So right here where we are, maybe this very stretch of highway we are driving on, is the exact center of the whole world, what everything else spirals out from.

Ms. Fairchild said, No, Evelyn, that's just the way the map is made. She said they just as easily could have put India in the middle, or Africa for that matter. She said she had seen maps that have Australia at the top and Greenland at the bottom, and those maps are also right, just in a different way. She says the map on her wall probably has the United States in the middle because it was made in the United States.

I don't know. I've never seen a map with Greenland at the bottom. I think maybe Ms. Fairchild is wrong, and that the United States really is in the center, not just on maps, but in real life, because we are here on purpose. I feel so lucky to live here, right in the center and on purpose, and Eileen says, Yes, it's just another of the many ways we've been blessed.

At the school in Topeka, we have to wait in line for registration. Eileen starts to talk to the people behind us, the family of a boy in overalls from Hill City. He has two little brothers, and all of them, even his parents, look tired and sunburned. I feel bad for them, the whole family, because I have never even heard of Hill City, and I know it must be in western Kansas, small and far away. The boy tells me he and his parents had to get up at six o'clock in the morning and drive for four hours, and now his older brothers are bringing in his triptych from their truck.

"Can I see yours?" he asks.

I nod and unfold my triptych for him, amazed once again by the orderly perfection of it, so many different colors on the graph. Eileen is holding my box of lima bean plants, and she opens the lid to show him. The boy nods and smiles, tells me good luck.

When we get to the front of the line, I am given a number to put around my neck. I am to set up my triptych on a table with the corresponding number in the gymnasium. I have twenty minutes to set up my experiment and display. The judges will walk around then, and will put a special yellow sticker on those they wish to consider finalists. I glide into the gym, Traci's shoes on my feet, the new and improved triptych in my arms. I think about God putting on the headphones, tuning in.

But looking around, I start to get worried. The girl on my left has a triptych much larger than even Traci's, clearly labeled HYPOTHESIS, OBJECTIVE, METHOD, OBSERVATIONS, and CONCLUSION. It appears to be made out of something metal, the edges lined in black. It stands behind her, at least six feet tall. On the ground in front of her is a small, intricate maze, the walls inside made of what looks like wooden rulers, sawed in half. Just off to the side of the maze are three cages, each with a small white rat inside. One cage has a bright lamp shining into it, and the two others have a navy blue cloth over their lids. Large red letters read THE EFFECTS OF LIGHT AND DARK ON PROBLEM SOLVING IN RATS.

My mother's eyes drift over to the rats. They are nibbling on the metal bars of their cages, looking up at us with pink eyes. "Poor things," she says.

The boy from Hill City appears, directing his brothers, older and bigger versions of himself, also wearing overalls, as they carry his triptych to the table on my right. The hinges squeak when they unfold it. The boy himself is now holding a large plastic tray of lima bean plants, maybe twelve of them.

I walk up to him slowly.

"You did lima beans too?"

"Yeah," he says, arranging the plants on the table. "I did it for 4-H, so I already had some done."

I watch him move his plants from the plastic case to the table. Some of them are even taller, even greener, than my best plant. "You have twelve?"

He looks away. "Twenty-four, actually. I wanted to find the best possible growing environment. You know, how much water in the soil, direct or indirect sunlight. That kind of stuff."

I look at his chart. EXPOSED TO SUNLIGHT BETWEEN 10 A.M AND 2 P.M.; FERTILIZER WITH NITROGEN; FERTILIZER WITHOUT NITROGEN; FERTILIZER WITH NITROGEN WITH HEAVY WATERING; FERTILIZER WITHOUT NITROGEN WITH LIGHT WATERING.

"Yours is good too," he says.

I hear a hissing sound from across the room, and then a loud pop. A black boy in a red-and-white striped shirt is dragging a tape measure across the floor to where a small model rocket lies on its side, still smoking. He seems pleased, smiling at the numbers he is reading and then writing down. I glance quickly at the graph on his triptych: ESTIMATED TRAJECTORIES BASED ON TYPE OF FUEL.

"Smile, honey!" Eileen aims a camera at me, her middle finger pressed down over one of her eyes. I hear the click, and I see my mother's eyes catch mine.

"What's wrong?" she mouths, and I can't believe this, that she could be so stupid.

"I want to go home."

Her eyes move around my face. "What? Why?"

The judges are coming down the aisle now, two men and a woman, all of them holding clipboards, looking at the rockets and the triptychs, writing things down. They stop in front of the girl with the rats, and she pushes a button that releases one of the rats into the maze. The judges lean over the maze to see, and I can hear them saying "Ahhhh!" in a very good way. One of them hands the girl a yellow sticker.

They walk past me, their eyes moving over my lima bean plants. One of the men smiles, but that's it. No yellow sticker.

I will not get to meet Ronald Reagan. I start to pick up my lima bean plants, putting them back in the box. "I want to go home."

"Honey? Are you sick?" My mother reaches over to feel my forehead.

I pull my head away. "Yes. I want to go home."

"Okay," she says. She looks at Eileen and nods. "I guess we're going to go." She does not seem too sad about this, and I know that she is ready to go home too. All morning she has kept her hand on her stomach. She is really the one who doesn't feel well. She wants to go back to Kerrville so she can get back into her nightgown with the stains on it and lie around on the floor.

"We'll go home right away, kitten," Eileen says, taking the lima bean plants from me. "Right away."

We get out to the registration area, and when the woman at the door sees us, she gives me a funny look, her head tilted. "You're leaving already?"

"I don't feel well."

She glances down at my triptych, folded under my arm. "You're not leaving because you weren't selected as a finalist, I hope."

I say nothing. I take the number card off from around my neck and try to hand it to her.

"Because that's not the point of the fair. You should go around and read what the other kids have done." She smiles. "Maybe you'll learn something."

"She wants to go home," my mother says, using the voice that makes some people jump. The woman takes my number card and reaches into a box behind her that says HONORABLE MENTIONS and takes out a certificate with a blank line in the middle. She writes my name on it and hands it to me.

On the way home, we are quiet. Every now and then, Eileen smiles at me in her rearview mirror and tries to say something nice, like how getting an Honorable Mention is pretty darn good in her opinion. She says she hopes I am proud of myself, and that she is proud of me, and that the girl with the rats and the maze looked like she might be an Oriental and that they should only let real Americans be in it. My mother puts her hand over her eyes and makes a sound like she might be sick again.

I look down at the certificate—swirling calligraphy with an official seal at the bottom, my name written on a blank line in blue ballpoint pen.

I hereby solemnly swear, on the twenty-first day of July, 1982,
EVELYN BUCKNOW received an Honorable Mention
in the Kansas State Fourth Grade Science Fair

On the highway, we pass a billboard that says ONE KANSAS FARMER FEEDS 87 PEOPLE . . . AND YOU!!! The 87 part of the sign is in a different color paint than everything else. You can tell they change it all the time. Eileen says the number gets higher every year, never lower. The poor farmers, she says. They're having a bad time. It's the Zionist bankers, she says, pushing the farmers out, making a killing.

She asks my mother what the matter is. My mother says she's fine. It's quiet after that, but I watch Eileen's face in the rearview mirror, the crooked side of her mouth starting to pucker, her eyes moving back and forth.

"You're pregnant," she says.

My mother says nothing. I look at the statue of Jesus, still friendly and waving between them, like if they get into a fight, he will try to break it up.

"Are you, Tina? Am I right?"

"Can we discuss this later?"

"If you are, she'll know about it soon enough."

My mother moans and puts her arms over her ears. "I don't want to talk about it. Okay?"

I look back out the window, feeling cold, my forehead pressed against the glass. My mother shouldn't be pregnant. You're supposed to have a husband.

"Déjà vu all over again," Eileen says. "You're a piece of work, Tina."

My mother fingers the silver handle on her door, saying nothing. Eileen pushes a button on the dash that goes *click*, and the lock on my mother's door goes down.

"Who's the father? Do you know?"

"Yes I know. God, Mom. God!" She puts her arms back over her head.

"Well, is he going to help out? Maybe even marry you? Try something different this time?"

My mother shakes her head. "Stop talking, okay? Just stop talking."

"Is he? Does he know?" Eileen looks at my mother, and when she does, the car veers to the right of the road. "Is it the man who gave you the car?"

My mother knocks her head against the window glass, hard enough for it to crack. But it doesn't. My stomach starts to buckle in on itself, and I work hard to focus on the statue of Jesus, still waving and friendly, steady on the dash.

"He's married?" Eileen's voice is strained, panicked.

When my mother doesn't answer, Eileen slaps the seat in between them, and my mother jumps. She's in trouble. You're not supposed to have a baby with someone else's husband. You're not even supposed to have a baby without a husband of your own, and she has already done that once before, with me. If you have too many babies without a husband, you're a welfare queen. Ronald Reagan says he is tired of welfare queens having babies without husbands and driving around in Cadillacs while everyone else has to work hard.

We don't have a Cadillac. Not yet.

"You and your accidents," Eileen says, looking at my mother. "That's great. You thought he would stay and take care of you, maybe leave his wife? You thought you'd just help him along. Well, is he going to now? Is he?"

My mother says she doesn't want a baby. Her voice is soft, like a little girl's. She says she can't have a baby, not now. Eileen says she should have thought about that earlier. "Stupid, stupid, stupid," she says. She keeps looking over at my mother, straying out of our lane, and she is still so mad that I think she will slap the seat between them again, or maybe unclick the lock on my mother's door and let her go rolling out onto the road, her head cracking open on the pavement.

We pass a sign nailed to a fence that reads WE ARE FARMLAND'S LAYED OFF FAMILIES. I know it should be "l-a-i-d" instead of "l-a-y-e-d," but then again, that isn't really the point of the sign.

$\mathcal{M}$Y MOTHER KNOWS I DON'T like her anymore. She has stopped trying to get me to smile at her, and when I say I want to eat dinner in front of the television instead of with her at the table, she shrugs and says fine. But she is still my mother, she says, still the boss around here, and when she goes across the highway to get more milk from the Kwikshop, she makes me come with her, holding my hand tight in hers. She has to pay Carlotta with nickels and dimes she has found in the pockets of coats and under the cushions of the couch. The coins have lint on them, dirt, dried gum, and Carlotta touches them only with her nails.

When we get home, she waters down the milk so it will last longer. It tastes bad.

She doesn't sleep. When I am in bed at night, I can hear her footsteps moving back and forth on the carpet in the hallway, the toilet flushing. She wants to flush the baby, I know. She would if she could.

One morning, the sun already hot and bright in my window at eight o'clock, I wake to her standing over me, saying my name. I open my eyes and we look at each other, but neither of us smiles.

"Get up," she says. "We need to go on an errand." She is wearing only her bra, underwear, and a shower cap. Sweat glistens between her eyebrows.

"Where?"

"Downtown. I can't leave you here by yourself."

"How will we get there?"

"Walk."

"It's too hot."

But she has already gone back out into the hallway. I get out of bed and follow her to her room. She keeps her window shade down in the daytime now to keep the heat out, the bottom of it tucked against the top of her fan. A pile of clothes lies on the bed, dresses and shirts inside out and tangled over each other, but she is still taking more out of the closet. The fan makes a steady tapping sound, like water dripping from a faucet.

She tries on the yellow dress, the one that she wore to Wichita when the car broke down. It's tighter than it was. Her whole body looks swollen, puffed up, especially her face. "You'll need to wear tights today," she says, fastening the belt. "We have to look nice."

"Why?"

"Because I said so."

"It's too hot for tights."

"You'll be fine, Evelyn. I'm wearing panty hose. You can wear tights."

I say nothing to this. She's being stupid. Yesterday it was 102 degrees, and the man on the news said the sidewalks were cracking in the heat, like bread in an oven.

"Go put them on," she says. She lies down on her bed by the pile of clothes, pulling her nylons on, her legs kicked up in the air, toes pointed, like the letter *V*.

"No."

She gives me a moment, just a moment, to take it back, her right eyebrow high on her forehead. Then she stands up quickly, pulling the nylons up to her waist, a run shooting up to her knee. She looks down at the run and starts counting to ten.

I watch.

When she gets to ten she says, "Evelyn, you have to understand something. I am really..." Her voice is shaking, and I can see she is about to cry. "I am at my limit, okay? I don't care how hot it is. Go put on your goddamn tights."

But I don't want to go where she's going, and it's too hot for tights. I'm up and out of her room in a second, sliding on the linoleum of the kitchen, around the corner, into the bathroom. I hear her coming after me, her footsteps heavy, one nylon leg swishing across the other. I lock the door.

She knocks so hard the mirror rattles against the bathroom wall. "Evelyn! Open the door." She is crying now. Some of me feels sorry for her, but most of me doesn't.

"It's too hot for tights!" I yell. "Too hot!"

I hear more crying, then footsteps back to her bedroom, her door slamming. I look at myself in the mirror, at my sleepy eyes and mean little mouth. Ms. Fairchild thinks I'm nice, but if she could see me now, if she really could look into her crystal ball, she would think differently.

But that's how it is sometimes. Sometimes you have to be mean.

There are 368 tiles on the bathroom floor. I am beginning to count the tiles in the shower when I hear her in the kitchen.

"We have to go now. You win." Her voice is still breathy, but quieter now. "You're a brat."

"I'm not," I say. I can see my reflection in the doorknob, my face like a monster's, upside down. "I don't have any shoes to wear. I told you that a long time ago. I told you I needed new shoes."

She pauses, and for a moment I'm not sure if she's even still there. "What about the red shoes? You've been wearing those."

"They're too small." This is a lie. They fit perfectly still, but I can't wear them if we are going into Kerrville. I imagine Traci seeing them on me, pointing at my feet so her mother will see. I would be arrested. I open the door, just a crack, and look up. Her cheeks are tear-stained, her eyes red.

"Are you coming or not?"

It is uncomfortable in the apartment, the humid air still and heavy even in our darkened rooms, but outside, under the bright, stinging sun, it's worse. The sun burns too hot on the top of my head as we walk along the highway to Monroe Street, lined with gas stations and Laundromats. I run my hand along a chain-link fence that keeps in a golf course. We walk past fast-food restaurants and the Pine Ridge Shopping Plaza. I look for Travis in the parking lot, but he isn't there. Closer to town, on McPhee Street, a man leans out of a car window and yells, "Whoo baby."

"I'm thirsty," I tell her.

"Me too," she says, and keeps walking. "What, Evelyn? We're almost there."

"My feet." I point at my shoes. Tiny spots of blood have soaked through the toes of the canvas.

"Jesus," she says, as if this is a surprise, as if I have not told her about my shoes. "Oh honey." She bends down, and the run in her nylons grows larger, spreading across her knee. Her yellow dress is see-through now, wet with sweat. "Okay," she says, wiping her forehead. "I have to get these off of you."

"I can do it myself, Mom. I know how to take off my shoes."

But it's like she doesn't hear me, her fingernails already picking at the knots. She has pushed her sunglasses up into her hair, and when she bends down, I can look down and see myself in them, the sun bright behind my head.

"Oh God, look at your feet," she says. "Your toes. I'm going to have to carry you."

I want to argue with her, to tell her this is a bad idea, that I am almost eleven years old and far too big to be carried. But her arms are already around me, lifting me up. "Hmmph," she says. I can feel the muscles in her back tighten under her dress. She leans one way and then the other, breathing hard. I keep my arms tight around her neck, feeling her sway a little, hearing the unsteady clicks of her heels on the sidewalk. She walks like this for two more blocks, until we get to a brick building that says KERRVILLE COUNTY WELFARE SERVICES across the top in silver letters.

We go inside. Welfare. It is happening.

She sets me down in front of the drinking fountain in the lobby, and my toes curl up when they touch the cool tile. A lady sits behind a desk, her eyes closed, a fan blowing her yellow-orange hair straight back so it looks like she is riding in a convertible car. There are brown chairs against the wall, and my mother and I fall into two of them.

"You have an appointment?" the lady asks. She has to yell over the sound of the fan.

"Barbara Bell, eleven o'clock."

"Everyone with an eleven o'clock appointment should be in the audio room to the left," the lady says, pointing to a white door on one side of her desk. "If your appointment is at eleven, you were instructed to arrive at ten forty-five, so you could listen to the tape in its entirety."

My mother stares at the lady. I am worried that she is counting to ten in her head, and that maybe both the lady and I should go to the other side of the room. But my mother says nothing. She stands up, holds her hand out to me, and leads me through the door.

There are about a dozen people in the next room, their chairs in a circle. This time the chairs are orange. In the center of this circle is a cassette player, playing a tape of a man speaking very slowly. No one is listening to the tape. Some people are talking, and some people are sleeping, their heads tilted back on the chairs. One woman is trying to lullaby a baby, singing a song in Spanish. We take two seats by the door, and I try to think about how good the air-conditioning feels, my feet set free from the shoes, and not about where we are, what Ronald Reagan would think if he could see us here now.

"How are your feet?" my mother asks.

The lady from the first room sticks her head in and says, "Shhh! You-all are supposed to *listen* to the tape." She points at her own ear. "No talking!"

But we can't hear the tape because people are talking, and two different babies are crying. Someone opens a different door and calls my mother's name. We walk down a long green hallway to a room with four desks, a woman sitting behind each one. Three of them are busy with other people. The fourth one waves us over. "Helloooo?" she says. "Come on. Let's go."

She wears red-framed glasses that sit on the tip of her nose. The nameplate on her desk says MRS. BARBARA BELL, INTAKE, and when she sees us, she looks me up and down carefully, puffing out her cheeks like a chipmunk. "We'll have to do something about shoes for you," she says. She looks at my mother. "Name?"

"Christina Bucknow," my mother says. She is all of a sudden using her nice voice, which I have not heard in a while. "Here's the form they told me to bring. I did the best I could with it." She smiles. "But some of it was pretty involved. See, this is my first time doing this so—"

Barbara Bell pushes up her glasses and flips through the booklet. She gets out a calculator, her fingers tapping against the buttons quickly. I think she looks very smart, wearing red glasses and punching a calculator like this.

"You're twenty-seven?"

"Yes."

"This is your daughter?"

"Yes. This is Evelyn."

"From a prior marriage?"

"Not exactly."

"Meaning?"

"No."

Barbara Bell nods and looks back down. "And she's ten?"

"She'll be eleven in August."

"And you receive no child support from her father?"

"No."

"But you've entered the father's name in a search, correct?"

"Yes. A long time ago. No luck."

Barbara Bell leans back in her chair. "And the father of this pregnancy?"

"This new one?" My mother points at her belly.

"Yes. This new one."

"It doesn't matter." My mother smiles.

"Actually, it does. Ms. Bucknow, I have to exhaust all of your other means of support before the state gives you financial assistance. And really, if we could get some child support mandated, that would help you out more than food stamps."

My mother looks around the room, at the people at the other desks. "It was a bad situation," she says, her voice low now, almost a whisper. "I'd really rather not say. I sort of made a mistake, and I'd rather not make that mistake go any further. You know?" She nods in my direction, the way she might do with Eileen to say, *Let's not talk about this in front of her.*

I get up and go to the other side of the room and look at the pictures on the wall, at a map of Kerrville stuck up with tacks. A little red circle is drawn on the map, and next to it, YOU ARE HERE in red letters. I don't want to be here. I don't want to be here.

My mother is smiling now, trying to look at Barbara Bell as if they are friends, in cahoots. Barbara Bell does not smile back.

"I'm afraid you're going to need to be candid with me if I'm going to help you, Ms. Bucknow."

My mother shakes her head. "Well, I'm afraid I can't get too particular. Given the situation, I think this could make things pretty awkward for him and . . ."

"His comfort level isn't really my concern."

"He's gone anyway."

"He's left town?"

"Yes."

"No forwarding address? No number?"

"No."

"Surely you must know someone who . . ."

"No."

Barbara Bell looks back down at the booklet, her glasses down on her nose, her fingers drumming on the desk. "If you could give me a first and last name, I could enter that in a search."

"He's married, okay?" my mother says.

"But it's a different man than the father of your first child, correct?"

"Yes. That was *ten years ago*. Jesus."

"I'm just trying to get the information I need, okay? No one is judging you. But given that you can't give me the name of the father, I have to ask you if there is some confusion on your part."

"What?" She says this so loud and sharp that everyone else in the room stops talking. "Look," she says, leaning over Barbara Bell's desk, knocking over her nameplate, maybe on purpose, maybe not. "Let's get something straight here. I'm not confused. I know who the father is. I just don't want to tell you. It's not your business, okay?" She leans in closer. "It's not your business."

I would be scared, if my mother were that close to my face and yelling like that. But I don't think Barbara Bell is. She looks bored. "Ms. Bucknow," she says, her voice still calm, bored even, setting her nameplate straight again. "I couldn't care less what you want to tell me. In fact, I can assure you my interest in your personal life is negligible at best. But if you want money from the government, you're going to have to answer these questions to the best of your ability. They're cutting back our programs; they're upping our eligibility requirements. We have to be careful."

My mother stands up and tells Barbara Bell she doesn't give a fuck about eligibility requirements. She says she won't be talked to this way; she would rather starve. Barbara Bell says that is her prerogative, but she will be glad to speak with her again when she is feeling calmer.

And then it's like Wichita all over again. She takes my hand and pulls me back out into the long green hallway, past the room full of different people listening to the same scratchy tape, past the receptionist's desk with the orange-haired lady and the fan, out the door, out of the air-conditioning, into the sharp, stinging heat. I have to run to keep up with her, her hand tight around my arm, and the white sidewalk is like fire under my feet.

"My feet! Mom! My feet!" I twist my arm out of her grip. She stops so quickly that her head goes forward even after her body has stopped moving.

"Wh— Oh! Oh God, I'm sorry. I forgot. I forgot you had no shoes. How could I forget that?"

She looks weird, even for her. Her eyebrows are pushed down behind her sunglasses, and she looks as if she is concentrating very hard on something, her forehead wrinkled, her mouth open. I can hear her breathing.

She bends down and puts her hands under my arms. "Hmmph," she says. But this time, she can't get me past her knees. She sets me back on the grass, stumbling backwards. "I'm sorry, Evelyn," she says. She wipes more sweat off her face, and her hand looks too pink against her white face, like her hand and her face belong to two different bodies. "I just can't . . . I just can't carry you anymore . . ."

She is swaying a little now, back and forth. I know I should move forward, maybe take her hand. But I am also worried she could fall down right on top of me. I step back.

"I don't know what to do," she says. Her sunglasses have fallen off one of her ears. They sit crooked across her face, the pink strap hanging around her neck. She does not try to fix them. Instead, she sits down, right there on the grass between the sidewalk and the street. One of her black high-heeled shoes comes off, and the way she is sitting, I can see her underwear.

"Mom, get up. Let's go find somewhere to sit. A bench. Let's get a place in the shade."

Instead she lies all the way down, curling her knees up to her chest. "I don't know what to do."

There are cars now, slowing down, people looking out their windows. I try poking her, hard enough to hurt. "You have to get up. Get up now."

A man rolls down his window and leans out. "Honey, is your mom okay? Did she fall?"

"Mom, *get up!*" I want to kick her.

She is still on the ground when a police car slows and pulls over to the side of the road, lights on, no sirens. The other cars move around it, people watching us.

"Hi there," the policeman says, getting out of his car. "Is this your mother?"

I nod. He doesn't look old enough to be a police officer, even in the uniform, so many things swinging off his belt as he jogs toward us—a stick, a gun, a radio. He is wearing a hat, but I can see he has acne, swollen red marks and open scabs on his throat and cheeks, so much that it looks like it hurts. He gives me a bottle of water and tells me to go sit in the shade and drink it.

"Ma'am?" he says, kneeling beside my mother, his hand on her arm. "Ma'am? Do you need me to call an ambulance?"

She props herself up on her elbows. "No," she says. "No, no. I just need to lie here for a minute. I'm okay."

"Okay, well, we have to get you someplace where it's cool. We have to get you out of this sun, get you some water. Do you have any family I can call?"

She sits up quickly. "Where's my daughter? Oh my God, where is she?"

"I'm here," I say.

She sees me and lays her hand on top of her heart. If you were just driving by now, seeing her lying on the grass with her hand like this, the policeman kneeling next to her, you might think she'd been shot.

"She's fine, ma'am," the policeman says. "But she needs to get inside, and you do too. You need to stand up and walk with me so we can get your daughter inside where it's cool."

This is what does it. She stands up, leaning on him for just a moment before she waves me over, and we walk to his car together.

Finally she is embarrassed.

We are in the police car, both of us sitting in the back. My mother is drinking her second bottle of water. I am on my third. The police officer tells us we have to keep drinking it, that heatstroke is nothing we want to fool with. His car is magnificently air-conditioned, and I ask him to please turn it all the way up, to make sure it's on maximum. He laughs and says, "Of course!" and then I can feel it all around me, the coolness filling the air like smoke.

"It must have been the heat," my mother says. "I really don't know what came over me. Thank you so much for the ride."

He says that the heat has been making people act crazy all week. People have been fainting in their own homes—sunstroke, heatstroke—dropping like flies, he says. But he keeps asking her questions, looking at her in his mirror: Does she really want him to take us back to our house? Does she want him to take us to Social Services down at the station? Or the hospital, maybe?

No, she says. No. She'll be fine if he just takes us home. He asks her if she thinks she can take care of me, and she says yes. She tells him about the shoes, and how we had to take them off because they were too tight. She had tried to carry me, and the heat had just gotten to her. That was all.

When he pulls up to our house, he gives her his card and tells her she can have him paged if she starts to feel bad again, or if there is anything she needs. We get out of the car, and he rolls down his window, asking her again if she thinks she will be able to look after me.

"Yes," she says, her arm cool around my shoulders. "Yes, I'm sure."

The next morning, there is a pair of Keds in front of our door, left there in the middle of the night. They are a size too big, but this is better than too small. I stuff toilet paper in the toes so they will fit and show them to my mother, but she doesn't smile. She stays in bed all day, her eyes open, looking up at the ceiling, still wearing the yellow dress. She doesn't even get up to eat. I don't want to go into her room, dark and humid, starting to smell. She sleeps on just her mattress now, her broken bed pushed to one corner.

I eat cereal with the watered-down milk for two days, and leave her alone. I stay up late, watching television until they play the national anthem and the stations go blank.

On the third day, there is no more cereal, no more milk. I go back into her room and jump on her mattress. I yell at her and tell her she has to get up. When I pull off the sheets, she rolls over and turns away from me, the yellow dress pale and wrinkled. Her hair is awful, the back tangled in red-brown knots.

Finally, she stands up, her hands in her hair, looking not at me but at her reflection in the mirror. She closes her eyes and opens them again. "Okay, Tina," she says. "Come on."

She goes into the kitchen and finds some powdered milk. She fries an egg for me. She tells me not to worry. She will try to fill out the yellow-and-blue booklet again. She should not have talked to the lady at the desk like that. She says she is just having a bad time right now, but she still loves me. I am her little light in the world, she says, and she will always take care of me. Everything will be okay.

I eat my egg and watch her move around the room, listening to her talk. Everything will not be okay, I know. She has lost her job. She is going to have a baby, Mr. Mitchell's, and he has moved away with his wife somewhere, probably to get away from her. She sat down on the sidewalk downtown and cried like a little girl with her underwear showing until the police had to come.

I don't say anything, but in my head, things have changed. I've drawn a line between us, the difference between her and me. It's like one of the black lines between states on maps, lines between different countries on the globe. They don't really exist. You don't really see a long black line when you cross from the United States into Mexico, from Kansas to Missouri. But everyone knows where they are, and they are important, keeping one state separate from the other, so you can always tell which one you're in.

$\mathcal{I}$T'S JANUARY, AND LONG, SHARP icicles hang down from the roof. Eileen says she had a friend who was killed by an icicle; it fell off the building just as he was coming out the door, and it went through his head like a knife, split it right open.

My mother and the new baby are still gone. He was born too early and too small, with a weak heart and lungs that don't work by themselves. He has to stay in the hospital, a respirator breathing for him, in an incubator to keep out germs. My mother has to stay because her blood is too thin, and she needs rest. She'll be fine though, Eileen says. She'll be home soon.

Eileen has come up from Wichita to stay with me. She says the baby, Samuel, is most likely an angel who will only visit Earth for a little while before he flies back up to heaven. But it will be okay since he is a baby, she says, pure and innocent. He will go straight up, no problem. It will only be sad for the rest of us.

But she turns away from me when she hangs up the phone after calling the hospital, and acts like there's something in her eye. She cooks for me, makes me anything I want, but she doesn't eat. She wraps her entire plate up as a leftover, and says she will eat it in the morning, but never does.

"He'll go straight up," she says, getting out the aluminum foil. "Straight on up to a better place."

I go outside to the common yard and lie down in the snow, my arms spread wide, watching snow fall from the sky onto my face. I tell Eileen I am making snow angels, but really I am just lying there, thinking of the baby, wondering whether he has flown back up yet or not, if he can look down and see me lying here, looking up, trying to see him.

But the new baby doesn't fly up. After just a few days, they take him off the respirator, and he starts breathing all by himself.

Eileen takes me to the hospital in Kansas City, but we are not allowed to touch him, or even go in the room. There is a little window to look through, though, and when Eileen holds me up I can see him, squirming and gray, much smaller than you would think a baby could be. He looks more like one of the baby hamsters in a cage at school than a person. I put my hand up in front of the glass, and just my hand, stretched pinkie to thumb, is as long as he is. One of his legs is like two of my fingers put together.

He has hair already, thick and dark red like my mother's, but it is shaved on the sides, and a tube goes right into his head, burrowing right under the skin of his scalp. Another tube goes into his arm, another into his belly. There are wires attached to his chest, and he has a glass box over his head, with a hole at the bottom for his neck. On top of the box is a bright yellow teddy bear, a rainbow on its chest. He doesn't look at the bear.

I try waving, tapping on the window. I can see he's awake, his tiny hands squeezed into fists, one leg thrashing, his chest heaving up and down. His cheeks pucker like he is trying to suck in air through a straw, but there isn't enough. He kicks his good arm and his legs, like a beetle that has flipped over on its back and can't get up. I saw a grasshopper like this once, half of it run over by a car, its yellow-green insides squished out, the other half still alive, still moving. I stepped on it, killed it so it would quit hurting.

"Maybe there's not enough air in the box?" I ask.

"No," the nurse says, standing behind Eileen. She is the nice nurse, the one who asked us if she could get us something from the pop machine in the nurses' lounge. "There's more oxygen in the box than outside of it. It's just that his lungs can't get enough of it in."

I hold my breath for as long as I can, until I feel dizzy, until it hurts.

"Poor baby," Eileen says, her fingers on the glass. She has been crying so much that the crying seems like a part of her face now, like her nose or her mouth. When old tears dry or fall off, new ones grow in her eyes, spill over. But she talks like she is not crying, though anyone can see that she is.

The other nurse comes out of the room where Samuel is, pulling a mask down off her face so she can talk to us. They have to wear the masks because if the baby gets any germs on him, even just one, he will die. They are monitoring his blood, she tells us, making sure there isn't too much sugar or salt. They are watching for jaundice. They are checking the veins in his eyes. She doesn't want to get our hopes up, she says, looking right at Eileen. It's still hard to say which way things will go.

Eileen nods and smiles at the nurse, says thank you. But after the nurse leaves, she tells me that the nurses actually don't know what they're doing. They can't help him at all with all their needles and machines. Only God can help the baby now, Eileen says. The only thing we can do is pray.

So we do, every night at the kitchen table when we come home from the hospital, Eileen's small hands pressed over mine. She prays to Jesus to help the baby and my mother, not God. Jesus is God's son, but they are also both the same person. I don't understand this, how two people can be different people but still just one person. Eileen says that's because they're not people.

In my head, God has dark red hair and a beard. He doesn't wear clothes, but it's okay, because you can't see below his shoulders anyway. Everything else is always covered by clouds. Jesus looks exactly the same only he has blond hair and wears a white robe and sandals. This is how you can tell them apart.

And Jesus, I understand, is nicer than God, a little less likely to kill you if you do something wrong.

A week goes by, and the baby doesn't die. Eileen takes me to visit my mother in the room she shares with a blond woman who is pregnant with twins. This woman's belly, covered only by her thin gown, rises up so large out of her small body that at first I think she has put pillows underneath the sheets. But no, the woman says, pulling back the covers, showing me, she's really that big. She can't even walk anymore, won't be able to until they come out.

Her husband, a large man with a beard, comes to visit. He brings her flowers, yellow roses, and says hello to us when he comes in, shaking snow off his jacket.

"The least he can do," the blond woman tells us, smiling, holding up her cheek for him to kiss.

My mother is on the other side of the curtain from this woman, and she keeps it pulled shut. Sometimes she is asleep when we come in, but sometimes she is sitting up, awake, staring at the wall in front of her, not even looking up at us when Eileen says, "Knock knock? Tina?" There is a television on her side of the room, but she does not turn it on.

"Tina honey? I brought Evelyn in to see you. Are you awake?"

My mother looks at me and Eileen as if we are a light that is too bright. She tries to smile. Polaroid pictures of Samuel in his incubator are tacked above a bag that runs clear liquid through a tube into her arm, like she is a blender or a radio, something that needs to be plugged in to work. The liquid in the bag looks like water, but it could be anything.

"Are you okay, Evelyn?" she asks. I am standing far away from her, behind Eileen even, feeling bad for her, but still. The black line between us has stayed there, grown thicker and darker the whole time she was pregnant, sick all the time, crying in her bedroom at night. We had to go back to the welfare office, had to see Barbara Bell again. And now it is this, sick in the hospital with a sick baby, two strings tied together into a tight knot. Whatever was frightening or ugly about her before is doubled now, with her zombie eyes and the IV in her arm. Her hair smells like medicine, like sickness. So does her breath.

"I'm fine," I say. "Eileen's taking care of me."

This seems to make her more worried, not less. She opens her mouth to say something, but then looks as if she is suddenly too tired, or does not even know what it was she wanted to say.

The nurses say that the next few days will decide everything for Samuel— he'll either get better or a lot worse. No matter what, they tell us, they won't put him back on the respirator. And if his kidneys go, that's it. Eileen nods like she understands, but she starts crying again, her hand tight over her mouth.

But his kidneys don't go. He gains half a pound in less than a week, and the nurses try to explain his other improvements in words we can understand. A red light that did not blink the day before is blinking steadily now, and this is a good thing.

"Well, his heartbeat is stabilizing, and his lungs are getting stronger," the doctor tells us. "Things are looking up. The surgeries were successful, and we've had some luck."

Eileen almost starts laughing, or maybe she is just trying to catch her breath. She looks up, smiling, and claps her hands twice.

The doctor has wrinkles on his forehead, two small L's facing outward, and I can see how he got them, his forehead pushed down with concentration as he looks at the notes on his clipboard, reading the numbers on the machine with the blinking red light. "But he's a very sick baby, even for a preemie. I'm still worried about a hemorrhage in the brain. And his kidneys. And his eyes. He'll need more surgery, and even then . . ."

But Eileen is already crying again, her hands folded, head bowed. "Thank you," she says. "Oh thank you." She looks up again, and I can see her crooked smile surprises the doctor, who was not smiling, and is not, still.

The following Sunday, my mother still in the hospital, Eileen takes me to church. I understand that she is taking advantage of my mother's absence, doing something that my mother, if she were at home, would not allow.

"There's no need to say anything to her about it," Eileen says. "She's got enough on her mind. But we're helping her, really. More than she knows."

Eileen's pastor in Wichita has recommended a church for us in Kerrville, the Church of the Second Ark, which, it turns out, isn't really in a church at all, but in a roller-skating rink rented out Sunday mornings, the disco ball still hanging from the ceiling, folding chairs lined up along the glossy white floor. Eileen says she would rather come here, and be with real Christians, than have to go someplace where the Scripture has been watered down and as good as thrown out the window, just so she can look at a steeple and a bunch of stained glass.

"If you're going to follow the Bible, you have to follow the Bible," she says. "There's no point in going halfway. Especially when you've got a sick baby."

When we walk in, a man in a light blue suit—jacket, pants, vest, tie, everything light blue—is standing in the middle of the rink playing an accordion. I can't tell what song he's playing. Sometimes he stretches the accordion out and it sounds like the legs of a table being pushed across a floor.

"That's Pastor Dave," Eileen whispers. "He's the one I talked to. I like him a lot." She squeezes my hand. "He knows his stuff."

He nods at Eileen when he sees her, but does not put the accordion down.

"Morning, Pastor," she says, walking toward him, her shoes slipping a little on the smooth floor. "I'm Eileen Bucknow. We spoke on the phone."

"Yes, Eileen." He lets go of the accordion with one hand, holding it out to her. There is a strap around his neck that holds it up. "I'm so glad you could come!"

"This is my granddaughter, Evelyn, the one I was telling you about."

"Evelyn!" He smiles at me, taking my hand. He is younger than my mother, with straight blond hair and blue eyes and pinkish skin, not sunburned, but just naturally pink, the way other people look when they're embarrassed. His face is smooth, unwrinkled, but he has a mustache, thick and darker than his hair. It looks like it may not even be his, but something you could buy in a store and paste on, a mustache another man grew for him. "So glad you're here with us today," he says. "And the baby?"

"Doing better, praise Jesus." Eileen closes her eyes while she says this. "He's out of the woods."

Pastor Dave tilts his head back and pushes the accordion in and out. I am mesmerized by the accordion, all the buttons, the different sounds it can make, the way it moves in and out, folding up and out again like a chest, someone breathing. "I have to say, I'm not surprised," he says. "Not surprised at all. You-all be sure to sit in the front row," he says, pointing to the folding chairs. "You're our VIPs."

There is already a large man in a flannel shirt sitting in the front row, and Eileen makes it so I have to sit right by him. He turns and holds out his hand. "You-all new?"

Eileen explains she is from Wichita, and that I am her granddaughter, and that she is just in town visiting because my mother is in the hospital with a new baby.

The man frowns, looking at me quickly. "Everything all right?"

"He's getting better. We think they both might come home soon."

"Well I hope so," the man says. "You'll be in my prayers." He reaches into the pocket of his shirt and hands Eileen a small yellow card.

ED'S TV AND SMALL APPLIANCE REPAIR
"Cheaper than buying a new one"

"Wait a minute," he says, taking a red pen out of his pocket. He draws a cross on the card before handing it back. "Just bring that into my shop if you ever need anything fixed," he says. "I give a thirty percent discount to Second Arkers."

"Oh, how nice," Eileen says, taking the card. She pats me gently on the leg. "Evelyn, these are the nicest people in the world," she whispers. "You'll never see so many kind people together in one room as you will in a good church like this."

I watch the other people file in, men in ties that do not match their jackets, women holding hands with children who are picking their noses. There are three rows of ten chairs, and so some people have to sit on the floor. Only the men sit on the floor. The women and children get the chairs.

Pastor Dave moves behind what I think is the DJ's table when the roller-skating rink is in session, the record players and switchboards covered with a white cloth with JESUS IS LORD stitched in gold letters. "Good morning!" he says, thumping his hands on the table and then clapping them together. He sounds so happy that he looks like he is maybe going to start singing instead of talking, his arms raised above his head like Maria in *The Sound of Music*. "Sorry you-all have to put up with me on the accordion again. I'm still working on bringing in a piano or at least a keyboard Sunday mornings."

"You sound fine, Pastor," someone says.

He shrugs, his mustache moving up when he smiles. "Well, I wish I were better at it. It's a beautiful instrument in the right hands. Does anyone recognize the song?"

Nobody says anything. Pastor Dave looks around.

" 'Amazing Grace'?" someone asks.

He shakes his head. "No. No."

" 'Simple Gifts'?"

He looks down at the accordion. "No." He laughs. "It was 'Onward Christian Soldiers.' Let's give it a try with you-all helping me out, okay? Maybe it will sound more familiar."

We stand up to sing. I don't know the words, but Eileen and the man beside me do. I listen, mouthing along, trying to get the melody. Eileen squeezes my hand, and when I look up at her, she winks. It's so easy to make her happy. And I like that I am here, where my mother does not want me to be. Just by my being here, we are not the same.

We finish the song and sit down.

"Nice!" Pastor Dave says. "Very nice! You know, I've been thinking about this song all week. This week in particular, it was on the news. Anyone hear it?" He pushes the accordion in and pulls it out while he is waiting for an answer. "It was playing as President Reagan finished the wonderful speech he gave last week to the National Association of Evangelicals. Anybody see that?"

The man next to me and a few other people start clapping, nodding their heads. I wish I would have seen the speech. I would like to clap and nod.

Pastor Dave ducks to take the accordion strap from around his neck, setting it down on the sheet-covered table. It rolls over to one side, and he has to move quickly to catch it and push it away from the edge of the table so it doesn't fall. "Well, if you didn't see the actual speech, I'm sure you saw clips of it on the news. That speech has a lot of people angry. But I, for one, am glad to see somebody putting the 'God' back in 'God Bless America.'"

Everyone claps this time. "Amen," Eileen says. "Amen."

Pastor Dave holds up a finger, just one, like he is testing to see which way the wind is blowing, even though we're inside. "But a lot of people don't feel this way. A lot of people are a little *angry* right now, because President Reagan had the guts to go ahead and call the Evil Empire what it is." He shakes his head, stroking his mustache with one hand. "People don't like that word anymore, it seems. 'Evil.'" He pretends to shiver when he says this word. "They think it's a little . . . harsh, even for the Soviet Union." He shrugs, sticking his thin bottom lip out, like there is a possibility this might be true. "They say just because the Soviets are officially godless, officially anti-Christian, doesn't mean they're necessarily bad."

He pauses, looking around the room. "Are they right? Or, as the president says, is this Cold War really a struggle between good and evil, clear as daylight?"

We are all quiet for a moment, like when a teacher asks the class a question and nobody knows the answer.

"He's right!" the man sitting next to me says. "Reagan's right."

I think of Russia, cold and gray, people wearing dark coats and hats and never smiling, standing in long lines. I understand that they want to kill all of us, or at least make us wear dark coats and hats and stand in lines too. Eileen says they don't care about anyone, the Russians, even their own children. They don't care if they get blown up or not, because they don't believe in God. Still, it's sad to think that if there's a nuclear war they'll all go to hell. I would like to go over there, and tell them the way things really are so they won't want to bomb us and take over anymore.

"Well," Pastor Dave says, "I won't get too into politics here, but I imagine most of you are with me when I say I *know* there's a struggle between good and evil going on here in the world, and when one country tries to follow God, and the other one says there isn't one, it's not too hard to see which side is which, is it?"

The man next to me claps again, says, "That's right."

"Amen," someone says. "Amen." I like this, how people can just yell out when they agree with something. I wish we could do it at school. I want to try saying it now, but I have never done it before, and I worry that I will look stupid. None of the other kids are doing it. I'm not sure if you have to be an adult to yell out "Amen" or not.

Pastor Dave says he agrees with Ronald Reagan. You can't do business with godless people, because they lie and they cheat, just like godless people in our own country. He says right here in America we've got people giving out birth control to teenage girls and telling teenage boys it's A-OK to be homosexual, it's A-OK to ignore the Ten Commandments and act as if there are only four or five. When he says this last part, he pounds his fist on the table, trying to look mad now, even mean. But he can't. Even with the mustache, he looks like John Boy Walton. His voice isn't loud enough to be scary.

"It's not A-OK, is it?" he asks.

"No sir!" a woman yells. "No!"

The disco ball turns slowly, reflecting circles of sunlight around the room. Pastor Dave looks up at it, then out the window. "What are we going to do about America today? Read the paper, and you might be able to confuse this once great, God-fearing nation with Sodom and Gomorrah."

Eileen makes a clicking sound with her tongue and nods.

"Well, let me tell you something. If you-all think fire and brimstone was bad, that's nothing, *nothing,* compared to what's coming, when God comes down from the Heavens to separate the faithful from the sinners once and for all."

"Hallelujah," someone says. "Praise be."

Pastor Dave closes his eyes and raises his baby blue arms above his head. "But the righteous should have no fear," he says, the words rolling out of his mouth. "For the Good Lord knows what names are written in the book of followers, and they shall be flown on the wings of angels into everlasting peace, while all the rest will be damned by his terrible swift sword to everlasting contempt."

When Pastor Dave gets to this last part, he clasps his hands together and swings his arms quickly, the way you would swing a bat, or maybe a swift sword as well. I try to think about what it would really look like, all those angels coming down, God swinging a sword from over his shoulder, cutting off the heads of all the homosexuals and Russians, Jesus standing behind him with his hands over his eyes. "My name's in the book!" I would yell, and God, still cutting off other people's heads, would smile and say, "I know, Evelyn, I know."

Pastor Dave has taken the microphone off the DJ stand and clipped it to the front of his baby blue jacket. He's free to walk around now, and he does, slowly, circling the folding chairs. We can always hear his voice because of the microphone, but we have to keep turning around to see where he is. He says Lot's wife had her chance to get away from Sodom, but she went and turned around even when she'd been told not to. All she had to do was to keep walking and not look back at her friends and neighbors as they were getting rained on by fire, but then she did, and so she got changed into a pillar of salt.

I have never seen salt in pillar form, and am not sure what it would look like. I don't know if she was still shaped like herself, or if she just turned into a big pile of salt that you would never know used to be a person. It's scary to think something like that could happen to you, just for not listening to directions.

He moves to the center of the rink, directly under the disco ball, shaking his head. "All this insanity that you see in the papers, the declining moral values of today—this is all part of the prophecy. If you watch the news, you can see it all unraveling before you. Deadly wars are brewing in Lebanon. The children of Israel are back in their homeland, and the stage is set for the final scene." He looks out the window again, at the cars on the highway.

"But Lot survived the fire and brimstone," he says, quiet again, almost whispering. "And Noah survived the flood. And just by being in this room, just by staying true to the Scripture, we've built ourselves an ark, haven't we? Haven't we?"

"We have, Pastor. We have."

"Yes. We have. So you have nothing to fear. Scripture tells us that when the storm comes, only the faithful will be ushered through the wind and rain to live in perfect salvation. Like Noah, we will be chosen not to suffer, because we, in our lives, have chosen to live rightly."

Noah and the ark is a difficult story to imagine, all that water coming out of nowhere, then disappearing just as fast. Last year the Kaw River flooded its banks, and when the water finally went down, the news showed dead cows lying in muddy pastures, their stomachs bloated, flies buzzing around their heads. The people who had to move the cows were wearing handkerchiefs over their noses and mouths, and even the reporter kept one held up to his face when he wasn't talking.

It must have smelled like that when Noah's flood went down too, but worse, because there would have been not just cows, but people too. Lots of them. Even with the rainbow in the sky, when Noah first came out of the ark and looked around, things would have been pretty gross.

"Everybody else drowned?" I ask Eileen. We are in the car, going home. At the end of the service Pastor Dave gave me a Bible, green with gold letters. I hold it carefully in my lap, feeling its weight.

She nods. "Everybody who wasn't on the ark. But they got to bring two of each kind of animal. That's why we still have animals today."

We pass a field along the highway where horses are grazing, three brown horses and one gray. There is grass inside the fence, but all four of them lean their long necks over it to get at the tall grass on the other side.

"Only two horses?"

"Yes. A boy horse and a girl horse, sweetie."

"Two of each kind?"

She runs her tongue along the bad side of her mouth. "There weren't as many different kinds of horses back then, I think. Only when people started breeding them."

"And polar bears?"

She nods again. "Mm-hmm." I'm not sure if she is listening. She is thinking about the baby.

"Did they bring ice and snow for them so they wouldn't get too hot?"

"Mm-hmm."

"Two dogs?"

"Yep."

"All the different kinds? Saint Bernards? Poodles?"

"Yes."

"They were in cages?"

She pauses, just for a moment. "Yes."

"Things like tarantulas? Mice? Rats?"

"Yes, honey. Two of everything, except the fish. The flood didn't bother them one bit."

"Grasshoppers?"

"Yes."

I squint, looking out the window. "Wouldn't the tarantulas need to eat the grasshoppers? What would the tigers eat?"

She scratches her head. "They probably brought extra of stuff like that."

I picture Noah walking around with his staff and sandals, trying to organize the whole mess, giving orders, ducks quacking, kangaroos jumping around.

"How did Noah know which tarantulas were boys and which were girls?"

Eileen lights a cigarette and rolls down her window. "God knew, honey."

"And all the other animals died?"

"Mm-hmm." She looks in the rearview mirror. "He had to show he meant business, give the world a good cleaning." She takes one hand off the steering wheel and makes tiny scrubbing motions.

My mother took me to see *Black Beauty* last year, and I cried during the part where the old horse is whipped because it can't pull fast enough anymore. But the true stories are always the worst, and this one about Noah is really terrible, all the horses in the world getting killed except just the lucky two. I picture thousands of them trying to swim, frantic and kicking, the water rising up over their ears. I imagine myself standing next to Noah before the rain came, me wearing my normal clothes, looking at a field of horses, all of them staring up at me with their lovely horse eyes—old horses with swaybacks, skinny colts, the rain already starting to fall. *Two, Evelyn,* Noah would say. *You can pick only two.* But how could anyone pick just two out of so many? No matter which two I chose, I would be killing all the others. There would be no way to choose the best two because all horses are good.

You would just have to close your eyes and point.

And finally, doors would have to be shut, sealed off, even when the other people came knocking and then pounding, dogs, even puppies, scratching on the wood. *Let us in! Let us in!* But you would have had to just close your ears to them and not open the door. Because if you did, the ark would sink under the weight of everyone in the world, and there would be no one left at all.

Mrs. Rowley stands in her doorway, Jackie O in her arms. "How's the baby?" she asks.

"He's getting better," I say. I am walking to the bus stop, but I stop and look at her, surprised that she wants to know. "They might let him come home pretty soon. But he's still pretty sick. And my mom too."

Mrs. Rowley nods quickly, as if she understands more than I have told her. She has gotten thinner since Mr. Rowley left, the sash of her robe wrapped twice around her waist. The last time I talked to Travis, he told me that his father had a new girlfriend in West Virginia, and this woman, seven years younger than Mrs. Rowley, was sometimes in the pictures he sent to them of Kevin.

She catches my eye then, looks right at me. "That's what she gets," she says quickly.

I start to walk again and then stop, look back. "What?"

"That's what she gets." She tightens the sash of her robe and goes back inside.

They let my mother come home first, bringing her out to Eileen's car in a wheelchair. When she sees me, she leans forward and holds me against her chest until I am able to pull away. The nurses had to cut her hair short, so the curls look like mistakes now, coiling out from her head in all different directions, only brown now, no more red.

"I missed you," she says, taking my hand. "Oh honey, I missed you so much."

I smile weakly, say nothing. *Adultery,* I think. I looked "adultery" up in my dictionary, after coming home from church. The broken bed was a warning. Adulteress. Not just a horse.

Samuel comes home a few days later. He is still so small, and now two scars, pink lines, crisscross his chest. But he is beautiful, even so, lovely to look at because of his eyes. They are like blue stained glass, the light shining from somewhere behind. Already he has eyelashes, so thick and dark that they catch ahold of one another when he blinks.

My mother keeps him close to her at all times, carrying him around the house in the crook of her arm. She sleeps with him next to her on her mattress, a stack of blankets around him so he can't roll. When I try to touch his face, she pulls him away from me, her hand over his eyes. "Wash your hands first," she says. "You have to be careful, Evelyn. We're lucky he's still with us. Very lucky."

Just by looking at him, you can see he is still sick. His left arm doesn't unbend at all, and most of the fingers of his right hand stay curled beneath the palm. Just the one pointer finger, instead of curling under with the others, stays straight.

"He's like E.T.," I say, leaning forward to touch the tip of his finger.

My mother frowns, pushes my hand away. "What a nice thing to say, Evelyn."

So I leave them alone. I stay back in my bedroom, doing my homework, reading my green-and-gold Bible. I read a page a night, starting in the beginning, with the seven days and Adam and Eve and the subtle serpent. That story is also difficult to imagine, a snake talking like that. Animals talk in cartoons all the time, and sometimes in movies, but not in real life. Except for parrots. I would have liked to have lived when animals talked.

In all of the stories, God likes some people, and he stays on their side. He likes Abel, Noah, Abraham, Joseph, and Moses. He doesn't really like the other people as much, right from the start. He doesn't like Egyptians at all.

Pastor Dave made it sound like when Noah and all of them came out of the ark and saw the rainbow they were all happy forever, but it wasn't like that. Noah got drunk and fell asleep the way Mr. Rowley used to do, only Noah was naked. One of his sons, Ham, saw him, and instead of Noah getting in trouble for lying around drunk and naked, Canaan gets in trouble, even though he wasn't in the story in the first place, and he has to have a special mark on him and be a servant for the rest of his life, just because he's Ham's son.

Really, it's not important if you do bad things or good things. Some people are just blessed, and some aren't.

I keep reading, every night, and now I have already finished Genesis and Exodus and Leviticus. I am already up to Numbers, the part where God helps

Moses kill all the Midianites. The Midianites are not blessed, so they have to die, even all the boys, even all the women Midianites who have already known a man by lying with him. This, I think, is a nice way of saying women who have had sex. Adulteresses. Moses says they have to die, but the other women get to stay alive.

My mother knocks quickly and opens the door before I tell her to come in, Samuel quiet in her arms. She is still wearing the nightgown with the ketchup stain, although now it has faded.

"You're supposed to knock and wait," I tell her. "It's my room, not yours."

She clicks her tongue, using her free hand to point at the Bible in my lap. "What's this?" she asks. "When did this start?"

I take a deep breath, getting ready. *In me I have the strength of the Lord, and I fear no evil.* "Pastor Dave gave it to me."

"Pastor Dave." She keeps standing there.

"Pastor Dave at the church Eileen took me to while you were in the hospital."

She nods slowly. "The church Eileen took you to while I was in the hospital." She waits, maybe counting to ten in her head. "What church would that be, Evelyn?"

"The Church of the Second Ark."

"Ahhhh." She bites her lip. "The *Second* Ark."

"Are you going to repeat everything I say?"

She moves Samuel to her other arm. "Everything I say?"

I don't smile back. I'm sick of her and her jokes. She thinks she's funny, but really, there's nothing for her to laugh at. "Just because you don't go to church doesn't mean I can't."

Samuel starts to whimper, his cry high-pitched and shrill. She shifts him again, blowing lightly on his face. "Well, who's going to drive you there? Because I can tell you, Evelyn, I've got a new little baby here, who's still very sick, and I've got other things to do with my time than take you to the Church of the Second Ark. Super sorry."

"I've got a ride," I say. It's true. Pastor Dave's wife, Sharon, gave me a hug at the end of the service and told me they would be *happy* to give me a ride to church. *More* than happy. They are going to come early, so Sharon can French-braid my hair.

"Were you going to tell me about this?"

"I'm telling you now."

She leans against the door frame. "Let me get this straight. I go away for three weeks, almost die in the hospital, come back home, and you've turned into a carbon fucking copy of my mother."

Evil. She is evil. Don't turn back. I sigh and look down at my Bible. "Please don't use that kind of language in front of me."

She starts to laugh, her hand over her eyes, then backs away, shutting the door between us.

She is giving Samuel a bottle in the front room the next morning at eight-fifteen. I wait in my room until the last possible moment, but I have to go past her to get my coat.

"Just a minute," she says, holding up her hand. "How do I know who these people are? I don't know how I feel about letting you ride off with total strangers."

"Eileen knows them."

"Great," she says. "Great."

I look over her head, out the window. Pastor Dave's wood-paneled station wagon is in the parking lot, and he is standing beside it wearing the light blue suit again, squinting at our building. My mother follows me outside, shielding Samuel's face from the cold with her hand.

"Well hello!" Sharon says, already stepping out of the passenger seat. She wears a pink coat over the same dress she was wearing last Sunday, nylons, pink flats, and pink earrings that look like large buttons. Her voice makes me think of water running through a faucet, a whistling sound, happy and light. "You must be Evelyn's mother!"

"I am," my mother says. She does not look at Sharon when she says this, but at the bumper sticker on the back of the station wagon: WARNING: THIS CAR WILL BE UNMANNED IN THE EVENT OF RAPTURE!

Pastor Dave is on the other side of the car. "Evelyn's a lovely little girl," he says, resting his arm on the roof of the car. "You won't mind if we borrow her for a few hours?"

"I guess Evelyn will have to do what she wants."

"Well, we'd love it if you'd join us too. I don't know what Evelyn has told you about my accordion playing, but really, it's not that bad."

Sharon laughs. "I think he's getting better!"

"No," my mother says, not even trying to be nice. "No thanks." I am so embarrassed by the way she looks. She sleeps in her clothes now, and you can tell.

Pastor Dave nods and gets back in the car.

"Bye now," Sharon says, rolling up the window.

Even when I am in their car, my mother stays outside, watching me. I can actually feel her eyes on my head. Pastor Dave starts up the engine, catching my eye in the rearview mirror. "What about your father, Evelyn? Would he like to come to church?"

"I don't have one," I say. He and Sharon look at each other. I like this, the way this surprises them. I want them to know exactly what I'm up against, how bad she really is. I know they like me already, and the worse they think she is, the more they will think I am amazing to be so different.

"What about the baby's father?" Sharon asks, turning around, still smiling. "Is he home?"

"No. The baby doesn't have a father either."

"Oh," they say, both of them at the same time, not looking at each other now, not needing to. Pastor Dave puts the car in gear, and we shift smoothly into first, no problem at all as we glide away.

nine

$\mathcal{P}$ASTOR DAVE AND SHARON PICK me up every Sunday before church now. I worry they'll get sick of having to come all the way out of town to get me, but Sharon says, "No, Evelyn, no. Don't be silly."

I wish they were my parents.

When I am not at church, and not at school, there's nothing to do but watch my mother sleep or carry Samuel around the house. When summer comes, I want to walk into town with Travis, but my mother says I can't because I'll get hit by a car. I tell her I don't care, because I know if I die I'll go to heaven and that's why I'm not a coward the way she is.

"That's why you can't go," she says.

Travis sometimes comes over, and we go sit up on the roof, watching cars on the highway. He tells me stories about the strip mall. He wants to get a skateboard, a nice one, but he doesn't have the money. He has started stealing again, and every day there are close calls with security guards.

"I'm going to get one of those tarantulas," he says.

"How are you going to steal that?"

"I don't know." He throws pebbles on top of the roof of Unit B, at the windows of his own apartment. It makes Jackie O bark, and when Mrs. Rowley opens the door to look up at the sky, Travis and I lie down on the roof so she can't see us.

"Who is that?" she says. "Who's there?"

I let Travis throw the pebbles, but I don't throw any myself. God is watching us at all times, can see our every move. "You shouldn't," I whisper. "Travis. You shouldn't do that."

He puts his fingers to his lips, tosses another pebble. If it were anyone else doing this, I'd make them stop. But I can't yell too much at Travis for throwing the rocks, or go back inside, because if I do, he might not come back.

The door opens again, and Mrs. Rowley leans out of the balcony. She is wearing a white cotton nightgown, her shoulder bones like metal rails to hang something on. "Who's there?" She looks up, right at us, but doesn't see us in the darkness. She goes back inside.

Travis throws another pebble, and another. She opens the door again, and for a quick moment, she does not look like herself. Standing there in her white nightgown, her thin arms pale in the darkness, she looks different, not so skinny as much as small. I have known Mrs. Rowley my entire life, heard her yell, watched her watch us with her mean fish eyes. But I've never seen her just listen, not wearing her glasses, just being still and looking up at the sky.

Travis says her name softly, his voice low, stretching it out like a ghost in a movie. *"Becky . . ."*

"For God's sake, who's there?" She is scared now. Jackie O sees us, looking up at me with iridescent eyes.

"Rebeeeeeecaaaaaa. Rebeeeeeeeeeecaaaa."

She leans over the cement railing, squinting up into the darkness. "Dad?"

Travis puts his face into the neck of his shirt. I shake my head and give him a mad look, but I can tell from the way his ears rise up he's laughing.

"Is it you?" She leans farther over the balcony, looking up at the sky.

Travis reaches up and presses his hand against my mouth, his arm hooking quickly around my neck. I can feel his breath against my cheek, warm and humid. I say nothing.

When she goes back inside, he lets go of me, still laughing. "Come on, Evelyn. It's nice for her. She liked her dad."

"He's dead?"

He smiles, his ears rising. "Not tonight."

I won't laugh, even though I can still feel where his arm was on the back of my neck. "You shouldn't do that, Travis. It's wrong."

But the next day, Travis says his mother is being nice all of a sudden, speaking to him in soft, careful tones, as if there were a camera, or someone from child protection, right there in the room. And instead of lying in bed the way she usually does, she got up early and made breakfast for the two of them. She even brushed her hair.

When school starts again, Samuel is eight months old, but you can't tell. He's still small, and when you smile and talk to him, he doesn't smile back. He doesn't even look.

Still, whenever my mother takes him anywhere, strangers come up and tell her how beautiful he is. At the grocery store, they look over her shoulder and smile and make kissing sounds as if really, they know him well, maybe better than we do. Carlotta at the Kwikshop tells my mother he is the most gorgeous baby she has ever seen, and other people say the same thing. *"Look at those eyes!"* they say. *"What beautiful eyes!!"* People we don't even know try to touch his face, and my mother has to turn quickly and explain that he has been sick, and that she has to be careful about germs. When we're at the Laundromat, a woman asks if she can hold him, and my mother says only if she washes her hands first. The woman says fine, and she does. She goes into the bathroom of the Laundromat and comes out drying her wet hands on a paper towel. This is how much people want to hold him.

But people talk only about his eyes. They don't talk about how one of his arms still won't unbend, or how his fingers stay curled underneath his palms so his hands look like claws. My mother has to pry his fingers open every night to wash his hands and trim his fingernails. She pats baby powder on them so he won't get a rash. Sometimes she blows on them with the hair dryer. Still, his fingers smell strange, as if he has been holding pennies.

People in grocery stores and at the Laundromat never talk about how he doesn't smile, and how he doesn't look back. But I can tell the moment they realize it, that something is wrong, because their voices get louder and they talk about his eyes more and more, about how beautiful they are, the most beautiful eyes they have ever seen.

The Day After is going to be on television in November. It's about nuclear war. The people who made the movie picked Kansas because we're in the middle, and that way it would scare the most people. I've been to Lawrence. My mother and I stopped there once and got pizza on Massachusetts Street.

The commercial for *The Day After* shows Massachusetts Street turning black and white in a flash and then just going to darkness. A man keeps saying, "This is Lawrence, Kansas. Over. Is anyone there? Anyone at all?" No one answers, and you can guess that's because everyone else is already blown up and dead.

I want to watch it, but I don't think I'll be able to because the school sent home a note.

Dear Parents,

As you are probably well aware, The Day After *is going to be on television next week. The film attempts to depict what would happen to a small town in Kansas in the event of a nuclear war. Because the film is primarily set in Lawrence, Kansas, only fifty miles away, we at Kerrville Middle School are concerned that the program, meant to be realistic and upsetting, might be a little too realistic and upsetting for young people in our community. When deciding whether or not to allow your child to watch* The Day After, *please take into consideration his or her ability to deal with anxiety and fear, as well as his or her understanding of fiction versus reality.*

My mother reads the note and looks at me carefully.
"What?" I say. "I'm fine."
My mother says I can't watch it. I have to stay in my room while it's on. I scream and yell, but it doesn't matter. Sorry you don't like it, she says. That's the way it is.

She watches it, though, sitting out in the front room with Samuel in her arms. I listen to what I can through the door. There are just people talking at first, but then there are sirens, loud crashing sounds, people screaming. Sometimes there's laughing and music playing, but it's just the commercials.

When I come out of my room to go to the bathroom, I can see her face, tear-streaked and watching the screen, holding Samuel close as if the bombs were really going off, not just on television, but all around her, right there in the room.

Even when he's a year old, he can't roll over. My mother says it's because of his bad arm. His legs are weak too, still so small, she says. The doctor says yes, maybe that's what it is. But he'd like someone from the university to have a look at him, just to make sure.

Two women come over. They are very nice, and both of them wear long overcoats with blazers and turtlenecks underneath. They carry clipboards. One of them has a green ball, and she tries to get Samuel to take it. They hold him on their laps, and they tell my mother how beautiful he is, especially his eyes.

My mother sighs and crosses her arms. She is tired of hearing this.

And, one of the women says, putting down her clipboard, there seem to be some developmental delays.

"Right," my mother says. "That's what I'm worried about."

The woman nods, keeping her eyes on my mother's face. "Of course, there are the physical disabilities, but I suspect mental delays as well. We would have to do more tests, but I imagine they're fairly severe."

My mother stares at the lady with the green ball, her face still with fear. I understand, just from the quiet in the room, that this is very bad, what the woman is telling us. Samuel is retarded. That's what she's saying. He will ride the short bus with the kids who use crutches, wear crash helmets. When you do something stupid at school, you get called a retard, and this is what they mean. They mean Samuel. There's nothing to be done.

My mother looks at Samuel, still lying in the other woman's arms, and makes a whimpering sound, something inside her crumpling up, or getting pulled apart.

One of the women gives my mother a card with a phone number on it. She says the sooner she calls, the better, the more they can help. They have special classes. My mother winces when they say "special," and she goes to the door and stands there until both of the women put on their overcoats and leave.

She gets her own green ball. For days, she tosses it lightly in Samuel's lap, again and again, saying, "Catch the ball, honey! Catch!" as if all he had to do was catch it, just once, and that would prove them wrong.

When I go to church now, I pray for the baby, because he is still innocent and does not deserve to be retarded. Pastor Dave says we should wait and see, and not listen to everything so-called experts say just because they are from so-called universities. They don't know everything, he says. And miracles happen every day.

Driving me home from church, he says he has thought about Samuel, prayed about him, and has heard from God himself that we should not give up. He says I should try to get my mother to bring Samuel to church next Sunday. They are bringing in a faith healer from Arizona, one of the very best. "We're so blessed to have him," he says, looking at me in the rearview mirror. "Harry Hopewell."

"What a marvelous name for a healer," Sharon says, turning around. "Hopewell. Hope-well!" She is wearing blue earrings shaped like telephones, the receiver hanging onto the outside of her ear, the cord a hoop underneath her earlobe.

"He saved the life of a man in Nevada, dying of so-called cancer," Pastor Dave says, scratching his mustache. "The doctors had given up hope, but then Hopewell laid hands on him"—Pastor Dave holds his own hands up for a moment, letting go of the steering wheel—"and the man was cured. Boom. My brother in Texas saw it with his own eyes."

The next time Eileen comes to visit, I tell her Harry Hopewell is coming. Her mouth goes in the shape of a capital O, her eyes wide. "Harry Hopewell? In Kerrville? Oh Evelyn, he's amazing, truly amazing," she says, her hand over her mouth. "He's the one who's been curing all those boys who thought they were homosexuals." When she says "homosexuals," she leans forward and whispers, as if really, she doesn't want me to hear. "He put the spirit of God in them, and they don't think that way anymore. Some of them are already married." She's holding Samuel while my mother is in the bathroom. He is awake, but you can tell this only because his eyes are open. For him, that's the only difference.

Eileen sways him gently back and forth. "If anyone can help this baby, it's that man."

"She won't come, Eileen," I say. "She hates church." Really, I don't want her to come. She'll ruin it, contaminate it just by being there. Pastor Dave and Sharon like to remind me that my mother is always welcome at the Second Ark, and that I should keep inviting her. When they say this, I shake my head sadly, and say I don't think she'll ever come. They hug me then, and they tell me how amazing it is that I have turned out the way I have.

But now my mother is coming with us to church, and she's bringing Samuel. Eileen got her to come. She said all she wanted for her birthday this year was for all four of us to go to church together. She said it would be nice if we could *all do something together,* and when she said this, she nodded in my direction.

"Fine," my mother said. "Just this once."

And already it is just as bad as I knew it would be, her coming with us. When she sees the church is also a roller-skating rink, she starts laughing. She says the Second Ark might be more successful if they let everyone bring their skates. The pastor could stand in the middle and preach how everyone was going to hell while the congregation glided around him, bending down to do the cold duck, grabbing hands and spinning in pairs.

I glare at her. Eileen shakes her head.

"Sorry," she says. She looks down at Samuel. "You thought it was funny, right?" His blue eyes gaze up past her head. He is her only friend these days, the only person who isn't mad at her, trying to get away.

When Pastor Dave and Sharon see us, they walk toward us quickly, their hands reaching forward. "Tina!" Sharon says. "We're so happy you could come today. It's so good to see you!"

"What a beautiful baby!" Pastor Dave says. "Look at those eyes!" Pastor Dave is holding the accordion, but Sharon reaches over the blanket to touch Samuel's face. My mother pulls him away.

"Sorry," she says. "He was sick for so long. I have to be careful."

Pastor Dave and Sharon look at each other quickly, then back at my mother. She tries to smile. "If you wash your hands you can hold him."

I close my eyes, and pray to God to make my mother disappear, for her to be zapped by a bolt of lightning, smited by a laser from above. She doesn't belong here. All of the other women are wearing dresses, but she's wearing cords and a blue sweater that is too tight. And now this, telling Sharon, lovely, pink Sharon, who is so much cleaner than she is in so many ways, that she has to wash her hands.

Harry Hopewell is a tall, black-haired man with sideburns that make him look a little like Abraham Lincoln, and I think maybe he has done this on purpose. He wears a black suit and a red tie, a gold cross stuck in the middle of it. His voice is deeper than Pastor Dave's. Words come out of his mouth like he is pounding on a drum.

"Are you all ready?" he asks, standing behind the DJ table, his arms stretched out wide. "Are you all ready to witness the healing power of the Lord?"

Pastor Dave starts to play something on the accordion, and my mother leans over and taps me on the arm. "Evelyn," she whispers. "What's that man's name?"

I frown at her. She is like Ray Watley at school, talking in class. "Hopewell."

My mother looks back up at him, squinting. "You're not going to believe this," she whispers, "but I swear, I mean I *swear,* that guy was on a soap I used to watch."

I scoot my chair away from her, closer to Eileen.

"I'm afraid I'm having trouble hearing you," Harry Hopewell says, cupping a hand around one of his ears. His voice is so loud you can hear it over the accordion, and he hasn't even turned on the microphone. "What I need to know is, are you all with me today in the spirit of the Lord? Are we going to do some healing? Are your hearts bound in faith? You all have to be in the spirit for this to work."

There is a growing hum in the room now. People are stamping their feet, clapping hands, calling out "Amen." It's exciting. But I'm worried my mother will ruin everything. You can tell just by looking at her face she's not in the spirit. She's looking up at Harry Hopewell, at the disco ball, and at me, and her face looks like she is going to laugh and also like she is still trying to remember the name of the soap opera.

Harry Hopewell steps down from behind the table and asks who wants to go first. A lady in the back row raises her hand, and Pastor Dave plays "When the Saints Come Marching In" on his accordion as she walks between the folding chairs to the front of the room. Harry Hopewell looks at her carefully, and then closes his eyes. "What ails you, child?"

"Headaches," she says, her voice more like she is asking a question than giving an answer. "I've been getting headaches right here." She points to one of her temples. "I get them almost every day, for about a year now. They're very painful."

Harry Hopewell puts his hands on each side of her head like it is something he can squish together, and for a moment, I think this is what he is going to do. "In the words of Luke," he says. "The spirit of the Lord is upon me. He hath anointed me to preach the Gospel to the poor, to heal the brokenhearted, to preach deliverance to the captives, and recovering of sight to the blind, to set at liberty them that are bruised."

Even my mother is quiet now, jiggling Samuel on her knee. Harry Hopewell asks us to bow our heads, to let the spirit of the Lord enter the room, for each of us to pray for this woman to be set at liberty from her headaches. I pray as hard as I can, holding on to Eileen's hand. You are supposed to close your eyes, but I open mine long enough to see that my mother's are still open. If this doesn't work, if the lady still gets headaches, it will be her fault.

"Do you feel this?" he asks, still squishing the lady's head. "Do you feel this coming from my hands, this heat?"

She waits, her eyes closed, face tensed, as if she is listening for a sound from far away. Then she opens her eyes. "I do," she says. "I feel it!"

Eileen jumps a little in her chair, both hands cupped over her mouth.

"I feel better!" the lady says, to us now. "I feel better! I really do."

Pastor Dave starts playing the accordion again, and the lady dances down the aisle, her arms raised high in the air.

The next man who goes up won't say exactly what his problem is; he will only say he is suffering from wicked thoughts in his mind and heart, but Harry Hopewell nods quickly, as if he knew what the man would say before he even opened his mouth.

"You know," Harry Hopewell says, taking off his glasses, rubbing the lenses with his red tie, "Jesus, while on Earth, stilled a storm. He had the power to calm both the land and sea. Does he not have the power to purge this man of the thoughts that torment him, to bring him back into the light?" When we don't answer, he looks up at us. "Well, does he?"

"Yes!" we say, all of us together, except for my mother, who says nothing.

He places his hands on the man's head and tells him he won't suffer from wicked thoughts anymore if he is in fact a true believer. The man says, "Okay," and goes back to his chair. A woman with arthritis goes up next, and then even Sharon and Pastor Dave take a turn. Sharon starts crying, up there in front of everyone, and it's so strange to see her like this, mascara tears running down her pink cheeks. She's crying so hard that you can't really understand her as she explains what the problem is, but then Pastor Dave says that they haven't been able to have a baby, and that they want one, more than anything else in the world. They'll give up anything to have a baby, he says. Harry Hopewell says if this is true, then they'll be able to have one.

My mother leans over me to poke Eileen on the knee. "This is stupid," she whispers. "That's mean, for him to tell them that."

I look at her, unbelieving. It's pretty bad, what she said, even for her. You can't call a reverend stupid, especially when you're in church. The walls could fall down, tumbling down just on her head, leaving everyone else alone. And then, maybe because we're in church, she gets what she deserves.

"In the back there?" Harry Hopewell asks. "Ma'am? With the baby?"

The accordion stops playing. My mother shakes her head quickly, sitting up straight. "No. Nothing. I'm okay."

But Eileen waves at Pastor Dave, motioning him over. "Go on up," she says, pushing on my mother's arm. "Go, Tina. It's free, anyway."

My mother brings Samuel closer to her chest, his empty eyes staring off past her shoulder. She shakes her head. "No, Mom. No. Stop it."

"Come on. What would it hurt to try?"

Pastor Dave is moving toward us, smiling and squeezing the accordion in and out as he walks. He stops when he gets to where we are and puts his hand on my mother's shoulder.

"I'm okay," my mother says. She keeps her head still, but she moves her eyes so she's looking at his hand on her shoulder. "Really."

"Tina," he says, still holding the accordion in his other hand, his fingers pressing lightly on the keys. "You said your baby was sick. Don't you want to help him? We're coming to you with love. Just love, Tina. Nobody's judging you for what you may have done wrong in the past. We only want to help you and your baby come to Christ."

"Come on, Tina," Eileen says, her hand on my mother's knee. "Just give it a try."

My mother is still looking at Pastor Dave's hand on her shoulder, her eyes wide. "No thanks." She pulls the edges of Sam's blanket over his face. "Go away, okay?"

The people in front of us have turned all the way around in their folding chairs to see. My mother starts to stand up, but there's nowhere for her to go. She tries to scoot her chair back, but she can't.

"God wants you to be happy, Tina," Pastor Dave says. He kneels beside her, his hand still on her shoulder. "Christ died to wash your sins away, but you have to let it happen. You have to say yes." He takes his hand off her shoulder and reaches toward Samuel.

"Okay," my mother says, raising one of her arms like she is getting ready to ask a question, or to volunteer. "Okay," she says again, looking at Pastor Dave's hand. "If you touch my child . . ." She pauses, like she is trying to decide what will really happen, like she isn't sure yet and has to think about it. "If you touch my child, I'll hurt you. I really will."

Pastor Dave stands up and moves back. It is hard to believe. All of us watching take in one deep breath at the same time, like a choir getting ready to sing. You can't say you're going to hurt a pastor right in the middle of church.

And then, again, it's like Wichita, her hand suddenly tight around my wrist, pulling me up beside her. But I don't want to go with her this time. "I'm staying," I say, trying to twist free.

She leans down and looks at me, her slightly crossed eyes inches away from mine. "No, Evelyn. I'm your mother, and you're coming with me."

No one comes to save me. She pulls me outside, out into the parking lot, into the cold late-morning drizzle. She does not even try to dodge the puddles, but kicks right through them, dragging me behind.

"I hate you," I tell her. "You ruin everything."

"I know, Evelyn. I know."

Eileen jogs out behind us, holding our coats. "Tina!"

My mother tries the door handle of the car, but it's locked. When Eileen gets to the car, she hands us our coats so we can put them over our heads, but then we all just stand there.

"Mom, take us home," my mother says, her hand over Samuel's face. Even with the raindrops falling right onto him, he hardly blinks.

"You could at least try."

"Take us home."

Eileen puts one hand on my shoulder, and we face her, the two of us. "Tina, I know you don't want to hear this. But I think Samuel has a . . . specialness to him, and—"

"He's retarded, Mom."

"Tina—"

"He's retarded. He's retarded, he's retarded, he's retarded." She puts her own hand against her ear and nods. "He's not special. He's retarded. That's how it is. That man in there can't do anything about it."

They both stand there for a while in the rain, looking at each other. Then Eileen unlocks the car. We get in, and she drives us home.

ten

$\mathcal{I}$ AM NO LONGER ALLOWED to go to the Church of the Second Ark. If I want to go to a normal church, my mother says, fine. But no more Second Ark. She tells me this while she is trying to get Samuel into a clean T-shirt, and he is crying, loud and angry, flailing his legs and good arm.

"I'm a Second Arker, Mom," I tell her. "I don't want to go to some so-called church where the Scripture has been as good as thrown out the window just so I can look at a bunch of stained glass."

"How original," she says.

I go to my room and slam the door. But I am too mad to stay there. I come back out again, running down the hallway toward her. I could hit her. I'm that mad. I stand over her, my fists clenched, ready to burst. "Pastor Dave and Sharon are going to come out here and get me. I'm going with them."

She picks Samuel up, her free hand resting on the small of her back as she stands. "I don't care if they send a goddamn limo out here. You're not going."

"Freedom of religion!" I yell, going back to my room. "Where's my free-dom of religion?" I slam my door, and then open it and slam it again.

It does not seem fair that she can do this, here in America.

I stay in my room for the rest of the day. I don't even come out to eat. I can stay in here forever if I need to. I am like Moses in Egypt, and I have righteousness and God on my side. My mother is the Pharaoh, Samuel only one of the plagues to visit her, all of which, it seems to me, she deserves.

I'm happy when school starts again, because at least it's an escape from her. I am taking French this year, and so is Travis. We use it as a code to talk about our mothers, right in front of them.

"*Bonjour, Travis, ma mère est trés bête.*"

"*Bonjour, Evelyn, ma mère est un chien mechant.*"

But my favorite class is science. Mr. Torvik has a model of the solar system hung up around the room, and when he turns a switch, the planets revolve around the sun, the baseball-sized Earth spinning on its axis. The planets glow in the dark, and if we are good, if we do our homework and do not pass notes while he is talking, Mr. Torvik shuts out the lights for the last five minutes of class and turns on the switch, so we can just look up and watch the planets move.

"Lovely, isn't it?" he asks, the light of the planets reflecting off his glasses.

In the spring, he takes us outside and has us bring in leaves to put under the microscope. He shows us how to tell how old a tree is by counting the rings of the stump, the wider rings being moist years, when the tree grew the most. He tells us the names for the different kinds of clouds—cumulus, cirrus—and we learn about warm fronts and cold fronts and wall clouds, how tornados are formed.

We watch films about dogs and wolves, how they are different, how they are the same. They belong to the same *genus,* he says, but are not the same *species.* Snow rabbits are white because that makes them blend in with the snow and harder to see. Mr. Torvik says the reason there are white rabbits where there is snow is because all the rabbits who were different colors couldn't hide in the snow and got killed before they could have babies.

I raise my hand. "This is before Noah's ark, or after?"

Traci Carmichael turns around, and again there are the thin lips, the blue-gray eyes. "You've *got* to be joking," she says. She looks at Brad Browning, who is already laughing, shaking his head. I feel my neck flush, my throat go dry. Half of me thinks, *We'll see, Traci Carmichael, we'll see who's laughing when the bombs go off, and only my name is in the book,* but the other half of me knows I have said something stupid.

Mr. Torvik opens his mouth and closes it several times, like he is trying to yawn instead of speak. "It's separate," he says finally, his hands making quick, chopping motions in the air. "Two different things."

He shows us a film of lions hunting, circling a herd of antelope. The antelope are too fast for the lions to catch, except for one with a hurt foot, and the lions all move quickly after this one, surrounding it, as if they already had a meeting and knew exactly what they were going to do. Traci puts her hands over her eyes during this part, and so of course Libby Masterson, who does not have her own brain, does too. But I watch, something in me wanting to see the look in the limping antelope's eyes as the lion's paw grabs it by its throat, the rest of the herd running past, only scared for themselves, no time to stop.

"It's so sad," Libby says, even though, really, she didn't see it. "It's terrible."

But Mr. Torvik says it isn't sad. It's just nature. This way, he tells us, the lions get to eat and the antelope rid themselves of an imperfect specimen. Nature has to get rid of imperfections in the womb, or soon after, to make certain that imperfection isn't allowed to mate and reproduce itself. Otherwise, there would be a bunch of antelope with bad legs limping around.

He squints at the VCR, trying to find the rewind button. "You wouldn't want that, class, now would you?"

Mario Cuomo is on television at the Democratic National Convention, and my mother won't let me change the channel. He looks really mad when he talks, and I like Ronald Reagan better because he's usually smiling and making jokes. But Mario Cuomo says we cannot let Ronald Reagan be president again, because he's already talking about spending billions of dollars putting a shield around the shining city on the hill. Mario Cuomo says this shield won't work, and anyway, there really are two cities in America these days, and half the people live in the other one, which isn't shining, and isn't on a hill. He says go ask the people who sleep in the streets if they live in a shining city; go ask the woman who can't get the help she needs because we just spent it on a tax cut for a millionaire or another missile.

"That's right," my mother says, trying to clap. She can't really, because she's holding Samuel with one hand and the fingernail clippers in the other.

He is still retarded. All this year I have been learning so much, he has learned nothing. My mother spoon-feeds him oatmeal, carries him around the house as if he were a part of her body, his legs dangling below her arms.

"Can we watch something else?" I ask, my hand already on the dial. I'm sick of Mario Cuomo. The Democratic Convention has been on all week, canceling my shows.

"No."

I glare at her, yawning, loud and on purpose. I scratch my head with the hand that is holding a Rubik's Cube, and Samuel makes a screeching sound.

My mother stops looking at Mario Cuomo and looks at Samuel. She leans forward, turns the television off with her foot. "Do it again," she says.

I put the Rubik's Cube back on my head, and again, he makes the sound, like a pterodactyl, his good arm reaching toward me.

She takes the Rubik's Cube from me, without asking, and offers it to him. But he doesn't want it. He goes back to the way he always is, zombie-eyed, just staring. I put the Rubik's Cube back on my head, and again, he makes the sound. My mother takes it from me and puts it on her head. He cries out.

She confiscates the Rubik's Cube permanently, carrying it in the pocket of her bathrobe at all times so she can put it on her head whenever she wants him to look at her. She starts making the pterodactyl sound as well, imitating him, like she is trying to show him they are both the same species. She does this when she thinks I'm not looking, but sometimes I am.

"Oh shut up, Evelyn," she says.

"I didn't say anything."

She loses the cube. She spends the whole day looking under cushions and behind furniture, saying, "Find it! Evelyn, we have to find it!," Samuel riding on her hip, staring off over her shoulder. Out of desperation, she tries one of her slippers, puts it on her head. He groans, and does something with his mouth that is maybe a smile. She tries different objects—a fork, a cup, a pack of gum, one of my notebooks. The shinier the object, the louder he groans, but it has to be on your head. She takes a hat that Eileen knitted for her last Christmas and sews a red patch on the front, covering the patch with glue and then glitter, so it sparkles in the light.

Now when she holds him, he stares up at the hat, and she can at least pretend he is looking back at her.

· · ·

I haven't seen Travis since February, when he got in trouble with Ed Schwebbe, his friend with the blue-and-white van who sometimes gives him a ride to school. He had to go back to the group home, this time for seven weeks, and they didn't even let him come home on weekends.

By the time he comes home, it's almost May, warm enough to sit up on the roof again, even at night. He tells me the whole story, how one morning Ed was driving him to school, and they started talking about whether or not Ed could jump over a picnic table in just one jump if he got a running start. Ed said he thought he could. Travis said he didn't think so.

"I knew he could probably do it," Travis tells me, throwing pebbles again, but not at his mother's window. They land on the hedges below us, making no sound. "He's pretty tall. I just didn't want to go to school."

But Ed found a picnic table in a park and jumped over it by eight-fifteen, which left plenty of time to get to school before the first bell. So Travis said he wasn't sure whether or not Ed's feet had touched the picnic table as he jumped over it, and the only way to be sure would be for Ed to jump over a table again, but this time it would have to be on fire. He told Ed that he had seen someone do this on television, which was not true. So this was why Travis and Ed had put the picnic table in Ed's van and driven out of town, stopping only to get some kerosene, to the middle of a plowed soy field. They got a good blaze going, but Ed never got to jump because a state trooper saw the smoke rising from the highway. And so Travis and Ed ended up appearing before a judge, who wanted them each to have seven weeks at the group home to think about what they had done.

"And did you?" I ask, hitting him on the shoulder with one of my flip-flops. "Did you think about it?" I'm trying to act disappointed, but really, I'm just glad he's back.

He nods, watching the highway. His face has grown more lean in the last year, so his eyes seem larger now, catlike. He is wearing only shorts, no shirt, and just lately, maybe while he was in the group home, he has gotten dark hair on his chest and underneath his arms.

"I thought about it." He smiles, rubbing his chin.

"What did your mom say?"

"She called my dad. Told him." He laughs again. "I guess I won't be going to live in West Virginia this year either." He throws another pebble. "Poor me."

"Well, I'm glad you're staying," I say. *So we can get married.* "But you should really go to school." I'm worried about this, how much Travis gets into trouble. In my mind, Travis has to start going to class regularly, so he can pull his grades up, so we can be boyfriend and girlfriend in college. Then he will start coming to church with me, then we can get married. When we are old and married, we will tell people that we have been friends since we were little, and that we went to Homecoming and Prom together in high school. Travis will smile at me, and say, *She turned my life around. I was always in so much trouble before Evelyn.*

Travis leans back, looking up at the sky. "Which one is that?"

"Venus," I say. "It's so bright because it's close. Especially right now."

I'm learning more and more about the stars. I got Mr. Torvik for science again this year, still balding and hushed-voiced, still with the miniature solar system hanging from his ceiling. He gave me a book to read about planets and stars. "You seem so interested," he had said. And I was. I sat open-mouthed the day he explained light-years to us, shutting off the light and then turning it back on.

"See how fast light travels?" Mr. Torvik whispered. "It takes no time for the light of the lightbulb, from the moment I turn it on, to reach your eyes. It actually takes time, but not very much." He paused, flipping the light switch again, on and off. "The closest star to Earth, the very closest, is just over four light-years away, which means when we look up and see it, we're really seeing the light that was made in 1981.

"Can you imagine that kind of distance?" he asked us, taking off his glasses. "Can you *imagine*?"

I couldn't. Not really. It was like when someone said "forever" and you tried to imagine it both ways, forever in the future and forever in the past. Mr. Torvik said there are stars in our own galaxy that are ninety thousand light-years away. I think if you really sat down and tried to imagine that much space, or that much time, you would go crazy.

Mr. Torvik told us they used to think that the Earth was in the middle of everything and that everything else moved around it. But now they know that it's actually the Earth moving around the sun, and that the Earth isn't really in the middle. It just looked that way from here. Galileo was the one to figure out that there are moons around Jupiter. He got in trouble for it, because the moons around Jupiter didn't have anything to do with Earth, and so that meant there were other things out there that didn't have anything to do with us at all.

But if you think about the size of the universe, or even just one galaxy, Mr. Torvik said, it's pretty obvious that there's quite a bit that doesn't have anything to do with us. The universe is so big that there may not even be a middle. If something goes on forever, there can't be a middle, a top, or a bottom.

"Venus," Travis says, looking up. "Huh. There's the Big Dipper. I know that one."

I watch his neck move when he talks, the soft outline of his Adam's apple shifting underneath his skin. They made him cut his hair short again in the group home, and he's mad about this, but I think it looks nice. You can see his face again, the angles of the bones in his cheeks. He is beautiful. *Please God,* I think, looking up. *I will love him forever. Please.* I close my eyes, and when I open them, I see a streak of light shooting across the sky. It's already gone.

"Did you see that?" Travis asks. His hand is on my arm.

I open my mouth, but I can't speak. Mr. Torvik told us that shooting stars are not really stars at all but meteorites, burning their way through our atmosphere, sometimes landing in the oceans and in the middle of farms. He said you could make wishes on them if you like, but they are really just pieces of rock falling down from the sky, and they could land on your head and kill you just as you look up to make a wish. Really, they're just rocks. They don't care about your wishes at all.

But still. It's too much of a coincidence, to see a sign like that in the sky, just as I was asking for what I want the most. It was over before I knew what I was seeing, but now I know that, again, I've been blessed, quick as a wink from above.

When summer comes, there is a new girl in Unit A, Deena Schultz, from Lincoln, Nebraska, and she is also going into eighth grade. She came here to live with her grandmother because her mother went to follow the Grateful Dead for a while and didn't think it would be a good idea if Deena came too. It was only supposed to be for the summer, but it's August now, and her mother still isn't back.

The first time I go over to Deena's, she shows me a picture of her mother, looking happy and tan, with blond hair down to her waist. She is holding a tambourine in one hand and a Mountain Dew in the other. On the back of the picture it says I LOVE MY BABY in swirling, purple letters. Deena says that her mother has done so many drugs that she says she can hear smells and see sounds.

"I don't know," Deena says, shrugging. "Maybe she can."

Deena is nice, but really, the first thing you notice about her is that she's pretty. She has the face of someone in the movies. She tries to act like she doesn't, walking stoop-shouldered so it looks like we are the same height, and wearing large sweatshirts with sleeves that are too long so just her fingers show. But it doesn't matter. Even with the sweatshirt, you can see she is tall and long-limbed like a ballerina, with a ballerina's face to match. She has large dark eyes that always look a little wet, her eyebrows two half moons high above them.

She says her father is Filipino, and this is where she gets her dark hair. It hangs down to her shoulders like one piece of smooth ribbon, and she could be in a magazine with this hair, selling shampoo, even though she is only fourteen and that's just the way it grows out of her head.

When I tell my mother about Deena's mother, she gets so mad she almost puts Samuel down. "What is this with people up and leaving their kids behind?" she says. "What is the *deal*?" She looks at Samuel and then at me, as if one of us might know the answer. He stares up at the glitter hat.

When my mother meets Deena, she is further outraged.

"My God," she says, after Deena has left, "she's such a beautiful girl. How could you want to leave such a beautiful kid?"

"I know," I say. "It's so much easier to leave an ugly one."

My mother frowns. "Evelyn. You know what I mean."

Deena's grandmother's apartment is very clean, with wooden crosses in every room, and a picture of a crying Mary. The rooms smell faintly of bleach, and there are framed brown-and-white photographs of unsmiling people in uncomfortable-looking clothes set on a lace runner on top of a table in the hallway. Her grandmother speaks mostly German, and even when she does speak English, I don't understand her. It's fine though, because she's usually asleep in bed by the time I come over. It's like Deena lives by herself, except she has to whisper and play music on her headphones instead of out loud.

"Grandma's okay," Deena says. "She just needs to sleep a lot. She's almost seventy."

Their apartment has the same layout as ours, but it looks completely different because it is so dark and quiet, heavy drapes over the windows, so many creaking chairs and tables that you have to zigzag to walk across the room. But Deena's room is the opposite: pink everywhere. Pink bedspread, pink pillows, even a pink throw rug. There are two lamps with pink light-bulbs in them. Deena says plain white lightbulbs make everything ugly, and she has to have a lot of light in her room or she gets depressed.

She has bought copies of *Tiger Beat* magazine and taped up pictures from it on her walls, boys without shirts looking out thoughtfully, the flash of the camera reflected as a glint in their eyes. Deena has seen *The Outsiders* seven times, and has pictures of all of the stars: C. Thomas Howell, Rob Lowe, Tom Cruise, Ralph Macchio. She knows their names from the movie: Soda-pop, Ponyboy, Johnny. She memorized the poem that Ponyboy says at the end when he's dying, "Nothing Gold Can Stay," and she recites it for me, looking up at the posters. She wrote the cast of *The Outsiders* letters, and some of them wrote back, sending her more photos of themselves with their real signatures on the bottom. She has taped these up as well.

"Are you going to send them pictures of you?" I ask. "It seems fair."

She laughs, and her laugh is the opposite of what you would think it would be for someone so pretty. She makes loud, wheezing sounds, her mouth open wide. "You're a nut."

We go to her house at night to do homework. "Because it's *quiet* there," I tell my mother. "You can actually *think*." But really, I am the only one who does homework. Deena reads *Tiger Beat*, or paints her fingernails, or her toenails, or my toenails. Sometimes she gets out a book and looks at the pages, but she plays her Madonna tape in her Walkman loud enough so I can hear it, moving her lips to the words of the songs, not the words on the page.

She does not do well in school. The teachers are nice to her, smiling at her even when she doesn't say anything, and when they hand back quizzes and tests, they have to fold hers in half so no one can see her grade. I don't know if she really isn't smart, or if she just doesn't try very hard. Or maybe she doesn't try very hard because she knows she isn't very smart so what's the point. She doesn't seem worried about it. "Madonna didn't go to college," she says.

"Neither did my mother," I say, and we both know what this means. Deena likes my mother, but no one would want to be like her, on food stamps with a retarded baby, always changing diapers and wearing her robe, even in the middle of the day, so it is too embarrassing for Deena to come to my house and that is why we always come here. My mother is the opposite of Madonna.

"But I hate school," Deena says, lying back on her bed. "I really, really, hate it." She rolls her essay up into a sort of telescope, looks at me through it, and then back up at the posters on her wall.

So we are not the same, but still it is wonderful, having a friend like this. Travis is my friend, but he is not always around, and lately I am so nervous about what I say around him that sometimes I can't say anything at all. I don't want to say anything dumb. But with Deena, I can say anything, and she'll just laugh.

They've built a McDonald's across the highway in the field next to the Kwikshop, where I used to see the deer. Deena and I watch its construction with anticipation, realizing that once its doors open, we will have somewhere to go, somewhere to be besides where the school bus takes us. But I am also worried about the frogs and the white-tailed deer and stray cats, where they will go now, what they will do.

"They'll just go somewhere else," Deena says. "They'll be fine."

And it is nice, once the McDonald's opens, only two months after the bulldozers first started digging holes in the ground. Neither Deena nor I can afford to go out to dinner every night, but we're happy enough to just sit in a booth in the warmth and bright lights, doing our homework, looking up to watch people come in from off the highway, jingling car keys in their lucky hands. Trish, the dining-room attendant, calls this loitering, and doesn't think it's okay.

"This isn't a library, girls," she says, her voice loud, embarrassing us on purpose. Trish's face is a little frightening, and easy to make fun of when she turns around. She has lost her real eyebrows, by her own fault or by accident, and drawn new ones on in a strange color of orange, much higher on her forehead than real eyebrows could ever be. This gives her the look of always being wide awake, even slightly alarmed. So when she says anything to us, anything at all, we turn away quickly and laugh.

We have learned, over time, how to stall Trish, how to make it more difficult for her to kick us out. "We aren't done with our pops yet, see?" we say. And then Trish says, "Well, hurry along now. We've got paying customers." And we say "Okay," and then sit there for another hour, until there isn't even ice left in our cups and we've chewed our straws into little pieces of plastic.

The truck drivers who stop in off the highway sometimes ask us if they can buy us anything, always looking at Deena.

"No," she says quickly, not even thinking it over. "No thanks."

They are older than Eileen, some of them, but they sit in booths across from us, sipping coffee, watching her, not even caring if she can tell.

"Gross," she whispers. "Grossorito." She has a long pink pen twisted into a heart on one end, and she uses it to write something on a napkin.

Two o'clock. Grandpa Joe wants you to sit on his lap.

When I look up at the man, Grandpa Joe, it's clear that he is looking at Deena, and that she is the one he wants to sit on his lap. But this is the way Deena says things. Men are looking at us. Trish is just jealous because we are young and pretty, and still have our real eyebrows. We both know this isn't altogether true. I still have my eyebrows of course, and am still young. But I'm accepting slowly, a little more every day, that I am not pretty, at least not beautiful the way Deena is. I still look sleepy, even unhappy, all the time. There is nothing I can do about this but try to keep my eyes wide, like I'm surprised or very awake, and then I just end up looking like Trish.

Deena says blue eyeshadow will help. She has some that sparkles like there is glitter in it, and she looks pretty when she has it on, but she also looks pretty when she doesn't wear any at all. She applies it carefully to my eyes in her pink room, holding my chin firmly with one hand. "There now," she says, stepping aside so I can see my reflection in the mirror. "If you wear it to school, I will too. And everyone will fall in love with us."

We both look in the mirror, frowning. It doesn't look the same on me as it does on her. She scratches her head, coming toward me again. "Let me try to rub it in."

I tell myself I will be a late bloomer. It will be like one of those stories that movie stars tell. *Really, when I was a kid, I was ugly. I was hideous. People made fun of me.* Morgan Fairchild said this to the man interviewing her on television. They had shown a picture of her as a child, and really she had been ugly, with big thick glasses, and just look at her now. She can sit and joke about how ugly she used to be because really, the whole time she had been beautiful. It had been hidden inside, waiting to come out.

I have to think this same thing will happen to me, because it's too terrible to think that it won't, that I might have to go through my whole life being ugly. It would be like somebody telling me I was going to be poor my whole life, no matter what I did. It would be a hard thing, going through your whole life ugly, and I don't think God would do that to me. But looking around, I can see it happens to other people all the time.

My mother says the thing about Deena is, she really is just as sweet as she looks.

She likes Deena because Deena likes babies, and even though Samuel is two now, he is still like a baby in almost every way. He's just bigger. When Deena comes over, she asks my mother if she can hold him, and although he usually cries when my mother isn't the one holding him, with Deena, he doesn't.

"You're a natural," my mother says. She looks strange to me, my mother, standing there with nothing in her arms. I am used to seeing her carrying Samuel, and without him, she looks almost naked, or even like she is missing a limb. She stands there awkwardly, rubbing the small of her back.

"I love babies," Deena says, kissing Samuel on his pale, soft cheek. "I had a lot of little cousins in Nebraska. I got to take care of them all the time."

Deena does not get tired of putting things on her head for Samuel so he will make his screeching sound, and she would do this the entire time she was over if I let her. She waits until later, when we are back in my room by ourselves, to ask me if there is anything wrong.

"He's retarded," I tell her. "He was born premature, and it messed up his brain."

"Oh," she says. "That's sad." She is lying on my bed, her dark hair wrapped up underneath her head like a pillow. We are supposed to be studying, but she did not bring any of her books. "How come you don't have any posters on your walls?"

"I do," I say, pointing to the star chart on my ceiling. CONSTELLATIONS IN THE SUMMER SKY: A MAP OF THE HEAVENS. Eileen got it for me for Christmas.

"No, like boy posters," she says. "I have extra. Tell me who you like, and I'll give you some."

I make a face. "I like real boys."

"Ahhhh." She smiles, rolling over so she is lying on her stomach, her hair falling back around her shoulders. "Like who?"

I wait, unsure of what to say next. I have never told anyone else that I know I am destined for Travis Rowley, that he is destined for me. I still know this is true, especially now, because of the shooting star.

"Who?" she says again, sitting up on her knees. "Tell me." I can already see by her face that she will be hurt if I don't tell her, maybe even mad.

"Travis Rowley. He lives in Unit B." I point out my window at his. There. I've done it.

"Does he go to our school?"

I shake my head. "He's in ninth grade. And he gets rides from a friend, so he's not on the bus. I don't know if you've seen him."

"Look at you turn red." She narrows her eyes. "What does he look like?"

Beautiful, I want to tell her. *The most beautiful boy in the world*. But I know if I say this I will sound dumb. "He's got brown curly hair and green eyes. He's a little taller than I am."

She shakes her head. "I've never seen him. Do you know him, or is it just a crush?"

Deena has a lot of words like this, like "crush." She gets them, I think, from reading *Tiger Beat*. "We're friends." I say. "We've been friends since we were little."

She leans her head off the edge of my bed. "But you've never made out or anything?"

"No," I say, embarrassed. I understand now that I have given her the wrong impression. If Travis could hear me talking right now, he might get mad. He would say, *What are you talking about, Evelyn? Why are you saying things that aren't true?*

"We're just friends," I say. "I don't even know if he likes me like that. He probably doesn't."

"I bet he does," she says, smiling like she knows, even though there is no way she could.

"Actually, I don't even know if I like him like that. I mean I just really like him as a friend."

This is a lie. I feel stupid, now that I have said "Travis Rowley" out loud. It's one thing to wish for something in your head, but it is another to tell someone else. If you tell someone else what will happen as if you know for certain and then it doesn't end up happening, it's worse. Because not only do you have to worry about being disappointed, but about looking stupid too.

"Don't tell anyone."

"I won't."

I can't do my homework until she leaves, so we listen to records, and she paints my toenails bright red, which is okay because it's almost winter, and no one will see.

$\mathcal{I}$F I HAD GOTTEN ARRESTED with someone for setting a picnic table on fire, I don't think my mother would let them still come and pick me up for school. But I guess Mrs. Rowley doesn't care. She's got a job now, working the desk of a motel in town. I see her walking to it in the evenings, coming home in the morning. She puts the flat of her hand over her eyes like a visor, and looks right into the rising sun.

Ed Schwebbe comes out in his van every morning now to pick up Travis for school, and sometimes he comes at night too, just after Mrs. Rowley leaves for work. I don't know where they go. If he sees me in my window, he waves quickly, and that's it. It's okay, though. I can wait. Next year, we will be in the same school again, and then maybe.

But one night, finally, I see him. Deena and I are in a booth at McDonald's, studying for a history test, and in he walks with Ed Schwebbe. They are laughing about something, wiping snow off their jackets. He sees me and waves with a red mitten.

Deena looks up. "What?"

"Don't turn around."

She turns around. "What?"

I shake the sleeve of her sweater, but she is already laughing, her hand over her mouth. "Sorry," she says.

"That's Travis."

She turns around again. "The tall one or the short one?"

"The short one. Don't stare." Travis is not short, but he looks that way standing next to Ed Schwebbe. It is the first time I have ever seen Ed standing up and not sitting in the blue-and-white van, and I can see now that if anyone could jump over a picnic table on fire, it would be him. He is thin as Deena, but so tall that he has to duck when he comes through the doorway of the McDonald's, and a woman walking out the door looks up and says, "My, my, how's the weather up there?" He smiles and rolls his eyes, and you can tell he has heard this before.

They go up to the counter to order, and I watch them, holding my book up so I can look back down if they turn around. "Don't act weird when they come over, okay?"

She nods and looks down, fidgeting with something on her face, and when she looks up again, she has a plastic straw sticking out of each nostril. "What do you mean?"

This is how she looks when Travis and Ed walk up, holding their trays. Travis opens his mouth to say hello, but when he sees Deena with the straws in her nose, he and Ed start laughing again. She pulls the straws out of her nose and puts her hands over her eyes. "Okay," she says. "I'll just go ahead and die now. Don't worry."

"No no, it's cute," Travis says. He nods at me. "Hey, Evelyn, this is Ed. Can we sit?" I nod and scoot over. Already I am having trouble speaking, trying to think of what to say.

"We went to a movie," Travis says. "*Godzilla 1985*."

"It was awesome," Ed says, very slowly, like he is a radio running low on batteries. I could say six words in the time it takes him to say one. "It was so fucking cool."

"I thought it was kind of dumb," Travis says. "They did the dubbing wrong, so the Japanese people's mouths kept moving when the words stopped." He does an imitation of this for us, saying, "Look out!" with a Japanese accent, forming more words in silence. Deena laughs when he does this. His eyes move quickly across her face.

"This is Deena," I say, pointing at her. "She lives in Unit A. How can they make a remake of *Godzilla*? Didn't they kill him at the end of the first movie?"

"They nuked him back to life," Ed says, and again, it's very slow. "He's just asleep on this island when they do this test bomb, and that wakes him back up. He's all radioactive and shit. It's cool."

Travis makes a face, looking at Deena. "Just so you know, Ed liked *Rambo*."

Ed smiles, and I can see one gold filling, right in front. "A lot of people liked *Rambo*, Rowley. That movie was awesome too." He makes his hands into fists, tapping them lightly on the table. "They need to send that dude down to Nicaragua and let him kick some serious ass."

Travis rolls his eyes, unwrapping his hamburger. He offers us his french fries, and I notice, the way you notice that you might be coming down with a sore throat but maybe not, that he keeps looking at Deena. A strand of hair falls in front of her eyes, and she brushes it away.

"I've seen you around, you know? But I didn't know you were Evelyn's friend. I didn't know you lived out here."

There's a lilt in his voice. I haven't heard this before, this lilt.

Deena says she has to go to the bathroom. Ed scoots over to let her out, and we all three watch her walk away, just her fingers sticking out of the sleeves of her sweatshirt.

Travis leans over, his hand on my arm. "Oh my God, Evelyn, she's so cute." He places his other hand over his heart, as if he is getting ready to have a heart attack, or maybe say the Pledge of Allegiance. "What's her name again?"

It takes me a moment to hear what he has said, to understand that this is his hand on my arm, but these are the words coming out of his mouth. Inside my head, I am realizing, for the first time, that I am a fool. Trish is standing on the other side of the dining room, mopping, her alarmed-looking eyes staring at the floor.

"Deena," I say, so softly that he can't hear me. "Deena," I have to say again, loud enough.

"Does she have a boyfriend?"

No no no. No no no. "No," I say, still looking across the room, at Trish pushing the mop back and forth. She looks up, catching my eye. "I don't think so."

"Hmm." He straightens up, bobbing his eyebrows up and down at Ed. His ears bob also. "This is good to know."

Ed smiles, finishing his hamburger. I am distracted only by how quickly he is able to eat. I watch him consume a second hamburger in four bites, and I decide this, Ed eating too quickly, is somehow another thing to be miserable about. It is somehow connected.

Deena slides back into the booth, glancing at me and then down at her history book. I know she must understand what's happening. She probably knew even before I did. Men have been looking at her like this forever, and she would know the look Travis was giving her, recognize it. But she is still staring down at her book, as if all of a sudden she cares about the history test tomorrow, which I know she doesn't. She is actually pulling her hair in front of her face, still looking down at the history book, her eyes moving too quickly to take in any of the words.

Ed empties almost an entire carton of french fries into his mouth, his head tilted back so it rests on top of his seat. When he brings his head back up again, he starts to cough.

Travis pushes a Coke over to him. "You okay?"

"Yeah," Ed says, taking deep breaths. "Dude, I thought you were going to have to do the Heimlich again."

"Again?" I ask brightly, still trying, still hoping. There is a chance, if I am friendly and Deena is not. There is still a chance. "You did the Heimlich on somebody?"

Travis smiles. "Against my will."

"Oh, dude, it was so cool," Ed says, excited now, speaking a little more quickly. "When we were in the group home, there was this guy, Officer Pickervance. Oh man, he was such an asshole. Peckervance. He was all like"—Ed straightens his posture, and makes his face look stern—"'I'm going to teach you boys a lesson.' So one day we're all sitting around eating hot dogs, and Peckervance starts to choke." Ed puts his hands around his own throat, pretending to choke. "He was all turning blue and shit. And dude, Travis did the Heimlich fucking maneuver on him. Saved his asshole life."

Travis shrugs and pretends to be embarrassed, but I can see, my stomach a rock inside of me, that he's happy Ed told this story in front of beautiful Deena, who has finally looked up from her history book, her half-moon eyebrows raised in surprise. Ed keeps eating and talking, telling us how Travis finally pushed so hard on the officer's abdomen that the piece of hot dog had gone flying across the room, hitting another delinquent right in the eye.

"The guy was like 'Ow! My eye!'" Ed holds his hand over his eye.

Deena laughs at this, one little snort, in and out.

Travis's eyes move quickly around her face. "What a great laugh you've got."

She stops quickly, biting her lip, and looks back down. "Well, Evelyn makes me laugh all the time. She's so funny."

It's pathetic, this attempt. His eyes are still focused on her face, sparkling now, love struck. She's doing her best to help me, trying to be a good friend, but there's no point now. It's like gravity, pulling him toward her, the laws of nature. There's no one to be mad at, even. It's just the way it is.

"Evelyn *is* funny," Travis agrees.

I turn and look out the window, but I can still see all four of us in its glossy, dark reflection. I listen to Deena and Travis talk about how funny I am. This is all I can do. They talk about nothing, about the difference between Nebraska and Kansas, the difference between eighth grade and ninth. They are looking only at each other. *Love at first sight.* I imagine a cartoon lightning bolt between them, tapping into both of their brains, making their eyes light up, creating a force field no one else can enter. Everyone else in the restaurant, even me and Ed, could blow up and die, and they wouldn't even notice.

Ed scrapes the cheese off the wrappers of the Big Macs, licks his fingers, and then sucks on the straw of his empty Coke until the cup implodes. After this, he leans back in the booth, eyes closed. "Oh man, I feel so much better," he says, picking up his car keys. "That was awesome. Okay, let's go."

Travis looks at the car keys in Ed's hand, then back at Deena. "Why don't you guys come?" He turns to me, looking at me for the first time since Deena came back from the bathroom. "We're just going to drive around for a while. Come on, Evelyn." He pinches my cheek lightly. "Have some fun."

"Oh, I don't think so," I say.

He pinches my elbow lightly, lowering his voice. "You okay?" He gives me a pleading look, and I can see he's asking me to help him out here, to be a friend. Clearly, he did not know about the love affair between us. And at this point, this is the only thing I have left. The goal now, I decide, is to maintain dignity.

I smile. "I'm fine. I just need to study. We have a test tomorrow."

"Well then, come on." He reaches around my back and closes my history book. "You need to have a little fun. You've sat there reading all night. I'm sure you're ready for your test or whatever."

"Evelyn is so smart," Deena says, nodding quickly. "I'm serious. If she didn't help me with my homework, I don't know what I'd do."

"She is smart," Travis agrees. They look at each other again and smile. I look out the window, at the snow coming down. I don't want to go. I don't want to go drive around in Ed's van. I want to go lie down on the highway and let a truck run over me.

"Evelyn, come with me to call my grandmother," Deena says. She is trying to wink, but she isn't very good at it, and it just looks painful, like there's something in her eye. "Let's see if we can go."

I follow her outside. We stand by the pay phone, shivering in the cold. It is January, but she is wearing a miniskirt with pink legwarmers pulled up only to her knees because of the movie *Flashdance*, which neither of us has actually seen. I tried making a pair for myself, cutting the top off a pair of tights—perfectly good tights, my mother complained. But they still didn't look like legwarmers; they sagged down around my ankles, and when I was in math class the next day, old Mr. Delph, so blind that he couldn't tell when Candy Vistoli's big sister showed up to take her tests for her, asked me in front of everyone if I had sprained both my ankles, and did I know my bandages were coming unwrapped.

"Are you mad, Evelyn?" She is leaning down, trying to see my face in the floodlight over our heads. And even under its yellow-orange glow, she is beautiful. Of course. If I were Travis, I would choose her too.

"It's not your fault."

She leans in closer. "But..."

I wave her off. "It's not that big a deal. Really. I mean, it's not like we were dating or anything. It was just in my head." I shrug. "Really, it's okay. Just don't tell him, okay? I feel stupid."

"I won't," she says. "I promise."

I start to walk back inside. She stops me, her hand on my arm. "You're sure this is okay, Evelyn? If it isn't, just tell me. And we'll go home right now. I won't ever talk to him again." She rubs her lips together, watching me closely, even though right now I can't look back. "You're my best friend, Evelyn. You're my only friend."

"It's okay," I say.

She is trying to be nice. But when it comes to people liking each other, being nice has nothing to do with it. Despite her good intentions, this is the way things work. This is just science here, biology at work. Even if I say no, eventually it will make no difference.

We do not just drive around for a while in Ed Schwebbe's blue-and-white van. He drives straight to a snow-covered field less than a mile away, parking behind a burned-out barn, and takes out a bag of marijuana from a case for sunglasses clipped onto the visor. I know it is marijuana because a police officer came to health class only a month before and showed us some. "Don't do this," he had told us, waving the bag around. "Don't ever do this." He played a video for us of Nancy Reagan in a red dress telling us to "Just Say No."

"You know that's illegal?" I ask. Ed Schwebbe looks at me, and then back at Travis. Travis and Deena are sitting together on a small couch in the back of the van, his hand resting on her knee.

Travis leans up and touches me on the arm. "Evelyn, you need to relax a little bit, okay? We're out here in the middle of nowhere. It's fine. And if you don't want to have any, you don't have to."

I cross my arms. The police officer warned us about this exact kind of scene, someone offering us drugs. Marijuana is the beginning of the end, he told us, a slippery slope. You start smoking it and the next thing you know you'll be doing cocaine and maybe trying to kill your own parents because you'll be addicted and willing to do whatever you can to get your next fix. He'd seen it a thousand times. We are supposed to just say no, but Deena, her hand resting on Travis's arm, hasn't said anything yet.

"She gonna be okay?" Ed asks, looking at Travis, like I speak a funny language that only Travis can translate.

"She's fine, Ed. Really."

Ed taps out a bit of the marijuana from the bag onto a small white paper, rolling it into a tight cylinder. He hands it back to Travis and makes another one for himself, lighting the tip with a match as he inhales from the other end, his eyes closed. I can see the fiery tip shriveling up, disappearing.

"You know that's really bad for you?" I ask. "It kills your brain cells, and if you get caught, you'll never get financial aid in college."

Ed laughs at this, three short exhales, smoke coming out of his nostrils. "Okay," he says. "What's your name again?"

"Evelyn." I don't see what's so funny.

He nods and smiles. "Okay, Evelyn, you need to relax."

"I don't want to."

"Just say it. Just try. Come on. It's alllllllll goooooooood."

I hear Deena coughing in the back, and when I turn around, I see Travis holding her shoulder, offering her a sip from his Coke. "It's okay," he's saying. "It'll get better."

The police officer and Nancy Reagan told us that if someone ever offered us drugs, we should say no and leave immediately. *Call your parents if you have to,* Nancy Reagan said. *Call anyone.* But there is no way to call my mother or Nancy Reagan out here in Ed Schwebbe's van, and it's too far to walk in the cold. There's nothing I can do but sit, and wait, and maybe study. I open my backpack, get my history book out.

"You're going to do your homework now?" Ed asks. He looks at me from under his long bangs, his eyes two little slits. "You're so weird. You're such a weird kid."

"Excuse me if I care about my future," I say. But really, I know I don't need to study anymore. I have an A in history. Mr. Graham likes us to memorize important dates of important wars and then write essays about them as if the people who lost the wars had won, and the people who won the wars had lost. Some people don't like this, but Mr. Graham says it is important to understand that history books tend to be written by the people who won or killed everybody else. He liked my last essay very much: "How the Native American People Kept the European Invaders Off Their Land."

Ed watches me read, still smoking. It's very annoying, but when I look up, he smiles. "You sure you don't want any of this?"

I narrow my eyes. "Are you trying to use peer pressure on me?"

He inhales again, pinching what is left between his finger and thumb. "What? No, it's just—"

"What?" I ask. He's speaking so slowly. It's driving me crazy. People should talk at a normal speed or maybe not at all.

"Okay," he says, closing his eyes again. "Okay, I know I've only known you for like an hour." He inhales again. "I don't want you to take this wrong."

I could be getting things done in the time between each of his words. I could get out and run around the van and jump back in in the middle of one of his sentences, and I wouldn't miss a thing. "Just tell me," I say. "Spit it out."

"It just seems like you need to smoke pot more than anyone I've ever met in my life."

I wave the smoke out of my face. "What?"

He nods. "It's sad that the people who won't smoke pot are usually the people who need it the most. I mean, somebody like you, if you smoked pot every day for like a year, you might be normal at the end of it."

My glasses have slid down to the tip of my nose, but I leave them there, so Ed Schwebbe looks smaller through them, like something you might see at the bottom of a microscope. "I'm abnormal, Ed? Is that what you're telling me?"

He scoots closer to his door and bends one of his long legs up on the seat. "Whoa. Okay, don't get mad. I'm just saying that I can, like, look at you and *see* how uptight you are. I mean, I can *see* it." He puts his hands up to his eyes, like I'm the sun, too bright for his eyes. "It's like this bad vibe you give off. It's so intense." He turns away. In the back, Travis and Deena have gotten quiet, and I'm not sure what they are doing. I don't turn around.

The van is hazy with smoke now, getting into my nostrils, seeping into my brain. If the police catch us, they will do drug tests, and I will never get financial aid. We'll all get in trouble. No one will believe that I was being good.

I don't care. I don't care about my brain cells anymore.

I look up at the dark, starry sky, and I think about the *Challenger*, how it blew up, leaving just a huge white cloud in the sky, white streaks snaking out of it. Mr. Torvik rolled in a television so we could watch the news reports, but all they kept showing was that same white cloud, the people in stands, the families of the astronauts, looking up at the sky and crying. Mr. Torvik was crying too, because this was the first time they were going to take a teacher up in space. He'd applied to be on the *Challenger* himself, and had even made it to the final rounds and gotten an interview, but in the end they'd chosen someone else.

"Ed, I need to ask you a question."

He nods and looks at me slowly. "Sure. That's fine." His eyes are glassy, shiny, almost like Samuel's, the skin around his eyes puffy and pink.

"Okay, you need to be honest with me. Don't worry about my feelings, or my vibe or whatever."

He nods again, looking down at his hands. "That's cool. I can do that."

I take a deep breath, thinking of what exactly it is I want to know, how I want to ask it. I want to know, right now, just how bad things are going to be, once and for all. "Okay," I say. "What would I be on a scale of one to ten, as far as, like, general attractiveness goes? Besides the vibe thing."

He looks at me carefully, still smoking, for so long I am not sure he understands what I am asking. Finally, he frowns and shakes his head. "I don't like that kind of question," he says. "I don't like that, giving girls numbers. I think it's bullshit." He taps a long, thin finger on his chest. "It's who you are, Ellen. There are no numbers for that."

I roll my eyes. "You know what I mean. Just tell me what you think somebody else would say, who did believe in giving girls numbers, okay? Go ahead. One being like totally disgusting no way, and ten being somebody like . . ." I nod in the direction of the backseat but do not turn around. "Somebody like Deena."

He shakes his head. "Deena would be more of a nine. Christie Brinkley would be a ten."

I nod, impatient, bracing myself. "Fine. What would I be?"

"Well . . ." He looks at me carefully. I can see he does not want to hurt my feelings, wincing for me, as if he is the one about to get the bad news. "Well, I guess, maybe, like a . . ." He bites his lip. "A four?"

"A four." I nod, seeing a number line in my head, one through ten, four so close to nothing, to hideous. So there it is. I am the limping antelope. I cannot be allowed to reproduce.

Ed leans toward me, touching me on my arm. "Hey, don't get mad. Come on. You told me to tell you." He closes his eyes and knocks his head against the headrest of his seat. "See? That's why I totally hate that number shit."

I look at my face in the mirror on the visor, at my sad, sleepy eyes. A four is probably about right. "No, it's okay, Ed. Thanks for being honest."

He shakes his head and gets out the Baggie again. "Okay, but you know what it is that makes you a four? It's not so much the way you look. It's that vibe I was talking about. I mean, you've got to get rid of it. Seriously." He reaches out his hand and moves it in quick circles above my head. "It's like I can see your aurora, and it's all black and shit."

I stare at him, trying to understand. "My what?"

"Your aurora. It's black, man. Black."

"You mean my aura?"

He nods, closes his eyes again, and holds up his hands so both his palms are facing me. "Yeah. You're so uptight. Wow. I can feel it too. I mean, I can actually feel it."

I am trying hard not to cry now. "I'm not uptight, for your information, Ed. I'm a Christian."

Ed nods, inhaling again. "That's cool. It is. It's cool. You know what I think?"

I look out my window, away from him, wiping tears off my cheeks. "No, Ed. Tell me."

"I think if Jesus would have been alive today, he would have been all about pot. I think he would have really grooved on it, and that's why he would have gone to jail today."

I shake my head. The moon is just a sliver in the sky, the edge of a saucer. "Well, I think that's a really offensive thing to say."

He shrugs. "Well, that's what I think. I'm allowed to think that if I want to, just like you're allowed to think what you want. It's all supposed to be about peace and love, right? Right?" He squints at me. "And man, I have to tell you, your vibe doesn't have anything to do with peace or love, man, and it is *in-tense.* It's freaking me out."

I have to wait before I answer, to get a hold of myself. When I'm ready, I turn and look right at him, at his puffy little eyes. "Okay, well, Ed, your aura tells me you smoke too much, and you're a stupid pothead who talks too much. How about that?"

"Whoa. Whoa." He opens his eyes and holds both of his arms out straight, his palms facing me again, but this time overlapping each other, blocking my face from his view. "You know what? You've got some bad energy. You really do."

I lean forward so I can look at him and say something back, but he moves his hands again, covering his view of my face.

"I don't think I want your energy in the van," he says, almost yelling now. "Really, not to be rude, but you've got to get out of the van." I move, and he moves his hands again, the rest of him huddled against his door. "Please, okay? I'm asking you. Vacate the van."

Travis's head appears between us. "What's going on?" His sweatshirt is on inside out.

Ed brings his hands in closer to his face, covering his eyes. "Get her out of the van. She's got bad energy. She's freaking me out. She's got to get out of the van."

"Fine," I say, shutting my book. "I'm leaving. I'll walk."

"Hold on," Travis says. "We'll walk with you, Evelyn. But just wait a minute." He looks at Ed again, who still has his hands over his eyes. "Wait outside."

I slam the door behind me and walk to the back of the van, watching the exhaust drift up and dissipate into the cold night air. Travis and Deena stumble out, Deena still trying to put on her hat, both of them laughing. "I'll call you tomorrow, Ed," Travis says, sliding the side door shut. "It'll be okay."

The van pulls away, the back tires kicking up muddy snow. Travis turns in a small circle, Deena orbiting around him, holding his hand.

"I'm over here," I say.

"Jesus, Evelyn, what'd you say to him?" Travis asks, laughing. But he doesn't really care. He is preoccupied, trying to help Deena put on her gloves.

I rub my head with my mittens. "It wasn't me. It was my bad aurora."

"We've got so far to walk," Deena says, her voice like a little girl's, singsongy and soft. "I need to sit down for a minute." She starts to go down into the snow, but Travis stops her, pulling her back up by her elbows. "No no," he says. "Let me give you a piggyback ride. Come on. We'll all go together."

So we stumble through the snow like this, the three of us, Deena up on Travis's back, me walking alongside, like a camel, or a mule. Halfway through the field, Deena slides down off Travis's back into a pile of snow. She looks up at Travis, laughing, her hat crooked on her head, still adorable, maybe even more so. He stops and sinks down to his knees and then onto her. They roll around like that for a while, like puppies, pushing snow in each other's faces.

I keep walking. I will not watch for cars when I get to the highway. If I make it, I make it. If I don't, I don't.

"Evelyn! Wait!" Both of them are shouting my name, still laughing, trying to stand up, falling into each other.

But I keep going. I walk the rest of the way home by myself. The stars are out, bright and numerous, but they are all still. There are no falling stars tonight, no asteroids, no flaming rocks hurtling through the atmosphere. The stars stay right where they are, twinkling high above, and none of them have anything to do with me.

"Bullshit," my mother says, her arms crossed. She looks like she's been crying. "I called McDonald's, and I talked to Trish. I know you left at ten, Evelyn. I know you left with two boys, older boys, and I know now"—she looks at her watch—"it's after midnight."

I shake my head. Her voice seems shrill, the light from the kitchen too bright.

"Do you have any idea how scared I've been for the last hour? What thoughts have been running through my head?" She points at her head. "You're fourteen years old, Evelyn. Fourteen. I need to know where you are in the middle of the night. Okay? That's basic."

I say nothing. Usually I can come right back, say something quick and sharp, but now my tongue feels heavy in my mouth, and I can't think of anything to say at all.

She shakes my arm. "Do you understand what I'm saying?"

I step away from her. "You'll wake up Sam."

"Don't worry about Sam. I'm talking to you right now."

Her face is close to mine, her eyes only inches away. *She has such large pores,* I think. I've never noticed this before, but now that I have, I can't stop looking. They're huge. Enormous. I touch my own nose softly, wondering if I have pores this large and have just never noticed before.

"Evelyn? You're acting really weird."

"I'm fine," I say, still looking at her. Her hair has changed too. There are lighter strands, wiry and sticking out from the curls. Gray hairs. She's thirty years old, and she's getting gray hair. I move toward her, holding a strand of her hair between my finger and thumb. "Mom, you're getting gray hairs. Did you know that?"

She swats my hand away. "Evelyn?"

I close my eyes, nod. Everyone can see it. "I've got a bad aura, Mom."

This stops her. She moves her hands up to her face, cupping her cheeks. "What?"

I nod again. "It's black. My vibe, my aura, is black." I shrug, looking over her shoulder. "Do we have some chips or anything? Pretzels?"

She leans in close to me, sniffing me, like I'm a flower in a vase. "Evelyn, have you been drinking?"

"No."

She holds my chin steady and moves my face from side to side, looking at me from different angles. She looks puzzled, almost amused, her eyebrow high on her head. "Evelyn. Have you been smoking pot?"

I laugh, turning away. But inside, I am scared. *She has extrasensory powers,* I think. *She really does.*

She turns me back around, sniffs my hair. She steps back. "Evelyn?"

"I didn't. God. Everyone else did. But I didn't. It was too cold to roll down the windows."

She sort of falls backwards when I say this. Luckily, the couch is behind her. "I'm having a nightmare," she says. "Oh my God. You're fourteen."

"Honest, I didn't. It was because of my bad aurora." I point at my head, laughing. I can see how this is funny now, this whole night. You've got to be able to see the humor in things, I realize, and I do now. I really do. "Can you see it? My aurora? My evil vibe?"

Her eyes are slightly crossed, staring hard at me, but I can tell, just by looking at her, that she doesn't see the humor in things. She is no longer amused. "You're so grounded," she says. "You don't even know how grounded you are."

"We're all grounded, Mom," I tell her, walking back to my room. I'm not sure what I mean by this exactly, if I mean anything at all. "We're all grounded now."

The next morning, she is standing over me, still in her robe. I try to close my eyes again, to make her go away, but she doesn't. She walks back and forth alongside my bed, one hand in her hair, the other one stretched out in front of her, as if she were a blind person, feeling for walls.

"Okay," she says. "Let me just start off by saying that even without the pot thing, I feel like I don't understand you at all. I don't know you anymore. I know I used to have this nice girl, this nice little girl. And now, you're . . ." She stops walking and looks at me as if she has just realized that I am really from Mars, or Russia. "One minute you're reading the Bible for three hours a day in your bedroom, which is weird, okay? And then you come home last night, and you're high. You're talking about *vibes.*"

I pull the covers over my head. She pulls them back down.

"So, as your mother, I'm having a little trouble keeping up, Evelyn. I was wondering if you could help me out. Is this a completely new personality, or just an extension of the old one?"

I start to close my eyes again, but she claps her hands in front of my face.

"I didn't smoke anything. I told you that. I was just in the car with them, and the windows were up. It was cold out."

She nods. "Who were the boys?"

I shake my head, saying nothing. If I tell her it was Travis, she will call Mrs. Rowley. More humiliation. Even more. It is unthinkable.

She waits. But I wait too, and we both know, from experience, that I can wait longer than she can.

"Well," she says, "whether or not you want to tell me, we still need to talk." She sits down on the foot of my bed, rubbing her eyes with her thumbs. "I didn't think I'd have to talk to you about this yet. But you're out with older boys, doing drugs, and I don't know where you've been."

"Mom, I didn't smoke anything."

She makes a quick, cutting motion with her hand, like a conductor telling an orchestra to stop playing. "Just let me talk, Evelyn. Okay? Shut up for a second, and let me talk. I want to tell you that I've learned some things the hard way, especially lately. And I would rather you not learn them the hard way too."

I am horrified, suddenly realizing where this is going. She is going to talk to me about sex. About morals. My mother, adulteress, welfare queen, not a horse but a whore, is going to talk to me about morals. I stare at her, waiting, wide awake now. This should be good.

She looks up at the ceiling, at the star chart above my bed. "I know you think I'm a bad person, Evelyn. You've made that clear. Maybe you're right. I'm aware that you've seen me do some pretty stupid things, and that of course makes this conversation that much harder." She looks at me. "But I'm still your mother, and I still care about you, and I'm going to tell you something that I wish someone would have told me when I was your age, whether you like it or not."

"Can I eat breakfast first?"

"No. When I was your age, I spent a lot of time trying to figure out exactly what I was worth to other people. Exactly how beautiful I was. Like if I had a boyfriend who loved me, or said he did, it was going to fill up this worry in me, this nagging in me that I wasn't worth all that much."

Samuel starts to cry from their room. "You woke up Sam," I say.

She waves her hand, her eyes still on me. "He can wait. Just this once, he can wait. Look Evelyn, I'm not even talking about virginity and all that crap. That's not what's so precious, okay? It's you. You are precious. I know it doesn't always seem like it. I know that other people may make you feel like you aren't. And I even know that maybe there have been some times when I have made you feel like you aren't. But you are, okay? You are."

I say nothing. I am still glaring at her, still rolling my eyes. But in my head, I am again wondering if she really does, in all her evilness, somehow have ESP, or a surveillance antenna on top of her head that follows me wherever I go, or a mind that can decode my cryptic reference to the bad aura, eyes that can see right through me.

"I know we fight a lot right now, and I have to tell you, Evelyn, in my opinion, you've been pretty hard to take as of late. But you're precious to me. And you've got to see yourself as precious. If I would have known that at your age, if I would have really been able to feel that, things would have been very different."

"You mean you wouldn't have had me."

"I would have had you later."

"But maybe it wouldn't have been me anymore."

She waves her hand again. "And maybe it would have been. Water under the bridge."

"And then you wouldn't have had Sam."

She looks irritated. "Right. You get my point. But here you are, and I love you. I know you've been pissed off at me for a very long time, and maybe I deserve it, but still, I want you to know that." She is looking at me, waiting for a response. I try to avoid her eyes, to avoid having to reply to all of this one way or the other. My head feels fuzzy and light, and I don't have a response. But she is looking at me, waiting, and even though I am usually the one who can outwait her, something tells me that this time, she will not look away until I answer, even if we both have to sit here all day.

"Okay."

"You're sure? You're sure you understand what I'm saying?"

I nod. "Yes. God. Are we done?"

She tells me I am grounded. No McDonald's for a month. After that, she says, we'll try it with a curfew, and see how it goes. Samuel is still crying, louder now, and she starts to move toward the door, then stops and turns around. Without warning, she dives toward me, a firm hand on each of my cheeks, and kisses me on the forehead.

After she leaves, I do not go back to sleep. I can still feel where she kissed me, a tickle on my forehead, just above my eyes. I raise my hand to wipe it away and then stop, decide to leave it.

twelve

*I*T'S SPRING NOW, AND TRAVIS and Deena are still in love. They have to be holding hands at all times, as if one of them is really a helium balloon and will float away if the other lets go. Travis is especially obsessed with Deena's hair, and even when I am standing right there trying to talk to one of them, he has to reach over and push it out of her face or pick imaginary objects out of it in a way that reminds me of a television special I once saw about chimpanzees.

Deena and I still eat lunch together, just the two of us, but even then she looks at the clock on the wall and says things like "Only three hours and forty-five minutes until I get to see Travis." Next year, we'll all be in high school, and they'll get to be chimpanzees together all day long. No more interruptions.

But Deena is my only friend. Star left last year, at the end of seventh grade, because it took that long for the insurance money to come through and to build a new house to make up for the one that the hurricane got. After she moved away, she wrote me letters for a while, on pink stationery that smelled like Love's Baby Soft, her loopy handwriting, with large hollow circles over the *i*'s, telling me how happy she was to be back in Florida, how sorry she felt for me in the snow and the cold. "It's so much fucking better here!"

she wrote. She sent me a picture of herself, standing on the beach in a lime green sundress and matching sunglasses, her skin tan, her long hair cut short. She wrote once a week, then once a month, and then the letters stopped, but I thought of her when I was sick of the snow in the winter, a lime green Star standing in the warm sand, making up more lies to tell, the tide swirling around her feet.

But Betsy, the lunch attendant, says Star was pregnant when she went back to Florida. I tell her no, that's a lie, because I still have the picture of Star in her sundress, standing on the beach. But Betsy says it sometimes takes a while for a pregnancy to show, especially on a body that tiny, only thirteen years old, and that I can't possibly know these things because I'm still an innocent. Betsy says Star's parents didn't know and didn't know and didn't know, and when they did know, her father wanted to know who who who and Star told them it was her uncle back in Kansas, and that he had made her.

And they couldn't believe it. Neither could the teachers in the teachers' lounge. But Betsy the lunch attendant could.

"It happens," she says, shrugging. "It happens all the time. Count yourselves as lucky."

The uncle cracked when they called, Betsy tells us, crying to his wife, saying he was sorry, saying she had made him do it, that she had egged him on since they moved in, but that he was so sorry, so very sorry.

What a load of crap, Betsy says.

So they let her get rid of the baby. An abortion. But then, Betsy says, get this: it turns out she's pregnant again, and this time, she can't blame it on the uncle, because she's been back in Florida now for over a year. This time she can't cry and say none of it was her fault. But still, she's only fourteen, so messed up from what happened in Kansas, and her father wants her to be able to get rid of this baby too, and they're fighting it out in courts, and nobody knows what will happen.

When I tell my mother this, she stares at me for a long time, her hand over her mouth. I ask her if she remembers Star, and she says, yes, oh my God, of course.

The summer of 1986 is the summer of the cats—too many of them, with nowhere to go. People have been leaving dogs and cats in the field across the highway from Treeline Colonies, I guess because they don't want them anymore. I've seen this happen. Cars stop, and someone pushes a dog out the door, or someone gets out and puts a blanket down in the middle of the field and hurries away, and the blanket starts to move after the car is already gone. The dogs try to chase cars, and sometimes they get smashed flat on the highway with the possums and the skunks and the raccoons, and sometimes they stand around the parking lot of the McDonald's, eating out of the garbage and barking until somebody calls the pound.

My mother has been getting madder and madder about this, and lately she has been going over the line. She runs outside now when she sees it happening. "Irresponsible!" she yells, throwing rocks with one hand, holding Samuel with the other. Her aim is bad, and she's always too late to actually hit anyone, but still, she shouldn't be trying. When she comes back in, she says things like "'How the fuck can people do that? Don't they feel bad?" Even though it's pretty obvious already that no, they don't.

I tell my mother that maybe she should spend her time worrying about bigger problems, people for instance. There are children starving in Ethiopia. You see them on the news. My mother says she does feel sorry for the children in Ethiopia, but it doesn't help them out for her to not care about the animals getting run over right in front of our own house. It's not like you have to choose which one to be worried about, she says.

My mother doesn't like my French teacher, Mrs. Blanche, because she lets her lab, Daisy, have a litter of puppies every year. Last autumn, Mrs. Blanche sent each of us home with a card that said FREE PUPPIES TO A GOOD HOME!, her phone number on the bottom. My mother saw the card, and I had to grab it out of her hands and tear it up into little pieces so she wouldn't call Mrs. Blanche and tell her to get Daisy fixed.

"Tell her I've got a whole field of free puppies," my mother said, pointing across the highway, Samuel's eyes following her hand. "Tell her to come scrape them off the highway and we can see how she likes free puppies then."

I relay this message to Mrs. Blanche, in much softer language, and she tells me, in French, that she lets Daisy have puppies because it's nature, and because she wants her children to witness the miracle of life. *"La miracle de la vie!"* she says, her hands cupped under her pointy chin. And, she adds, in English, Daisy is a good breed. People want her pups, and are willing to pay for them. The mixed breeds, she says, are the problem.

My mother doesn't believe this. "The miracle of life," she mutters, hoisting Sam up in her arms. "That's great. Tell her to come down here and I can show her the miracle of death. What a smart woman. I'm so glad she's your teacher."

"She just teaches French."

Now every time we see a dead animal in the road, my mother points at it and says, "Look, Evelyn, ze meeracle of life!," trying to do a French accent.

But some of the cats make it across the highway. They hide in the crawl spaces under the stairs of the apartment buildings, creeping around only at night, their bones jutting out of mangy fur, their green eyes shining if you catch them with a light. We hear them mating sometimes, and my mother and I agree it sounds like someone getting murdered. In the morning, garbage bags lie scattered in the road, torn and gutted in the night for milk cartons and TV-dinner trays.

So now someone has started poisoning them, and it's pretty gross. They go into convulsions before they actually die, their cat legs sticking out straight and stiff, flies buzzing around their mouths. When this happens, my mother pulls the sheets down over the windows and tries not to look.

"People make me sick," she says, no French accent this time. "They really do."

She gets mad about things more now, even about things that have nothing to do with her. She is still mad about the nuclear bombs, and now she's also mad about the Contras. The Contras are in Nicaragua, fighting the Communists, and Ronald Reagan says they are like America's founding fathers and that we have to do whatever we can to help them. I think so too. We can't have the Communists in Nicaragua, or they will come into Texas and that will be the end. The Contras are good, and the other people, the Sandinistas, are Communists.

My mother says no, Evelyn. You can't believe everything Ronnie says. It's not that simple. The Contras are bad, too. They blindfold people and shoot them, just for being in the way, even old men and little children. They kill nuns and cut off women's arms in front of their children, and we shouldn't be giving them a dime.

I don't know what to think. Maybe that's what founding fathers have to do. Maybe the mothers were Communists. But still, it seems pretty mean, and if I could see them doing this, cutting off the arms of mothers, I would make them stop. Even if the nuns and mothers were Communists, you can't go around doing things like that.

On the first day of ninth grade, Deena and I walk past two dead cats on the way to the bus stop. One is an orange tabby, the other black with white spots.

"Grody," Deena says, turning away. "Gross out!"

But I feel bad just leaving them there, lying in the road. I push both of them into the grass, and stretch them out so it looks like they are just sleeping, except for the bloodstains around their mouths. Deena says I will get rabies.

"Fleas too," she adds.

Travis is already down at the bus stop. When we walk up, he takes his cigarette out of his mouth and pulls Deena close to him. They get started right there, hands groping, eyes closed, at the bus stop at seven-thirty in the morning, right in front of all the little kids with their brand-new Big Chief tablets and unsharpened pencils squeezed against their chests, right in front of all the cars passing on the highway. One car honks.

"Are you guys sure this is the best place for that?" I ask, shifting my book bag to my other shoulder. "It'd be a shame if you misplaced your tongues on the first day."

They stop and look at me, both of them smiling. But they are still holding hands, Travis's thumb rubbing Deena's palm. They are so in love that everything is funny, especially me.

"It's kind of gross," I say, looking down the highway.

Travis winks at Deena. "Sorry, Ev." He takes out another cigarette, and Deena asks if she can see my schedule.

"Hey!" She wraps her finger around the belt loop of my jeans, pulling me closer. "We're all in algebra together at the same time. All three of us! That's so cool."

"You're still in algebra, Travis?"

He looks at me, long and steady, the flicker of hurt there for me to see. "Yes, Evelyn. I am."

I say nothing, pretend to just watch for the bus.

"It's not that it's hard," he says. "I actually don't mind algebra. I just don't like going." He frowns. "Sellers is a terrible teacher. I'm serious. I passed all the tests last year, but he won't let me out because of poor attendance. He has to let me out this year, though. He has to. It's getting ridiculous, being in there with all those little kids."

I want to point out to him that the little kids are ninth graders, and that Deena is in ninth grade, and that right at this moment, he has his hand in the back pocket of her jeans, which really, if you think about it, looks dumb at any age.

But I don't. I don't say anything. I have already hurt him once this morning, and that's enough. If I do it again, we would all know that it was just my unhappiness talking, the scratching claw reaching out from my own sad little heart.

Travis was right about Mr. Sellers. He's not a very good teacher.

He looks smart: he has gray hair and glasses that make his eyes look larger than they really are. On the first day, he wears a three-piece suit, with a used Kleenex poked in one of the buttonholes. He has a glass of water on the chalk tray, which he does not actually drink out of, but uses to occasionally rinse his mouth out, spitting the water back in the glass after swishing it between his teeth.

We watch him do this, saying nothing.

"My name," he tells us, looking at us with his enlarged eyes, "is Mr. Sellers, and I have been educating young people at this institution for over thirty years." He stops and picks up the glass of water, and still we are silent, half hoping he will gargle again in front of us because it is so disgusting that we still can't believe he did it the first time, half hoping he won't for the same reason. "So I know all the tricks," he says, wagging his finger. "Don't try anything funny."

"Like this?" Ray Watley asks. He waves his hands up by his head, his tongue hanging out of his mouth. It is supposed to be a joke, and though Ray's jokes are usually bad, this time it's a little funny. But Mr. Sellers doesn't laugh. He turns around and stares at Ray with his bug eyes until Ray looks back down at his desk.

He starts writing equations on the board. He doesn't talk very much, and when he does, we can't really hear what he's saying because he is still facing the chalkboard, so we all just sit and watch.

Class goes on like this the next day, and the day after that. Since he never turns around, it's like study hall, and we can do what we want. People talk, play hangman. Ray takes naps, his arms flat out in front of him, drooling on his desk. I do my homework, and so does Traci Carmichael. Twice, Travis gets up and walks out without Mr. Sellers's noticing. Deena follows, and he doesn't notice that either.

But after the first test that even I get a C on, people get mad. They are not mad because I got a C; they are mad because they are failing. Deena, who would have a hard time in algebra with a normal teacher, is terrified of Mr. Sellers. She tried raising her hand to ask a question once, but since he was facing the board, he didn't see. She sat there with her long, thin arm raised for fifteen minutes, her hand hanging this way and then that, then slowly going back down, giving in to gravity until it fell on her desk with a thud.

Traci Carmichael is the one to finally say something. "Mr. Sellers?" she says one day, tapping on her desk with her pencil to get his attention. She has cut her braids off into a fluffy bob, and she wears glasses too now, gold-rimmed. They make her look smart, like a young journalist.

He turns around, startled, like he has forgotten we are there.

"Mr. Sellers, I don't understand some of the things that are going to be on the test on Friday. I don't know what we're even working on right now." She holds her hands up, gesturing at the rest of us, sitting silently around her. "*No one* knows what we're working on right now."

He turns completely around, looking just at her. This alone would be enough to make Deena cry, but Traci just gazes back at him with her blue-gray eyes. Already she has the face of a small adult, the voice of someone in charge.

Mr. Sellers licks his lips, squinting. "Did you do the assignments, dear?"

"Yes," she says. "I mean, I did the ones I could."

"Well then, if you're reasonably intelligent, you shouldn't have any trouble." He brings the glass of water up to his lips, sucks in, spits out, and turns back to the chalkboard with a little laugh. "Numbers don't change, after all. If it works once, it will work every time."

Traci stares at the back of his head, her mouth slightly open.

Something is going to happen. I know, better than anyone, that Traci Carmichael may look like a princess, but she is also the kind of princess who hits back. Even if you are a teacher, you can't say something like that to someone like her.

Before the end of the hour, there is a note moving around the room:

The first official meeting of S.O.S. (Sick of Sellers) will be held immediately after this class by the flagpole. We don't have to put up with this! Our parents' taxes pay his salary. And he sucks!!

I still don't like Traci, but I remember her understanding of the power dynamic of the PTA, how it aided us in getting rid of Stella, the hated bus driver with the broomstick back in third grade. After class, I go to the flagpole.

"We need to get a petition together," she tells us. I am amazed to see that she has somehow already obtained a clipboard for the petition, a pen tied to it with a string. She passes it around for us to sign. "My mother will call. She's seen the homework, and she thinks it's ridiculous. Everyone needs to get their parents to call. That's the most important thing."

I tell my mother this when I go home, while she is giving Samuel a bath. He's three now, big enough so she needs help getting him in and out of the tub, but once we get him in, I move away and stand in the doorway, because he likes to splash. She leaves the faucet on so he can hold his hand underneath the rushing water, and he makes the pterodactyl sound, his eyes rolling back in his head. I have to yell so she can hear me.

"I don't know, Evelyn," she says, massaging his scalp with a washcloth, her hand over his eyes. "I can't go calling the school every time you don't get an A." She is wearing the red glitter hat, and Samuel stares up at it, open-mouthed. His blue eyes look even larger with his hair slicked back and wet.

"Traci's mom is calling."

"Well then," she says, reaching for a towel, her mouth curved in a half smile. "I'm sure that's all you'll need."

But it isn't true. Mr. Sellers is more difficult to get rid of than Stella the bus driver. The principal, Dr. Queen, is on his side.

I kind of like Dr. Queen, though I do not tell anyone this, ever. It is not okay to like the principal of the school. I have never really spoken with her, because you have to talk to her only if you get in trouble. But I like that she is principal and everyone is a little scared of her. And I like that she has a name like Dr. Queen. I would love to have a name like that.

Dr. Queen has black hair with a tight permanent wave and a gray streak right down the middle, and it does not look like she has her hair cut so much as clipped, the way you would clip a hedge. It goes out at least four inches in every direction above her ears, and sometimes people call her Frankenstein's Bride, but never to her face. She wears business suits with big shoulder pads, and she carries a briefcase to work in the morning. For a long time, I wanted to be a principal, just because of her, but one day I saw her in the teachers' lounge with Mrs. Evans, and before they shut the door, I saw Dr. Queen fall down on the couch with her hands over her head and say, "Claire, I hate my job. I hate it, I hate it, I hate it."

Traci said that when her mother called to complain about Mr. Sellers, Dr. Queen told her that he was a respected educator, that he had gotten his degree in mathematics at Duke, that he was in his thirty-fifth year of teaching, almost ready to retire.

"She wants to compromise," Traci told us, rolling her eyes. "Principals are total politicians."

But Mrs. Carmichael showed up at Dr. Queen's office the next day, un-announced, on the way home from a tennis game, and escorted Dr. Queen down to our classroom so they could watch Mr. Sellers teach.

"Just watching!" Mrs. Carmichael said, waving at him from the back of the room, her car keys jangling in her hand. She was wearing shorts and a sweatshirt, carrying a tennis racket. Traci turned around, and her mother pointed the handle of the racket at her and winked.

By the end of the week, we had a new teacher.

The new teacher, Mr. Goldman, is shorter than Dr. Queen, not even including her hair. He is young enough to be Mr. Sellers's son, or even grand-son, and he has dark eyes and dark hair, cut short on the sides but longer in front. He wears a crisp, ironed gray shirt and a matching gray and green tie. None of the other male teachers match like this.

"Class," Dr. Queen says. "Class." She does not have to clap her hands to get our attention because just her voice is like hands clapping. "Mr. Goldman will be in this room for the rest of the year. He's going to be helping... learning from Mr. Sellers. He's from *New York City*." She pauses, eyebrows raised, letting this information sink in. "Right, Mr. Goldman?"

"That's right," the new teacher says, his words coming out quick, cut off at the end. He stands beside her, smiling at us. "And now here I am." His thick eyebrows form almost a straight line just above his eyes. He doesn't look or sound like anyone I know.

Dr. Queen turns to the chalkboard to write Mr. Goldman's name on the board for us, and Libby Masterson holds up a piece of paper for Traci to see: MAJOR BABE.

"Do you have a question, Libby?" Dr. Queen asks, turning back around. She has an eye like a sparrow, Dr. Queen. Mr. Sellers is already looking at the chalkboard longingly, his arms flapping at his sides. He doesn't like to be away from it for this long.

Travis raises his hand. "I have a question."

"Shoot," Mr. Goldman says, tilting his chin up quickly. The eyebrows go up too.

"Are you Italian or something? Greek?"

Dr. Queen winces and holds up her hand. "Are there any appropriate questions?"

"I'm Jewish," Mr. Goldman says. He points at his face, and then at his name on the chalkboard. "Goldman? You know?" He says this like we are supposed to know that the last name Goldman means he is Jewish, like we are stupid if we couldn't figure that out by ourselves. But I don't know if I've ever seen a Jewish person before. I didn't know they had special names either. And I didn't know you were supposed to be able to tell, just by looking at someone's face. Anne Frank was Jewish, but she just looked normal.

Eileen says Jewish people are from the land of Israel, and God's chosen people. Abraham and Moses and all of them, they were Jews. Every time in the Bible when God was helping someone win a fight or a war because they were blessed and someone else wasn't, those were the Jews. God helps them more than other people. Helped them, actually, Eileen said. Not anymore. They *had been* chosen, she said, but then they'd messed it up and killed Jesus, so now it was the Christians who were chosen because we had the ears that could hear and the eyes that could see. That's why there was all that sadness going on in Beirut, she said. Because some people have eyes to see and some people don't, and when you've got that many people who don't know Jesus living together in one place, of course there's going to be trouble.

But Mr. Goldman has eyes and ears, and everything seems to be open and working. He is still smiling at us, his teeth straight and white.

"Are you really from New York?" Travis asks.

Mr. Goldman nods. "Manhattan."

"And you came here?"

Dr. Queen says she doesn't like Travis's tone, but this does not stop him. "Why would you come here from New York? Aren't there schools in New York?"

"No shit," Ray Watley says. Dr. Queen stiffens, and it is clear she heard this word, but not where it came from. She stands in front of the room with her hands on her hips, scanning our faces.

Mr. Goldman shrugs and shows us the wedding band on his hand. "My wife's from Kansas. Her father's sick, and she wanted to be here for a while."

Libby Masterson quickly writes another note, holding it up for Traci: THAT IS SO SWEET!

"So here I am." He looks around the room again, and the way he is looking at us makes me think of the show *Voyager,* where the little boy and the man travel around in a time machine, going on missions. Every time they come to a new place, they stand by the time machine for a while, just looking around, not sure yet where they are, what year it is, or what it is they're supposed to be doing.

When I come home from school, there is an orange-and-white-striped kitten curled up on the sofa. It looks up at me, yawns, and tucks its head back under its paw.

"What's this?" I yell, putting down my backpack. "What's this cat?"

My mother answers from the bedroom. "We'll be out in a minute," she yells. "Hold on."

I sit down on the sofa next to the cat, not seeing the bowl of milk that was sitting on one of the cushions. I knock it over and try to set it upright, but it's already seeping in under the upholstery. The kitten starts to lick what it can.

My mother comes out of her room, Samuel on her hip. She is smiling, wearing the glitter hat, jeans, and the gray sweatshirt. "Oh, Evelyn, didn't you see the milk? I had it there for the kitty."

"No. That's why I sat in it. If I would have seen it, I wouldn't have sat in it."

"Okay, Evelyn. Okay." She dabs at the wet part of the sofa with her hand and sits down, Samuel's legs hanging over the edge of her lap. "No use crying over it. Ha ha."

I point at the kitten. "What's it doing here?"

Instead of answering, she picks up one of the kitten's paws and makes it wave. "Hi there!" She is speaking for the cat as if it were a Muppet, her voice high and squeaky. "I'm a little kitty!"

"We're not allowed to have pets here."

She looks at me like this is my fault. "The Rowleys have had Jackie O for years, and nobody's said boo about it." She takes Samuel's hand and guides it down to the kitten's fur, her voice going up high again. "My name is Tiger! Pet my fur, Sam! Feel how soft I am!" Samuel screeches, his curled fingers pushing into the kitten's fur.

I look at the damp spot where the milk spilled. This is only the beginning, the beginning of so much mess. "Cats smell."

My mother frowns. "You're mean!" she says, still speaking for the cat, making it point at me with its orange paws. Its eyes have taken on the same disinterested glaze as Samuel's, allowing my mother to move its limbs this way and that. "You're the mean one! They told me about you!" She stretches the paw forward to tap me twice on the leg. "They told me you would try to throw me out, but you seem to be forgetting who's really in charge around here." She points to herself with the kitten's paw. "She is! And I'm here to stay!"

I sigh. "I can see your lips moving, Mom. You're not fooling anyone."

She shrugs. "We're keeping the cat."

Of course, it doesn't end there. The next day, she looks out the window and sees two more orange-and-white kittens darting across the highway, narrowly missing the tires of a passing semitrailer.

"Here," she says. "Take Sam."

"What are you doing?"

She puts on dishwashing gloves and runs outside. I watch her through the window, Samuel heavy in my arms and already crying. The kittens have ducked into the drainage ditch between the mailboxes for Treeline Colonies and the highway, and my mother gets down on her knees in the grass, twirling dandelions to get their attention, luring them toward her. When they get close enough, she tucks them under her arms and runs back to the apartment. She pushes open the door, and the kittens fall to the ground, crouching low, eyes wide.

"You're kidding." I hand Samuel back to her. "Mom, they probably have diseases."

"I'll take them to the vet. They're just babies." She leans down to touch one of them, and they both run under the couch.

"With what money?"

She sighs, and leans Samuel's head against her shoulder, patting him on the back. "Evelyn, they're Tiger's *sisters.*"

We sit quietly, waiting. One of the kittens appears from under the couch, sniffing the air, flinching at any sound. It sees Tiger lying in a square of sunlight in the middle of the room and creeps toward him. The other one, half an ear missing already, follows. When Tiger sees them, he flips his tail and rolls over on his back.

"We're breaking the rules," I tell her. "And three is too many. You're going to become a cat lady. I'm serious. It's a certain kind of person."

She nods and leans over to rub one of the new kittens behind the ears. It closes its eyes, purring. "Okay, Evelyn," she says, "you go ahead and choose which one you want me to throw out."

Within a few days, they have taken over. There is cat hair in the silverware tray; one of them has thrown up behind the couch. They lounge on the sofa, all three of them stretched out so there is no place to sit. If you tell them to move, they get up slowly, looking irritated and vengeful, as if they have just as much right to be there as anyone else.

Mr. Goldman is a big improvement to fifth-period algebra. Not only is he unusual and therefore interesting to watch, but our collective test scores have gone up as a result of his ability to actually explain things. All through class now, Mr. Sellers sits in the back of the room and reads until he falls asleep, his book, *Oppenheimer's Legacy,* facedown on his lap.

Mr. Goldman uses his hands when he talks, one hand raised at shoulder height, palm facing the ceiling, and he moves it rhythmically, almost like he is juggling. I don't know if he does this because he is from New York or because he is Jewish or maybe just because, but none of the other teachers move their hands like this. When he turns back to the chalkboard, Libby Masterson performs accurate imitations of him, her hands moving quickly in front of her. Traci ignores her now; she's serious about bringing her math grades back up. But Libby continues to write notes: HE IS ADORABLE!!!

The other teachers don't think Mr. Goldman is adorable, though, I know. My locker is just around the corner from the coffee machine in the teachers' lounge, and I can hear what they are saying even when the door is shut. They liked him okay at first, but now they're mad because they think he balks. This is the word they use. He balked about parent-teacher night, because it was scheduled on a day that was a holiday for him but not for us, and they had to reschedule it.

"I had a sitter lined up," Mrs. Hansen told Dr. Queen. "If he's going to balk about every special holiday, this is going to be a pain in the ass."

Mr. Goldman also balked about Christmas, about how the proposed title for the annual winter musical was "Christmas Around the World." I heard him balk about this myself, making photocopies in the teachers' lounge.

"Ignoring the fact that the title isn't exactly inclusive," he said—and though I couldn't see him, I imagined his hands were probably moving—"it's also pretty inaccurate, wouldn't you say?"

"Oh Jake," Mrs. Hansen said. "We've done it that way for years. You don't have to be so careful with these kids. Everybody celebrates Christmas out here."

"Well," Mr. Goldman had said, stacking his photocopies. "I'm here now."

No one said anything until after he left. He smiled quickly at me as he passed my locker, shutting the door to the teachers' lounge.

"Give me a break," Mrs. Hansen said. "He's too sensitive. Nobody's burning crosses."

They wait until he leaves the teachers' lounge to say things like this. They are nice to his face, and he is nice to theirs. With the other teacher no one likes, Ms. Jenkins, nobody bothers pretending.

Ms. Jenkins is different from the other teachers in a lot of ways. She is maybe fifty, but she isn't married, and she doesn't have any children. All the other teachers eat at one lunch table together, even Mr. Goldman, but Ms. Jenkins sits by herself. I don't know who started this. Maybe they won't sit with her, or maybe she won't sit with them. She does not buy hot lunch, but brings a salad in a Tupperware container in a cloth bag that says JUST BAG IT!, and while she eats she reads magazines that don't have any pictures. She has a floor-to-ceiling poster of Mr. Spock on her door. She is a vegetarian. Also, she is very tall, and does not wear makeup. She scratches her head when she talks, and her hair stays in the direction that she scratched it, sometimes sticking straight up because of static electricity, even when everyone else's hair is fine.

I like her, though. She hands back my lab reports with smiley faces drawn in red ink with words like "Impressive!" and "Quite good!" across the top. She has colorful posters of extinct and endangered animals along one wall of her classroom, and whenever an animal or insect or bird gets taken off the endangered species list, she brings a bag of Snickers to class. Another wall is covered with Far Side comics, and if you finish your test early, you get to go over and read them until the bell rings.

But the best part of Ms. Jenkins's room is the beehive. She made it herself. It's just a plastic container with a tube that leads directly to a sealed-off window, so the bees can go in and out as they please. But the plastic is see-through, so we can watch them when they bring back their honey in round balls they carry with their feet. When they come back into the tube from outside, sometimes they stop where they are and spin in circles. It looks like they are dancing, or maybe confused, but Ms. Jenkins says really they are communicating with one another, telling one another where the good flowers are. Two circles to the right mean one thing; three circles to the left mean another. If you want extra credit, you're allowed to stay in during lunch and watch them, taking notes on which way they turn.

I do this sometimes. I don't need the extra credit, but I think it's amazing, watching the bees. They really do spin in circles the way Ms. Jenkins says, telling one another things, and it's like watching something secret. I look at bees more carefully now when I see them outside, even when I see just one, resting on a flower. All my life, I've seen bees buzz around, and I never really thought they knew where they were going, but apparently they do.

Deena and I sit at her grandmother's creaky kitchen table, newspapers spread out beneath our pumpkins and carving knives, careful not to make too much noise. We had to buy our pumpkins at the Kwikshop, and it wasn't the greatest selection. My pumpkin is bad, but Deena's is worse. It has a brown scar on one side, the other side is covered with some kind of fungus. She squinted at it for a while in the Kwikshop, tracing the moldy spot with her finger.

"I'll make it the mouth," she said.

Deena's good at things like this. Art is the only class she likes. For the pottery unit, we each had to make a vase in the shape of an animal, and Deena made a baby bird, its beak stretched up and opened wide. She had spent hours texturizing the wings with a No. 2 pencil, and by the time she finished, it looked as if a real baby bird had survived the kiln and was still waiting to be fed, its downy wings small and unfolded.

Mrs. Toss had carried Deena's bird slowly around the room, cradled in her hands. "Isn't it lovely?" she asked us. "Isn't it?"

I had tried to make a swan, with a long, thin neck, but I made the neck too long, and the head fell off in the kiln. Mine was the only animal without a head, and I got a D−. My mother took it out of the garbage and put it on her dresser, and now she keeps safety pins in it.

"I think it's nice," my mother told me, not even cracking a smile. "I like it."

I watch Deena draw on her pumpkin with a ballpoint pen. The swirling lines she's making don't look like anything yet, but I know they will. She never messes up.

"You're so good at things like this," I tell her.

She looks up quickly, like I have surprised her. "No," she says. "Not really. Did I miss anything in English?"

"Nope. We all just sat around. It's just not English without you."

She squeezes a pumpkin seed between her finger and thumb, hitting me on the cheek. "Very funny. What did I miss?"

I shrug. "You've missed a lot. We're on the third act of *Othello*. You're going to have a hard time with it, trying to read it by yourself."

She squints at her pumpkin. "I know. I know."

I cut into my pumpkin and tell her that she should come to English, not just because she has to but because sometimes it's fun. Mr. Adams jumped up on his desk today, holding a yardstick up like a sword, pretending to be Othello. *"Put down your swords or the dew will rust them!"* he had yelled, jumping off his desk, both of his feet hitting the floor at the same time.

Deena rolls her eyes. "Whoopity-do."

I say nothing, looking down at the jagged line I am cutting into my pumpkin. She has been doing this lately, talking to me like I am a little kid, instead of the same age that she is, as if everything I think is interesting is actually kind of dumb. I don't know if she's doing it on purpose or not. I finish the circle on top of my pumpkin and try to pull it off. The green stub twists off in my hand.

"Well, what's so great about whatever you and Travis do all day?"

She sets her knife down and looks at me, a slight smile on her glossy lips. She is trying not to laugh. "You really don't know?"

"No." I wipe my hands on the knees of my jeans. "I really don't know."

She leans in close, her eyes on mine. "We're having sex, silly goose." She laughs her goofy laugh, pushing her hair back over her shoulder. "That's what we do all day. That's what's so great."

I stop cutting, my knife stuck into my pumpkin where the nose should be. I'm not ready for how much this hurts me. I've gotten used to seeing them together by now, his arm around her waist when we walk back from the bus stop, their feet wrapped around each other's under the table in the cafeteria. But now, hearing this, it's like I just swallowed a needle and can feel it moving down my throat, a long, slow, and sharp descent.

"Sex? Like real sex?"

"Shh!" She nods in the direction of her grandmother's door. "If my grandmother hears you, she'll come out and call me a little *schlampe*." She picks up her knife again.

"Every time you skip, that's what you're doing?"

She laughs again. "Mmm. Not every single time. Sometimes we do it, and sometimes we just go out to Dairy Queen and he buys me a Mr. Misty." She moves her eyebrows up and down. "Either way, I come out a winner."

"Where?"

"Where what?"

"Where do you do it?"

I hear her talking as if I am not really in the room with her, just watching her on television. Mostly in Ed's van, she says. And no, not with Ed in it. Once in her bedroom, her grandmother sleeping in the next room. "We were *very quiet*," she says, giving me a knowing look, even though we both know I don't know anything. I imagine them lying together under Deena's pink sheets, Deena with a finger pressed against her lips like a librarian. The needle is in my chest now, turning slowly.

"Don't look at me like that, Evelyn."

"Like what?"

"Like you think I'm a terrible person."

"I don't." This is a lie. You're not supposed to have sex before you're married. "It's just weird, that's all."

She takes her pumpkin off the table and cradles it in her arms, making quick, short jabs into its skin. "What's so weird about it?"

"Because. Because, for one, you're only fourteen."

"And?"

"And you could get pregnant."

"I'm on the pill." She glances up at me. "Travis and I went to the clinic together, for your information. You know, sometimes you act like you think I'm stupid, Evelyn."

"I don't think you're stupid." Another lie. "But you could get a disease. You could get AIDS."

She snorts once, hard and fast. "We're not homosexuals, Evelyn. I'm sure."

But I've heard stories. Patty Pollo said her cousin had a friend who went down to Fort Lauderdale for spring break and met a man who was so nice to her she couldn't believe it. She was a virgin, but she had sex with him because she knew she loved him right away. When she woke up the next morning he was gone, but he had taken her red lipstick and written on the bathroom mirror WELCOME TO THE WONDERFUL WORLD OF AIDS.

I remind Deena of this story. She laughs again.

"Do you really think Travis is going to do that to me?" Her half-moon eyebrows stay raised, amused. "We're very careful. Don't worry. Nothing bad is going to happen."

I frown, watching her carve. This doesn't seem exactly fair. "What's it like?"

"What do you mean?"

I stare at her, annoyed.

"I can't really explain it," she says. "It's one of those things that you can't explain."

"Try."

"What do you want to know?"

"Did it hurt?"

She shakes her head. "Not as much as everyone makes it out to. Getting my ears pierced hurt more. I think they just tell you that to scare you." She wags the knife in her hand like she is Groucho Marx holding a cigar. "I know I'm hooked."

Her pumpkin is already amazing. The mouth she has cut is wrinkled and menacing, baring fangs instead of teeth, small, swirling lines spiraling beneath it to look like a beard. I tried to make lines swirl out of the circle-shaped mouth on my pumpkin, but all the cuts ran together, and now it's just one big hole, too big to be any reasonable facial feature.

She looks up at me. "What else do you want to know?"

"How long does it take?"

She laughs again. Everything is funny now, apparently. "A little longer every time." She picks up her pumpkin. "It's like this, Evelyn. I'll show you." She holds the pumpkin in front of her, pushing its grinning mouth against her neck and chin. "Oh, Travis," she whispers, rolling her eyes back, shutting them. "Your head is so ... orange and round ... and your stem! Oh, your stem! Oh Travis!" She arches her back, holding the pumpkin close to her throat.

I look away. "You're a weirdo, Deena."

She smiles and puts the pumpkin down. "You're the one who asked."

When we are both finished, she gets candles from her grandmother's nativity scene, packed away in a box in the closet. With the lights out and a lit candle behind its eyes, Deena's jack-o'-lantern looks like a real person. The eyes she made are wide, asymmetrical, curvy lines radiating outward so they look like seeing suns. Mine is not as good as hers, but still, the candle helps. The jagged triangles turn into shining eyes above a smirking mouth.

We sit in the darkness, silently watching them, their faces flickering light and darkness around the room.

$$thirteen$$

$\mathcal{R}$ONALD REAGAN IS IN A lot of trouble.

Even when he got shot, he was making jokes, telling the doctors he hoped they were Republicans and telling Nancy sorry he forgot to duck. But now he stands in front of a blue curtain and behind too many microphones, his face white, his voice shaking.

"Listen," he says. "We did not, *did not,* trade arms for hostages."

But now it looks like maybe they did. When the reporters ask him questions about the money from Iran going to the Contras in Nicaragua, he looks like he is mad at them for asking, and also like he just remembered he left his keys locked in his car with the engine running. Oliver North is a Marine, and he says he would stand on his head if the president asked him to because that's how much he loves this country. But nobody asked him to stand on his head. Somebody asked him to get money to the Contras in Nicaragua, even though Congress said not to, and he did it. He found a way. Maybe Ronald Reagan asked him, but maybe not. If he did, he's in trouble.

Deena says Oliver North looks like Mel Gibson, but my mother says really, that isn't the point. She leaves the news on when she feeds Samuel his dinner in the front room, watching reporters yell questions to Ronald Reagan as he walks from the White House to his helicopter. He waves and cups his hand over his ear like he can't hear their questions because the helicopter is too loud, but he keeps walking, and you can tell that really, he just doesn't want to hear them.

My mother is happy and mad about this at the same time. "Now who's the cheater, Ronnie?" she says, eyes glittering. "Tell me who the liar is now."

But I feel bad for Ronald Reagan. When I look at his face and hear his voice, I can see in his heart that he really is trying to be a good person. My mother says that's because he's an actor, but I think it's real. When he says "God bless America," I think he means it so much that in some ways, he is almost crazy, like maybe in his mind he sees a ray of light coming down from the sky, shining down on America and no one else, just because he loves it so much. So then he would have to lie and cheat to save Texas from the Communists, and he would still be as good as Moses, smiting down the Midianites, even the little children. It gets confusing, because that's why he hates the Communists in the first place. Because they lie and cheat. But if America is really blessed, then it's different for us.

I'm sure God loves people in Nicaragua, almost as much as he loves us. But it would be a bad thing if the Communists came to Texas, so maybe some of the Nicaraguans have to die to keep that from happening.

But I probably wouldn't think that way if I lived in Nicaragua.

The reason Travis and Deena don't get in trouble for missing so much class is because the school spent five thousand dollars on a computerized attendance system this year. The teachers said it was worth every penny, because now all they have to do is mark "absent" by your name on the slip that goes to the office, and the computer automatically calls your house. The computer called my house one day, when I really was sick. My mother, thinking it was a person she was talking to, said, "I know. She's right here. She's sick," getting madder and madder before she figured out she was talking to a machine.

But Deena's grandmother doesn't hear very well anymore, so Deena just turns down the volume of the ringer on the phone before she leaves for school in the morning. She tested it a few times, calling from the pay phone at the Wendy's across the street from the high school. If nobody answers the phone when the computer calls, it sends a letter right to your house, but Deena brings in the mail for her grandmother every day, so that's not a problem, at least for now.

The attendance policy at Kerrville High says that you are allowed to miss thirteen days of each class each semester. You get thirteen sick days, no questions asked, whether you are sick for real or just sick of school. It sounds like a lot, but if you go over thirteen, you fail that semester, no matter what, even if you get pneumonia and are really about to die. But Travis figured out that the computer can only count: it can't tell if you miss different classes on different days. So really you can miss thirteen gyms, thirteen algebras, thirteen biologies—and they don't have to be on the same day. Since thirteen free sick days each semester mean twenty-six free sick days each year, Travis says he and Deena can get away with never going to a full day of school for almost the entire year without ever getting in trouble with anybody but the computer.

So really, two years of freshman algebra taught him something after all.

But Mr. Goldman is catching on, and he's starting to balk. "Where are they?" he asks, looking at me. The dark eyebrows lower, and I know he knows I know. He's figured out that I'm the one turning in their homework, all of it done in Travis's handwriting.

"I don't know," I say. But I do, of course. They are either at Dairy Queen, or worse. Either way, Deena comes out a winner.

Mr. Goldman doesn't like this answer, and he keeps looking at me, pulling on his red tie. "Do their parents know how much they miss?" he asks. "What's going on here?"

Mr. Sellers cuts in to rescue me. "Mr. Goldman," he says, not even looking up from his book, "let us not bother the industrious Miss Bucknow with the whereabouts of her less industrious peers. If they choose to miss, they choose to miss. Their parents have been duly informed. Life, and class, will go on without them. We should focus on teaching the students who are actually *here*."

But just then, just as he's saying this, the door opens and Deena shuffles in, smiling at Mr. Goldman, her hair wet from the snow. "Sorry," she says, like she really means it. "My watch broke."

Mr. Goldman frowns, not just at Deena, but at Mr. Sellers too. "I already marked you absent and sent the sheet to the office," he says. "You have to be here on time."

"Yes sir," she says, looking back at him, very seriously, until he turns around.

Mr. Goldman goes back to the chalkboard, telling us that it isn't so important that we memorize the quadratic formula, but when we see it written down, we should be able to recognize it for what it is and plug the right numbers into the right spaces. But if you do want to memorize it, he says, it helps to know that you can sing it to the tune of "Row, Row, Row Your Boat." And of course he does this for us, his voice low, straining on the high notes. This is what he is doing when all of a sudden he looks out the window and freezes, the chalk in his hand resting against the board.

We turn around, all of us. Outside, just across the street, Travis and Ed Schwebbe are walking slowly, their hoods pulled up over their heads and their hands in their pockets.

"Hold on for a minute," Mr. Goldman says, setting down the chalk. "I'll be right back."

Ray Watley runs to the window the moment Mr. Goldman leaves. Deena gets up next, and then we all do. Mr. Sellers tells us to sit back down, but we don't care about him anymore. Already we can see Mr. Goldman outside, jogging after Travis and Ed, his red tie flapped up over his shoulder, leaving footprints in the inch of snow that has fallen on the sidewalk since they shoveled it at lunch. He shouts out to them, and they turn toward each other, Ed saying something quickly and then running ahead, disappearing behind the Wendy's. But Travis just stands there, smoking a cigarette, watching Mr. Goldman run toward him.

When Mr. Goldman catches up to him, he takes the cigarette out of Travis's hand and throws it on the ground. He points at Travis and then back to the school as if Travis were just lost and maybe needed directions. Travis says nothing, his hands in his pockets. I can't see his face from here.

They walk back together, Mr. Goldman still talking, not even acting like he is cold although he must be, in just one of his crisp colorful shirts with snow falling on his dark hair. We move quickly back to our seats, everyone in place before they get to the door. Travis takes his seat in the back, his eyes steady on the back of Mr. Goldman's head for the rest of the hour, the hissing radiator the only sound in the room.

The protesters show up the next day, chanting loud enough for us to hear them in health and family life. The snow has turned into a cold March drizzle, but they are out there anyway, walking in slow circles in the school parking lot, carrying signs: DON'T LISTEN TO JENKINS; LISTEN TO JESUS!! DON'T MONKEY WITH FREEDOM OF RELIGION!

Mrs. Hansen pulls the curtains over the windows and turns on the air conditioner so the hum of it will drown them out, even though our hair is still wet from walking from the buses.

"Who are they?" Traci asks. "What do they want?"

Mrs. Hansen rolls her eyes. "Ms. Jenkins wants to teach evolution. It gets people stirred up."

I am silent, taking this in. I don't know what the protesters are mad about. I want to ask, but I'm worried if I do it will be like asking about Noah's ark, and Traci will turn around and say, "You've *got* to be joking" again.

I am most disturbed by the sign that says you have to listen to Jesus instead of Jenkins, like Jesus is on one side and Ms. Jenkins is on the other. Ms. Jenkins has just handed back my report on the different kinds of cloud formations with an A+ and GREAT WORK written across the top, underlined three times. She's my favorite teacher besides Mr. Goldman, but if she's on a different side than Jesus, well then.

I have biology third period, and all through class, I watch Ms. Jenkins carefully. She moves around the room like nothing is happening, like we don't all know that there are protesters outside with her name on their signs. She talks about chlorofluorocarbons and the ozone layer, scratching her graying hair so it sticks up at the sides. I am thinking that Ms. Jenkins doesn't believe in God, and this is why the protesters are mad.

Eileen says she feels sorry for people who don't believe in God, just plain sorry for them. I don't know if she would feel sorry for Ms. Jenkins or not, if she met her. I can't imagine them in the same room. I can't even have both of them in my head at the same time. They are like two parallel lines that should never cross each other, but keep going on side by side, always on different tracks.

At lunch, Mr. Goldman sits by himself, reading *U.S. News & World Report,* sipping orange juice through a straw, his green tie flipped up over his shoulder so he won't spill anything on it.

"I hate that fucker," Travis says.

I give Travis a look. I don't like his calling Mr. Goldman a fucker. He's nice. If anyone is confused about a math problem, he stays during lunch and helps them, eating a sandwich with one hand, writing on the board with the other.

Last week, he caught Libby Masterson passing a note to Traci. Usually this is a good thing for everybody else, because if a teacher like Sellers catches you passing notes, he takes it from you and reads it out loud to everyone. It can be very interesting. But when Mr. Goldman took the folded-up note out of Libby's hand, she looked up at him with her rabbit face and said, "Please, *please*, don't read it," and just looking at her you could see that the note had something about him in it, and that if he read it, that would be it for her as far as being embarrassed. Sellers was in the back of the room, and he started snapping his fingers and saying, "Bring the note to me," and we were all saying, "Read it! Read it!" But Mr. Goldman just wadded it up and threw it away and told Libby to keep her mind on math.

I was one of the people saying, "Read it! Read it!" and now I feel bad.

Deena does not say yes or no about whether Mr. Goldman is a fucker. She's preoccupied, reading an article in *People* about Fawn Hall. Fawn Hall was Oliver North's secretary, and she was supposed to shred the documents about Iran and Nicaragua but did not. The article is not about this, but about how Fawn Hall is not just a secretary but also a part-time model with a red sports car and a license plate that says FAWN 1. She drives around Washington, D.C., in this car with the windows down because she smokes. If there is a movie made about all of this Iran-Contra business, the article says, she could be played by Farrah Fawcett, or maybe Vanna White.

"She's so pretty," Deena says, looking at the picture.

Travis takes the magazine from Deena, shaking his head. "You're prettier," he says.

She smiles and places a raisin on the tip of his tongue.

I eat my yogurt and look at the clock. This is how it goes. I have to eat lunch with them when they stay on campus because they get mad if I don't, but when I do, they say things like this to each other, and they have to be touching or feeding each other at all times. Right now his hand is on her knee under the table. I can tell this just by the way they are looking at each other. This look between them has everything to do with their having sex in Ed Schwebbe's van every other day while I am sitting in algebra.

The protesters are still outside, the paint on their signs bleeding downward in the rain. They are all wearing jackets and scarves and hats, wrapped up like colorful mummies, and they have stopped chanting. Now they just talk to one another, holding the signs up with mittened hands.

Travis sees me watching them through the window, and he grins. One of his front teeth is crooked, yellow. This should make him look ugly, but it doesn't. "Your old buddies out there?" he asks, taking a bite of his sandwich.

"What?"

He rolls his eyes. "Your church friends. The people who used to come and pick you up in the station wagon. With the bumper sticker. I recognize the car."

Of course. I had not thought of this before, but of course Pastor Dave and Sharon are outside. I put down my yogurt, a wave of nausea passing through me.

"Maybe they'll cancel it," Deena says, turning a page of the magazine. "Biology, I mean. That's what I vote for."

Ms. Jenkins is on the other side of the cafeteria, eating a salad, her glasses pushed up into her hair. She catches me looking at her, and before I can look away, she smiles.

When school gets out it's still raining, and we have to wait under the portico for the buses to come. Traci Carmichael watches the protesters, her thin mouth curled at one end. "Idiots," she says to Libby. Libby nods in agreement.

At this very same moment, I hear one of them calling my name. I can tell from the voice that it's Sharon, even though she's wearing a ski jacket and a green scarf wrapped around most of her face. She holds a sign that says EVILution: DON'T BELIEVE THE LIE! In the other hand, she holds a Styrofoam cup.

She isn't pregnant yet. Harry Hopewell didn't help.

Pastor Dave stands next to her, holding an umbrella over both their heads. She touches him on the shoulder and points at me. He waves, taking care to keep the umbrella steady. They start to walk toward me but stop when they get to the sidewalk. "You have to come over here to talk to us, honey," he yells, waving me toward them. "We're not allowed to cross the sidewalk." They stay right there, their toes on the edge of the grass. Traci and Libby turn around, verifying that yes, he is speaking to me.

I pull on the hood of my jacket and step out from underneath the portico, moving toward them, but not all the way, stopping well before the sidewalk.

"It's so good to see you!" Pastor Dave calls out. "We've missed you so much, Evelyn. Hey, do you need an umbrella? We've got plenty in the car."

I shake my head and show him the folded-up umbrella in my hand. "I'm just going to the bus."

They both nod, still smiling. They are getting hurt, I think, wondering why I am not coming closer, crossing over the invisible line. "How's your grandmother?" Sharon yells, her hands cupped around her mouth.

"Good," I say. I turn around to see the windows of Ms. Jenkins's classroom. She could be looking down from them, but she isn't. "Good."

"Good," Pastor Dave says, his eyes steady on my face. "Would you mind telling her what we're doing out here?" He points behind him, at the people carrying signs. "She's welcome to join us. We'll need all the help we can get in the next two weeks."

"I'll tell her," I say, turning around with a wave. "Well, that's my bus."

"We could use your help too," he calls out. But I am already walking toward the bus, and I pull my hood closer around my head, pretending I don't hear.

If Eileen could see the way that Travis acts in algebra now, she would say he was being a pill. *That little pill,* she would say, shaking her head. Meaning his behavior is hard to take.

He comes to algebra now because he has to, but he does little things that probably make Mr. Goldman wish he would have just let him stay outside, smoking with Ed Schwebbe in the snow. Travis has joined forces with Ray Watley. They each sneeze loudly every five minutes and say "Bless you" to each other every single time. He doesn't do his homework. He doesn't even bring his book.

After three days of this, Mr. Goldman balks. "Travis," he says, "where's your book?"

Travis takes his time responding, his fish eyes moving slowly around the room. "Forgot it," he says.

Mr. Goldman rests his hands on his waist, leaning heavily on one foot. "Okay," he says. He walks back to Mr. Sellers's desk and pulls an algebra book out of one of the drawers. The drawer squeaks loudly, but Mr. Sellers doesn't wake up. "Here you go," he says. "We're on page two thirty-six."

Ray Watley sneezes.

"Bless you, Ray," Travis says.

Deena's eyes catch mine. Travis sneezes.

"Bless you, Travis," Ray says.

Traci Carmichael rolls her eyes, so Libby does too. Mr. Goldman goes back to the chalkboard, where he has drawn a graph with red and blue chalk. He is talking quickly, chopping off the words the way he always does, his hands moving in front of him. I like the way he talks about math, all breathy and excited, like he is letting you in on a secret and you are lucky to be able to hear it.

But only a minute later, he stops talking. "You going to open that book, Travis?"

Travis looks down at the cover of the book, as if he is considering this question for the first time. He yawns and leans his head to the right. "In a while," he says.

Mr. Goldman nods, scratching the back of his neck. "Go ahead and open it now."

Travis opens his book to the first page. Ray Watley sneezes again.

"Bless you, Ray."

Mr. Goldman looks down at his shiny shoes, his mouth moving as if he is trying to do some sort of deep-breathing exercise. "Okay," he says, clapping his hands together one time, "let's try this. How about I give you guys the rest of class to work through the problems in this chapter in groups of three. That was going to be your homework for tonight, but you can do it now. If you have questions about tomorrow's test, just come up, and I'll help you individually."

This is quite a deal, a generous offer, and we know it. Deena and I move our desks together, and she nods at Travis to join us. But he's still looking down at the first page of his book, which has nothing on it but the acknowledgments and copyright dates, and he's dropping his pencil on his desk over and over again, hard enough for it to bounce up on its eraser. Traci looks up from her paper, nudging Libby.

"*Fifth grade,*" she whispers.

It's true. I hate to admit it, but she's right. Mr. Goldman waits five minutes before he says anything, and when he does, his voice is quiet, calm. "Travis, you can work by yourself, or you can work in a group. But I want you to use this time to work on your assignment. You can't just sit there."

Travis catches the pencil in midair and points it at Mr. Goldman. "I'll do it later."

It's so quiet now that all you can hear is the *ticktock* of the large electric clock on the wall, counting off the seconds, and the sound of Travis's pencil bouncing on his desk.

"I want you to do it now, Travis."

He bounces his pencil again. "Well, I want to do it later."

Ray sneezes again, though even Travis has given this up by now. That's how dumb it is.

"Then you can leave. You're absent, okay? You're not here today mentally, so you're not here at all." He walks to the door and opens it, one arm gesturing toward the hallway. "Just go."

Travis laughs, tucking a stray curl behind his ear. "Wow. First you want me to come back, then you want me to leave. You need to make up your mind, Mr. Goldman."

We wait, watching Mr. Goldman's face. He looks tense, tired. "Dude," he says suddenly, his hands resting in front of him, palms up, as if he were waiting to catch something falling from above. "I'm trying to work with you here, okay? It's my job to teach you, and I want to do that. But you've got to work with me, okay?"

Travis remains seated, but his face changes. There is almost a smile, and I hope this is a sign that maybe he is finally starting to see that Mr. Goldman is trying, that he is acting dumb.

"Okay?" Mr. Goldman tries again.

Travis tilts his head to the side. "Um, did you just call me dude, Mr. Goldman? Dude?"

Ray sneezes.

Mr. Goldman looks down at the floor, rubbing his chin. "Just get out, Travis. Just leave."

"Okay, dude." Travis stands up slowly and takes his backpack off the back of his chair. He gives Mr. Goldman the thumbs-up. "Right on, my man! Out of sight!"

Everyone is looking at Travis except for Mr. Goldman, who is looking at some point over Travis's head toward the back of the room. He walks away from the door before Travis can get to it, and sits back down at his desk.

"You got it, dude. Far out," Travis says, flashing the peace sign from the doorway. Ray Watley is laughing, but no one else is.

Mr. Goldman doesn't look up. "Don't come back until we talk."

"Okay, dude." Travis waves, his backpack slung over one shoulder, opening the door. "Bye, dude. Righteous, man. Righteous."

And then, the terrible thing happens. One of the straps of Travis's backpack catches on the doorknob as he is walking out, and since the other strap is already around his shoulder, part of his body is jerked back as the rest of him tries to go forward. His head hits the doorknob on his way to the floor, and everyone hears him yelp.

Deena's hand goes to her mouth. Traci laughs, one loud *Ha!,* but the rest of us just sit there, looking down at Travis hanging from the doorknob, his face twisted with pain.

Mr. Goldman gets up quickly, moving to the door. "You all right?" he asks.

"I'm fine," Travis says. He keeps his eyes lowered as he stands up, rubbing his head. He does not look up once as he unhooks the strap of his backpack so he can try to exit again.

That evening, a little gray car pulls into the parking lot of Treeline Colonies, moving slowly in front of Unit B, the driver squinting at the numbers on the doors. It takes me a moment to see it is Mr. Goldman, because he is wearing a hat and a black fisherman's jacket and no tie. I close my book, and move closer to the window.

He walks up the concrete stairs to the Rowleys' door and knocks. Mrs. Rowley answers, Jackie O barking in her arms. She shuts the door, and Mr. Goldman walks back to his car in the parking lot, his arms folded across his chest. I think maybe she's lied to him, told him Travis wasn't home, but the door opens again, and Travis comes out, yawning and pulling a sweatshirt down over his head. He takes his time coming down the stairs. Mr. Goldman sits on the bumper of his car, one foot resting on the knee of the other leg, leaving enough room for Travis. But Travis stays standing, looking at his shoes, his hands pushed deep inside the pockets of his jeans.

Mr. Goldman talks, one arm moving back and forth between them, like a bridge for his words to fall onto and bounce more easily into Travis's ears. They stay like this for a long time, Mr. Goldman's breath turning to steam in the cooling March evening. When the sun starts to set, I have to squint to see their faces, turning gray and then shadowed against the dusking sky. Travis leans on one foot and then the other. And then, maybe just because he's tired of standing, he sits.

fourteen

TRAVIS WON'T TELL ME EXACTLY what was said between him and Mr. Goldman. He only says they have worked out a plan: he will come in and work with Mr. Goldman during study hall for each day of algebra he has missed this year—thirteen last semester, nine this semester. If he does this, and if he passes the final exam, Mr. Goldman will move him right up to tenth-grade math with the rest of the class, which is good, because already he's a year behind.

"He's not so bad," Travis says.

But of course I already know that Mr. Goldman isn't so bad. This is now something to worry about, though, because it turns out he is on Ms. Jenkins's side about the evolution business. I know this because Traci Carmichael raised her hand in the middle of math and asked him what he thought about Ms. Jenkins's teaching us evolution, even though that's about science, not math. He was handing out our quizzes, still warm from the photocopier, and he smiled and said, "Ah, Ms. Jenkins, the Copernicus of Kansas. I wish her the best," and Traci smiled back like all of a sudden that made them friends.

I have looked up evolution in the encyclopedia in the library, and now I know why they're fighting, why the protesters are mad. Evolution says that we came from monkeys, not Adam and Eve, which is what the Bible says. I don't know what to think about this.

All ninth graders have been given a letter from Dr. Queen, written on lavender stationery to take home to our parents. It was stapled closed when Ms. Jenkins handed them out, but I opened mine as soon as the bell rang.

Dear concerned parents,

I'm writing this letter to let you know how we at KHS hope to resolve the debate surrounding our science curriculum. Although I appreciate the many parents who have called in to share their concerns with me over this issue, I have decided not to prohibit our teachers from teaching evolutionary theory. Our science faculty points out that human evolution is overwhelmingly supported by the larger scientific community as the best possible explanation of the origin of the human race, and also that students will need to be familiar with this theory should they go on to college. Our science faculty feels strongly that the scientific evidence that supports this theory must be presented to all students, regardless of an individual student's religious beliefs.

However, since so many parents and religious groups have expressed concern over the possibility that teaching evolution could also be used to undermine religious teachings, I have asked a member of our teaching faculty who is active in his local church to sit in on the biology classes that will focus on Darwin and evolution. It is my hope that Mr. Jim Leubbe will represent other views in the classroom, and that his presence will ensure that no one's personal views are attacked, demeaned, or dismissed.

Several parents have also suggested that the Genesis story of creation at least be given equal time in our science curriculum. Although I appreciate the willingness to compromise that this suggestion shows, the science faculty has made it clear that teaching the Genesis story should not take place in the science classroom. It is my hope that by next year we can have an elective course on religion offered to seniors to counterbalance the heavy emphasis on science and math for sophomores and juniors.

Sincerely,
Dr. Joan B. Queen
Principal, KHS

I thought Dr. Queen's letter was okay until I got to the part about Mr. Leubbe sitting in on Ms. Jenkins's classes. Mr. Leubbe is the gym teacher, and lately, when we have been running laps around the gym, he blows his whistle and says, "You-all run like orangutans! I'm going to talk to Ms. Jenkins about her monkey theory. Maybe there's something to it after all!" He is just joking, but this kind of joking does not go over well with Ms. Jenkins, who hardly laughs at all, and when she does it is just a lifting up of one side of her mouth so you have to be watching carefully to even see it.

Mr. Leubbe graduated from Kerrville High only ten years ago, and there are still pictures of him in the trophy case, wearing a Kerrville High football jersey and kneeling, his football helmet at his side. If he didn't have blond hair, he would look exactly like Superman. He has that kind of jaw. When we complain about having to go outside for gym class because it's too hot or too cold, he tells stories about playing football in freezing snow, and he says we should quit our whining because when he had to play outside in bad weather he loved every minute of it.

"Those were the days," he likes to say, his hands behind his head so his big arms form a triangle at each side. "I'm jealous of you all, of your youth. I really am."

Mr. Leubbe saved someone's life once. Two years ago, a car went off a bridge on the Kaw River, just when Mr. Leubbe happened to be jogging by, and he took off his running shirt and jumped in, even while everyone else was still just standing around, trying to think of what to do. He just went home after it happened, but enough people saw what he did and the governor came down from Topeka to give him a medal and there was a picture of him in the newspaper.

LOCAL FOOTBALL LEGEND SHOWS VALOR OFF THE FIELD

Mr. Leubbe told the newspaper that he didn't think of himself as a hero because he was just doing what anyone would have done, which was kind of a dumb thing to say, because there were a bunch of other people standing around when the car went into the river, and they didn't do anything.

He is pretty nice as a gym teacher. He picks teams for us when we play basketball, and I think he does this because he feels bad for the people who never get picked. He didn't make me climb the rope because I couldn't even get myself up past the knot at the bottom, but at the end of class, he took me aside and said, "Listen, Bucknow. I'm not going to make you climb the rope, because at this point, I don't think you can. You've got chicken arms, okay? I'm not saying that to be mean. But there it is. You've got to start developing your arm strength, or what's going to happen is you're going to become one of those little old ladies who can't even push their grocery carts in front of them. I'm just telling you, okay?"

The only problem I have with him is the only problem almost everyone has with him, which is that he likes to sneak up on people and scare them. He is very good at it, and you never even know he's there until his fingers are on the backs of your elbows, his voice loud and startling in your ear, saying *"Gotcha"* so loud your heart stops right where it is.

I jump when he does it. Everyone does. Even the large, deep-voiced football players, juniors and seniors, who like Mr. Leubbe very much when he is standing in front of them, jump when he comes up from behind. They laugh, but they step away from him quickly, and you can tell they wish he wouldn't do it anymore.

Knowing that he can be behind you at any time makes gym class somewhat frightening. We run laps looking over our shoulders. Even in the hallways, at lunch, you have to be careful. He snuck up behind Dr. Queen in the cafeteria once and made her drop her tray.

"Whoa, whoa, sorry there, Joan," he said, helping to pick up her Tater Tots, rolling on the floor. "Maybe a little too much coffee these days?"

Dr. Queen's hands were shaking, one of them over her heart.

He is also a back slapper. I think he does it to be nice, because usually he does it when he is making a joke or telling you good luck when it's your turn to run relays. He slaps hard and fast, usually three times, right between the shoulders. You can hear the slap echoing off the walls of the gymnasium, and when he does it to me, I can feel it in my teeth.

He used to slap Mr. Goldman on the back, but he doesn't do it anymore. Mr. Goldman slapped him back. I saw it happen. They were walking outside together at the end of the day, looking like they were getting along, Mr. Leubbe wearing his red shirt and his whistle around his neck, almost two heads taller than Mr. Goldman. Mr. Leubbe was saying something, and then he started slapping Mr. Goldman on the back. He was smiling, but he slapped him so hard that Mr. Goldman pitched forward for a moment, his tie lifting up off his shirt. Mr. Goldman straightened up and slapped Mr. Leubbe on the back, just once, but hard enough for us to hear it down by the buses, and hard enough to make the gum that had been in Mr. Leubbe's mouth fly out and land on the sidewalk in front of him. Mr. Leubbe smiled and slapped him again, three times, and Mr. Goldman slapped him back again, smiling too, and for the first time in my life, I saw Mr. Leubbe wince.

So he doesn't slap Mr. Goldman anymore, but he still does it to Ms. Jenkins, especially after he makes a joke to her about us running laps like orangutans. When she doesn't smile, he keeps slapping, and says, "I'm just joking with you, Constance. No harm meant to you or your monkey theory."

And still she doesn't smile. But she almost does later, when she tells us that contrary to what Mr. Leubbe believes, it isn't her monkey theory. She'd like to take credit, she says, the half smile rising, but really, she's not the one who came up with the idea.

The first day went okay. Mr. Leubbe stood next to Ms. Jenkins while she took attendance, his hands on his hips, wearing the same clothes he wore that morning in gym, a red shirt and tan shorts, the whistle on a string around his neck.

"Look, troops," he said. "I'm just here to make sure everybody gets a fair shake, okay? That means Mr. Charles Darwin *and* the man upstairs." His eyes moved across the room, to the endangered species posters, to the bees buzzing in their plastic hive. "I'm not going to pretend to like this monkey business any more than a lot of your parents. Nonetheless, I want everybody to be good sports, to be polite to Ms. Jenkins and to myself and to one another. As far as I'm concerned, we might disagree, but we're all on the same team, okay?"

Ms. Jenkins must have seen what was coming, his big arm rising up behind her. She tried to step away in time, out of arm's reach. But he got her, right between the shoulders, one, two, *three,* and all you had to do was look at her eyes when he got to the third slap to see that as far as she was concerned, they weren't on the same team at all.

But for the rest of the class, there wasn't a problem. He just sat in the back row, eating trail mix out of a Ziploc bag, making notes in his notebook. He's too big for one of our chairs, but he sat in one anyway, his knees sticking up on each side. Ms. Jenkins talked about finches and the Galápagos Islands, and he didn't seem too worried about anything she had to say about that.

But the next day, she started talking about "our watery origins," and that's when the fight started.

"So when did monkeys first start talking?" he called out, not even raising his hand. "That's what I want to know." He was smiling at all of us, like we were all with him, all of us in on the same joke. He popped a raisin in his mouth. "And how come some of them stopped?"

Ms. Jenkins had been facing the chalkboard, and she flinched when he said this, the chalk in her hand making a small white mark on the board. It was like he had snuck up behind her, even though, really, she must have remembered he was back there.

"No," she said, turning around. "Monkeys didn't talk, Mr. Leubbe. That's not the argument. The argument is that our lineage can be traced back to a shared ancestry with the simian family." She gestured at the chart on the wall. "Studies of human DNA and simian DNA have supported this idea."

He was quiet again until the next day. Ms. Jenkins was talking about how *Homo sapiens* came before *Homo erectus*. He didn't really actually say anything, but we could hear him giggling in the back row. We all turned around again, and finally, he got so loud that Ms. Jenkins had to stop talking.

"Sorry," he said, his hands raised in front of him. "It's just that..." He shook his head, his eyes wide, like Rodney Dangerfield telling a joke. "I don't know about you guys, but I don't know if I'm comfortable being called *homo* anything."

Ms. Jenkins scratched her hair. Even after she was done, a large strand of it remained upright, rising up toward the ceiling like a puff of smoke. Then she put her chalk down and walked out of the room.

Traci Carmichael called her mother from a pay phone at lunch, and by the next day, there was another note for us to take home to our parents, on light green stationery, this time not from Dr. Queen but from the Kerrville County School Board.

On April 4, 1987, we will hold a town meeting in the KHS gymnasium at seven-thirty, The purpose of this meeting is to let the community express its views on how different theories on the origins of life should be presented in KHS classrooms. The school board will be arriving at a decision the following week.

Now the Channel 6 news has come to the school parking lot, and when I go home, Dr. Queen is on television. "It's out of my hands now," she says to reporters, holding up her hands like she wants to prove that really, there's nothing there.

Eileen has already found out about the meeting. She calls to tell me she is driving up from Wichita to meet with some people from the Second Ark. They will pick me up in the church van at seven, just before the meeting. "Don't you worry about that Jenkins woman," she says. "We'll take care of her."

"I don't think kids are allowed to go to the meeting," I say, my hands tight around the receiver. My mother and Samuel are in the front room watching *ALF,* but my mother hears me say this and looks up at me, one eyebrow raised.

"They can't keep you out, baby," Eileen says. "It's your school, after all. You have the right to be there. And we're bringing a little surprise for you too."

I have to act like this is a good thing, because I love Eileen, but I don't want my surprise, and I don't want to go to the meeting. I have secretly read the chapter on evolution in my science book, even though we are not supposed to yet, and there are pictures of fossils and skeletons, human bones too old to be Adam and Eve. I have believed everything Ms. Jenkins has told us this year about mitochondria and ATP and chromosomes and the rain forests in Brazil. She's never lied to us about anything before, and I don't see why she would start now.

But if she isn't lying, then Eileen is. And then that means that maybe Genesis is a story that somebody made up. But if you start to believe that, then you also might think there is a chance that no one is upstairs, wearing headphones and looking out for us, choosing good from bad. Maybe we are just on our own. But then if we aren't, and you listen for a minute to what Ms. Jenkins is saying and start to wonder, and you happen to get run over by a bus just at that moment, well then.

It would be easier, maybe, if you just didn't think at all.

My mother is doing this stupid thing all of a sudden where she is letting me do whatever I want. I have emphasized repeatedly to her that not just Eileen is coming to pick me up for the school board meeting, but Pastor Dave and Sharon as well, and people coming up from Wichita.

"The people from Eileen's church," I say again, slowly, so she can understand. "And Pastor Dave. From the Second Ark."

"Huh," she says. But she only looks at Sam. He has been coughing for the last three days, and she is trying to get him to swallow a spoonful of Robitussin. He doesn't want it, and he keeps turning his head, swinging at her with his good arm.

"They're coming to pick me up in a van," I add, thinking this will somehow scare her more.

She turns to me, holding Sam's arm away from her face. "Evelyn, are you saying you don't want to go?"

There is something about her face when she says this that infuriates me. Maybe it's just her nose, but I feel like she's laughing at me, or like she will, the second I leave the room. One of the cats moves in a slow figure-eight pattern around my feet. "I'm saying I thought you didn't want me to go anywhere with them. Geez. Make up your mind."

She cups her finger and thumb around Samuel's chin, forcing him to open it wide enough for the spoon. "If you don't want to go with them, you can just tell Eileen. Just call her up and tell her you're not comfortable."

"I didn't say that. I didn't say that I'm not comfortable."

Sam screams when he tastes the cough syrup, and tries to spit it back out, but she tilts his chin up and gives him some water from his sippy cup. "Well, good then," she says. "Have a nice time."

My surprise is a blue T-shirt that says LIGHT on it in white letters, so big on me it goes down almost to my knees. Eileen slips it over my head before I am in the van.

"Perfect," she says, leaning down to kiss me on the cheek. "Just perfect." She is wearing a T-shirt that is exactly the same, only hers says BE.

When she opens the door for me, the interior light comes on, and I see that everyone else in the van has a blue T-shirt also, each with a different word printed on the front. The woman sitting next to the window has a shirt that says THERE, and the man next to her has a shirt that says LET.

"Let . . . there . . . be . . ." I read, trying to sound excited.

"Light, kitten," Eileen says, buckling her seat belt. "That's you."

Sharon is sitting in the passenger seat, and she reaches back to squeeze my hand. "Evelyn, honey, it's so good to see you! Are you sure your mom doesn't want to come?"

"I'm sure."

Pastor Dave is in the driver's seat, and he says the important thing is that I am here, especially since I am LIGHT. "We'd look pretty silly without you," he says, winking at me in the rearview mirror. His shirt says GOD, and Sharon's says SAID. He tells Sharon to show me the back. She leans into the aisle between their seats to show me a picture of a monkey wearing glasses and reading a book. There's a slash through the whole picture, like in the ad for *Ghostbusters*. I reach behind my own shirt to feel if this picture is ironed onto the back of mine. It is.

"I like your hair," Sharon says, turning back around so she can see me. "It's really cute."

This is a lie, what Sharon is telling me. My hair does not look cute. Deena convinced me to let her try to do a home perm on my hair, and the rods she used were too small. Now my hair is so thick and curly on the bottom that it sticks out like a Christmas tree, like Gilda Radner's. It's okay for her because she's trying to be funny, but I'm not.

Deena and Travis are not coming to the school board meeting. Deena said no way was she going to school any time she didn't have to, and Travis, pulling her onto his lap, even though we were sitting in the cafeteria and Dr. Queen had been on the intercom just the week before saying there should be no public displays of affection on school grounds, said he was sure I would be fine on my own.

But I won't be fine. I can see that now, sitting in the van with all of them, Eileen's thin arm around my shoulders, her hands tapping along to the radio on the back of the seat. I won't be fine, and I'm not on my own.

I know that sometimes when you are really worried about something, it ends up not being nearly as bad as you think it will be, and you get to be relieved that you were just being silly, worrying so much over nothing. But sometimes it is just the opposite. It can happen that whatever you are worried about will be even worse than you could have possibly imagined, and you find out that you were right to be worried, and even that, maybe, you weren't worried enough.

There are more people at the meeting than I expected, people in suits I've never seen before, people in suits with notepads in their laps. There are newspaper reporters, and also two television news teams, one from Topeka, another from Wichita. When we come in, a photographer for one of the newspapers sees our shirts and asks if we can line up together for a picture before the meeting starts. I tell Eileen I have to go to the bathroom.

"Sure, honey," she says, smoothing my hair. "Go."

I don't really have to go, and when I get to the bathroom, I lock the door behind me and just stand there for a while, looking at myself in the mirror. The T-shirt is too big for me, and the blue is too bright. I look pale and washed out underneath it, smaller than I really am. The letters on the front are backwards in the mirror, and it looks as if it doesn't spell anything at all.

Someone knocks lightly on the door. "Evelyn, honey?" Eileen asks. "Are you okay? The meeting's about to start."

I open the door, looking up at her face, her crooked mouth, her worried eyes. She is already opening her knitting bag to look for an aspirin or a Tums or whatever I might need. I could ask her for anything. I could say, "Eileen, give me all of the money in your wallet." And she would. I could take the sweater she has been knitting for the last two months out of her bag and unravel it right in front of her, and she would only look at me and say, *Why are you doing this, kitten?* She has always loved me this much.

"I'm fine," I say, trying to smile.

The gym is completely full by the time we get back. Every chair is taken, and now people are lining up along the walls, sitting on the floor. But Pastor Dave was able to secure eight chairs in a row so people would be able to read our shirts in one complete sentence, left to right. Sharon waves to us, pointing at two empty seats, her pink coat spread over them.

I see a lot of parents, but not too many kids. Robby Hernandez is in front of us with his parents and little brothers and sisters, a priest on one side of them, two nuns on the other. Traci Carmichael sits on the other side of the aisle, between her mother and father. Her mother is frowning at us, wearing a skirt and matching red jacket, her blond hair up in a french twist. Traci's father wears khaki pants and a black sweater. His face is just like Traci's, the same thin lips and steady blue-gray eyes. I can feel all three of them watching us, taking in the T-shirts.

You are on the good side, I tell myself. *You are on the good side; they are on the bad. There is no reason for you to be embarrassed. Traci Carmichael has always been a bad person.*

The five members of the school board sit up front at a long table, facing a podium with a microphone. Dr. Queen is the first person to go up to the microphone, and even though she is usually frightening, people just keep talking and taking pictures, even after she has been standing there for a while, clearing her throat. She finally has to clap her hands together and say, *"Hey!"* and then the room goes quiet and everyone looks up.

She smiles, lowers her voice again. "I want to thank everyone for coming out tonight. If you signed up to speak, you'll get five minutes, and I'll wave this white flag when your time is up." She waves a little white flag over her head, still smiling, as if she were at a football game or a parade. She is dressed up, I notice, wearing a blue suit, and her hair looks like it's been recently clipped, the gray stripe exactly in the center. "I hope this meeting can be a productive exchange of ideas, and not a shouting match. I think we can do it if we try. My father used to tell me that it was important to show respect for others, particularly those you disagree with. I hope we can all remember that tonight."

Everybody nods and seems to agree with this, but Ms. Jenkins is the next person to go up to the microphone, and before she even says anything, people forget all about Dr. Queen's father and start booing. I hear Sharon humming "Onward Christian Soldiers" under her breath, and after a few notes, Eileen joins in.

"If you'll let me speak," Ms. Jenkins says, pushing her glasses back up on her face. She looks around the room, at our row of bright blue. I try to lean forward, hiding behind one of the nuns. "Listen, people," she says. "I'm just trying to teach your children what's commonly accepted in the larger scientific community, okay? Most scientists agree that *Homo sapiens* have been walking around on Earth for over half a million years, only after having evolved from simpler mammals through a process of natural selection. That's it, pure and simple."

Mr. Leubbe is sitting with his wife in the third row, and although Ms. Jenkins has said *"Homo,"* this time he doesn't even smile. But people start to boo again, and Mrs. Carmichael has to turn around, her fingers to her lips, and say, "Let's be adults."

I feel bad for Ms. Jenkins getting booed up there, dressed like a teacher, in a brown jacket that doesn't really match her pants, her hair sticking up the way it always does, so you know the people who don't like her are going to make fun of her for that too. She scans the audience with her small eyes, talking about carbon 14 and the difference between a hypothesis and a theory, not even having to look down at her notes. She speaks slowly, the way you would talk to someone either very young or not very smart, saying "Okay?" after each sentence. Every now and then, Traci's mother nods her french-twisted head and says, "Exactly."

I understand that what Ms. Jenkins is saying makes sense, but if I nod my head, even once, I will be on the same side as the Carmichaels, and on the opposite side of Jesus and Eileen. I try to map it out in my head the way you can do with a story problem in math, hoping to find a space on the same side as Eileen and Ms. Jenkins and Mr. Goldman, but not with Traci and her mother. But there is no space like that. The lines keep crossing over one another. They would have to be curvy to make it work.

"I'm just giving facts now, people, okay?" Ms. Jenkins says, holding up her hands. "Those are just facts, which is what I'm concerned with, as a science teacher. I don't barge into your churches Sunday mornings, so please, don't barge into my classroom." Dr. Queen waves the white flag then, and Ms. Jenkins walks away from the podium, but she keeps talking on the way back to her chair. "They've found fossils, okay? Nobody's making this stuff up."

Pastor Dave goes next. He begins his speech by thanking Ms. Jenkins for her illuminating introduction, but he says "illuminating" in a way that you know he didn't really think it was. He tells the school board they are making an important decision, that they are standing at a crucial fork in the road.

"The wisdom of thousands of years and the faith in a higher power is this way," he says, holding an arm out in one direction, "and some half-baked theory that tells children they come from slime is the other." He holds his other arm in the other direction, so that both are raised, and he stands just like this for a moment, like he is getting ready to hug someone, or maybe do a back flip. The newspaper photographers take pictures of him like this, and I know it is because his T-shirt says GOD, and he is standing by himself, his arms spread wide like that. Tomorrow people will look at the newspaper and think that Pastor Dave thinks he's God, not knowing that we're all down here making up the rest of the sentence.

Mr. Goldman goes up to the microphone next, and the Carmichaels clap and smile even before he says anything at all. He is wearing a white shirt and a bright green tie, but it's hard to tell if he tried to dress up or not because he looks exactly the same way he does in algebra, crisp and polished, smiling down at us with his straight white teeth.

"Good evening, folks," he says. "Um, I know I'm a newcomer, but still, I have to say right off the bat that the fact that this is even a controversy is . . . flooring me." He opens his mouth again to say something else, but for a moment, no words come out. "I'm . . . I'm having a hard time understanding how there can really be a debate in this day and age." He looks at us as if there should be some reaction, but there isn't. Everyone just keeps looking back at him, waiting. They don't know what side he's on.

"Of course we have to teach evolution," he says. People catch on, start booing. But Traci and her father clap, and Mrs. Carmichael, to my surprise, puts two fingers in her mouth and whistles.

"Look," he says, raising his voice, his hand over his heart, "I'm a religious person, too, okay? But you can't pretend those fossils don't exist. They do. You can't tell your children they don't and call it religion. You can't call it anything but lying. What about truth? What about intellectual curiosity?"

Eileen touches me on the knee. "Evelyn, honey, what's that man's name?"

I know, right away. I know about last names now. I pretend I don't hear her, even though she's right next to me, her nicotine breath warm on my cheek. I keep looking at Mr. Goldman, and I am thinking about Anne Frank, about whether Eileen would say she doesn't have any eyes and ears either.

She pokes me again. "What's his last name?"

I look at her carefully, watching her eyes. "Goldman."

She nods, a little smile on her crooked mouth.

Mr. Leubbe goes up to the microphone next. People start clapping before he even opens his mouth because everyone, even the people from the television crews, remember that he is the one who pulled the little girl out of the river. He has to hold up his hand to make everyone be quiet so he can talk, and he looks embarrassed. "Thanks," he says, raising the microphone. "Thanks. Um, since my colleague here said he had some trouble understanding what the controversy was, I'm going to try to clear it up."

People go crazy when he says this, clapping, saying, "You tell 'em, Jim!" He can't talk for a little while because people are so loud, and I don't know if this counts as part of his five minutes or not. "The controversy," he says, "for your information, is that a lot of people *around here* don't really take to their children being taught that Genesis is all a bunch of lies and in reality we all came from monkeys." When he says *around here,* he stretches it out a little, moving his hand in a tiny circle as if he were getting ready to throw a lasso. "Maybe in *other places* they're okay with that," he says. "But not *around here*."

People clap so much when he says this that his five minutes get taken up, and Dr. Queen looks at her watch and says, "I'm sorry, but we've got to move on." Pastor Dave stands up and says, "Wait a minute! That's not fair," and as soon as he does this, the photographers start taking pictures of him again.

Mrs. Carmichael goes up next. When she gets to the microphone, Traci's father takes a picture. She smiles when the flash goes off, but even when he's done, his camera back in his lap, she does not turn around and face the school board the way you are supposed to. Instead, she takes the microphone out of the holder, still facing us. The television crews come out from behind the table, moving in front of her quickly.

"Do you-all realize," she asks, "that the *entire nation* is laughing at us right now?" She pauses here, and it's almost like she's Pastor Dave in church, waiting for us to answer. "I've got friends from college on both coasts, calling me and laughing because Kerrville, Kansas, is on the national news. We look like a bunch of hicks." She shakes her head, looking directly at our row, at all of us in our blue T-shirts. "Do you know how hard they're laughing at us in New York?"

I try to picture it, people in taxicabs going past tall buildings, thinking about me and Eileen, shoulders shaking, their eyes wet with tears. *"They're so stupid,"* they would say to one another, eating hot dogs on the sidewalk, watching the Macy's Thanksgiving Day Parade. *"I can't believe they're so dumb!"*

Mrs. Carmichael steps away from the microphone, silent, her eyes closed. "Look. We all care about our children. That's why we're here. I love my daughter, and I want her to be able to apply to the best colleges when she graduates. And I don't want people laughing at her."

I am just sitting there, thinking about how much I don't like Mrs. Carmichael, about how I don't care about Traci's college applications at all, when all of a sudden I feel Eileen standing up next to me. I know this won't be a good thing. My hand moves quickly to her, but she jerks her arm away.

"Lady," she says, her voice surprisingly loud, "if you really love your daughters, you won't let them be led astray."

Both television cameras swing around, two dark eyeballs focusing on Eileen. Dr. Queen waves the white flag and tells Eileen to sit down and wait her turn.

She doesn't. She holds her arm out straight in front of her, pointing up at Mrs. Carmichael. "You think having people laugh at them on college applications or whatever is bad for them," she says, her voice wavering now, holding back a sob. "But how bad is it for them to risk spending eternity in hell?"

I am very still. Everyone else in the room, Mr. Goldman, the nuns, Traci, everyone, is watching us. I look at the cameras and pull on her arm. "Eileen. Please. It's not your turn."

Mrs. Carmichael shakes her head, her hand over her eyes. "Okay, this is exactly what I'm talking about." She looks at Eileen. "This is a civilized meeting with rules, ma'am, not a tent revival. You'll have to wait your turn."

But now Eileen is really crying, tears on her face. The cameras move closer to our row. "I come all the way up here from Wichita to protect my little granddaughter, who I love so much," she says. She reaches down and grabs my arm by the wrist, trying to pull me up beside her. I pull back. She lets my hand go before I think she will, and I hit myself in the face with my own hand.

No one moves. I hear the newspaper cameras clicking, taking pictures. I tug on her arm again. "It's not your turn," I whisper. "You have to sit down."

She sort of falls back into her chair when I do this, finally silent. Mrs. Carmichael says she should get to start her five minutes again, and Dr. Queen waves the white flag over her head and says it's only fair. Mrs. Carmichael doesn't look at Eileen while she talks, and Eileen doesn't look at her, either. For the rest of the meeting, she just sits next to me, crying quietly, her hand wrapped tightly around mine.

By the time we are back in the van, going home on the highway, Eileen has fully recovered. She is even smiling, squeezing my hand in her lap. Sharon tells her she admired her courage, and Pastor Dave says she stole the show.

"Really?" she asks, her hand over her mouth. "I hope so. That lady just made me so darn mad. I had to say something."

Pastor Dave agrees, and says he found Mrs. Carmichael's apparent superiority complex more than a bit ironic. I look out the window, at the dark sky and full, yellow moon. This is all I can do. People will see me hit myself in the face on television, wearing the blue shirt. They will ask me about it tomorrow at school.

"That one fellow that said he was religious and oh so educated was Jewish," Eileen says. "Did you notice that?"

I sit very still, keeping my eyes on the moon.

Pastor Dave nods and sighs, turning on his blinker to switch lanes. "Not a big surprise. There's all kinds of religious." He lowers his voice. "The blood be upon them."

The van is too hot all of sudden, too small. I reach over Eileen's legs, crack open a window. I know what Pastor Dave is saying is from the Bible, the part where Jesus is killed on the cross. But it's not right. It's almost funny, trying to picture Mr. Goldman with blood on him, on his hands, on one of his crisp white shirts and colorful ties. *What's this?* he would say, looking down at his shirt. *What's this mess?*

"Evelyn, honey," Eileen asks. "You okay?"

"I'm fine."

I want to get out of the van, and walk home by myself underneath the yellow moon. There is no blood. It says that in the Bible, but that's just because somebody wrote it down. I could write something down, and that wouldn't make it true. I want to say this to Eileen, to Pastor Dave. But if I try to, they will just come up with more quotes. They will just keep quoting and quoting and quoting until there is nothing left to say about anything at all.

Eileen smiles at me, smoothing my hair off my face with one of her small hands. I look at her hands, and then down at my own. My hands are larger than hers, my fingers longer.

I watch cars pass us on the highway, their headlights illuminating the inside of the van, shining on our faces. I could just as easily be in any one of those cars, going in the other direction. And then this van would not be anything special to me; it would be just two headlights on the highway, a pulse of light I would not even think about, something else to pass on the road.

fifteen

WHEN WE GO BACK TO school the next week, Dr. Queen tells us that if you want to be in Ms. Jenkins's class, you have to have a permission slip from your parents saying it's okay. If it isn't okay, you can just sign up for an extra hour of study hall or gym. This way, Dr. Queen says, everybody can be happy for a change.

But no one is happy. Both sides have people standing in front of the post office and grocery stores, handing out petitions.

"It's better than nothing," Eileen says. She is finishing the hem of a skirt she made for me, and she keeps the pins she isn't using clamped in the good side of her mouth, pushing me in slow circles in front of the mirror in my mother's room. The skirt is very pretty, dark red with purple flowers hand-embroidered at the knee. "At least they can't force that Jenkins woman down your throats."

My mother looks at me but says nothing. She does not smirk, or even smile, and I am grateful for this. She signed the permission slip I brought home last week.

Eileen says what they should really do, if they want to be fair about it, is offer a Bible study class for credit, and let us take that instead of sitting an extra hour in study hall, twiddling our so-called opposable thumbs. But she doesn't think the school is interested in being fair at all. She says you can take one look at that Jenkins woman and know that her idea of fair would be for us to be fed to lions in the middle of the Colosseum.

"I just hope her monkeys are there to save her at her moment of judgment," Eileen says, but she says this in a way so you know that, really, she hopes they aren't.

It's summer again, and Oliver North is on television all the time now, wearing his Marine uniform, getting yelled at by senators, his eyes filling up with tears when he talks about how much he loves America. They have canceled a lot of the daytime soap operas so we can see this, but my mother says really Iran-Contra is just another soap opera, going on and on and on, only this one doesn't have any women in it unless you count Fawn Hall and the mothers in Nicaragua with their arms chopped off.

But she can't stop watching it. She folds the laundry in front of the television, throws balled-up socks and underwear at the screen when Oliver North says something she doesn't like, which is pretty much every time he opens his mouth.

But not everyone is mad the way she is. Just from walking around I know that someone, somewhere, is making T-shirts that say GOD BLESS OLIVER NORTH, and a lot of people are wearing them.

We have renamed one of the cats Ollie, because he is on the television all the time too, sitting on top of it, his fluffy orange tail hanging over the screen. Sometimes my mother moves him off so we can see the real Ollie, but then Samuel starts screaming. Just like he likes us to have different things on our heads, he likes the cat up on top of the television set. We don't know why. Not too much has changed with him. His eyes are still a glassy, brilliant shade of blue, and he still doesn't look at us with them. We know he can see, because when the television is on, he stares at it, and he cries when we shut it off. He makes his screeching sound when something big happens on television, cars exploding, guns firing, anything loud. But you can stand right next to him, waving your arms and shouting his name, and he won't even blink. My mother says sometimes he looks at her—at her, not at the glitter hat—but I think she could be imagining it. Or it could have just been a coincidence. She could have been standing where he happened to be looking.

I know I am supposed to love my brother, but sometimes he is just like a big, limp doll, only he can scream and needs his diaper changed for real. He doesn't talk. When he's hungry or tired, he can scream so loud that you think that you're the one screaming, but that's it. No words. He's getting bigger too, not as big as a four-year-old should be, but big enough so that my mother, after carrying him around on her hip for a full day, winces when she sets him down.

My mother has called back the women from the university. They did not come back themselves, but sent a tall, snub-nosed graduate student to our apartment the next day. Her name is Verranna Hinckle, and she wears only turtlenecks, a different color every day. On her first visit, she looked right at my mother and said there was a chance Samuel would never talk. She said my mother should watch for any attempt he made to communicate, not just by talking, but by his hands or his eyes, even his feet.

"If he gives you a flick of the wrist," Verranna Hinckle told us, flicking her own, "assume it's a wave. Take any inch he gives you and stretch it into a mile. Once he understands that it's possible to communicate, that you're out there and listening, that's half the battle."

"Okay," my mother said, nodding quickly. "That makes sense."

So now she pretends that Samuel is pointing at things, even though really he isn't. His hand is still shaped like E.T.'s, one long finger sticking straight out, and if his arm happens to flail in a certain direction so that this finger is aimed at something—a book, a fork, a potholder, one of the cats—she gets up and brings whatever it is to him right away.

"This is a potholder, Samuel," she says, kneeling down beside him. "It's soft, isn't it? Is this what you were pointing at? Is this what you wanted?"

I change the television channel with my foot, watching him out of the corner of my eye. Nothing. She points at the potholder herself, tapping it with her finger, shaking her head so the glitter on the red hat will flicker in the light. "Potholder. I'm pointing at a potholder."

He looks up at the red glitter hat, his mouth open, drool sliding down his chin. The cats crouch behind my mother, their eyes large and dilated, focused on the potholder.

But she doesn't stop. She takes pictures of various objects in the house and tapes them to the back of a cereal box, their names printed in large letters underneath: TELEVISION, BED, RADIO, BATHROOM, DRINK, FOOD. Twice a day, she sits down next to his beanbag, the radio in one hand, the cereal box in the other.

"This is the radio, Samuel. Do you hear the music?" She places his hand on the radio, letting him feel the vibrations, and then turns it off. "This is a picture of the radio. If you want the radio, you have to point to the picture. See?" She points at the radio. "I'm pointing at the radio. That means I'd like to have it on." She turns on the radio. "Now you try, honey. Okay? Now you."

Samuel stares at the floor, unmoved, his finger in his mouth.

When we go back to school in the fall, there are large yellow posters in the hallway that say HEY SOPHOMORES! LET TRACI C. BE YOUR VOICE IN STUDENT COUNCIL! next to an enormous picture of Traci in a Guess? sweatshirt, smiling so you can see her braces. Libby Masterson is running for vice president, and doesn't get a picture.

When Travis sees these posters, he is able to keep a straight face and point out that it makes sense Satan should seek offices of power at an early age. When no one is looking, he draws a red tail coming over Traci's shoulders, arching her eyebrows so she looks as evil as we know she truly is.

"Don't," Deena says, trying to take his pen. "That's immature."

I get out another pen, give Traci a set of fangs.

New posters go up the next day. At lunch, Traci and Libby hand out Xeroxed copies of her campaign promises:

VOTE FOR TRACI C!

SHE WILL WORK FOR:

* Sophomores getting to vote for the theme of Homecoming and Prom!

* Making miniskirts (for girls) and shorts (for guys) okay when the weather is warm!!

* Allowing fast-food chains to open booths in the cafeteria, with a portion of their profits going back to Student Council Events and Planning!!!!

"Here you go, Evelyn!" Traci says, smiling at me with her metal teeth. I take the paper and throw it away while she is still watching. Travis does the same thing. Deena won't do it though. She takes one of the flyers from Traci and says thank you, reading it over slowly.

"Kiss ass," Travis says, kicking her lightly on the back of her knee.

Deena shrugs, opening her Thermos. "She's never been mean to me."

"That's because you haven't been here long enough," I say. Travis and I give each other knowing glances. We, on the other hand, have.

There are a lot of things like this now, things that Travis and I understand that Deena does not. Like French. And imaginary numbers. Deena failed algebra and has Mr. Goldman again, but Travis passed the final exam, so now he's in geometry with me. Mr. Goldman and Travis are friends now, and when they see each other in the hallway, Travis gives him the peace sign and says, "Right on, dude," like everything that happened between them the day he hit his head on the doorknob is now just a joke for them to laugh at together.

Travis goes to all his classes this year, not just math, which means no more Dairy Queen or anything else for Deena in the middle of the afternoon. She isn't happy about this. She says it's hard to get through a full day of school, now that she's gotten so used to taking breaks. But it isn't like she can go anywhere without him; there is nowhere to go and no way to get there, so sometimes she doesn't come to school at all.

Her father sent her a television for her room for Christmas, and when I go over to her apartment after school to give her her homework, she is usually sitting up in bed watching MTV, sometimes eating ice cream. She makes me a bowl and we watch videos together for a while. I like watching videos, and I wish we had cable so we could have MTV too, but after watching them for an hour, I get sick of them. But Deena can just sit there all day, no problem, going back and forth between MTV and soap operas with her remote control.

When she does come to school, she doesn't pay attention. She acts like she's listening to the teachers when they talk, taking notes, but really she is drawing flowers in vases or using her calligraphy pen to write things like *"Mrs. Fredina Rowley, Mr. and Mrs. Travis Rowley, Deena Sobrepena Schultz Rowley, Mrs. Deena Schultz Rowley."* When the teachers ask her questions, she looks up, startled, as if she isn't sure where she is, and says she doesn't know.

• • •

I wake up late on a Saturday and come out to the front room to see Samuel in his beanbag, his eyes open, my mother kneeling at his feet. Various objects surround them on the floor: the radio, plastic measuring cups, a box of plastic wrap, my mother's winter coat. She stands up when she sees me, the glitter hat crooked on her head. "Evelyn," she says, her hand on my arm. "Look what he's doing."

I look at Samuel. He is sitting in his beanbag, eyes glassy, mouth open and drooling.

"That's really neat, Mom."

She slaps me on the shoulder, hard enough to hurt. "Just wait. Wait."

We both stand there for maybe half a minute, watching Samuel sit. But then, slowly, his arm begins moving upward, his hand dangling in such a way that his E.T. finger appears to be pointing at the kitchen.

"See?" she says, moving toward him. "See?" She follows the line from his finger to the telephone on the kitchen wall. She picks it up and walks toward him, stretching the cord behind her. "Telephone. This is the telephone." She looks up at me, the glitter hat still crooked on her head. "He knows."

I look back at Samuel. His eyes are staring over our heads, at nothing. I'm not sure about this, and I don't know what to say. But again his hand moves, his finger this time pointing in the direction of the brown love seat in the corner of the room. My mother nods quickly at him and gets behind it. "Give me a hand with this," she says.

I hesitate, putting the phone back in its cradle. "This is kind of making a mess."

She snaps her fingers, the way a rude person would call a waiter at a restaurant. "Just do it, okay?"

I get on the other side of the love seat, and we push it toward him, the wheels snagging on the carpet, two cats still asleep on the cushions, going along for the ride. When we get it within arm's reach of Samuel, my mother gets back down on her knees. "This is a couch, Samuel. You pointed at a couch." She presses his fingers against the upholstery. "Couch."

His eyes remain blank, still as a doll's. But then his hand rises again, his finger pointing maybe at the television set, or maybe just pointing.

"I can't believe it," my mother says. Her eyes are wide, her hands pushed up under the glitter hat. "I can't believe this is happening."

I stay silent, watching his doll eyes. My mother is never this happy any-more, and I don't want to ruin it for her. She thinks she's found a key, a way in, and proof that something is going on behind the blank blue sky of Samuel's eyes. I don't want to steal this from her. But I think she's tricking herself, seeing something because she wants to see it, not because it's there.

But Verranna Hinckle is impressed with the pointing, even more excited about it than my mother. She comes over and takes pictures with a Polaroid camera, watching Samuel's arm move this way and that, writing down notes on her clipboard. This pointing is a very good sign, she says, an important step. She likes what my mother is doing with the radio.

"You just don't know," she says, pushing up the sleeves of her turtleneck. "There was a girl in Pennsylvania who never talked and never looked back. Severe autism. But then, finally, somebody thought to give her a pen, and the first thing she wrote was a sonnet." She nods at my mother proudly, as if she herself had something to do with this miracle. "It rhymed and everything. Fourteen lines."

I am standing in the doorway eating an apple, watching Verranna Hinckle carefully. I am suspicious of her now, with her little snub nose and her clip-board and her notes for her dissertation. I don't like her getting my mother's hopes up. I take a pen and slide it into Samuel's hand.

Nothing. He doesn't even look at it. He bangs his fist though, and we have to take the pen away from him so he won't stab himself. I look at Verranna Hinckle, and she looks back at me. She wears glasses too.

"Well, it's not always that drastic, of course," she says. "Sometimes it's just a blinking of the eyes, but at least then you're communicating. At least then you know he's in there." She keeps talking, looking only at my mother. "Right now we should concentrate on the basics, meaning self-care. I want you to keep his hand under yours when you feed him. Let him get the feel of it. We won't know what he can do unless we give him a chance." She squints down at Samuel, tapping her fingers on the counter. She tells my mother there are people just as disabled as Samuel who have learned to feed themselves, to use sign language, to use the telephone in an emergency. My mother nods, holding Samuel's twisted hand. She is believing this. She believes that Samuel might be able to use the telephone.

If I weren't so mad I would laugh. As if, when someone answered, there would be something for him to say.

• • •

I think Travis actually wants to be Mr. Goldman now. I am only waiting for him to show up on the bus one day with his hair long in the front but short in the back, wearing an ironed shirt and a tie, a U.S. News & World Report tucked under one of his arms. All of a sudden, Travis wants to travel. He says Mr. Goldman has been to Italy and Japan. He's gone looking for kangaroos in Australia.

"You're not going to believe this story," Travis says, leaning over the back of his seat on the bus. "This is great."

The story is that when Mr. Goldman was just out of college, he and two of his friends went to Australia together, and they drove into the outback to try to find kangaroos. They spent a whole day, looking and looking, but the only kangaroo they saw was the one they hit with the jeep they were driving home. *Thunk*, and that was it. They felt bad, but then finally decided they should at least take a picture of the dead kangaroo, since that's what they had come out there to see.

"Gross," I say.

"Just wait," Travis says, pinching my shoulder. "Listen."

Mr. Goldman and his friends thought it might make a funny picture if they picked the kangaroo up and held it in between them with his sunglasses on its face, so it would look like the kangaroo was having a good time instead of being dead. They ended up putting his sunglasses and his friend's jacket on the kangaroo. But when the flash of the camera went off, the kangaroo came alive and punched Mr. Goldman right in the eye. It took off jumping, and all three of them ran after it, but they couldn't catch it. They'd left the keys to the jeep in the pocket of the jacket they put on the kangaroo, so they had to walk forever, and when they finally got to a police station, the Australian police just sat around and laughed.

"No way," I say, trying to imagine this, Mr. Goldman, his tie flipped over his shoulder, running after a kangaroo wearing sunglasses and a jacket. "He made that up."

"He showed me the picture! You can see the kangaroo, right before it woke up!" We're both laughing now. If there's a picture, then maybe it really happened. It's a great story, if it's true.

"You know what Deena said when I told her that story?" Travis asks. "She said, 'What country is Australia in?'"

We laugh harder, Travis slapping his forehead with his fingers. But even while I am laughing, I think of Deena, what her face would look like if she could hear us, if she were on the bus instead of sick at home watching MTV, her large brown eyes widening with hurt.

But I deserve to be able to laugh a little, after all she has gotten, and all I have not.

Verranna Hinckle wants my mother to get Samuel a wheelchair as soon as possible, preferably a lightweight one. She says one of his legs is very strong, and there's no reason he shouldn't be able to pull himself around.

My mother has found a wheelchair just like this in a catalog. She tore out the page and stuck it to the freezer with a magnet shaped like a banana. It's been up there for a month, just a picture, too expensive to buy. Eileen says if my mother really wants the wheelchair, all she has to do is write a letter to any church and tell them she needs a wheelchair for Samuel, and they'll come through for her, lickety-split. That's what churches do.

But my mother says no way. She's not about to write out some sob story and make us sound pathetic.

"We are pathetic," I remind her. It's just a joke, but the look on her face makes me wish I hadn't said anything.

The next week, Eileen brings the same wheelchair from the catalog over to our house, a red bow tied to one of the wheels, a card taped to the seat:

To Tina, Evelyn, and little Sam,

You are in our hearts.

Love,
The First Christian Church, Wichita, Kansas

My mother eyes the wheelchair with suspicion, reaching forward to touch its shiny aluminum wheels. "No strings?" she asks.

"No strings, honey," Eileen says. "They're just being nice."

My mother smiles, trying to hide it. She gives Eileen a peck on the cheek.

After a few days of tantrums and tipovers, Samuel learns to get around in the wheelchair. He uses his good leg to scoot himself forward and then plants his heel in the carpet to pull the rest of his body along, like a slow-moving hermit crab dragging its shell. He likes to sit by windows, we notice. We didn't know that, before he had the chair.

The new wheelchair makes life both easier and more difficult for my mother. She does not have to carry him everywhere now, which is good. But he can move around quickly, get himself into trouble. He pushes himself into walls, and, not understanding how to back up, just keeps pushing, screaming to himself, his face pressed against the plaster. He inches into the kitchen when my mother is cooking, reaching up behind her at the handles of pots on the stove.

So she has tied a little bell to the side of his wheelchair, to better track his comings and goings. It works well, but it also encourages the cats to stalk him. They crouch like lions under the sofa, waiting for him to wheel by, their eyes wide, their tails twitching.

"Bad kitties!" my mother yells, swinging a dish towel at them. "Leave him alone!" They hiss and scatter, looking for new hiding places so they can do it again.

Verranna Hinckle says that my mother is doing an excellent job, and that Samuel is making, relatively speaking, substantial improvements. She tells my mother to keep her hand over Samuel's whenever she is doing something for him—feeding him, brushing his teeth, washing his hair, pulling on his diaper, changing his clothes—so he participates in his self-care. *Agency,* Verranna Hinckle calls it. *Give him agency.* Verranna Hinckle has a lot of words like this.

"And by all means," she adds, "keep up the talking. He understands more than you think."

I say nothing. Verranna Hinckle is pretending to know something that she does not. For four years now, I have listened to my mother talk to Sam, telling him every day how much she loves him, what a good boy he is, that this is the way you brush your teeth, this is how you lift a spoon. Still, we get nothing. He cries when he wants something, and he stops when he gets it. That's it.

But I suppose if my mother wants to think that he understands her words, fine. She isn't hurting anyone, and I think that, maybe, she is the one who needs to hear them.

Three days before the student council election, Mr. Leubbe puts us in pairs so we can do sit-ups for the Presidential Fitness Exam. "You and you," he says, pointing at Traci and then at me. We hesitate for a moment, and he slaps us on our backs—me with his left hand, Traci with his right—so hard we almost bump into each other, and tells us to get a move on.

"I'll go first," I say. I am the one in charge.

"That's fine," Traci says, her voice too friendly, too nice. She places her hands lightly on my feet and starts counting off my sit-ups in fives. Each time I come up, she smiles. I look only at her metal teeth, not at her eyes.

Travis will have a good time with this story when I tell him. He will say I had Satan binding my feet, and will examine my ankles for welts and bruises. But she's really bothering me, still smiling at me, not looking away. I do the sit-ups more quickly, pretending that I care very much about the Presidential Fitness Exam.

She clears her throat, forces a laugh. "Remember we got in that stupid fight in fourth grade?"

I pause mid–sit-up and look right into her blue-gray eyes, her contact lenses swimming in front of them. "Yeah, Traci. I remember."

She looks a little shaken. I am proud of this, the lowness of my voice, my ability to make her nervous. But she keeps talking, her thin lips pushed into a smile. "It was so stupid. I can't even remember what it was about."

I do another sit-up, and when I come up again, I stop and look at her carefully, wondering if she really believes what she is saying, if she could really be that dumb. "You made fun of my mother, the day I won the science fair." I go back down to the mat, starting to count where she left off. "I won, and you were mad about it. You said they let me win because they felt sorry for me for being poor and not having a father."

She looks down, at her hands on my shoes. She wears a small silver ring on one of her fingers, some kind of red jewel embedded in it. Nothing has changed. I think of her stolen clothes, still folded neatly in my bottom drawer. I'm glad they're there.

"I'm really sorry," she says.

I keep doing sit-ups. I don't want her to say this to me.

"I'm really, really sorry," she says. "I guess I was being a dumb little kid. I just didn't know any better. I didn't even know I was being mean."

I give her a doubtful look. She is not counting anymore, and that's her job. *35 Satan 36 Satan 37 Satan.*

"I mean, I know I shouldn't have said that. I wouldn't say that to you now." Her fingers are light on my shoes, barely touching them. "I don't even know your mother. And I know about your brother—"

I sit up quickly enough to make her lean back, lifting her hands from my ankles.

"You still don't know anything about anything, Traci. Don't even talk about my brother. Don't even bring him up."

Mr. Leubbe blows his whistle, pointing at us from across the gym. "Troops," he says, "settle down."

"You don't talk about Samuel," I whisper. "You don't understand anything about that. And don't try to be nice to me. I know what you are."

She winces, and now I can see the beginning of tears. But I don't care. I have never done sit-ups so quickly in my life. I feel amazingly energized, unsprung. I could do sit-ups all day.

"Why do you hate me so much?" she sniffs. "I haven't done anything to you since then. And I'm sorry. I said I was sorry."

I am open-mouthed, almost laughing at her nerve, her evil, Traci Carmichael nerve. "I'm not going to vote for you, Traci."

She shakes her head. "That's not what this is about."

"Of course it isn't."

Her small, even features freeze, and I think for a moment she is going to start really crying, right there in the gym. But she doesn't. Maybe she can't pull it off. When it's her turn, she does her sit-ups without complaint, me holding her feet and counting. Mr. Leubbe blows the whistle, and we go back to the locker room to shower and change.

I come home from school to see my mother still in her bathrobe, sitting with Samuel at the kitchen table, in the exact same position they were in when I left in the morning. The only difference is that now there is oatmeal everywhere. There are clumps of oatmeal in her hair, in his hair, drying on the wall, on the table. A carton of vanilla ice cream, half melted, sits on the floor, held steady between my mother's bare feet. Samuel is writhing and screaming, his face red with anger, pointing at a bowl of ice cream just out of his reach.

She nods to me when I come in, but that's all. No smile. Samuel thrashes in his chair, his good arm swinging in my mother's direction. The cats are all under the table, licking oatmeal off the carpet with their quick little tongues. I set my backpack on the counter. "What's going on?"

She picks up his thick-handled spoon, pushing it into his hand. "C'mon, baby, show Evelyn what you can do," she says. Her voice is hoarse, almost gone. "You almost did it just now. Do it again." He screams again, rocking so hard in his chair that my mother has to put one of her legs behind it so he won't tip over. He reaches for the ice cream, his fingers almost touching the sides of the bowl.

I put my hands over my ears. "Why won't you just give him some?"

"If he wants ice cream, he has to use a spoon."

Samuel groans and lets his head fall over the back of his chair. He is worn out. I can see the pulse in his neck, thumping beneath his pale skin. "That's mean, Mom. What if he can't? What if he's hungry?"

She shakes her head. "He's had lunch. I'll feed him if he wants more carrots and oatmeal, and he knows it. But if he wants ice cream, he has to get it himself."

I step away, watching her face. A combination of many factors—the oatmeal in her hair, the look in her eyes, and the way she is speaking—makes me nervous. I have seen her be crazy before—that day she laid down on the sidewalk when I was little—but this, what I am seeing in her now, looks like an entirely different kind of crazy. She looks like an entirely different kind of person.

"He almost did it," she says. "Just before you came in." She closes his fingers around the spoon. Samuel yells, throwing the spoon on the ground. She picks it up again, sets it by his hand.

"Mom, I don't think—I think he needs a rest." I wait. "I think you need a rest."

Samuel's chin is shiny with drool, but she cups it in her hand, turning his head toward hers. "Listen," she says. "You can have all the ice cream you want. But you have to use the spoon. Okay?"

"I'm going to my room," I say, no one listening to me. Even down the hall, even with my door shut, I can hear him howling, his fist banging on the table. I turn on the radio, lie down on my bed. Madonna is singing, "Open your heart." Deena has this song on tape, and she has been saying she will make me a copy, but it's two months now that she's been saying this, and she hasn't yet.

I look up at my wall, at all I have tacked up on it over the years to cover up the bad walls of my room, the peeling paint, the corners water-stained from the apartment above us. I still have the star chart Eileen gave me tacked to my ceiling, the ends of it curling up and almost over the red thumbtacks. I bought a calendar, *The Ends of the Earth, 1987: Postcard Pictures from Around the World,* and I cut the pictures off the top, hanging each of them up on my wall like posters, faraway places that look nothing like here. In these pictures, there are people who do not know us, people who have never heard of Kerrville, Kansas, wearing berets and carrying bread; there is a beach in Mexico, palm trees shading the sand; there is a castle in front of a blue lake in Switzerland, mountains towering high above. I close my eyes, imagine myself walking alongside the lake in Switzerland. If you are good at imagining something, it can be almost like it is happening. In a way, there is no difference at all.

But just as I am thinking this, the door swings open, and now I know I am not in Switzerland but in my room, looking up at my mother, her eyes wide, chocolate syrup on her cheek.

"What?" I say. "What is it?"

"Evelyn. Evelyn." She leans down and grabs my arm, pulling me up off my bed.

"What? Is he hurt?"

We run down the hallway together. Samuel is not hurt. He is sitting in his chair, his mouth covered with ice cream and chocolate syrup. It's dripping off his chin, onto the napkin tied around his neck. He gazes out the window, his spoon moving down to the bowl of ice cream in front of him on the table, slow and steady.

He brings the spoon back to his face. It hits his cheek first, then finds his mouth.

"Oh my God," I whisper, not even thinking, and my mother touches my hand.

His spoon moves down to the bowl again and back to his mouth. He groans, eyelids fluttering. I can hear my mother breathing next to me, smell the oatmeal in her hair.

"You were right," I say, still watching him. "You were right."

"Yes," she says. "Yes, I was."

He keeps going, the spoon trembling in his hand. He spills more than he swallows, but my mother and I stand perfectly still, not talking, not doing anything. We watch until we hear him scrape the bottom of the bowl. He starts to cry, pounding the spoon against the table.

"You want more, baby?" my mother asks, moving toward him. "You can have all you want."

His napkin is soaked, sticking to his shirt. Globs of chocolate syrup hang down off his chin, his hair, even his ears. There is ice cream and chocolate syrup on the carpet, and it will be difficult to clean. But I say nothing. I know this is amazing, what I am seeing before me. It is just a small thing, him feeding himself, just a little something he has learned, something she has taught him.

But if she could teach him this, then there is no telling what else is there, wrapped up inside him like a present, and outside of him as well.

sixteen

CHRISTMAS BREAK COMES AND GOES, but for Deena, it just stays. She gets sick on the first day of January and misses the entire first week back at school. Travis says she is faking.

When I stop by to give her her copy of *Lord of the Flies* for English, her grandmother answers the door, fully awake but squinty-eyed, wearing a dress with a zipper that goes from the hem at her knees to her throat. "Deena sick," she says, shaking her head. "No play."

But Deena comes out of her room, pale and coughing, wearing one of Travis's sweatshirts. "I'm so sick," she tells me. "I feel like crap."

Her grandmother says something sharply to her in German. Deena apologizes.

"Maybe it's mono?" I ask. If it is, she won't be able to come to school for weeks, maybe months.

"Just the flu." She swallows, looking pained. "Have you seen Travis?"

"Not really. In class, I mean, and on the bus. But that's it."

"Have you talked to him?"

"Not really." This is a lie. Travis and I got to work as partners in geometry today, taking a timed test. We beat Traci Carmichael and Brad Browning by five minutes, and high-fived each other on the way out the door.

"Me neither," she says, coughing again. "I'm here dying, and he doesn't even care."

She's sick again the next day, and again, it's just me and Travis on the bus. He's the oldest person on the bus now, the only junior, and also the tallest. When he walks down the aisle, the yarny ball on top of his ski hat skids along the metal brackets of the ceiling. "Someday . . . ," he says, sliding in next to me. "Someday I'll have a car. When I'm old and have money, I'm going to find some poor kid who's in high school and still has to ride the bus and give him a car."

"A car-lorship," I say, making room for him.

"That's right. A car-lorship." He takes off his hat, his curly hair springing out from under it. He has a red scarf, a hat, and mittens, but that's it. All winter long, he has gone without a coat. I can't tell if it's because he thinks coats are stupid or because he doesn't have one.

Through the windows, we watch Adele Peterson's red Honda Prelude pull out of the parking lot, Traci Carmichael in the passenger seat. Adele Peterson is a junior, and she lives next door to Traci and across the street from Libby in another brick house with too many windows. Adele got this car for her sixteenth birthday. I know this because Traci talked in a loud voice in geometry about how she was there when Adele first saw the car. Her father had parked it in the driveway the night before, and tied a white ribbon around it while Adele was inside sleeping like the little princess she is, her last night of being fifteen. And when she came out in the morning for school, there it was.

"She came outside," Traci said, talking just to Brad Browning, really, but loud enough for everyone to hear, "and she was like, 'Oh my God.' "

Adele gives rides to both Traci and Libby now, and they pass us on the bus when the road goes to four lanes on McPhee Street. They look like the Go-Go's in a music video, the radio playing loud, the windows rolled down even when it's cold out. Traci sits in the passenger seat every day, no matter what. Libby is taller than Traci, but she sits in the back. She has to put her feet up on the seat so her chin rests on her knees, and when they go past the bus, she looks up at us from the backseat like she is looking up out of a basement.

"You notice it's a red car," I say, nudging Travis, and this makes him smile. We have expanded on our joke that Traci Carmichael is actually the

Devil, sent down in the form of a fifteen-year-old girl to challenge good with evil. We have taken note that she wears colored contacts now: some days her eyes are blue; some days her eyes are brown. Travis says that at night, when no one is looking, her eyes turn red, and if you look directly into them, even in the daytime, you can go blind or crazy. This, Travis says, is how she won student president.

"You know Deena wants a pair of colored contacts?" he asks me, pointing at his own eyes. "She wanted blue ones for Christmas." He shivers, making a face. "They creep me out. Your eyes should be the color of your eyes."

I nod in agreement, although if I could make my eyes look different, not so sleepy-looking, I probably would. "Have you talked to her?" I ask. "She's really sick."

"Yeah, she's real sick. She was healthy all through break, you notice."

I think of Deena, wrapped in her quilt and coughing. I know she really is sick this time, but I don't say this to Travis. She has faked being sick other times, and this is really the point. "She says you haven't gone to see her."

"Not true. I went over there three days ago. If she even is sick, she's probably contagious, right? I'll get whatever she's got." He rolls his eyes. "I'll catch laziness."

I say nothing. He picks at the green covering of the back of the seat in front of us. "She has to understand that I can't just sit around with her all the time." He puts one of his mittened hands over his eyes. "I don't know."

"Are you guys in a fight?"

"No. No. But you know I've been talking to Goldman. I've been thinking about stuff, stuff I want to do."

"Like what?"

"I don't know." He reaches over me and slides open the window. "I want to go to fucking Australia."

"I hear it's a wonderful town," I say.

He smiles again, the second time on just this bus ride, because of something I've said. "I don't know," he says. "It's just weird. I just keep thinking that this is always how it is. People try to drag you down."

I nod, waiting for him to say it. But he doesn't.

"You think Deena's dragging you down?" I ask.

He waits. "No. Maybe." He glances at me again, lowering his voice. "This is going to sound weird, but, okay. I guess I keep thinking that this was how my dad felt when he left, you know? Like I've been so mad about it, my whole life, thinking he didn't have to leave us just to stop drinking. But I don't know. Maybe he did."

I think back to Mr. Rowley, when he used to fall asleep on our doorstep, setting his own clothes on fire. "You didn't make him drink, Travis. You were just a little kid."

He nods, still picking at the seat cover. "I know. That's exactly what I'm saying. Deena's not a bad person, but it's like, I don't know. I want to get through school, maybe even go to college or something. But she's mad because that's not what I promised her six months ago. And now I can't get it back. It's like she's locked that into her brain." He has succeeded in pulling off an entire section of the seat in front of him.

I have to work to keep my face the same. "You might break up with her?"

"I'm just talking. Don't say anything to her, okay? But whatever happens, it's over when I graduate." He looks up at me, and he doesn't look away until I am embarrassed.

"Anyway, I miss getting to hang out with just you."

Oh.

And now, coming from the inside of my own head, there is a small, electric hum, steady and pleasant, and I think about the terrible night in the McDonald's, the night Travis met Deena and they wouldn't stop looking at each other, the force field between them lighting up their eyes.

Perhaps this is how it feels to be inside of it.

Deena lies on my bed, *Lord of the Flies* open and resting on top of her face. She is only on page fifty-four, and the test is tomorrow. "I hate this book," she says, her voice muffled under the pages. "I hate it so much."

"It's good," I tell her. "And it's fast, too. If you start reading now, you can finish."

She shakes her head under the book. "There aren't even any girls in it. And there's no way I can finish it by tomorrow."

I know in Deena language, this means she wants me to tell her what happens in the book so she can write her essay tomorrow. I am tired of doing this for her. I have done this for her with *Billy Budd, Of Mice and Men,* and "The Rime of the Ancient Mariner." I am considering making something up this time, telling her that the book is about the boys on the island learning to be nice to one another, starting their own business selling seashells to people who stop by on their boats. But I look at her lying there underneath the book, her thin arms flailed out to her sides, and I know I won't really do this.

Lately, I have been feeling sorry for Deena. Her eyes are still large, but instead of thinking of them as just beautiful, now I think of them as looking a little bewildered. Her irises are such a deep, dark brown that it is difficult to tell where the pupils in the center end, and so this makes her look as if her eyes are dilated all the time, like she is one of the cats, trying to see in the dark.

She takes the book off her face and sets it down on the floor. "Do you know why Travis is being such an ass lately?" She pouts, scooting the book farther away with her foot. "He's always in a bad mood. He's always busy."

I say no without looking up from my book, trying to make the moment of my answer pass quickly. I'm not doing anything to her. It's just that things are starting to shift. Travis tapped on my window last night, and I am still sleepy because we stayed up so late, sitting on the roof in our hats and mittens, the knee of his jeans grazing against the knee of my leggings, maybe accidentally, maybe not. *Which one is that one? Polaris. Which one is that one?* He did not mention Deena once.

She yawns, tracing her finger along the edges of one of my calendar posters, a blue-and-gold picture of the pyramids in Egypt against a cloudless sky. "He wouldn't even help me with my homework tonight," she says.

"You don't need Travis to help you read a book, Deena."

"Actually, I don't need to read that stupid book. That's what I don't need."

"You'll need it to graduate."

She looks out my window, frowning. It is almost spring, but a winter storm moved in last week, covering the ground with a watery snow that has already frozen into hard clumps, caked with dirt from passing cars. The landscape of Treeline Colonies has not improved much, and in the winter, I get depressed just looking outside, at the leafless hedges planted by the doors, the frozen drainage ditch by the highway.

"You know we're going to move far away from here when we get married," she says. "Somewhere warm. By the ocean. Maybe Florida, or California. We're not even going to tell my grandmother or anyone else where we're going. But I'll tell you. You can come visit us." She rolls over and leans her head off my bed, her face upside down, her dark hair hanging to the floor in a way that makes me think of the tiny trolls attached to key chains for sale in the Kwikshop. She closes her eyes and smiles. "No more snow and no more cold."

She reaches over to pick at a strand of my hair, and I know she is doing this to check for split ends, the damage done to my hair from the terrible perm she tried to give me, which is only now starting to relax. I pull my head away. "Deena, you might want to double-check those plans with him again."

She rolls back up on her stomach, and I watch the color drain out of her face, down her neck, her hoop earrings falling back into place. "Why? Did he say something to you?"

"I just . . . I'm not supposed to say anything. I just think he's been thinking."

Her eyes stay on mine. "Evelyn? What did he say?"

I hesitate. I am not supposed to tell, but I feel bad for her. She shouldn't be whiling away her days dreaming about the life she and Travis are going to have by an ocean somewhere when he is thinking about college and Australia. I'm doing her a favor, although looking at her now, I can see she doesn't think I am.

"I just think he's going to keep his options open," I say.

"When did you talk to him?"

"A few days ago. Don't tell him I told you, or he won't ever tell me anything again."

She is still looking at me, eyes narrowed. I find it hard to look back. I have watched my mother long enough to know that there are all kinds of ways of being smart. Just because Deena reads slowly doesn't mean she can't see the little part of me that is happy about what I am telling her now.

"I'm only telling you this so you don't get too carried away, Deena."

But she's looking over my head now, out the window, past the ice-covered parking lot to Travis's dark window, though his shade is pulled all the way down.

My grandfather will turn sixty this February, and Eileen wants us to come to the party. There will be balloons and cake, she says. It won't last long. And it will mean so much, she adds, to him.

My mother's right eyebrow goes up. "Did he say that?"

Eileen nods, avoiding my mother's eyes. For her New Year's resolution, she is trying to quit smoking, and already she has bitten off all the white of her fingernails. "He said he'd be glad to have you, Tina. You and Evelyn and little Sam."

My mother frowns, looking down at Samuel. Now that he has learned to use a spoon, she is upping the ante: he has to answer her questions. She has attached a tray to his wheelchair, with a green circle taped to one side that reads YES and a red square on the other side that reads NO.

"Sam, we're going to have some ice cream," she says, speaking directly into his ear. "Would you like a bowl?" She takes his finger and points it in the direction of the green circle. "Yes?" she asks. She takes his finger and points it in the direction of the red square. "Or no?"

We wait, watching his hand slowly slide across his tray to the YES, like an oracle on a Ouija board. When his finger touches YES, Eileen claps. My mother scoops out two bowls of ice cream—one chocolate, one vanilla. "I have to offer him choices," she tells Eileen. "All the books I'm reading say that this is what's really important."

Verranna Hinckle has been giving my mother books to read: *The Special Child, Communicating with Your Child, A Doctor's Take on the Non-Verbal Child.* Each time she finishes one, Verranna Hinckle brings her another.

We wait again, watching Samuel's hand move slowly in the direction of the chocolate ice cream.

"Thank you for telling me you want chocolate, not vanilla," my mother says, the words loud and slow, like someone is standing behind us, holding a cue card for her to read. She slides the bowl of chocolate toward him and clasps his hand around his spoon. Eileen says I should have the bowl of vanilla. But I don't want it, and neither does my mother, so Eileen takes it for herself.

"Honestly, Tina," she says, waving her spoon at my mother. "You're doing such an amazing job with him. Really."

"Thanks, Mom. I'm trying hard." I see the ends of my mother's mouth twitch, almost a smile. She is hearing things like this more and more. Last week, Verranna Hinckle brought two other women from the university over with her, and they watched Samuel feed himself and point at what he wanted. They used the same word—"amazing"—as if he and my mother had performed a magic trick, pulled a rabbit out of an empty hat. I don't think my mother knows what to do with these compliments when she gets them, especially from Eileen. She's like a person without any hands getting flowers.

"So you think you might come?" Eileen asks. "To the party?"

My mother sits down in the chair next to Samuel. "No. I'm sorry, Mom. But no."

Eileen takes a small swallow of ice cream and sets the bowl back on the table. "It's his birthday, Tina. Just a couple of hours. It wouldn't kill you."

"It might," my mother says. She reaches over and dabs a napkin at Samuel's mouth. "I wish you'd leave this alone. If he wants to come out here and try to talk to me, he can. He knows how to get here, and he's a grown man."

"But maybe it's difficult for him to tell you how he feels, Tina!"

My mother laughs. "Actually, Mom, I think he's always been pretty good at that."

Eileen leans back in her chair, her arms crossed in front of her. She is finally starting to look older, like a real grandmother, the lines around her mouth growing deeper. My mother says it's from the cigarettes. "You know, Tina, you are a real puzzle to me. I find it hard to believe that you can be so kind to your little boy and have absolutely no compassion whatsoever for your own father." She points her spoon at my mother again. "He's going to be sixty, you know. His heart is bad."

"I'm sorry to hear that," my mother says. "Look, I'll tell you how it is. I just can't. Not with Samuel. Okay? I know how he'll look at him." She shakes her head, wincing as if she can actually see all of this in front of her, like a movie projected on the wall behind Eileen's head.

Eileen sighs, reaching over and pulling her fingers through Samuel's hair. "What about when he dies, Tina? How are you going to feel about you being so petty—"

"I'm not being petty. If he wants to call me and talk to me about it, he can. But it's a little hard to make peace with someone who doesn't actually think of you as a person. And you can't forgive someone who isn't even sorry in the first place." She shrugs, looking back at Eileen. "If he dies, he dies. I'll be okay."

Eileen makes a face like the kind you might make if you accidentally drank soured milk, or found a dead mouse behind the refrigerator. "That's a terrible thing to say, Tina. A terrible thing."

"It's the truth."

"No. You'll look back and you'll be full of regret. And it'll be too late."

I try to imagine the scene in Eileen's head, what she's imagining—my mother, dressed in black, reaching for her father's casket as they lower it into

230 · LAURA MORIARTY

the ground, pounding her fists against the metal, crying, *I'm so sorry. You were right. I'm not a person. I was a horse all along.*

"You will, Tina," Eileen says, reaching into her back pocket for the cigarettes that are no longer there. "You'll feel awful. But when death comes, it comes. And then it'll be too late."

My mother pulls Samuel out of his chair and onto her lap, pecking him lightly on the top of his head. "Well," she says, carefully. "I guess we'll have to wait and see."

Traci Carmichael is dead.

I am sitting in Mrs. Geldof's bright room, looking at Mrs. Geldof's watery eyes and the map of the world on the bulletin board behind her, the United States in the middle, Kansas in the middle of that. Traci's desk is empty, and so is Libby's.

There has been a car accident, Mrs. Geldof says. Yesterday, on the way home from school. Adele Peterson was driving, and she's dead too. They were going too fast, not wearing seat belts. Libby is alive, but badly hurt.

"What?" Ray Watley asks. There is a ripple in his voice, and although I think it's just because he doesn't believe what Mrs. Geldof is saying, it comes out as a laugh. "Are you kidding?"

"No," Mrs. Geldof says. She blinks, and there are tears. "No, honey, I'm not kidding."

I can feel my arms turning cold, someone running a feather lightly across my skin. I saw them yesterday, all three of them. Adele honked twice when they pulled up alongside the bus in the next lane. Traci's arm was hanging out the window, fingers snapping to the radio, three pink plastic bracelets around her wrist.

But I remember now. There were sirens only a few minutes later. Travis and I were still on the bus, laughing about something. Not about Traci. Something else. When we got to the street where the accident was, there was already a detour set up. We had to take another route, and it took longer. We got home late.

"They're dead?" Ray Watley asks again. Mrs. Geldof nods.

No one says anything. The truth of it, what this really means, starts to settle in slowly, moving into us through our open mouths, seeping in through our eyes when we look at the empty desks.

Ray Watley is quiet, not laughing now, his hands still on his desk in front of him. Deena turns around to look at me. She is already crying. Other girls are crying too, and I understand that I should be crying, that this is the appropriate response. But I am still just sitting and blinking, doing nothing, like a cartoon character hit on the head with something large. Even when people start to get up and move toward one another, clasping hands, I just sit there, still and dumb.

Mrs. Geldof comes over to me and pushes her wet cheek against mine, her arms tight around my rigid back.

"I know, honey," she says, still crying. "I know."

There is a picture of Adele's crumpled Honda in the newspaper. The front end is completely smashed in, the windows shattered. My mother moves around me quietly, making lunch for Sam. We've been given the rest of the week off from school.

"Evelyn, sweetie, don't look at that anymore," she says. "Put it away." She tugs on a corner of the paper, but I hold tight. According to the article, Adele was making a left turn after the light had already turned red, and the Honda slammed into an oncoming car, head-on. Traci actually survived the wreck, and was airlifted by helicopter to a hospital in Kansas City. Adele died on impact. The driver of the other car broke her foot in two places, but that was all. Libby Masterson was, of course, in the backseat, and is still in the hospital, in stable condition.

Libby had not been wearing a seat belt either, and Mrs. Geldof told us that the only reason she was alive was physics, a question of who was sitting where. The rest of us should not count on such luck and should wear our seat belts. Libby, Mrs. Geldof said, again and again, was very lucky.

"Yeah right," my mother says. "Tell that to the shrink she's going to need."

On Monday, we are supposed to go back to school, but I don't want to. I tell my mother I'm not feeling well. She holds her hand against my forehead only for a moment, biting her bottom lip.

"Evelyn, I can see you're upset."

I roll my eyes. "I'm just sick. I wasn't friends with any of them."

"I know. I know. But still, honey. I can see you're upset."

I go back to my room and lie down, and she brings me a 7-UP, plugs her tape player in next to my bed. But I don't play it. I know I am not really sick, but it is all I can do to just lie here and look up at the star chart on my ceiling with no sound around me at all.

I am trying to figure out whether or not I'm a bad person. There are some points that argue that I'm not: One, I did not make Traci and Adele die. They were in a car, going too fast, and I was on the bus. Two, just because Traci is dead now does not mean that she was a nice person before she died. Just because she is dead now does not mean she was never phony. All it means now is that she's dead.

I stare up at the star chart. I cannot go to sleep.

In driver's ed last year, Mr. Leubbe rigged up what he called a Seat Belt Convincer to the back of his truck. He made us all try it, one at a time, buckling each of us into an old car seat that slid quickly down a two-foot ramp. I had been amazed by how much it hurt, the strap holding me back as the rest of my body went forward. I had a red welt across my neck that stayed there for two days.

"You kids think you're immortal," Mr. Leubbe had told us. "You think you're going to be able to put out your hands and save yourself," he said. "But it happens too fast. That was only eight miles an hour. Try it at fifty, and your arms will break like twigs!" He had clapped his hands together, loud and sudden. "Your teeth will hit the pavement before you can think to shut your mouth. You'll bite off your own tongue!"

It is difficult to imagine Traci Carmichael like this, her blue-gray eyes hurled into the pavement and ended, just like that.

I lie there, still and silent for hours, until I hear my mother tell me good night, wheeling Samuel into their room. Only when the light in the hallway goes out do I get up and move across my room to my dresser. The clothes are still there, in the bottom drawer, underneath my own sweaters and shirts. The white jeans are still smooth and new-looking, creased where I folded them years ago, but the palm trees ironed onto the sweatshirt are cracked, starting to peel. And I am amazed by how small everything looks. The red shoes are so tiny, just half the size of my foot now.

I reach into the pocket of the jeans, and feel it there, the locket, a heart-shaped coldness between my finger and thumb, still hanging on its golden chain.

seventeen

*F*OR A WHILE, I AVOID Travis. A lot of our jokes aren't funny, now that Traci is dead. I feel a pain in me all the time now, a dull rock in my stomach. I don't want to feel bad about anything else.

The Saturday before Easter, I wake to the sound of a gentle rain hitting the roof, and then yelling, repeated knocks. Samuel is crying in my mother's room, but it's a woman yelling, not my mother. It's coming from outside. I move the sheet away from my window and see it's Deena's grandmother, already up and wearing the dress with the zipper, banging on the Rowleys' front door.

My mother peeks inside my room. "Evelyn? You awake?"

I nod, yawning.

"What's going on out there? Is Travis even home?"

"I don't know." I really don't.

"Is Deena over there?"

"I don't know."

She reties the belt on her robe and sits down on my bed, ducking so she can see out my window. Two of the cats stay just outside my door, eyeing the doorway with interest. My room is the one room they are not allowed to come into, and so this is the room they want to come into the most. I wave my foot at them. "Shoo, kitties," I say. "Shoo."

Deena's grandmother continues to knock, steady and strong. We realize she is not using her hand, but something metal and sharp, a large cooking spoon.

"I don't know what this is about, but she woke up Sam an hour early," my mother says. "I'm going over to her house tomorrow with a skillet."

The Rowleys' door opens, and we can see Mrs. Rowley standing in her doorway, holding Jackie O. Jackie O is old now, blind, her eyes clouded with cataracts. She barks at Deena's grandmother, her head turned in the wrong direction.

"No again!" Deena's grandmother yells, pointing as Mrs. Rowley's chest with the spoon. "No again!"

My mother and I look at each other, and then back out the window. Deena's grandmother does most of the talking, the rain falling on the shoulders of her zipper dress. When Mrs. Rowley opens her mouth to say something, Deena's grandmother raises her voice and keeps talking, so Mrs. Rowley has to just stand there and listen, her hand over Jackie O's muzzle. The cats creep slowly into my room, sniffing the carpet carefully. Just this once, I let it go.

"Huh," my mother says, squinting out the window, nodding, as if she can hear what they're saying. "Huh."

Deena's grandmother turns suddenly and hobbles down the steps, crossing the parking lot back to Unit A. The Rowleys' front door slams shut. There are loud thuds, more yelling. Travis yelling. We can hear Mrs. Rowley crying when she crescendos up, so shrill it makes the cats tilt their heads up to the window, searching the sky for birds.

The Rowleys' front door opens again, and Travis sort of falls out onto the balcony, wearing only shorts, no shirt, no shoes, the door closing behind him. He runs back and tries to open the door. He bangs and kicks, rain rolling down his naked back. The door opens again, and Mrs. Rowley throws a shirt and a pair of shoes down the steps to the parking lot. She slams the door shut, and he throws himself against it, kicking at it so hard we can hear the glass in their windows rattle.

Sam wheels into my room, bell ringing. He is wearing his red flannel pajamas, pointing in my direction, looking at the floor. The cats watch him, their eyes large with interest. "Glad you could join us, babe," my mother says, hooking her foot around his, pulling him the rest of the way.

Travis moves slowly down the steps, picking up the shirt his mother threw, already wet from the rain.

"Can he come inside?" I ask.

My mother frowns. "If he's all done kicking things."

I follow her out of my room. We are like a parade. Samuel jingling behind me, the cats bringing up the rear. I stop in the bathroom to brush my teeth and hair, keeping the door open to listen.

"Hey, Tex," my mother calls out, opening the door. I don't know why she calls him this. I don't think Travis has even been to Texas. "Why don't you come in here and warm up for a while? You can dry off. I'll make you some pancakes."

From the bathroom, I hear him say no.

"Why not?" she asks.

"I don't want to bother you."

"Oh, honey," she says, laughing now. "It's a little late for that."

"Is Evelyn awake?"

"She is. Come inside. I'll make you some breakfast. Whatever it is, it's not the end of the world."

I come out of the bathroom just as he walks in, his hair wet with rain. He doesn't look at me. My mother makes him take off his wet shirt, and she wraps one of Sam's blankets around his shoulders. He sits down on the couch, looking straight ahead, and with the blanket wrapped around his shoulders he looks like a man from the Bible, or a war refugee. The cats move around him cautiously, sniffing his toes.

I sit down next to him, tap him on the knee. "What? What happened?"

"Deena's pregnant."

I hear the pancake batter sizzle on the skillet. My mother shakes her head slowly, her eyes closed.

"What?" I laugh the way Ray Watley did.

He turns, looks right at me. He's breathing hard, rain still dripping off his nose. "She's pregnant."

I am angry, maybe at him. I try to remember Deena the last time I saw her, just on Friday, sitting in English class. She did not look any different. She could have made this up, told her grandmother a lie. "I thought you-all were being careful."

He closes his eyes, and now he laughs. "I thought so too."

"I thought . . ." I stammer. I don't know what I want to say, what it was I thought.

Through the window, I can see that Mrs. Rowley has come back outside. She stands on their balcony, looking around the way she did the night Travis threw pebbles on her roof, Jackie O licking the rain off her neck.

"Travis?" she says, her voice wavering. "Travis, honey? Where'd you go?"

My mother opens the door and tells her he's with us, and that she can come over too.

"Oh great," Travis says. "Great."

By the time Mrs. Rowley gets to our door, she is crying, her skin a blotchy red, her eyes a brilliant shade of aqua green, bright with tears. The cats notice Jackie O, shivering from the rain in Mrs. Rowley's skinny arms, and they form a circle, hissing, their hackles raised. Samuel makes a quick shrieking sound.

"Did he tell you?" she asks, looking at my mother. "About Deena?"

My mother nods, and new tears come to Mrs. Rowley's eyes. She turns to Travis. "I'm sorry I yelled, honey," she says. "I'm sorry. I'm just so damn sad for you."

Travis looks down at his muddy feet, at the tracks he made on our carpet when he walked inside. My mother tells Mrs. Rowley to sit down and asks her if she wants some coffee. Mrs. Rowley strokes Jackie O's head and keeps crying. "She tricked you, didn't she? Tricked and trapped. That's what it looks like to me."

My mother's face changes slightly, a weariness in her eyes as she pours the coffee, but Travis says nothing. If he would just look up at me, just once, I would nod. I agree with Mrs. Rowley. Tricked and trapped. She's right. I shouldn't have told Deena anything. Now it's too late.

"Are you sure it's yours?" she asks. "Can you even be sure of that?"

He winces and turns his whole body away from her. "I'm sure it's mine, Mom. Don't start that."

My mother hands Mrs. Rowley the mug I gave her for Mother's Day the year before. #1 MOM it says. "Cream?" she asks. "Sugar?"

Mrs. Rowley shakes her head no and takes a sip. She does not say thank you.

"Look," my mother says, pouring herself a cup. "Does Deena even know what she wants to do?"

There is a pause before anyone understands what she means.

"Oh, she'll have it," Mrs. Rowley says quickly, her hand shaking when she brings the coffee up to her mouth. "They've made up their little minds, her and that old German bitch. We've no say in the matter. No say at all."

Samuel wheels himself over to where Mrs. Rowley is sitting, trying to touch Jackie O. She growls, her eyes hazy and unseeing. My mother pulls Samuel's chair away.

"You don't have to marry her, honey," Mrs. Rowley says. "I know I said you did, but I was just mad. You don't have to. I don't care what she says about lawyers. We'll move. You can go live with your dad for a while."

My mother taps her fingers against her coffee cup. I know what she's thinking. Still, I'm with Mrs. Rowley on this one. Deena did this on purpose, because she cares only about what she wants. She didn't think about anyone else, what they might have wanted.

Travis does not even answer his mother when she says this. His face is still wet from the rain, so it is difficult to tell whether or not he is crying.

Again, Travis sits on the bumper of Mr. Goldman's little gray car. I suspect Mr. Goldman has come out here to try to convince Travis that it would be better for everyone, in the long run, if he stayed in school just one more year.

But it won't work, I know. Travis is going to marry Deena, and he has already told me what he would say to Mr. Goldman, to anyone, if they tried to talk him out of it. The baby is a sign, he said, his destiny, making him do what he's supposed to do.

"It's called Deena," I told him. "Not Destiny. She's making you do what she wants you to do. There's a difference."

He got mad when I said this, acted like I was being dumb. "You're not paying attention to the big picture, Evelyn," he said, looking at his hands and not at me.

I don't see this big picture. And if there really is a big picture, I guess I'm not in it. I don't see what any of this has to do with destiny. If Travis could have been sitting in my room the night I told Deena he might leave her, he would know that destiny really was the moment she looked out my window and started making up her mind.

I think of Travis now as a silver ball in a pinball machine, rolling in whatever direction he's pushed.

I have not seen Deena since we found out. She has not been to school. I am certain she is hiding from me, but I am watching for her, waiting for her to come outside. For days, I have been planning what I will say when I see her. I have made up long, sharp-worded speeches, and I imagine her face flinching when she hears them.

My mother says she feels sorry for both Deena and Travis. She thinks it's a bad idea for them to get married right now. She told me she doesn't think it's right to tether people together before they're ready. That was her word, "tether." She feels sorry for Deena because she doesn't know that Deena wanted to be tethered all along, whether Travis wanted to or not.

I move through my days, stunned, wide-eyed, as if someone has slapped me hard. I have dreams at night about different things being stolen—my favorite shirt, a ten-dollar bill. I set them down, turn away for just a moment, and they're gone.

Deena stands outside our door, her face pale in the sunlight. "Why haven't you come over?" She is already crying, her nose running. She wipes her face with her hand. I can't help but look down at her belly, as if I would be able to see it already, the pregnancy. But except for the crying, she still just looks like a normal fifteen-year-old girl, wearing cut-offs and a T-shirt on a nice day in April.

Behind me, my mother pushes Samuel's wheelchair by, bell ringing. When she sees Deena, she smiles. "Hi, honey," she says, reaching forward to squeeze her hand. "It's good to see you."

"I'll be outside," I say. I step outside, shutting the door behind me. A wasp has built a nest in the crack between our door and the stairs. It emerges quickly, hovering over our heads.

"You know?" she asks. She has the look of someone who has not just started crying recently, but for a long time, days maybe, the skin around her eyes puckered and pink.

I nod. "Mrs. Rowley came over here when she found out. I thought you were on the pill, Deena."

She looks confused for a moment, not saying anything. "I was. It just doesn't work sometimes."

I kick at the dirt on the concrete step. "When doesn't it work?"

She waits until I look up. "Sometimes." Her bottom lip is quivering, but I don't care.

"You guys are getting married?"

She nods. "I think so. His mom is saying no, but that's what everybody else wants."

"Everybody?"

She grimaces, blinks, and then, unbelievably, there are even more tears. It is amazing, the amount she can produce. "Why are you so worried about what Travis wants?" She presses one hand to her chest. "What about me, Evelyn? How long have you known, and you haven't come over to see me?"

I say nothing, watching her.

"You act like I did this all by myself. Well guess what? That's impossible. Okay? You should know that." She looks mad when she says this part, but then she just starts crying again, her shoulders shaking. "You're supposed to be my friend."

"I'm Travis's friend too." I look at her evenly. "You got pregnant on purpose, Deena. I told you he was going to end it. I'm the one who told you."

She makes a whimpering sound and pulls her hair so it covers her face, and even crying, she is pretty, her dark eyes looking darker now that her skin is so pale. If this were a made-for-TV movie, Deena would be the star, especially now that she is tragic as well as beautiful, pregnant at fifteen.

I know I am supposed to hug her. I am the supporting actress, the supportive friend. But instead I go back inside, shutting the door behind me, leaving her out there with just the wasp.

On the last day of school, we make cards for Libby. She is out of the hospital now, but Mrs. Geldof says she is still in a world of hurt. She is trying to walk without a walker now, and this summer, for her, will be long and hard.

I make myself think of Libby trying to walk when I feel sorry for myself now, which is pretty much all the time. I imagine her holding onto two side railings in a hospital hallway, stumbling, having to get back up again. I'm lucky, I know. I can at least put one foot in front of the other. And at least I'm not dead in the ground like Adele and Traci.

But I feel like I'm dead sometimes, underground. And it doesn't matter that I can put one foot in front of the other, because I have nowhere to go. When summer comes, I sit in my room in front of the fan, trying to read. I usually end up just sitting there, looking out the window.

Travis leaves for work early, seven-thirty, wearing a khaki jumpsuit with TRAVIS stitched in red letters on a white patch, carrying coffee in a blue mug that he brings home with him at night to be rinsed out and refilled with coffee again the next morning. His mother bought him a blue Datsun so he could get to work in the morning. It needs a new muffler, and the engine is so loud that the crows fly up from the corn across the highway when he starts it in the morning. My mother asked Mrs. Rowley when she thinks Travis will fix this, and Mrs. Rowley said Travis had enough things to fix right now, and maybe everyone should just leave him alone.

He gets home a little after six, the khaki jumpsuit stained with splotches of oil, walking quickly from the car. He does not look up at my window. Deena goes over around seven, knocking on his window, never the door. He comes out, and the two of them go for long walks together, up and down the highway. They don't talk, or maybe they wait until no one can see them before they begin. But they walk side by side, sometimes holding hands, sometimes not. She's cut her hair off, all the way up to her ears. Her neck looks even longer and thinner, like the stem of a flower. Sometimes she looks up at my window quickly, but I don't know if she sees me or not.

Travis says good-bye to her every night in the parking lot. Sometimes they kiss, and sometimes he just leans forward, bending his knees so that his forehead touches hers.

When Eileen hears about Deena, she says she thinks it's sad the way young people are going downhill today. She says if this country really wanted to put a stop to teen pregnancy, drug use, AIDS, and rap music, they'd put prayer back in schools and then wonder why we ever took it out.

"Case in point," she tells my mother, pointing at me. "Two girls, living right next door to each other. They're the same age. They're friends. One goes to church, at least when her grandmother can get her there, and the other one doesn't. One doesn't get pregnant at fifteen, and the other one does."

I watch Eileen talk, her crooked mouth forming the words. I would like to believe what she is saying now, that I am not pregnant because I am good. But I know that some of the reason I am not pregnant and Deena is is that she was born with large, dark eyes and a neck like the stem of a flower, and I wasn't.

"At least they're getting married," she says, unwinding her yellow measuring tape. She's knitting Samuel a sweater, a blue one, she says, to match his eyes. He reaches up for the tape, making his shrieking sound.

"Oh come on," my mother says. She is sitting on the counter, eating a grape Popsicle, wearing a denim skirt she has had since I was little. "They're both so young."

"Come on nothing, Tina. They created a child together. Now they can raise one. Or they can go through the nine months and give it up for adoption. Anyway, they're not so young. I was seventeen when I married your father. My own grandmother was sixteen on her wedding day, and she and my grandfather went on to have thirteen children."

Eileen looks proud about this, but my mother makes a face, reeling back in her chair. *"Thirteen?"* She looks at me. "Your grandmother had thirteen children? That's insane."

It's true, I think. My mother is right—thirteen is too many. Even their own parents would forget their names sometimes.

Eileen shrugs. "They were Catholic."

My mother rolls her eyes, chewing the end of her Popsicle stick. "Someone needs to give the pope thirteen babies. Just for a week or so. See how he likes no birth control then."

"People who have self-control don't need birth control, Tina."

"Well, apparently your grandmother did." She laughs, but Eileen doesn't.

"People need to learn to reap what they sow."

Reap what you sow. Eileen likes this phrase, this quote. She thinks people with AIDS are reaping what they sow too, getting what they deserve. She has said this to me before. She says, "Do you really think it's just a coincidence that homosexuals and drug users are getting it? Don't you see the lesson there?"

But I'm starting to think maybe this isn't true. In health class, Miss Yant showed us a videotape of people dying of AIDS in hospitals, too sick to eat, shaking under their blankets. Little babies have it now too, and they haven't even lived long enough to sow anything. So maybe Eileen is wrong. Maybe nobody is getting AIDS for a lesson. Maybe people are just getting it, and it's sad.

It won't really be like a wedding, Travis told me. It'll be more like an appointment, fifteen minutes from start to finish, four o'clock to four-fifteen.

Just at the courthouse, not at a church. But I think Mrs. Rowley got a new dress for it—blue with white flowers, with a sash in the back that she has left untied. She uses her hand to fan herself as she walks down the stairs to the parking lot.

Deena gets out of the car and waves up at Travis, turning in a little half circle to show him her dress. It's the dress she got for the prom. I remember when she bought it last year, on sale, seventy-two dollars with the shoes. She just happened to get a white one. Or maybe she knew, even then. Her stomach is still flat under the satin bodice. Spaghetti straps, tight against her tan shoulders, hold it up.

I duck below my window when she looks.

Travis is wearing a navy blue jacket, a gray shirt, a white tie, and dark gray pants that look like they have maybe been hemmed with safety pins. Deena's grandmother stays in the car, the engine running, but Mrs. Rowley has a small camera, and she motions for Travis and Deena to stand together. Travis puts his arm around Deena, and she leans her head on his shoulder.

I know that this moment, what I am seeing before me, will become a picture in a photo album. Their child, the one on its way, will look at this picture years from now, showing friends, and say, *This is a picture of my parents the day they got married,* touching Travis's and Deena's stilled faces with his or her fingers, seeing only how beautiful they both look, Deena's dress lifting in the breeze. They will think the picture is more important than it really is; they will think he or she exists because of the picture, instead of the other way around.

$$\boxed{\textit{eighteen}}$$

WHEN SUMMER COMES, TRAVIS AND Deena get approved for a Section 8, a two bedroom in Kerrville, just across the street from the garage where Travis works. It shouldn't be any different when they finally move—Deena and I don't talk, and Travis just works all the time anyway. But when they are actually gone, when I can no longer see them going on their long walks in the evening, I feel it. It's just me now.

But at least I'm finally old enough to work this summer, and that takes up some of the time. I turned in my application to the McDonald's in early June, but the manager, Franklin DuPaul, wouldn't even interview me at first. I had to bug him about it, by phone and in person, every day for a week before he dug my application up and waved me over behind the counter.

DuPaul is in his early fifties, tall and lean, the only black man I've ever seen in Kerrville, with a close-cropped beard that he rubs when he is thinking something over. When he interviewed me, he looked down at my application and not at my face while I explained that I needed to start saving money for college, and that I was a hard worker. He would not be sorry, I promised. Not sorry at all.

"Okay," he said, rubbing his beard. "We'll start you out, see how it goes."

He put me on fries, so this is what I do now, over and over for four-hour stretches at a time: I open a bag of frozen fries, pour them into the wire basket, lower the basket into the grease, and set the timer. While the fries are cooking, I sweep the floor, or I spray and wipe the stainless-steel counter behind me. When the timer for the fries rings, I lift the basket up out of the oil and dump the fries onto the warmer, add salt, and then shuffle them into different containers: small, medium, and large.

It is usually just boring, being at work, but sometimes it's hard. There are decisions to make. The fries go bad after about fifteen minutes, turning limp and soggy in the warmer, so I am not supposed to cook more than we need. But sometimes when I don't put enough in, buses pull in off the highway, and then forty-five people are waiting in the lobby, standing in five different lines in front of the counter.

"Fries," DuPaul will say, snapping his fingers. "Come on, Evelyn. Let's go. Let's go."

People have to wait too long when I don't make enough. Sometimes they say they are in a hurry and will just have an apple pie instead, but they look disappointed, or even mad, shrugging as they walk away from the counter, their heads hanging down.

But when I make a lot of fries, the lobby stays empty, and I have to throw them away. DuPaul can sense it when I have to throw fries away, no matter how far away he is. I try to bury them in the garbage, underneath hamburger wrappers and napkins. But he knows.

"Ms. Bucknow," he says, frowning, kicking the trash can a little so we can both see all the fries underneath the wrappers. "May I remind you that when we throw away our product without selling it, we lose money. It's a terrible waste."

"I know," I say, pushing my visor up so I can see him. "I know."

He tells me I have to learn to watch, to check for buses in the parking lot, to keep my eyes open. "Rhythm," he says, closing his eyes. "You've got to develop a rhythm."

Trish is no longer the dining-room attendant. She's the assistant manager now, and she gets to wear a special blue-and-white-striped shirt with a red tie. When I make mistakes, she isn't as nice as DuPaul.

"Are you stupid or something?" she asks. She pushes me out of the way and takes the fries out of the oil. They're burned, all of them, like little brown worms. "How could you forget to put on the timer?" Her eyebrows are still frozen high on her head.

"I don't know," I say. "I just forgot. I'm sorry." When Trish yells at me like this, in front of everyone, I have to work hard to think about something else so I won't cry.

"You're sorry." She dumps the burned fries in the garbage and puts another batch in. Her hands move quickly, and I can see raised scars on them, places she has burned herself. "You kids think you're so smart out in that lobby. But when it comes down to it, you don't know how to push a goddamn button."

DuPaul cuts in sometimes when she's like this. He tells her to go easy on me, to have a little patience. I'm still young, he says, still learning.

I hardly ever see either of them anymore, except for Sundays, when Deena drives Travis's no-muffler car to her grandmother's to do laundry. You can see she's pregnant now, a little slope sticking out of the middle of her ballerina body. It takes her a full minute just to get up out of the driver's seat. She carries the laundry basket on her hip, walking with her feet spread wide. The baby is due in November.

My mother is on the floor next to Samuel, helping him through his physical therapy exercises, pulling his legs when he does not want them pulled, and he is screaming. She looks out the window and sees Deena. "Poor thing," she says. "Honey, why don't you go help her?"

I shrug. "I'm busy."

"You're reading a magazine. When's the baby due?"

"I don't know. November." I glance outside. Deena is bent over, trying to pick up a shirt that has fallen out of the basket. She leans backward, one of her arms stretched out for balance, bending at the knees as if she were trying to get under a limbo stick.

"Evelyn," my mother says. "I don't know what this fight between you two is about, but at least go carry the basket."

"She's fine."

My mother leans across Samuel, grabs my magazine. Before I can believe she is really going to do it, she swats me with it on the back of my thigh.

"Ouch!" I stare at her in disbelief, and she does it again. I try to move away, but she leans after me, hits me again. "Knock it off!" I hold out my hands to shield myself, and she hits me there too.

"Go help your friend, Evelyn. You big meanie. Go help your friend." She stands up and swats me again, herding me toward the door. Samuel waves his arm from his beanbag, screeching. He's thrilled with this, all this violence.

"Mom, you're being crazy. Stop it."

"And you're being mean. Go help your friend." She opens the door, pushes me outside.

The door shuts behind me, and Deena turns around. "Hi," she says, surprised, squinting, her hand flat over her eyes. She is standing oddly, her legs crossed, the basket resting on one of her hips. She has not yet been able to pick up the shirt.

I reach behind me to try the door. Locked. "Hi."

"Haven't seen you for a while." She shifts the laundry basket to the other hip.

"Yeah. I've been busy. School and stuff."

I can see now she is sweating, beads trickling down from her new short hair. She leans heavily on the rail of the stairway, one of her hands resting on her belly. She might just be standing that way because she thinks pregnant women are supposed to.

"You need some help or something?"

She nods. "Actually, yeah. I have to pee. I have to pee right this very second. I don't think I'll make it if I have to carry this basket."

I jog across the parking lot, and she hands me her keys and the basket. She moves past me when I open the door, knocking the laundry basket out of my hands as she goes by.

"Sorry," she says, but keeps walking.

I kneel down to pick up the clothes, recognizing Deena's pink pillowcases from her old bed, Travis's orange T-shirt, his blue jeans. I pick them up, follow her in. Her grandmother's apartment has not changed. It's still dark, still crowded with furniture. I set the basket on the same table where we carved pumpkins.

She comes back out, sliding into a chair at the table. "Thanks," she says, breathing heavily, her eyes already closed. "Sorry about that. That's all I do these days is pee."

I'm not sure what to say to this. "Do you need some water or something?"

She nods, her eyes still closed. "It's a vicious cycle."

I get her a glass of water. "Where's your grandmother?"

"The movies. She says she goes to get out of the heat, but I don't know. I think she just doesn't want to see me." She pats her belly. "It bugs her, you know."

"Oh."

"At least she lets me come over." She shrugs. "Okay, I've got to put the laundry in." I watch her try to stand, leaning forward, pressing down on the sides of the chair with her arms. It looks difficult.

"Let me do it."

"You sure?" She sinks back down into the chair.

I bring her another glass of water. I can do this. It's just water. It's just giving water to a pregnant girl.

"Thanks," she says. "I say I'm coming over here to do laundry, but it's really for the AC." She grins at me, her eyes on mine. She's trying to act normal, but she's nervous, I can tell. "Feels good, doesn't it?"

I nod, sitting down. "I like your haircut."

She pulls her fingers through it quickly and rolls her eyes. "Travis is still mad about it. But if he likes long hair so much, he can grow his own."

We are quiet after this. It's not the same as it was before, her talking about Travis. My eyes drift away from her face, downward. The baby isn't due until November, but already, she's so much bigger than I remember my mother being with Sam.

"How does it feel?" I am always asking her this. She laughs. "Like you're carrying a basketball in between your knees. And it's always ninety degrees outside with eighty percent humidity and you're in a bad mood."

"Well, it really is ninety degrees outside."

"That's good to know. I thought it was just me." She fans herself with her hand. "I'm kidding. It's not so bad. I mean, physically, it's a drag. But it's kind of cool too. People hold doors open for you. Smile at you on the street."

Also, I think, watching her, *it makes it more difficult for your boyfriend to break up with you.*

"But I only have a couple more months," she says. "I keep dreaming I've already had the baby, and Travis is holding him. In the dream, I know everything went fine. So maybe that's a good sign. Anyway," she says, smiling again. "No going back now. One way or the other, he's coming out."

"It's a boy?"

She nods, her hand resting on top of her belly. I catch sight of the small diamond on her finger. It doesn't really sparkle. It may not even be real.

We are silent then, listening to the washing machine chug and spin. I don't know what to talk about. I don't know if I should talk about school, about McDonald's, or not. I can't think of anything to say. I stand up. "Well, I guess I'll get going."

She starts to smile, then lets it go, biting her lip. "Are you still mad at me, Evelyn?"

I don't know what to say. I never know what to say. I did not plan on having to talk to her today, and although I have been thinking about this question all summer, I still do not know the answer. Yes. No. A little. I sit back down. She pushes her lips together, and I can see she is trying not to cry.

"I miss you," she says. "I want us to be friends again."

Dead brown leaves rustle on the windowsill. They are already dying, the leaves of this year, dried out from the hot summer, not even bothering to change to red or yellow before they fall. I look at the sugar bowl in the middle of the table.

"It wasn't right, what you did," I say.

She rubs her eyes. "Oh God, Evelyn. You can be so mean, you know that? It wasn't like I had this all planned out. It wasn't like I did it on purpose. I just..." She stops. "I just didn't not do it on purpose." She frowns and shakes her head. "It sounds bad when I put it like that, but that's how it was."

This sounds fishy to me, this logic, but I don't tell her that. I don't want her to start crying. Not doing something on purpose would be doing something accidentally, accidentally forgetting to take the pills, accidentally throwing them away. I think about her doing this, coming home the night I told her that Travis was going to break up with her, walking through the sleet and slush to all this dark and quiet, her grandmother asleep in the next room.

But even though I have not said anything, she cries. Of course she does. "You're my only friend, Evelyn," she says. "Besides Travis, you're it."

This is terrible. The more she cries, the more I wonder if there is a possibility that I am actually the mean one. Or maybe we have both been mean. The washing machine buzzes loudly, and she starts to stand up.

I hold up my hand. "Okay. Don't. I'll get it."

"Thanks." She falls back into her chair, sniffing. I hand her a Kleenex, and she blows her nose. "Um, my pink blouse has to be set out. But everything else can just go in the dryer."

I open the lid of the washer. Inside, there are new blue-and-white-striped sheets, the pink pillowcases. Everything is tangled together. Deena's large, colorful maternity shirts are wrapped around Travis's underwear, her bras knotted up with his socks. Something about the cold wetness of their clothes, the clean smell of the laundry detergent and the way they are all tied together, makes me feel bad about touching them. Later there will be bibs and tiny shirts in the dryer too, all of their clothes spinning together, then folded neatly in the same basket, buttons and snaps fastened by each other's fingers.

It's just the way it is now. It's just the way it is.

"Does it look okay?" she calls out. "Nothing ruined?"

"No." I take out her pink blouse, lay it out flat on top of the dryer. "It's fine."

On the first day of eleventh grade, Libby is back, her long hair cut short and darker than it was. She can walk, but she has to use a cane. Dr. Queen asks me to share a locker with her, since we have both lost our partners. I move my things to her locker, to the shelf that used to be Traci's.

Because of the cane, Libby can't always get all the books she needs out of her locker and put others away at the same time, so I help her during passing time, holding her books. She shows me the leg exercises she has to do every night for her physical therapy, twenty-five on each side, a rubber band around her ankles for resistance.

"My little brother's got a rubber band like that," I tell her. "He has to do exercises too."

"They suck," she says. "Tell him I sympathize."

When the accident first happened, people kept saying how lucky Libby was, the sole survivor of the wrecked car. I don't know if she feels lucky or not. She told me that over the summer, Mr. Carmichael mowed the lawn every day, sometimes for hours, going over the same strips of grass two or three times, even when it was scorching out, the air humid with no breeze to blow it away. Every day she woke up to the sound of the mower, the blades racing over the grass that was already too short. She went outside once and saw him lying in the grass, right next to the mower, his hands over his face in the bright sunlight.

The Carmichaels are moving, she says. They're staying in Kerrville, but moving to a different neighborhood, maybe because of her. They don't want to have to see her all the time. Adele's family has already moved.

"I'm sure they're glad I didn't die too," she says, turning her cane in slow circles. A pink, sickle-shaped scar runs from the outer corner of her left eye to the top of her lip, and she runs her finger over it in class when she thinks no one is looking.

We have American government together third period, Libby and I. Mr. Chemsky is the teacher, young and with a red-brown beard, and he likes to use "so-called" as an adjective and "allegedly" as an adverb. "The so-called House of Representatives," he says, rolling his eyes, "are allegedly elected to represent the people's wishes in the legislative branch." He also makes quote marks with his fingers when he talks, sometimes twice in one sentence, and it is hard to tell if he is really quoting someone or if this is just something he likes to do.

He is doing this one sunny day in November when an office attendant walks in with a note. Mr. Chemsky takes the note from her, but waits until she leaves before he opens it, his hand cupped around it like it is from the FBI. When he is finished reading, he pauses dramatically, looking around the room. "Evelyn Bucknow, you're to go to the office."

I am scared when he tells me this, and then even more scared as I leave the room, walking down the long yellow hallway to the office. Too many bad things have happened this year. There can't be anything else. But of course, I know, really there could be. It's not like there are rules.

When I get to the office, the secretary says that a Dr. Love has called to relay the message that my mother had another episode and is now in the hospital, resting comfortably. My Uncle Bubba will be coming to pick me up in front of the school right away.

I am confused for only a moment, standing there and looking at the attendance secretary, who is wearing green eyeshadow, looking grimly back at me. And then, even from inside the school, I can hear the engine of Travis's blue Datsun.

He waves when he sees me come through the double doors, leaning over to open the passenger door. "Say hi to Daddy," he says. He is holding an unlit cigar.

"She had the baby?"

"Last night. Eight pounds, seven ounces." He thumps a gloved hand on the steering wheel. "Cutest little fucker you've ever seen."

"I get to come in? I get to see them?"

"You're the first person she asked for. Her grandmother went home last night and hasn't even come back yet, that bitch." A box of Dunkin' Donuts sits next to him on the seat. He sets the cigar on the dashboard, pulls out an apple fritter, and shoves it into his mouth while making a left turn. "Take one," he mumbles. There's a shadow of stubble from his ears to his throat, and he has the wild, frenzied look of someone who has been awake for too long.

"Have you named him?"

He inhales and exhales through his nostrils, grinning. "Jack." He turns on the radio. It's Prince, singing "I Would Die 4 U," and Travis sings along. I smile without thinking about it, for the first time in a while. This is not what I would have wanted, not what I imagined when I was younger. When I sat up on the roof with him, waiting for falling stars, I did not think that someday we would be riding in a car together, going to visit his wife and baby. But it really is good to see him this happy, after so many days of watching him go to work in the khaki jumpsuit.

When we get to the hospital, he leads me to the maternity ward, going the long way, pointing out where the pop and candy machines are, the elevator to the morgue, where he saw an old naked man being led back to his room by the nurses. He's been in every hallway, he says; Deena went into labor at eleven o'clock the night before, and he'd had so much nervous energy that the doctors hadn't wanted him around until the very end.

"What this place needs is a fucking arcade or something," he says, pushing the button for the elevator. "All the magazines are dumb. They keep the television on the goddamn *Nova* channel."

Samuel was in the neonatal unit in Kansas City, and I remember the walls and the floors being very, very white, but the maternity ward of Kerrville Memorial has light pink walls, with flowers painted close to the floor so maybe, if you were on a lot of medication, you might think they were real and really growing there. There are even oversized bumblebees, smiling, their eyes pleasantly dazed.

I follow him to Deena's room, right around the corner. It's still sunny out, but you would never know it in here, with dark, heavy curtains covering the window. She is lying in the bed by the door, her head propped up by large pillows, looking up at the television high in the corner of the opposite wall. The sheets and blankets come up to her shoulders, but I can see she's wearing her own pink robe.

"I think she's still pretty doped up," Travis whispers. "You should have heard her scream."

She turns toward us. "Evelyn? What are you doing here? Travis? What were you-all doing?" She squints, propping herself up on her elbows. "Where have you been?"

"You told me to go get her, remember?" Travis laughs, tousling her hair. "I called and pretended I was a doctor, remember?"

"Yeah. That's right. Hi, Evelyn." She smiles. "Wait. Where's the baby?"

Travis says he'll go find the nurse. The volume of the television is turned up loud, the opening credits to *General Hospital* blaring. I find the remote, push the mute button. "How you feeling, Deener?"

She crosses her eyes, makes her lips go crooked. "Like crapola. I feel like crapola."

"Travis said it looked painful. You want some light? You want me to open the curtains?"

She nods. "Yeah. I just feel out of it now. I told them to dope me up with everything they had. I told that nurse, I said, 'Look, I'm not into that natural childbirth shit. Just give me the juice. I don't want to feel this.' But I think she was holding out on me. It hurt like hell. Let me tell you."

"It seems like it would hurt." Stupid thing to say.

"Oh, it wasn't that bad. You'll want to have one too when you see him. You will. I'll let you hold him and then you'll want one for yourself." She lowers her voice. "Want to see something gross?"

I step away. "No."

But she is already lifting up her nightgown and pointing to her breasts, her nipples swollen and red against her white skin. "The nurses say I should keep breast-feeding, but I'm not going to do it anymore if he's going to try to chew off my tit like that."

A nurse walks in, holding the baby, Travis making faces at it over her shoulder. She puts the baby in Deena's arms like she is stacking teacups on top of each other, telling us that he has just fallen asleep. I smile at her, but she does not smile back.

Travis presses a button that makes a humming sound, and the back of Deena's bed starts moving up slowly, until she is sitting upright. "Pretty cool, huh?" he says, talking about the bed, not the baby. He pushes another button, and the bed starts to move down again. Deena tells him to knock it off, and he does.

"Evelyn, come look at him," she whispers. "He's like a doll."

The baby's face is pinker and flatter than I thought it would be, his eyes bulging and blue-green. I am amazed by how much he looks like Travis, the same shape of mouth, the same cheekbones.

"Isn't he cool?" Travis asks. Now he's talking about the baby. He rests his chin on Deena's shoulder, gazing down.

"You want to be gentle with him," the nurse says. She is an older woman, deep creases around her mouth and eyes. The nurses on *General Hospital* are wearing white hats that fold on the sides, but this real nurse doesn't have one. She wears a yellow cardigan and a name tag that says JULIA SHERIDAN, R.N.

"I know that," Deena says. "We don't need anything else, okay? I'll ring you when I get sleepy."

But Julia Sheridan, R.N., doesn't seem to want to go. She looks at Travis, and then Deena, me, and then at the baby. "Are your mothers coming back?" she asks.

"My grandmother isn't coming back, probably, if that's what you're waiting for," Deena says. "But since *I'm* the mother now, I guess we'll be fine. Thanks. Bye."

Travis says his mother will be back at three.

"Who are you?" Julia Sheridan asks, looking at me.

"She's my sister," Deena says.

Julia Sheridan looks at me and then back at Deena. She knows this is a lie. "Look, I don't mean to hassle you," she says. "But you have to understand, a baby's a delicate thing. You-all are just so young. I just wish you had somebody here to—"

"We're fine, okay? I said I'd ring you when I was tired."

The combination of Deena getting mad and still being kind of drugged up is no good. Her voice is shrill, her lips rubbery, not making the right shapes for the words. The baby starts to cry, high-pitched, urgent. Julia Sheridan frowns at me and leaves.

Deena blows on the baby's forehead, and Travis leans over her shoulder, telling him to try to be happy. For Daddy, he adds. But the baby keeps crying, poking a tiny pink fist out from the blankets, clutching at Deena's pink robe.

"Ugh. He's hungry. Here we go again." She moves aside her nightgown, putting his mouth up to one of her already red nipples, wincing in pain. "That's right, buddy, you go ahead," she whispers. "You like that, don't you? Is the evil nurse right?"

I don't want to be rude, but it's neat, watching this. I hadn't seen my mother nurse Sam; they were both too sick when he was born, and he had his nutrients pumped in through an IV and then a feeding tube, and then a bottle with enriched formula. But this baby is just fine, slurping steadily, his little fingers twitching against her skin. It seems strange to me that Deena's body can somehow suddenly produce food for him. It's like a magic trick, a secret talent she has always had that I didn't know about, like juggling or playing the violin.

I sit down on the foot of the bed. The room is nice and bright, little ducks and rabbits on the curtains, a fold-out shelf for changing diapers. Just outside, hanging in the hallway, is a large black-and-white poster of a baby's wide-eyed face. FRAGILE! HANDLE WITH CARE! is printed in large red letters beneath it.

"I got doughnuts while I was out, Dee," Travis says. "You want some doughnuts?"

She sticks her tongue out. "Doughnuts? Why'd you get doughnuts?"

"You like doughnuts."

"I need health food. I'm nursing a baby."

The soap opera is still on with the sound muted, the camera focused on a woman with long blond hair in a glittery black dress. She is very mad about something, pointing a gun at a man in a tuxedo, his hands raised in surrender.

"You watch this one?" Travis asks, turning the volume back on.

Deena shakes her head no. "I tell you all the time. I watch *Days* and *One Life to Live*."

Travis asks me if I watch this one, if I know what's going on. I shake my head, still looking up at the screen. "I'm in school when they're on."

They look at each other quickly, only for a moment, just long enough for me to see them do it. I didn't mean anything, but I know they think I did. I keep my eyes up on the screen, trying to think if I should say something else or just keep quiet.

A commercial comes on the television for Irish Spring soap, and we all pretend to watch it. No one says anything, but I can feel that they want me to leave.

"I guess I better get going," I say, standing up. "The buses leave in an hour." I don't know if even this is okay, to talk about the buses, to make any reference to school at all.

"Oh, okay," Travis says. He reaches for the car keys on the table, moving slowly enough so I have time to stop him.

"I can walk back," I say. "It's not far."

"You sure?" he asks, yawning. "Okay. I guess I am pretty tired." He smiles, pointing at the doughnuts. "My sugar rush is leaving me."

Deena says she's sleepy too, and asks me to turn the light back off on my way out. We hug each other, but lightly, with just one arm each, the baby still nestled in her arms. I wanted to hold him before I left, but now I don't think I should ask.

"Congratulations," I say. I feel suddenly large and awkward, like an adult ducking into a playhouse, too big to sit in the play chairs without breaking them.

"Thanks," she says, and the way she smiles makes me feel more this way.

When I am out in the hallway, I turn back to look at them through the glass window of the door. The room is dark, but I can see the back of the baby's head, his tiny head still nestled against her. I wave good-bye, but they are looking at the baby, tired-eyed and open-mouthed, and neither of them sees me.

nineteen

$\mathcal{I}$ DON'T HEAR TOO MUCH from them after they have the baby. I call sometimes, but usually Jack is crying in the background, and Deena just talks about how tired she is, how she's been up with him all night. He's a colicky baby, she says, and a light sleeper. When Travis answers the phone, his hello comes out as a yawn.

It's okay, I tell them. I'm busy too. I am still working at McDonald's. I told DuPaul I could keep working during the school year if they moved me down to part-time.

"Oh goody," Trish said, standing behind him. "Goody gumdrops."

I go in for two hours after school and eight hours on Sundays. It's a little better now. I have convinced DuPaul I would do better in drive-thru, simply taking money from people, and giving them what they want, no real grease involved, nothing to burn.

"At least you're not a leaner," he said, rubbing his beard, looking at JoAnne Steely at the front counter, who was right at that moment leaning on one of the counters and looking at her fingernails. "A lot of these people come in here, saying they want to work, and they just lean around. Like it's their lawn furniture or something. Like I'm paying them to lean."

DuPaul has three children, two of them in college. JoAnne Steely the leaner told me he's here because his wife died three years ago, and he moved here from St. Louis because they offered him more money. There are plaques by the time clock stating that he's won BEST STORE MANAGER in the Midwest District, two years in a row.

"I've got no time for leaners," he says, carrying in crates of orange juice from the walk-in. "No time at all."

Travis and Deena come through the drive-thru in the Datsun sometimes, Jack strapped into his car seat in the back. He has hair now, thin wisps of dark curls that make him look even more like Travis. They are starting to look alike, I notice, all three of them. They all have the same hair. When it's cold out, Deena and Travis wear matching blue-and-yellow jackets.

"Hey!" Deena says, looking up at me from Travis's window. "Can you get us some free food?"

"I don't think so," I say. Trish is already behind me, her hand flat against my back, steering me back toward the fry vat. "This isn't a social hour," she says. "You're on the clock."

Working this much does nothing good for my skin, and my mother has started leaving little packets of Noxzema in the bathroom. This is how it is now. This is my life. I do my homework on the bus.

I'm not sure yet what I will do with the money I am making, though I have been carefully saving it from the very start. I have bought only one tape this year, Tracy Chapman's, because I like the song "Fast Car," even though my mother says it's so depressing she can't stand it and would I please stop playing it over and over.

Ms. Jenkins is my science teacher again this year, and she says she thinks I can get a scholarship to KU, but still it seems as if this extra money from McDonald's will be good to have. If I do get a scholarship, I will still need a car to drive away in. I tell myself this when I am at work and Trish is yelling at me, her face too close to mine, and this way I don't hear her at all.

It's like swimming underwater, this whole year. I just close my eyes, hold my breath, and keep kicking.

Spring comes, finally. In April, the magnolia trees in front of the school bloom pink and white, their honey scent carried by the breeze. On the first warm day, Mrs. Evans opens the windows so we can smell them in sixth-period English. "Breathe deeply, class," she says. "Beauty is good for you." But before her class is even over, a storm rolls in, big and loud, the kind of storm I love. The sky turns a deep, dark gray very quickly, and streaks of lightning hit so close that Mrs. Evans jumps and says, "Oh my!" She shuts the windows and goes back to trying to teach us about iambic pentameter, but after a while, she gives up, and we all just sit there and look out the windows.

"Just a different kind of poetry," she says, more to herself than to us.

At the end of the day, when we are walking to the buses, it's already sunny again. If you looked at the sky, you wouldn't even know it had rained at all. But on the ground, entire branches of red buds and lilacs lie broken on the damp sidewalks. I pick up as many as I can, twisting them in two so they are small enough to carry. Libby stands in the line for the bus, watching me, leaning on her cane. I pick up more lilacs, and give some to her.

When I get home, I give a branch to my mother.

"Thanks," she says, looking at me strangely. "Do you know?"

"Know what?"

Samuel is in his wheelchair, and she has to hold the branch of flowers up, out of his reach. He tries for them anyway, banging his head against her leg. "Eileen called. My father died this morning." She is dry-eyed and even-voiced, a newscaster reporting a fire. "Heart attack," she adds. "You know he'd already had one."

Samuel reaches for the flowers again, groaning slightly. "No," she says, pointing at the ends of the twigs. "No, honey, they're sharp. Evelyn, help me get him into his beanbag." She puts the branch on the table and slides her hands under his arms, nodding at me to get his feet. I watch her carefully, trying to read her face, but she is looking down at Samuel, concentrating on the task at hand.

"Eileen sounded okay," she says. "But she might be covering."

"Are *you* okay?"

"Yeah. I'm fine." She tears a flower off the branch for Samuel and helps him get his fingers around it, holding it underneath his nose until he smiles.

Eileen comes up from Wichita three days later, after the funeral, not wearing black, but green, her hair pulled back in a ponytail. She says she needed to get away from all the people in the house. Daniel is twenty-two now, in the army and living with his wife and new baby, but they came to Wichita for the funeral, and they haven't left yet. My grandfather's two sisters came up from Oklahoma, and Eileen says they are not very pleasant people to be around for very long. There were too many guests, she says, and not enough bath towels. The people from her church have been good, giving her more food than she knows what to do with. She has brought some of it up with her—strawberry-rhubarb pie, banana bread, chicken dumplings, all of it in plastic bowls with plastic wrap stretched across the tops.

She hasn't even had time to miss him, she says. She says the same storm passed through Wichita that day, and she is sure it was my grandfather, his way of saying good-bye. The hospital called her just as the first drops of rain were starting to fall.

"I was still in my dressing gown, but I just tossed on my slippers and got in the car," she says, the smoke from her cigarette drifting to the ceiling. My mother is letting her smoke in the house. "All that wind, all that thunder. They hadn't told me on the phone, but he was already gone. I come out of the hospital maybe ten minutes later, standing there crying, and I look up at the sky, and there was the sun shining down through the clouds, everything green and shiny. There was a rainbow," she says, her voice lifting. "You think I'm making it up, but I'm not."

My mother says nothing to this. She does not roll her eyes. "Maybe you and the girls could think about moving up to Kerrville," she says, pouring Eileen some coffee. "Evelyn's going to KU, and she won't be far away."

"You should," I add. "I'd like that."

Eileen smiles and brings her cup up to her mouth. "Maybe," she says.

I give Samuel a bath, so my mother can stay in the front room with Eileen. I am still not as good with him as she is, and I don't do the bath right. I get soap in his eyes, and I leave the water on for too long. When it rises to his shoulders, he starts screaming, swatting at me, his head dipping underwater. I have to hold him close so he won't hurt himself, and this is what finally calms him, his soapy head under my chin. His hands clutch my arms, and we stay still like this, pressed together, his heart pounding so I can feel it, until the water drains back down.

"Everything okay in there?" my mother calls out.

"We're fine," I say. He gazes up in the direction of my face. His blue eyes stay focused, unblinking and brilliant. I don't know if they see me or not.

When I wheel him back out to the front room, a towel wrapped around his hair, Eileen is crying, and my mother isn't. "Thanks, Evelyn," my mother says. Samuel pulls himself toward her, his arms reaching vaguely forward. "Look at my boy!" she says. "Look at my beautiful clean boy!"

Eileen watches them, saying nothing, until her cigarette is all gone, turned to ash in the saucer my mother has set on the table. "You're really not too upset, are you?" she asks finally, really just asking, not mad about it. "You said you weren't going to be upset, and you're not."

My mother frowns, her hands pulling gently through Samuel's damp hair. "No. I'm really not."

"Seems like you should be," Eileen says, looking out the window. "Maybe it hasn't hit you yet."

"Maybe," my mother agrees.

"He had his problems, but he was still your father. He had his good points too."

"That's true," my mother says.

"Probably later I'll get really upset," Eileen says. "When I realize he's gone for good, not coming back. I'm sure it will hit me in a few days. That's what they say. I'm probably just numb right now."

"Probably," my mother says, catching my eye, looking away before Eileen can see her do it.

Samuel is going to start first grade through the special education program in the fall. I think back to my own first grade, and I remember putting together jigsaw puzzles of the fifty states in the union, letter books, and long pages of single-digit addition. It is difficult to imagine Samuel sitting in a classroom like this. I'm not sure what or how they're going to teach him. If someone gave him a jigsaw puzzle of the fifty states, he would just sit there, and maybe put some of the pieces in his mouth.

"They'll work on his independent-living skills," my mother says. She is sitting on the rim of the bathtub, leaning forward to help him brush his teeth, her hand tight around his. He doesn't like brushing his teeth, and she has to keep her feet wrapped around his ankles so he can't scoot away.

"But that's what you do," I say.

"Well," she says, reaching for the floss, "we'll give somebody else a crack at it for a while." She is all talk, though. When it gets closer to the first day, she gets nervous. They have already gone through a dry run in the summer: the bus for special education students, the short bus, came out and picked up my mother and Samuel so they could run through a simulated school morning, seeing his classroom, meeting his teacher. But now the real thing is coming up, and the school has sent out a letter, polite but firm, making it clear that no parents should be on the bus on the first day of school. They will send the same bus out again, and there will be two paras on board to assist the students on their way to school.

"They used to not have any of that," Verranna Hinckle told us, grinning as she scanned the letter. "It's because Kenny Astor's parents sued the district."

But my mother is not feeling very appreciative. She calls the school secretary several times a day, attempting to weasel her way not only onto the bus but into sitting right next to Samuel for the entire morning of school. I think they are getting tired of her calling.

"Yes I know," she says. She is sitting on the couch with Samuel on her lap, the telephone receiver in the crook of her neck. "But you don't understand. He's never been away from me. As in *never*." She pauses, and I can hear someone talking on the other end. Samuel reaches up to the phone cord, wrapping it around his wrist. "I know there's a first time for everything," she says. "I know that, okay?"

The night before the first day of school, my mother knocks on my door and tells me that Samuel probably won't get to start school tomorrow. She can tell he is already upset. He knows something is up, she says, and she expects he will put up a fight. She doesn't see how she'll be able to get him up and dressed and waiting for the bus by eight.

"It just won't work," she says, shrugging. "They don't understand." She is standing in my doorway, wearing the jean skirt and a shirt that is on backwards. I watch her for a moment, pushing my glasses up so I can really see her. She bites her lip, looks back at me.

"I'll stay home and help you," I say. "I can miss the first day."

The next morning, we get up at six, and even though she insists on being the one to lift him and help him brush his teeth, it really is a good thing I am there. He thrashes and swings when she lifts him from his bed to his wheelchair, from his wheelchair to the tub, and then up and over the rim of the tub into his wheelchair again. She leans him up against her so she can shimmy his pants up and over his hips, pushing his arms into his shirtsleeves, and he screams. I stand behind him, holding his arms down with mine, careful not to squeeze or pinch his thin skin. But still he grabs hold of her hair when we are coming out of the bathroom, and his grip is so strong that he is able to bring her to her knees before I can get him to let go. We wait until after breakfast to put on his shoes, because he is kicking wildly, swinging his legs with more strength than I thought he had.

He has never been like this before. He knows today is different after all.

When the bus comes, things go badly. My mother wheels him outside, and there is no doubt in my mind at all that he sees the bus, the lowered wheelchair ramp, and the smiling paras waiting on each side. He screams as if he is dying, holding on to my mother's shirt with his crooked hand until his fingers turn the color of bruised peaches. I am so busy trying to pry his fingers away that for a while I don't see that she is holding on to him too, her arm locked around his waist.

I touch her hand. "Mom."

One of the paras, a large woman wearing running shoes and a fanny pack, pats my mother on the shoulder. "Don't worry," she says. "We're going to take care of him. We're going to teach him things. I promise."

But he manages to pop the other para in the nose before they get him on the bus. She stands up for a moment, wrinkling her nose like a rabbit. "I'm okay," she says. "I'm fine." They strap his wheelchair onto the lift, and he starts to move upward.

"It's only for a few hours, baby," my mother says. She's crying now, not even embarrassed that the paras can see. "You'll be home by two."

They put him next to a window, both of them kneeling to buckle him in. I can see two other people on the bus, a little girl who looks normal, and a boy with a very large head. Samuel bangs his fist against the glass, and we can hear him screaming. My mother has to turn around and put her hand over her eyes until the bus pulls onto the highway.

"Are they gone?" she asks.

"They're gone." I put my arm around her. "You did a good job. He'll be home by two."

She is still crying, her shoulders heaving beneath my arm, but after a while she looks up at me, and even with the tears on her face, she looks like she could also be laughing. "Look, you're a nice lady and everything," she says. "But what have you done with my real daughter?"

I take my arm away, embarrassed. "Are you going to be okay?"

She wipes her face on the sleeve of her robe. "Yeah. I'll be fine."

It's true. By the next day, she has already gone across the highway and gotten a job at McDonald's, the lunch shift, ten-thirty to one. If she can get AFDC to approve her working without them taking everything else away, she says, she'll be able to make some extra money while Samuel is at school, and still have a full hour and a half to herself to shower and eat lunch before he gets home. She says this part, *a full hour and a half,* as if she has won a week at a health spa in Sweden.

Libby says all I missed on the first day was roll call and an announcement that the school will no longer be using the thirteen absences rule or the special computer. If you miss more than three classes in one quarter, the teachers themselves will call your house, and they will know exactly who they are talking to.

Also, Mr. Goldman is gone this year. He went back to New York with his wife. I saw the obituary for her father in the newspaper, so I guess that's why. They announced he was leaving at an assembly last year, and a lot of people were crying, and everyone was clapping for him, even the teachers who talked about his balking in the teachers' lounge. He smiled and said thank you, but sat down quickly. I think he was sick of us, and ready to go back home.

Libby and I are the only seniors on the bus. Brad Browning has a car this year, but Libby is not allowed to ride in it, and I have not been asked. We sit together, up front, because there are eighth-grade boys in the back who still throw spitballs, burp loudly, and laugh. We buy magazines at the store across the street from school and trade them back and forth: *Seventeen, Cosmopolitan, Glamour.* The models on the covers are flawless, shimmering, more beautiful than even the most beautiful girls in our class, and the words beneath them say things like YOUR BEST YEAR YET!, CELEBRATE LOVE!, and TWENTY-ONE DAYS TO A NEWER, SLEEKER YOU! We rub the perfume samples on our wrists, give each other the quizzes: WHAT'S YOUR SEXUAL I.Q.? WHAT'S YOUR FASHION PERSONALITY? ARE YOU A BITCH OR A DOORMAT??? These quizzes are hard to answer without lying, because it's easy to guess which answer is the right one, the one that will give you the most points in the good column: not a bitch, not a doormat, but just right. Somewhere in between.

1. A coworker embarrasses you in front of a client. How do you respond?
A. Fire back! Say something even more embarrassing or hurtful to her. See how she likes it!
B. Don't say anything. Maybe she didn't mean it.
C. Take her aside and let her know that she embarrassed you, and that you don't appreciate her disrespect. Listen to what she has to say in response, but don't back down.

Libby and I agree that the right answer is never this obvious in real life.

Homecoming is in October, but neither of us has a date. Libby says she couldn't go, even if somebody asked her. "I've got my partner right here," she says, tapping her cane on the floor of the bus. "He'd get jealous if I tried to dance with someone else."

She says things like this sometimes, but still, I go to great lengths not to mention the cane. I am also careful not to mention Traci's or Adele's name, even though I know that, really, this is stupid. It's not as if my not saying their names will keep her from thinking about them, about the accident. Traci was her best friend. It must be there, in her mind, all the time. But I don't want to say the wrong thing. Libby says if one more person tells her everything happens for a reason, she is going to beat them to the ground with her cane.

"It says here," she says, her finger pressed against a page of *Mademoiselle,* "that if you're feeling blue about being single, you should try doing something loving for someone who needs it. Not necessarily something romantic. And it has to be something you do, not something you buy."

We decide we will each do something like this. We shake on it. I will offer to baby-sit, once for my mother, once for Travis and Deena. Libby says she'll make a scrapbook for the Carmichaels. She will make copies of photographs she has of Traci and write down what she remembers about her.

"Edited, of course," she adds. "They don't need to know it all."

This is all she will say. She does not tell me what she is going to leave out, what things she knows about Traci that Mr. and Mrs. Carmichael would not want to know about their own daughter, even in their deepest grief. I am comforted all the same. Lately, painfully, I have been envisioning Traci Carmichael as an angel, her blue-gray eyes watching me sadly from underneath a halo, her body vague and not clearly defined. The teachers had already planted two trees on the front lawn, one for Traci, one for Adele. There is a plaque on the ground between the trees that says *For Traci and Adele, angels in our hearts forever.* When I pass it, I think about that day in gym when she had her hands on my ankles, and I feel guilty about everything bad I have ever done.

But really, it's difficult to imagine Traci Carmichael as a fluttering angel. It doesn't make sense. There is no way that Traci Carmichael could be floating around in the sky with a harp and wings and still be Traci Carmichael. She might be okay like that for a little while, but then I think she would get bored. She would start rolling her eyes. She would want to pass around a petition.

The only way I can really imagine Traci undead for all of eternity is to picture her just riding along in Adele Peterson's Honda, not being necessarily good, but not being bad either. She isn't thinking about me or even anything, just listening to the music on the radio, her pink-braceleted arm hanging out the window, her fingers spread wide in the breeze.

At McDonald's, my mother is a hit, a natural. She is fast at the cash register, and she does not forget to set timers. Her ice cream cones stand up perfectly, and she learns how to change the syrup in the cola machine the first week. In November, she is employee of the month, which doesn't seem fair. She only started in September, and I've been working there for over a year. DuPaul moves her up to drive-thru right away, because she makes the customers laugh, and then they don't get so mad when they have to wait.

We never work together, because she only works when I am in school, and I work after it. Still, the comparisons are made.

"Your mother is such a fast learner," Trish says, smiling. "She never makes any mistakes."

I lower a basket of fries into the oil and don't say anything. I know where this is going.

"Are you adopted?" she asks brightly, her eyebrows high up on her forehead, arched.

My mother says she will let me baby-sit for her when spring comes. If I am going to baby-sit Samuel for a full day, she wants it to be in May, when the weather is nice and she can go for a walk. I would think that she would be happy to let me baby-sit right away, no matter what the weather is like. She must be exhausted, I tell her, now that she is working at McDonald's and also taking care of Samuel. But she says she is less exhausted now that she is not with Samuel all the time. It's nice to get out a little, she says, and talk to other people.

"Some people, maybe," I say. "Not Trish."

"People in general," she says.

But when I ask Deena if she would like me to baby-sit, she says yes right away. She wants to know when. She says she has not been to a movie, not

266 • LAURA MORIARTY

one, since Jack was born. She says something else, but I can't hear her because Jack is crying.

"Sorry," she says. "Poor guy. His teeth are coming in. I said that would be really nice." She pauses, lowers her voice. "We could probably use a night out. Things haven't been going so well."

I wait for her to say more, but she doesn't.

She picks me up in Travis's Datsun, wearing mascara, hoop earrings, and a red velvet shirt with a neck so low you can see the top of her bra. There is something, maybe baby food, dried on a strand of her hair. She hugs me when I get in. "This is so nice of you," she says. "It's a big deal for me to get to go out. You have no idea. And we're paying you. I don't care what you say."

"No. You can't pay me. It's my favor," I tell her. "You look nice."

She glances up in the rearview mirror and smiles. "This is the one shirt I own that no one has thrown up on."

The apartment complex where they live looks amazingly similar to Treeline Colonies. It is only two miles up the highway, and also brown with black trim. They live in the basement, and Deena points out the four half windows that are theirs from the parking lot. I follow her down the concrete steps, her high heels stepping carefully over patches of ice. "Down to the dungeon," she says. "Watch your step."

Travis opens the door for us, Jack red-faced and crying in his arms. He is also dressed up, wearing a belt even, and clean shaven, his skin still pink from the razor.

"Hey Daddy-O," I say. Jack turns away, his face buried in Travis's shoulder. He's a year old now, but still all chubby cheeks and knees, his ears sticking out like handles on a cup. Travis leans forward to hug me, but it is difficult with him holding Jack, so he ends up just patting me on the back. Even this makes Jack cry harder, louder. Travis smiles and walks away with him, singing in his ear.

"We shortened his nap today so he would sleep for you," Deena says. "That's why he's such a grouch. Okay, here's the rundown." She points at a paper by the phone. "This is the number for the ambulance. I'm sure you won't need it, but just in case. This is our pediatrician. He's really nice, but don't call him unless it's something major. Call us first if you can. This is the number of the restaurant, and this is the number of the movie theater. The movie starts at nine-ten." She frowns. "This is Travis's mom's number, but call only if it's an emergency." She lowers her voice and smiles. "Let sleeping bitches lie."

Travis looks up, the expression on his face difficult to read. Jack isn't crying anymore, but gurgling softly, his small hand wrapped tightly around one of Travis's fingers.

"Also he's teething," she continues. "So if he looks like he's having a hard time, just sort of rub his gums with one of your fingers. It helps." She models this technique on her own mouth, her pointer finger moving quickly around the inside of her mouth, smudging her red lipstick. "He usually goes to sleep around eight-thirty. I would check his diaper around eight. If he seems like he wants another bottle, he can have one. There's a backup in the fridge."

I am silent, growing concerned. When I said I would do this, I pictured Jack sleeping, me reading a book. "How do I know if he seems like he wants another bottle? What does that mean?"

Deena frowns. "This kind of cry means he's hungry," she says. She makes a series of short, high-pitched sounds, opening her mouth wide.

"No," Travis says. "It's more like this." He makes, as far as I can tell, the same sound Deena just made. "And this kind of cry means he needs to be changed." He makes another crying sound.

"You guys don't sound like a baby," I say. "You sound like dolphins."

Neither of them laughs. They look at me the way Trish does when I forget to set the timer on the fries. "You can't hear the difference?" Travis asks.

"No." I'm more nervous now than before.

Deena looks at her watch. "We should probably get going."

"I just want to wait until he settles down to sleep," Travis whispers. "I'll put him in his swing."

Deena nods. "Okay, but the movie starts at nine-ten. We won't have time to eat."

They look at each other. "Evelyn can put him in the swing," Deena says.

As soon as Travis puts Jack in my arms, he starts to cry again. "Try the bottle," Deena says, handing it to me. The bottle is warm, decorated with tiny blue elephants. I hold the tip up to his mouth, aware that they are both watching. I feel stupid, like a bad imposter, and even a baby can tell the difference. "See the elephants, honey?" I try. I sound stupid.

Travis and Deena put on their hats and coats and stand in the doorway.

"Um, that isn't the way to hold the bottle," Deena says. "It'll give him gas if you do it like that."

Travis says I need to rock him a little when I hold him, rearranging Jack in my arms. "Didn't you take care of your brother when he was little?"

"Not really. Is it the teething thing? Should I put my finger in his mouth?"

Deena smiles and sighs, taking off her coat. "It was nice of you to offer," she says. "Really. Just the idea of getting to go out was good." She takes Jack from my arms, and right away he stops crying, the redness leaving his face. He gazes up at her with adoring eyes, sucking on the bottle that she holds at the correct angle, his tiny hands resting on her arms.

When Deena came to pick me up, she had been playing a regular rock station from Wichita, but when Travis starts the engine, he switches the radio over to country.

I point at the radio. "When did this start?"

He smiles, sheepish. "You ever hear that joke about what happens when you play a country song backwards?"

I shake my head. It is cold, even in the car, but he isn't wearing a hat or gloves.

"The dog comes back, the wife stops cheating, and all the beer reappears in the fridge."

"You guys had a dog?"

"You can't take it literally."

"And Deena's not cheating either."

"This is true." Once we are on the highway, he asks me to hold the steering wheel while he lights a cigarette. I'm not a big fan of this maneuver, but I do it. I have to get close to him, my arms crossed over his, and I can smell his shaving lotion, alcohol and mint.

"You see my mom lately?" he asks.

"Yeah. Jackie O had to have surgery or something. She's wearing this little doggie cast around one of her legs."

He laughs, taking the wheel again. "I know. I've heard all about it. That dog will outlive us all." He looks at me quickly, then back at the road in front of him. His face is changing, still handsome, but growing older maybe. He looks tired.

"Are you and Deena doing okay?"

He glances at me. "Why? What did she say?"

"Nothing. Really. I just wondered."

He shrugs. "I guess. I mean, it's okay. Jack's a cutie, isn't he?"

"He is."

Ten seconds go by without either of us saying anything. I count them off in my head.

"How's school?" he asks.

"Okay."

He rolls his eyes. "You can talk about it, Evelyn, really. It's fine."

"Well, you know. It's the same, more or less. I've got Duchesne for English."

"AP English, right?"

I give a little nod, but say nothing.

"College bound now, huh? Well good for you, Evelyn. Good for you." When he pulls into the parking lot of Treeline Colonies, he shuts off the motor and turns toward me. I wait for a moment, looking at him, because I think maybe he wants to say something. But then I think I am imagining it. Maybe he is just waiting for me to get out.

"Bye," I say finally, opening the door. "Sorry it didn't work out."

"No big deal. Thanks for trying, though."

He waits there until I have unlocked the apartment door, the Datsun idling in the parking lot. When I walk in, I hear my mother laughing. Samuel is in his pajamas, sitting in his beanbag, and my mother sits on the floor beside him. They are watching *Roseanne*.

"Evelyn, honey, you're already back? Sit down and watch this for a minute," she says. "It's really good. You're just like Darlene, I swear. It's like you're on TV."

I sit down on the couch and try to watch. The studio audience is laughing, and my mother is too, but I can't concentrate. I don't even hear what Roseanne says, or what Darlene says back. I have to read fifty pages of *Crime and Punishment* by tomorrow, and I think maybe this is what's bothering me, buzzing inside my head so I can't hear the television.

I brush my teeth and change into my pajamas. Two of the cats are asleep on my bed, and even when they see me standing there, yelling at them and clapping, they don't move. I have to scrunch in on one side of my own bed.

Even when I am tucked under the covers, my book in front of me, a glass of water by my side, I can't read. Sometimes you can feel it when someone is watching you, even if you are turned in the other direction. I don't understand how this works. You shouldn't really be able to feel someone's stare. But you can. I've felt it. Also, if I am staring at someone, they almost always look up. Ms. Jenkins said she knew what I was talking about, that she had felt this feeling herself, but she wasn't exactly sure how it worked. It wouldn't be any of the five senses, sight, touch, sound, taste, or smell. So maybe we are just imagining it, she said.

I pull back my window shade, peering outside into the darkness. The Datsun is still there. I can hear the engine running, and the faint music of the radio, still playing country music. Inside, the tiny circle of a cigarette glows bright orange, moving slowly, back and forth.

twenty

*E*ILEEN HAS HER OWN MONEY now, from the life insurance and the investments my grandfather made before he died.

"He was considerate, planning ahead for me," she tells my mother. "You have to give him that."

She's ready to do plenty of giving, now that all the money is hers. She bought Samuel a special chair for the shower so my mother won't have to lift him into the tub, and also a machine that actually says "Yes" when he presses the green circle and "No" when he presses the red one. The voice sounds like the voice of a robot, like the car in *Knight Rider*. She also bought us a microwave, a new coffeemaker, and a food processor. The UPS man comes to our apartment once a week now, delivering boxes. He's very tall, very handsome, and he smiles at my mother while she signs her name.

For Christmas, Eileen stays in Wichita with Beth and Stephanie, but she comes up the next day. She gives me too many presents—a Walkman, a pair of earrings, and a cream-colored cardigan with pearls for buttons. In the card, there is a check for six hundred dollars, my name spelled out carefully in large, childlike letters. On the memo line, she has drawn a heart.

"Eileen," I say, shaking my head. "It's so much."

"It's to help you with school." Her hair has just recently started to turn gray, but she is wearing it in two long braids, one on each side. She wears red and green glitter around her eyes. "For college. Save it up for next year."

"Pretty generous," my mother says, steering Samuel's hand away from Eileen's braids. He groans and hits the NO button over and over again. Now, because of the machine, we have to hear him say no as much as he wants to say it, the steady robot voice speaking for him, no no no no no no no.

"Well it's from your grandfather, really," Eileen says. "He's the one who made this all possible, God rest his soul." She looks up at the ceiling as if he is really up there, floating around like smoke. My mother nods solemnly, but as soon as Eileen turns away, she catches my eye, and raises both of her middle fingers toward the ceiling like they can fire bullets. She laughs silently, her mouth open wide. I make a quick hissing sound, and she puts her hands back in her lap.

She has been doing things like this lately, my mother, not acting like an adult. Two weeks ago, she came home from work and then called McDonald's on the phone, asking for DuPaul, plugging her nose to disguise her voice, saying she was from the Internal Revenue Service. She asked him why he hadn't yet turned in all the forms for 1988 yet, and if he knew about the special Kansas tax on condiments. She kept going and going with this, not letting up, not cracking a smile even though she could have because she was just on the phone and he couldn't see her anyway. But then he heard Samuel crying and realized it was her. When I went in to work the next day, he was still laughing about it.

"Your mother," he said, stacking cups by the soda machine, "is a piece of work."

He got her back the next week, getting all the other employees and five paying customers to individually tell her there was something in her teeth when really there was nothing. My mother thought it was hysterical.

But she is straight-faced again by the time Eileen stops looking at the ceiling. She tells Eileen it looks like I'll get a scholarship, and so I won't need so much money.

Eileen leans across the table, taking my hand. "Evelyn! A scholarship? That's wonderful!"

I nod. Ms. Jenkins helped me get a scholarship to KU; I'm going to major in biology. If you major in biology and you do well, you can apply to go to Costa Rica your junior year. The pamphlet for the Costa Rica program has pictures of students with backpacks walking through a dense forest, taking notes, looking at beetles the size of my fist. SEE THE DIVERSITY OF LIFE FIRSTHAND! is printed at the top. I want to do this. I want to go to the Galápagos Islands.

"She might get to go to Costa Rica," my mother says. Sam swings his fist back and forth on his tray, hitting both the YES and NO buttons, the robot voice speaking for him every time. No yes no yes no.

"Costa Rica?" Eileen says. "Goodness, why would you want to go there?"

I smile and shrug. "Just to go." There is no need to bring up Ms. Jenkins and biology with Eileen. I fold the check carefully, slip it in my pocket. "Maybe I'll go to Ireland too." I say this as I think it.

Eileen looks happy about this. "You could look up my mother's birth-place." She squints into her lap. "Mallow. That's where she was born. In County Cork."

I imagine myself going to Ireland, looking up Eileen's twelve aunts and uncles. I would have so many cousins. If I found the right town in Ireland, I might be related to everyone in it. There is a commercial on television where this happens: An American traveling in Ireland goes around to little cottages, trying to find his Irish cousins he has never met. When he finds the right cottage, they bring him in and give him beer. They make him dance with them while someone plays a fiddle.

Eileen frowns, shaking her head. " 'Course there wouldn't be anybody left from her side. They all died as babies. Just two of her brothers lived, and I think even they died in the war."

My mother and I stare at her. She isn't looking at us but is scratching her head, trying to remember the names of the two brothers. "Owen and Paul. Or Peter? It started with a *P*."

My mother puts her fork down. "The rest of them died? You said there were thirteen."

Eileen nods, spreading mayonnaise on a piece of bread.

"*Ten* of them died? As children?"

She shrugs. "They didn't have the medicine we do now, Tina, the anti-biotics. There was consumption, and not always a lot to eat. It was harder to keep your kids alive."

"Oh God." My mother crosses her arms on the table and puts her head down on them. "It's too horrible. I wouldn't have wanted to live."

Eileen takes a bite of her sandwich. "Yes you would have. You would have adjusted to the times. You would have found strength in the Lord the way they did, and you'd have carried on."

I think of Mr. Carmichael, lying in the grass and crying next to his lawn-mower. Ten times that.

"I would have tried to find strength in doctors," my mother says. "I think after the third one died, I would quit messing around."

"There wasn't a lot doctors could do back then, Tina. They just had to pray and hope. But let's not talk about all these sad things," she says, squeezing my hand. "It's Christmas. Look at this new camera I bought. Let's take pictures."

She holds the camera up. I put on the new earrings she gave me for the picture, leaning forward so Samuel and my mother will fit in the frame.

"Beautiful," Eileen says, and I hear the click. She is standing by the window now, the light hitting her face so I can see the glitter in her eyeshadow, creasing in her wrinkles when she smiles. "I want one of me and Evelyn."

My mother belts Samuel into his chair and takes the camera from Eileen.

"Aaaa! You're taller than me! My granddaughter is taller than me!" She looks up at me, her forehead grazing my chin. It's true—I've grown five inches in one year, suddenly taller than all of the boys in my class except Stu Svelden. It has taken some getting used to, being up this high. I'm still bumping into things.

My mother takes two more pictures, Eileen standing beside me, her arm around my waist.

I love having a Walkman. I can play my Tracy Chapman tape as much as I want, and I don't have to worry about my mother saying that if she hears it one more time she will have to put her head in the oven and end it all. By early March, it's warm enough to go walking, and I do, up and down the highway, the headphones snug inside my ears. I am reading a book on birds so I will know the names of the ones I see when I'm walking—red-winged blackbirds, dickcissels, indigo buntings. This spring alone, I have seen a fox, two deer, and a skunk, moving away from the highway, scurrying through the corn.

Sometimes I walk all the way to Travis and Deena's. Deena and the baby are always home, and she looks happy when she opens the door and sees it's me. She tells me to sit down anywhere I can find, that she is sorry about the mess. She offers me a Tab from the fridge, but warns me to keep an eye on it, to not get it mixed up with the other cans lying on the table. "Travis leaves his fucking butts in the empties," she says, shaking one so I can hear the cigarette rattling inside. She's grown her hair out to her shoulders again, but she has recently cut her own bangs, and I think maybe she cut them too short. Also they are not straight, but slanted across her forehead at a diagonal. Maybe she was tilting her head when she did it.

Jack is almost eighteen months old, walking now. It's like he was a baby one day, and then by the next time I came over, he had exploded into something else. Samuel is still in the wheelchair, still using the buttons and the robot voice to tell us yes and no, but already Jack can tell you no himself, with clenched fists and a red face, and say "I want juice," even "I love Mommy." I know my mother would give anything to hear this from Samuel, just once. But Deena gets to hear it all the time, and she just smiles and says, "I love you too, cutie."

She dresses him neatly, in little overalls and tennis shoes with pictures of the Teenage Mutant Ninja Turtles. He has a basket of books by the couch, and as soon as I sit down he hands me one and crawls up on my lap, as if this is a routine I should know. He still has Travis's eyes, but now he has teeth, and his smile looks like Deena's.

"Sun?" he asks, pointing at a sun on the cover of the book. The sun is neon yellow, with wide eyes and a large, smiling mouth.

"That's right," I say. "Sun."

The book about the sun is his favorite, the one he always chooses. It's about the smiling sun's journey across the sky; the only words in the book are the sun's greetings to everyone it wakes. "Good morning, rooster! Good morning, cow! Good morning, Farmer Joe!" He has it memorized. Halfway through the book, the sun moves on to different countries, waking Asian people in pointed hats, Africans watching it rise along the beach. "Good morning, Asia! Good morning, Africa!" At the end, the sun is back in America, saying good morning to the rooster again.

Jack flips the book back to the first page. He wants me to start again. "Sun?" he asks.

"Welcome to my world," Deena says. She's lying on the couch, eating a bag of Chee•tos. *L.A. Law* is on television, the sound too low to hear. She wears pink-and-white bunny slippers, her feet up on the armrest.

"You know, Deena, if you ever want to go out, I think I could take care of Jack by myself now. Really. He's older. I won't get freaked out."

"No no," she says, still looking at the screen. "All I want to do is lie here. I like being with him. It's just nice to have someone else here."

She doesn't say where Travis is, whether it would be nice to have him there or not.

I start coming over more, once a week. We watch TV. She paints my toenails. We talk about Jack, about what's on TV. We don't talk about school. I don't talk to her about next year, even though this is what I am most excited about right now, what I am thinking about all the time. I'm moving into the dorms in Lawrence on August 14, a hundred and thirty-two days from today. I already got a letter saying I will be in McCullom Hall, and my roommate will be Tia Boldrini, a girl I do not know, also a freshman, from Chicago, Illinois.

Libby isn't going to KU. She's going to Boston College, because that's where her father went. She says Traci was going to go to Wellesley, because that's where her mother went, and then they would be in Massachusetts together. They were going to have lunch together once a week in Boston and maybe go to museums and also on double dates. But now, like me, she'll just be on her own.

It's strange to think what it would have been like if the accident hadn't happened, if Traci and Adele were still alive. Libby and I would not have gotten to be friends, so she might not have been the one to tell me, but still, I might have heard they were going to go to expensive colleges in Massachusetts so they could have lunch together anyway, and I just would have hated them even more. I would have wanted something bad to happen to them in Massachusetts, something small, maybe just a car splashing mud on their clothes, ruining the lunch.

But now that something bad really has happened to them, I wish it all would have worked out for them. I wish they would be having lunch together in Boston next year, just the way they planned. Really, it wouldn't have hurt me for them to have had that. And it doesn't help me at all, now that they won't.

In May, Ms. Jenkins has to go to a conference at the university, and she gets permission for me to come with her, not to the conference, but just to the campus, so I'll be able to see my new home. She comes and picks me up in her little car, waving at my mother from the driver's seat.

"You're going to love college, Evelyn," she says, scratching her head, the air rushing in from the windows. She won't turn on the air conditioner. "It'll be a whole new world."

We exit off the highway and cross a bridge over a slow-moving river into Lawrence. It's a pretty town, not like Kerrville at all. There are a lot of small houses with shade trees, the campus on a hill in the distance. Some of the streets are paved with red bricks instead of asphalt, and Ms. Jenkins's car jerks unsteadily. She winces as we bounce along, but still, I like the way it looks.

I keep thinking about *The Day After*, though, how it was filmed here. I think of the voice on the commercial saying, "This is Lawrence, Kansas. Is anybody there? Anybody at all?" It must have been strange to live here when they were making the movie, to know that the whole world was going to see your town nuclear-bombed on TV. I see people sitting on their porches, in their cars at red lights, and I wonder if they got to be extras. That would be even more strange, to lie on the ground, pretending to die of radioactivity in the background while the real actors said their lines.

We park on campus. Ms. Jenkins gives me a map and tells me she'll meet me back at the information counter at five. It's a nice day, a breezy, cool Thursday morning. I buy a sandwich and a Coke and sit outside, on one of the large patches of grass. There's grass everywhere, neat and very green.

When the bells chime, the students come out of the buildings all at once, and there are suddenly more people walking on the sidewalk than there are in all of Kerrville, maybe more than I have seen in one place in my entire life. A lot of them look like people I would see in Kerrville, but there are also black people, people from other countries too, people speaking Chinese. A man with a beard and glasses walks by wearing flip-flops and a T-shirt that says STOP U.S.-FUNDED MURDERERS IN NICARAGUA NOW! They all have backpacks full of books, carrying them quickly from one building to the next.

I walk in and out of the large, yellow-bricked buildings, keeping up with the flow of people. I try hard to look not like a visitor but like a college student already, wearing comfortable shoes and a backpack, even though, right now, there is nothing inside.

I spend a long time at the Natural History Museum, moving up and down the silent stairways, looking at the displays. There are snakes on the second floor, including a live boa constrictor, green and black and large enough to eat a dog or maybe even a person, its body moving in one smooth coil around itself. On the next floor, there is a skeleton of a dinosaur, and the sign next to it says that most of the bones are real, dug up from under layers of dust. Its head is the size of a small coffee table, the jaws open wide, so it looks like maybe it was screaming when it died. The eyes are just empty sockets, large enough for me to stick my hand through. But the best display, the panorama, takes up the entire fourth floor. It's a large, dark, rounded room, quiet as under water, almost entirely surrounded by glass. Behind the glass is an even bigger room to look into, softly lit, a twilight sky painted on the background. A small river with real water runs down the middle, trickling over rocks.

The sign says the point of the panorama is to show all the life zones, from the Polar to the Tropical, all in one room. There are animals inside, and they must have been real at one point, I think, but now they're dead and stuffed. Someone has taken great care to put them in different positions—crouching in the grass, peering through branches—so they look as if they are still alive and are just being very still, listening for something in the distance.

The Tropical Life Zone is on the left, and inside there is a toucan and a three-toed anteater. I have to look at the signs. Something called a mantled howler monkey hangs from a tree. It gets a little cooler as you move to the right, and then there are deer and two mountain lions fighting, a cactus in the background. The changes happen gradually, one life zone fading into the next. The trees in the background change, from palm trees and Mexican figs to cacti and then cottonwoods. Then there are beaver and white-tailed deer, then mountains in the background, two rams and a moose. It gets colder and colder, or at least it looks that way, until you get to the right side of the circle, the arctic, and then it's just polar bears and seals, their coats sprinkled with white confetti that's supposed to look like snow.

I'm going to try to get a job at this museum. I have to do work-study for my scholarship anyway, and I would love it if I could work with the snakes. Also, I'm sure they need someone to go behind the glass and clean the panorama at night, at least once a week, and I want to be the one to have this job. I would dust the leaves off the Mexican fig, and make sure the water in the river was running smoothly. They would not have to pay me to do this. They might have to give me a key.

It would be like magic to get to walk around back there, from the arctic to the tropics and back again, easily stepping from one world to another, taking it all in at once.

· · ·

A week before graduation, it's still light enough at eight to walk to Deena's, the sky west of the highway gold and pink against the setting sun. I'm wearing the sundress Eileen made for me. It's the first night warm enough, and I love the way it looks, the skirt light and swirling above my knees. But a half mile away from Deena's, a car slows down, and a man with sunglasses leans out to ask me if I want a ride. I say no, not even looking at him or turning off my headphones, and cross to the other side.

Jack opens the door when I knock, wearing a T-shirt and diapers, jelly on his cheek. "Ebelyn," he says. He sets his cup down on the carpet, kisses me on the knee.

"Good boy," Deena says, waving at me. She is vacuuming the carpet, holding a Tab in her free hand. When she leans over to shut the vacuum off, Jack starts to cry. "Oh, okay, honey, I'm sorry. You want to do it?" She places the hose in his hand and turns the vacuum back on. "You want a soda, Evelyn? It's been in the fridge."

"Thanks." I go to the refrigerator, open the door. Inside, there are several six-packs of Tab, and several more of Pabst Blue Ribbon beer. There are two cardboard pizza boxes on the top shelf, and jars of baby food line the door. "How are you?"

"Good. Okay. I need a nap. How are you?"

"I'm good."

Her eyes drift back to the television. "Oh God, Evelyn, this show is hilarious. It's the funniest thing I've ever seen." She turns off the vacuum with her foot, and Jack starts to cry, still holding the hose. "No no, honey. Mommy's show is on." She picks him up and sits down on the couch, wiping the jelly off his face with the sleeve of her sweatshirt. "Come on, sit down. You've got to see this."

The show is a series of short clips sent in by people who have their own video cameras. There are children putting shaving cream on a dog, and then a bride sitting on a chair that isn't there, falling on the floor, her white gown popping up over her head. A studio audience laughs in the background, and Deena laughs when they do, pausing in between to kiss Jack on the head. He sneaks sips of her Tab when she isn't looking, pulling the glass down to his mouth with tiny, quick fingers.

"Where's Travis?"

She curls her lip. "He hates this show. He's back in the bedroom, reading. It's all very impressive."

"Is he staying in tonight?"

Jack slides off her lap, tottering over to his basket of books.

"Don't be ridiculous."

Jack hands her the sun book, its cover torn off the front now. Deena smiles, yawning.

"Are you guys in a fight?"

She takes a sip of her drink, thinking this over. "He's being a shit."

"Shit," Jack echoes, opening the book.

"No, honey, don't say that." She looks at me, trying not to laugh. "It's like having a freaking parrot."

Travis emerges from the dark hallway, rubbing his eyes. He looks like he is in a bad mood, or maybe just waking up. But he smiles when he sees me.

"Evelyn. Hey. You look nice."

"Thanks." I can feel Deena's gaze, moving from my knees back up to Travis's face. I pretend to have to bend down to tie my shoe, but I am wearing sandals.

"What?" he asks. "I can't even talk to Evelyn now?"

Even Evelyn. Like I'm a cousin. Or a dog.

Jack starts to cry again, and Travis reaches down to take him. "It's okay, buddy," he says, jiggling him lightly. "Come on. Nobody's mad at you."

Deena turns away from me and looks back at the screen, her arms crossed, and Travis says something under his breath. It's like I'm eleven again, sitting in the truck with Mr. and Mrs. Mitchell.

"Maybe I'll go home."

"No, stay," she says, pulling me back down. "It's so nice to have somebody who actually wants to spend time with me, who doesn't treat me like I'm an idiot."

Travis rolls his eyes and carries Jack into the kitchen. The video show comes back on: circus music plays along to a rapid succession of clips showing people falling down. A man on skis waves at the camera before crashing into a tree. A woman, walking and talking to her friend, accidentally steps off a pier into a lake. A clown riding a unicycle crashes into a wall. I can hear Travis consoling Jack in the kitchen. "You're my boy," he says. "Daddy's not mad at you. You're my tough guy." He swings him up in the air and back down again, making a whistling sound like a plane dropping a bomb until Jack is laughing, the tears not even dry on his cheeks. Travis carries him back over to Deena and sets him in her arms. "Good to see you, Evelyn," he says, grabbing his keys. "I'll see you later, Dee."

"Have a good time," she says, still looking at the screen. "I hope you have a really good time."

He stops walking, his hands over his eyes. "You want to come? Evelyn said she'd stay with Jack." He pauses, waiting. "I'm just going to hang out with Ed."

She stares up at him, unblinking, and though she says nothing, the look on her face is bad enough. Jack reaches up and pulls her glass over, spilling ice on her lap.

"I would like it," he says, the words slow and heavy, like he is a child in a school play, saying words he has memorized, "if you would come with me." He looks to me for help, but there is nothing I can say. He shrugs, turning away. "Good to see you, Evelyn."

Jack flinches at the sound of the slamming door.

"Bye, sweetie!" Deena calls out. "I love you too!" She leans forward and turns off the television, and we all three sit in silence.

"He hates me," she says finally.

I glance at Jack.

"Oh please. He knows. He lives here. He's not retar—" She turns away.

This is true. Clearly, Jack isn't retarded. But I am even careful with what I say around Samuel. You don't really know what's in there—what they hear, what they understand. There is no way to tell how much of this is seeping into Jack's brain, like water into a crack.

"You saw the way he looked at me," she says. "He doesn't think I'm pretty anymore. He thinks I'm stupid too."

"Deena, you're still pretty, and you're not stupid."

It's true. I'm not lying now. She is lovely still, even wearing green sweatpants and one of Travis's sweatshirts, the pink polish on her fingernails chipped and cracked. If anything, she is more beautiful than she used to be, her cheekbones more hollowed, her skin paler against her dark hair. But she frowns at me, looking down at my sandals.

Jack opens the book, pointing at the page. "Story?" he says. He looks worried. "Sun?"

She nods, and begins to read, but she's crying now, her voice cheerless, wrong for the words. "Good morning, rooster! Good morning, cow!" Jack keeps glancing up. When she gets to the last page, he hands her another book, holding her hand against the pages.

I am trying to think of a way to escape. I can tell she is mad, not just mad in general, but mad at me. I haven't done anything, but I can feel it, a heaviness between us. I could walk home, but it's already getting dark.

After four books, Jack's eyelids start to flutter. When they finally close, she stops reading and peers down at his face, her fingertips grazing his ear. She has told me before that babies actually get heavier when they fall asleep. I said that doesn't make any sense, but she said she can tell when Jack's asleep, just by the way he feels. "Let me put him to bed," she whispers, and she stands up so smoothly that he doesn't even stir.

But when she gets to the hallway, she stops and turns around, her eyes moving down to my feet and then up again. "By the way," she says. "Nice dress."

Travis gets home after midnight. I hear the Datsun rumble into the parking lot, the radio cutting off in the middle of a song. But he's quiet coming down the stairs, and Deena does not wake when he opens the door.

"Hey," he whispers. Deena is still stretched out on the couch, snoring lightly now, her mouth open, her brow furrowed, as if she had been getting ready to sneeze, or say something important, just before she drifted off. She lay down just after putting Jack to bed, and fell asleep immediately.

"Jack's in bed?"

I nod. "She put him down around nine."

He looks down at Deena, his hands in his pockets, his face difficult to read. "Well, let's let sleeping Deenas lie. I'll take you home."

When we get outside, Travis takes off his sweatshirt and hands it to me. "It got cool out. There's supposed to be a storm tomorrow. A big one." His sweatshirt smells like the detergent Deena uses. I stand by the passenger door and look up while I wait for him to unlock it. It's a clear night, the stars shining brightly as eyes against the blue-black sky.

"Evelyn, Evelyn, Evelyn," he says. "Evelina." I don't know why he says this. I don't smell the alcohol until after we have pulled onto the highway. He steers with one hand, whistling, his cheeks pink.

"Are you drunk?" I tug on my seat belt, making sure it will hold.

"No. Not drunk." He smiles. "Little Miss Serious. I'm driving fine." He turns on the radio, and country music comes on so loud it makes me jump. He laughs, turning it down. "Relax," he says. "Relax."

"Still with the country music," I say. "And now you're drinking too." I'm joking about this, but really I am a little mad. I cannot get killed in a car accident now, just before everything is about to get better for me. Eighty-two days until I move into the dorm. Eighty-one and a half.

"Oh, come on, Evelyn. You'll like this one. Just listen."

The man on the radio sings about his heart being broken years ago, a guitar strumming gently in the background. Travis starts to sing along, sort of kidding around, but mostly not. His voice is nice, low and earnest-sounding, better than the man singing on the radio, I think.

"You're a good singer, Travis."

He keeps singing. I wait for him to laugh, to start making fun of himself, but he doesn't.

If someone would have shown me this scene a few years ago, played it on a screen like a clip from a movie, I would have been happy. I'd have taken one look at me and Travis in a car on a starry night, listening to love songs on the radio, Travis singing along, and I'd have thought, "Oh good."

He's still singing when he pulls into the parking lot of Treeline Colonies, slowing the car far away from the buildings. "Stay a minute," he says, turning off the engine.

I lean back in my seat and look up at the apartment buildings, all four of them, A, B, C, and D, the concrete balconies stacked on top of one another, four on each side. A macramé plant holder on the top balcony of our building drifts back and forth in the breeze.

"Wow," Travis says. "Just look at the stars."

I nod, saying nothing. Deena is mad at me for wearing the dress. That seems a little silly. Eileen made it for me, and I have to wear it somewhere. And if anyone should be mad and jealous, it's me. It's still me.

Travis brings one of his feet up to the seat and turns so he is facing me, tapping his cigarette in the ashtray. "Graduation's coming up, huh?"

"Yeah," I shrug. "It's just dumb. It's going to be hot and boring."

He nods, his eyes on mine. "And then it's off to college for you."

"I guess so. I move into the dorms in August."

"You paying for it?"

284 · LAURA MORIARTY

"I got a scholarship. Ms. Jenkins helped me. I'll still have to work, but just part-time."

"Wow." He takes a long drag from the cigarette and exhales slowly, still watching me, still not looking away. "What are you going to do with your McDonald's money?"

"I don't know. Maybe a car. I might try to study abroad or something." I'm talking too quickly, my teeth almost chattering. "I might get to go to Costa Rica. We'll see."

"Costa Rica. Listen to you." He pokes my shoulder, and his finger lingers for a moment, twisting half a circle against my skin before pulling away. "That should be me going," he says. He is still smiling when he says this.

It takes a minute for me to register what he has said, the way he has said it. I'm not sure if it was mean, or if it just didn't make any sense. It's not as if only one of us could go to college. It's not like he's not going because I am. "You could still go, Travis. Get your GED, and then maybe."

He shakes his head. "Nope. I'm roped and tied." He reaches across my knees to the glove compartment, getting out another pack of cigarettes. I look at my knees, one of them scraped from when I fell yesterday afternoon. I tripped getting off the bus, thinking there were fewer steps than there were, and pitched forward, landing hard on the pavement, my hands out in front of me, breaking my fall. Libby picked up my backpack and helped me to my feet. "Listen," she said, pointing at me with her cane. "I'm the one who falls down around here."

"Deena thinks you hate her," I say quickly, pushing all the words out in one breath. "She thinks you're going to leave her with Jack."

"I won't leave Jack." He leans back, shaking out the match. "But yeah, I have to say, I kind of hate her." He looks at me, one side of his face lit up by the parking lot light, the other side dark.

"Why?"

"Don't act stupid. You know, Evelyn. She did it on purpose. You know that."

"She's sorry, though. She's sorry."

"I think we're both pretty sorry by now." He grins, wagging a finger at me. "But Evelyn Bucknow is going to college."

"Yeah." I try to laugh, looking away. "If I don't do anything to screw it up."

He finishes his cigarette, throws the butt out the window. "It's not fair. I was always smarter than you."

Again, I can't tell if he is joking. I look at him carefully, trying to see. He has gotten closer, I realize, his arm on the back of my seat. "Just kidding," he says quickly, looking away and then back again. "You know that's not true. I'm the biggest dumbass there is."

"Why are you saying that?"

He looks at me, green eyes wide, and then breaks into laughter. "I married *Deena*. I'm nineteen years old, and I'm fucking married to *Deena*. I love my kid, but hello, I'm not going anywhere for the next couple of decades."

I can think of nothing to say to this. It's like when we sat on the steps after his father left, me trying to think of something that was kind as well as true, coming up with nothing.

He flicks the keys on his key chain, still dangling from the ignition. "I wish I were with you and not her."

I could hit him. I have to hold on to the edge of my seat. He says it again.

"Oh stop it," I say. "Give me a break. You chose her. You chose her and not me." And I make myself remember it, the three of us walking home from Ed's van, back across the snowy field. I am angry, but also, terribly, hopeful. I want him to tell me something now that would take away the sting of that night, to say that really he always loved me, even then, even when he first put his hand over his heart and asked me to repeat her name.

"You chose her," I say, pressing, waiting. "You act like all of this just happened to you. Poor baby. But it's not true, Travis. You chose it."

He puts his hands over his face. "I know."

"Why?" I am crying now, though I don't want to. It's a terrible question, this why.

He looks like he doesn't understand, squinting at me in the darkness. "I thought she was pretty."

I feel the muscles in my arms and legs tighten, closing down. "Well, she still is then. You have what you wanted."

He closes his eyes. "I know, Evelyn. I know."

"Yes, I know you know. I know you've always known."

He looks confused now, befuddled, and I remember he has been drinking. But what I am saying makes perfect sense to me, even the bitterness in my voice makes sense, though I can see his lovely eyes are turning glassy, rimmed in red. He rests his elbows on the steering wheel, gazing out in front of him, at the shrubs in front of the mailboxes, at the Treeline Colonies parking lot, full of unshiny cars.

There is a chance, I realize, that Travis still does not understand my heart at all, that I am, and have always been, in this alone.

But looking at him, even with the scratching claw inside me, I feel bad for him. Maybe he didn't really choose this. Maybe he didn't get to choose at all. It could be that the decision was made for him, the first time he saw her. It's biology, after all, pushing us into each other, pushing us around. Sitting here, looking at him, I can understand better than anyone how you can be pulled toward someone even when you don't want to be, just because of the way his voice sounds, the way his skin is stretched across the bones of his face.

I think of dead moths inside of a porch lamp, lemmings jumping to their deaths.

"What?" he says. "What are you thinking about?"

"Dead moths. Lemmings."

He laughs. He goes to tap himself on his temple and pokes himself in the eye. "I have no idea what you're talking about. I never do. Did you know that? Even when we were little, I just pretended." He laughs again. "But I like you anyway." He says this warmly, turning toward me. But all I can think is that he is still saying *like* and not *love*. There is so much difference between these two words, a line you have to cross to go from one to the other.

He's close again, though. His arm rests on the back of the seat, his hand grazing my shoulder. I can smell his minty breath on my cheek, and I know that all I have to do is look up. The air that I am breathing in is air he has just breathed out, warm and dizzying, air I can almost taste.

All I have to do is look up.

I put my hands flat against the dashboard. The stars are still glimmering, still shiny as eyes. They are not eyes, though, just hot balls of gas, far, far away. But on the floor of the car, a baby rattle rests by my feet, bright yellow with a smiley face painted on it, a crescent of Jack's tiny teeth marks on one side. The car seat, I know, is in the back. I think of Deena, lying on the couch with her mouth open, and I imagine her waking up, yawning, looking around, the television turned off and nobody home.

"I have to go," I say.

"What? Why?" His fingers run lightly off my shoulder, up my neck.

"I just do. I have to." I open my door and stand up slowly. "I have to get up early tomorrow. I told my mom I'd watch Sam."

"Okay." He squints up at me. "Everything all right?"

"I'm fine," I say. "Thanks for the ride."

I shut the door without looking back, and put one foot in front of the other, moving quickly up the walkway. A small swarm of mayflies and moths swirls around the light by our door, and though I pass just beneath them, they are not disturbed.

My mother knocks twice on my door.

"Come in," I say. Finally. I have trained her.

"What's the story, morning glory?" She lifts my window shade quick and hard, letting it roll up with a snap. *"Zap!"* she says. Travis's sweatshirt hangs on the back of the chair to my desk, and my hair smells like smoke.

I yawn. "What are you doing? What time is it?"

"It's nine. Remember? You said you'd watch Sam today. Did you forget?" She stands in front of the mirror on my closet door, frowning. "Is this dress too tight?"

She is wearing one of her dresses from before Samuel was born, the flowered one, and the seams on the sides look strained and puckered, the material stretched tight across her hips.

"Mom, that dress is like eight years old. Maybe you should just get a new one."

"Dammit." She frowns at her reflection, patting her stomach down. "Dammit dammit dammit."

She looks nice though, really. She's not wearing the red glitter hat, and her hair has gotten longer. She's started wearing lipstick again, even earrings when she goes to work.

"I thought you were just going for a walk," I say. "What's the big deal?"

Instead of answering, she runs her hand along the books on my bookshelves. "Three months," she says. "Three more months and my baby's gone."

"Two months and twenty-one days." I watch her carefully. "Why are you getting dressed up? Where are you going?"

She shrugs. "I don't know. Maybe Kansas City or something. It's getting

288 · LAURA MORIARTY

ready to storm." She smiles and turns away, starting down the hallway. I stay in bed, thinking about this. She's acting stupid. And there's no reason for her to go to Kansas City.

I get up and go into the front room. Samuel is asleep in his beanbag, already dressed in his shirt and overalls, his hair parted neatly on one side. The television is on, President Bush is giving a speech. My mother stands at the sink, rinsing off the dishes from breakfast. She glances up at me and then down again. She's wearing mascara.

"Why are you going to Kansas City?"

She rolls her eyes. "I'm going with Franklin. Okay, Miss Nosey?"

Franklin. "DuPaul?"

She nods. She won't look up.

"Why?"

She shrugs. "Why not?" There's something in her face I have not seen in a while, a flush, a glisten.

"Are you guys *dating*?"

"I don't know." She squirts dishwashing soap on a sponge. "He wants to take tango lessons."

"What?"

"Tango," she says. "You know." She holds her arms up as if she were dancing with someone, one arm in an embrace, the other stretched out in front of her, still holding the dishwashing scrub.

I'm confused. I can't imagine this. "Are you going too? Is that where you're going?"

"I don't know." She shuts off the water, drying her hands on the skirt of the dress. "I mean, today, maybe. But I don't know about every week. I don't know what I'd do with Sam."

I am watching her eyes, trying to see if she is joking or not. They're just a little crossed, the way they always are. She's serious. But I can't really picture her dancing the tango, slinking around a ballroom in Kansas City with DuPaul. For so long now, I have only thought of her wearing the red glitter hat, tired and kneeling before Samuel, trying to put on his socks.

"I'll watch him."

She shuts off the water. "It's once a week, Evelyn. For the rest of the summer. Don't say you'll do it if you won't."

"I'll do it," I say. "Until I have to leave for school. I really will."

Samuel stirs in his beanbag. We wait to see if he will fall asleep again, but he starts to cry. "I'll get him," I say, holding up my hand. "Really. Go get ready."

She starts to walk back to the bathroom, but then stops and turns around. "Listen, Evelyn. I'd like to take the lessons if I can. If you're really serious, I'd appreciate it. It would be nice."

"I said I'd do it. Jeez." I try to look annoyed, but really, I like how I have surprised her. I have startled her, just by being nice.

"Thank you," she says. She looks out the window, tugging on her earring. "But don't say anything to Eileen, okay? I just don't want to hear that Tribe of Ham bullshit just yet."

"Okay."

She smiles, twisting one of her toes on the linoleum. "I like him a lot, if you want to know the truth, and I'll let her know pretty soon, when I'm up to it. Because I can tell you right now, there'll be a fight." She turns around and throws little punches up in the air, walking back into the hallway. "Buy your tickets now."

When I go to move Samuel, he pulls away from me, pointing vaguely up at the television. I can't tell what he wants. I start to change the channel and then stop. "Can I try a different channel?" I ask. "See what else is on?"

I wait for him to point to the YES or the NO, but he doesn't do either. I scan the channels. There is Billy Graham on one station, the weather report on another. On the weather report, a man points to a map of the Midwest, Kansas outlined in black underneath the animated clouds. There are tiny cartoon lightning bolts in the upper corner of the screen, and SEVERE THUN-DERSTORM WARNING blinks across the bottom. The weatherman talks about pockets of low pressure, barometer readings, low fronts and cool fronts. Radar blips in the background make things seem urgent, exciting.

But Samuel doesn't care about the weather report. He's pointing over my shoulder now, at something behind me. I don't know what he wants, and I can see he's getting angry. I try various objects from the counter, placing each on my head, one at a time: the phone book, a mug, a bottle opener, a box of matches. I try one of the cats. He shakes his head and keeps pointing, getting agitated, groaning now, red in the face.

"I don't know what you want, Sam. I'm sorry."

He bangs his head on the side of his wheelchair and points again. I look into his glassy blue eyes, hoping for hint, a flicker, something, but I see only blue, and my own reflection.

"Do you want to go outside with me and watch the storm?"

He rocks back and forth a few times before his hand slides to the green circle.

It isn't raining yet when I wheel him outside. The wind is strong though, and even over the sound of the highway, I can hear it rustling through the corn. The sky is interesting, cut in half. There is a deep, dark thunderhead in the distant west, but directly over our heads the sun is still shining, surrounded by a cloudless blue. The line in the middle of the sky between storm and clear is almost perfectly straight, as if someone drew it along the edge of a ruler.

I know from Mr. Torvik's class that this is called a wall cloud, and that wall clouds can turn into tornados, warm and cool air pushed sharply together on each side. But not always. Sometimes the two sides just sort of melt into each other, and they don't turn into anything at all.

A jet flies over our heads, high up in the blue part of the sky, leaving a thick white trail. Samuel points up at it, his eyes wide. I wonder if he thinks I can reach up and place the jet on my head for him, like a tiny toy just out of his reach.

Verranna Hinckle has been telling my mother more stories, filling her head with more distant miracles. She brought over a VCR and a videotape of a little girl with autism in Korea who didn't speak and didn't seem to know her own mother was sitting beside her, but she could hear Beethoven once and then play it on the piano. My mother got excited and bought Samuel a toy keyboard. She got it out of the box and placed it in front of him, pressing his hands against the keys. He just sat there, not even looking at it, his hand in his mouth, and then finally my mother got quiet and put the keyboard away.

Nothing.

Nothing yet, my mother said. It may be something else for him.

Thunder rumbles again, closer now, and both Samuel and I gaze up at the darkening sky. It's beautiful to look at, the clouds rolling into one another, lightning crackling on the horizon. But it's frightening too. Times like this especially, I hate to think that the Earth is just a rock spinning in space, and that if it ever stopped or even slowed down, that would be the end for everybody. The clouds, the cars, even the buildings would go flying, burning up or flying out into nothing at all.

But Mr. Torvik said there was no reason to think that this would happen anytime soon. If we don't mess it up, he said, the Earth should just keep spinning, all the plants and animals and people turning right along with it, safely tucked beneath the clouds.

He had stood on a chair one day and moved the little Earth in his classroom around the electric sun, his hand clutching the bottom like he was changing a lightbulb. He kept it tilted on its axis, so we could see how sometimes, depending on where the Earth was in its orbit, the light and heat of the sun would shine more brightly on the Northern Hemisphere, and then later, more on the Southern. If the Earth weren't tilted like this, he said, there wouldn't be seasons. He made the earth straight up and down and moved it around the sun to show us what this would look like, the band of light around the equator unchanging as he moved around the room. But this way, he said, tilting it back, everybody gets some light.

There is more lightning, a flash of brightness tearing across the sky. Samuel shrieks and points up, his eyes wide.

"It's pretty, isn't it?"

He doesn't answer, doesn't point to the YES or the NO. After a while, I feel the first drops of rain, cool and soft on my face. Already the clouds are moving toward us, spreading out across the entire sky, our shadows on the concrete disappearing.